LEO E. NDELLE

THE BRIGHT EYES

ACKNOWLEDGEMENT

Writing this novel has been a remarkable journey unlike any I have undertaken. I have had the greatest fortune of not embarking on this journey alone, though. I have so many people I am grateful to.

A special thank you to Stacey; for all you do, you're simply the best.

And to everyone who has read this novel, I say thank you so very much. Your unwavering encouragement and support have been the fuel that has brought me thus far.

DEDICATION

To you, Papa!

You are, and always will be, the greatest ever!

PART ONE

BEFORE THE BEGINNING

HE DESCRIBED HIMSELF, for those who needed a description, as a purveyor purpose and as such, he had given himself a purpose. An apprentice gone solo, he sought to express his identity in its fullness, especially now that Creation was at the cusp of a new vibrational dance, a new perfect cycle. This go-round, he would not fail. In this existence, he was called The Scribe. So far, there had been order, which was a mere extension of his arch nemesis and mentor, Akasha. How he missed her! He cursed in his mind.

All is not yet lost, he thought.

He accessed the Dimensions of Space and Energy so that the ethers that constituted his essence could vibrate at the highest frequency possible. In this state, his being merged with as much of Creation as his current level of evolution could allow because, in this state of heightened vibration frequency, Creation, which was everything ever manifested from the Un-Manifest, was laid bare as a singularity and that singularity only existed in the present.

The Scribe scanned Creation in an instant. Satisfied with his research, he returned to his former form.

I applaud myself for shielding me from Akasha all this while, he smiled wryly.

The Scribe accessed the Dimensions of Time and Ether. He sparked the ethers into what looked like a transparent, legless desk in front of him and, with a mighty will, he blew gently over the desk. He sparked more ethers into the past, present, and future and spread out these illusionary aspects of time on the transparent legless desk in front of him. After carefully studying the past, present and future, he conceded, again, at the remarkable order of everything. Creation was, for lack of a better term, a work of pure genius.

But who is the Creator? I am yet to behold this being, The Scribe muttered. *Anyway, when I am done with my plan for Creation, not even the Creator will survive.*

He picked a few points on the etheric display in front of him and inserted a few anomalies. These anomalies would serve as catalysts for the vibration of chaos that will wreck Creation in the form of a chain reaction he will set in motion from the Core of Creation to the Edge of Creation.

The chaos will be pure, the chaos would be unstoppable, the chaos would be perfect. After all, I am pure, I am unstoppable, I am perfect, and, most of all, I am Chaos!

The Scribe rubbed his proverbial hands in excitement and almost laughed out loud with evil joy. But he covered his mouth with his hands just in time. The last time he chuckled while in this state, many realms and dimensions had been reduced to nothingness. After all, he was one of the handful of multi-dimensional entities in Creation, able to access the Dimensions of Space, Time, Energy and Ether at will

Finally, I have my answer, he exclaimed in his mind.

He touched the 'past' section of the display that had formed on the desk. It enlarged itself across the entire desk. He zoomed in on a blue realm.

This will be my point of entry, he thought.

The Scribe then leaned back as a chair appeared to accommodate him. He held out the fingers of his left hand, the hand of the past, and sparked the ethers into a golden pen, which formed in between his fingers. He also sparked the ethers into a golden manuscript, which appeared and floated in front of him. Golden pages flipped open to one-fifth of the manuscript. The Scribe wrote a few golden glyphs on the page. The heading read *The Bright Eyes*. He then blew on the page, and the golden glyphs left the page, disintegrated in millions of tiny golden etheric particles. These particles floated into Creation and buried themselves into the etheric image of the young, blue realm that had appeared on the transparent, legless desk in front of him. The image of the young, blue realm pulsated six times in affirmation before returning to normal. The golden manuscript then closed itself and hovered in front of The Scribe. The Scribe smiled at the title on the cover of the manuscript. *The Soulless Ones,* it read.

This is my design for this section of Creation, he grinned.

The golden manuscript then disappeared along with the golden pen. The Scribe relaxed further in the chair, closed his eyes and smiled with satisfaction.

And now we wait, The Scribe said to himself.

CHAPTER ONE

ENTICED

THE PLANE TAXIED to a stop at the Dulles International Airport in Virginia. Jake Fellows and his team moaned with sweet relief as they stretched their muscles after a very long, exhausting, uneventful but gratefully, direct flight from Prague, Czech Republic; uneventful, except Mark Stone, the lead cameraman, had been a whiny prick. The internet-now-turned-network TV stars called themselves '*Myth Huntsmen*' comprising of Duke Wilson, the team's geek, Sam Cantor and Paul Holleman, both technical assistants, Eva Blades, the team's muscle, and Mark Willows, co-founder with Jake Fellows.

The *Myth Huntsmen* quickly rose to fame after capturing a strange, giant of a bird in the south section of Mount Kilimanjaro, in the Moshi Tribe region, that bore a striking resemblance to a pterodactyl. Screw Bigfoot and his cousins, the Sasquatch and the Yeti. This find was probably the next best thing since the first moon landing. Though scientific and expert analyses proved inconclusive regarding this creature being a pterodactyl, the consensus was that the avian specimen was, without a doubt prehistoric. Sometimes, it did pay to follow up on claims from local inhabitants. After three days of waiting for the perfect opportunity and the element of surprise, a massive dose of horse tranquilizers had put the creature to sleep. The fame was instant, the show's ratings went through the roof, and *Myth Huntsmen* received a new and sweeter contract.

A few months after the whirlwind of instant fame settled, life was back to normal for the team. Blades groaned in protest as Jake slid out of bed.

How dare he take his warmth away, she thought.

Beneath that macho-lioness persona of hers was a cute, feely, touchy kitten. Jake smiled at her cuteness and continued sorting through the mail;

Business before pleasure always.

Although sometimes, like now, it was business, pleasure and then more business. A dark, brown envelope caught his attention. He scooped it up and dropped the rest of the mail on the sofa. The envelope did not feel like paper.

This is odd, he thought.

He walked towards a desk in his office as he ripped open the envelope. He emptied the contents of the envelope on the desk. A thumb drive wrapped around what looked like a dried animal hide landed on the desk with a thud. Jake eyed the thumb drive with extreme caution.

Just like his email, his mailbox was always replete with 'evidence' of sightings of the mysterious, supernatural and even the paranormal from all over the world, and only the *Myth Huntsmen* could 'save the day.'

"Fans," Jake murmured. "Let them get in your head and that head will swell like crazy."

And that could just be as flattering as it could lead to one's fatality. Yes, their quest for the truth did involve considerable amounts of risks, some of which were life-threatening. But thank God Duke, the computer genius, was on their team. At age fourteen, Duke Wilson had remotely hacked into an NSA worker's computer. FBI agents and SWAT teams had stormed Duke's parents' house within the hour, only to find a one-hundred-and-fifty-pound, unperturbed teenager hunched over his laptop with a victory grin on his face. When asked why he did it, he said he was bored out of his mind. The NSA promised him a job instead of meting out federal punishment of some kind for his crime, a decision that could pass for an epitome of a miracle. Duke had declined though and eight years later, he joined *Myth Huntsmen.*

Jake separated the thumb drive from the flesh-looking thing and looked at it quizzically as if studying some alien object. He closed his fist around the thumb drive and foraged through the envelope, expecting to find something else in it. And then, the smell, trapped within the package for all God knows how long, hit him like a slap across the cheek. Jake almost gagged.

What the…, he almost cursed as he wrinkled his nose and held the envelope away from his face.

Jake rummaged again through the envelope just to make sure he did not miss anything. Satisfied, he tossed the envelope as far away as possible. Then, he stared at the thumb drive in his hand for a few seconds, as if unsure how to proceed.

Could be another virus, he thought.

Finally, he shrugged and sighed.

"Might as well," he said under his breath.

He slid into a seat behind his desk, turned on his laptop and inserted the thumb drive. There was a single folder in the drive, and Jake double-clicked on it. The folder opened to reveal a video icon, and Jake double-clicked on it, half expecting a computer virus attack and half expecting anything else.

"Blades," he tried to call out a few minutes later but his voice caught in his parched throat.

He cleared his throat and gave it another try.

"Blades," he called out again.

"What's your problem, man?" she sounded annoyed.

"You gotta take a look at this," he replied.

"Are you seriously waking me up for a video?" she asked almost angrily.

"Just get your butt over here and take a look at this!" Jake said.

The sense of urgency in his voice was all the motivation Blades needed to oblige. She flung the covers from her naked body and half-trotted, half-walked over to where he perched over his laptop. She hugged him from behind, and he could feel her bosom press against his bare back.

"What is it, babe?" she asked, gently stroking his head and kissing his right earlobe.

"Watch!" Jake replied and hit the 'Play' icon on the video player.

After the first minute of the video, she released him from her rear hug and knelt to his right, with her full attention on the laptop monitor. At the fourth minute, she cupped her mouth as if to stifle a scream and tried to say something but stopped short. When the video was over, six minutes, sixteen seconds later, she stared back and forth between the monitor and Jake.

"Is this… No. It can't be. Are you…" Blades spoke incoherently.

"Only one way to find out," Jake replied. "Let's get cleaned up and have everyone over here."

And for the first time in his career, Jake hoped that a video from a fan was a hoax.

Duke was just getting ready to take on the world of online gamers when his phone rang. He contemplated ignoring it but changed his mind. He accepted the call without even looking at the caller ID.

"Main Man Duke, how may I be of assistance to thee?"

"It's Jake. My place, right now! Bring Suzie with you."

"Whoa, hold on now partner. What's going on? It better be good 'cause I'm about to take on some cry-babies online right now."

"As possible as a gig of a lifetime," Jake replied. "Just bring Suzie with you."

"Aight, playa! But least you can do is gimme some headlines though.!"

When Jake finished with the seven-second synopsis of the situation, Duke was out of the house with Suzie in less than twelve seconds. He shaved forty-nine seconds off his average drive time to Jake's house. Sam and Paul showed up within an hour. Mark, of course, blamed his lateness on two red-haired, heavily bronzed, fake-busted chicks he had scored at the bar the previous night. He also made it a point to notice that Blades' hair was still wet and wondered aloud at why that was so.

"Not everyone is as hyped up as you are after your 'awesome night,' Mark!" Blades sneered at him.

"Could've fooled me, princess," Mark replied. "You can fool anyone here, but not me. I can smell sex on a female a mile away and you, my fancy, karate-feisty damsel, must have had some mad pummeling last night. Um hm."

Mark eyed her from head to toe in mock inspection, with immaculate, bleached, white teeth exposed behind a chiseled grin.

"Wouldn't you agree, Jake?" he asked, not taking his eyes off Blades.

"Whatever Mark," replied Jake with exasperation. "Can we just get on with why we're here, please?" he asked, trying to mask his embarrassment with a fake sternness of voice.

"Yeah, Right, let's get on with business," Mark said. "After I place this hairpin," he picked up a hair pin from the sofa and walked over to the laptop, "right where we all can see. Say, Jake, since when did you start using hairpins? Or is that where you and sweet pea over here started your jujutsu training last night?" he gestured towards the sofa.

"I can see how this played out," Mark added and burst into laughter. "You two walked in, your hand brushed against that fine ass of hers and then she gets all 'mad with rage' and tackles you to the sofa. But then realizes that y'all's clothes are in the way. So, you two start a race, who gets to take who's clothes off first and then-"

"Yeah, I'm sleeping with him," Blades spat. "Got a problem with that?"

"Not at all, sweet pea! Not at all." Mark replied.

He then turned his attention towards Jake.

"You broke the rule, bro," he said coldly.

"Look, we can talk about this later-" Jake offered.

"Try another strategy, bro," Mark was borderline angry.

Mark's outburst was justified. He and Jake went way back. Mark was the only other person remaining from the original team. It so happened that one of the other team members had left because things had gotten 'complicated' with Jake at one time.

"Look, Eva," Mark turned around to addressed Blades. "I ain't sure if Mr. Open Zipper told you about what happened a while back; about him and someone else on the team getting intimate. Somewhere down the line, things got complicated and emotions got involved. Next thing we know, she's leaving the team. That's why we can't have team members grinding genitals with each other for any reason whatsoever. She was a great team member and we all suffered from her leaving. You're an even better team member, and I sure as hell don't wanna look for your replacement someday just because Mr. Horny Monk over here couldn't keep his fly shut. We're great together beyond our differences. Hope ya understand where I'm coming from. My concern is for nothing else but the team."

Duke could care less if the team was having an orgy, Paul was laughing hysterically, and Sam tried to stifle a chuckle. But Blades was not sure how to react to Mark's words. A part of her felt embarrassed to have her business out in the open like that. But, at the same time, she was flattered by Mark's genuine and unexpected compliments. Sometimes, Mark acted more mature than all of them combined. Behind the sissy stance he took sometimes was a leader who knew when to take charge and keep everyone in line. He had the strength of heart, mind, and soul and when Blades realized that she was having a warm sensation in between her legs just thinking about this, it dawned on her that this could be why the girls were drawn to Mark like moths to a fluorescent lamp. Eva nodded and smiled.

"And as for you," Mark turned his attention towards Jake. "I shall have words with thee."

"Fine. Now let's just watch the video, please," Jake replied.

Jake walked to his sixty-inch TV screen and inserted the thumb drive into the USB port behind it. He sat crossed-leg on the carpet as the rest of the team sat on various seats.

"Hey Sam," he called out to Sam, twisting himself about his hip and looking over his shoulder at Sam. "Toss me the remote, will ya?"

Sam complied, and Jake selected the folder on the drive. He then selected the video and pressed the 'Enter' button on the remote control. The video started playing. He tried to focus on the screen despite Mark glaring icily at him. Mark was pissed and rightly so. The girl Jake had been sleeping with was Clara. The team was aware, though. Eventually, Clara had become pregnant on the pill and had refused to have an abortion. Unfortunately, Clara had miscarried two months later, and Jake had to admit, to himself, that he received the news with mixed feelings.

He had fallen in love with Clara, but he was far from ready to be a father. At first, she was not happy being pregnant, but her maternal instincts kicked in. The team agreed that she should not join the team on expeditions, to which she was compliant. Her miscarriage had devastated her, though. She sought comfort from Jake, but Jake was no expert in that domain. Months of therapy had helped her deal with the emotional and psychological toll of the miscarriage. Alas, she had left the team and had only found peace about two years later. Finding her replacement had not been easy. The team had then decided to ban

11

fraternization within the team.

The video was shot at night and whoever shot the video appeared to be adjusting the settings of the camera accordingly. The camera zoomed in on a clearing beneath a tree. Based on the voice behind the camera, the team concluded a man was recording the video. A couple was sitting on a blanket. They had a portable lamp with them that cast a glow around them. Beyond the glow from the lamp was darkness. The couple looked young, maybe in their twenties. They were naked and seemed to be having a romantic picnic in the middle of the night in the woods. The male appeared to have said something funny because the girl leaned her head back in laughter and spoke.

"Romanian!" interjected Sam a-matter-of-factly.

Everyone turned around in unison towards him with a look of surprise on their faces. Jake paused the video.

"Used to date a Romanian chick some years ago. Taught me a thing or two. Or three," Sam explained and burst out laughing, but no one else joined him.

"I bet," said Duke. "Okay, let's get on with the video. At least we may have a location."

"Agreed," Jake said and hit the 'Play' button on the remote.

The video resumed playing. The female stopped laughing and then slowly walked on all fours towards her male companion. Her partner propped himself on his elbows as if creating an accommodation for her. She stopped just short of his pelvis and started kissing her way up from his knees, groin and then to his chest; the entire time, she let her medium-sized breasts brush against his skin till they settled on his chest. The couple then locked lips.

"Hmm, didn't realize you brought us here for an amateur porn flick," spat Mark with sarcasm and was ignored.

The female suddenly let out a shriek before quickly scurrying away from her companion. Her companion also scurried away towards her and she crouched behind him. She pointed into the darkness and her companion appeared to squint into the darkness until he made out what she was pointing at.

"What are they saying?" asked Blades.

"I don't know," Sam replied.

"Thought you knew how to speak Romanian," Mark scoffed.

"Thought you didn't have a stick up your-," Sam spat but was cut off.

"Look," Dukes pointed at the screen.

Eva and Jake had watched the video already. So, what happened next did not surprise them at all. Yet, the tightening of their stomachs and the cringing of their bodies remained unchanged.

Another couple emerged from the shadows. The couple held up their hands, to indicate that they came in peace. The second couple appeared to be a little older than the first couple but looked a lot stronger, more toned and more beautiful than the younger couple on the blanket. They too were naked. They appeared to talk to the younger couple for like seventeen seconds or so and the tension seemed to ease a little. But then, the strangest thing happened. The second female walked over to the younger male on the blanket and the second male just stared at the younger female, who then rose from the blanket and walked towards him. Both the younger male and female behaved as if they were in a trance.

The older female straddled the younger male and started kissing him passionately. The older male and younger female locked lips and kissed passionately as well. The entire scene was like a weird, sinister erotic routine. The younger couple was consumed in this prelude to a sexual parody and they let go. That was until both the older male and female lifted their heads upwards and their eyes glowed like those of creatures spawned from the pits of hell itself. Mark and Duke gasped and let out a few expletives.

"Jesus Christ!" Sam and Paul exclaimed almost at the same time.

CHAPTER TWO

C. E. 30

TWO WEEKS INTO the month of Heshvan and rain was still a scarce commodity. Odd, but not a cause for alarm. The sun's heat was gentle on the skin and the plowing fields held a promise of huge harvests that year, much to farmers' and their families' content. It was also that time of the year to start slaughtering the fattened sheep. Children played outside, mothers tended to the affairs of the house, men remained busy with 'men's affairs' as always, and the young maidens took the liberty to gossip about puberty and betrothal. Life would have been paradise for the Jews, except for the blasphemous presence of their colonists: the Romans. How could the Jews be Yahweh's chosen people and still be under Roman rule? The cry for the Messiah, their savior, was as strong as it was silent, burning within their souls as a fiery lust for liberation and divine justice. But no one dared speak out for fear of being punished by their oppressors. Yes, that was what the Romans were: oppressors.

Perhaps Yeshua was the only Jew who remained unbothered by the Roman occupation of the Holy Land of Israel. He came from a lowly family. His father, Yosef, was a carpenter, his mother, Miryam, a home-maker and he had three younger siblings, Abimelech, Yizrela, and Elisha; nothing special about them. However, Yeshua was special, even before his conception, which, they claimed, was immaculate. One day, at age twelve, he went to the temple with his parents. His siblings elected to go with their uncle, Daniel, instead. At the temple, a regal-looking young man in expensive garbs walked up to him and his parents.

"My name is Ganesh Singh," he introduced himself to Yeshua's parents, but he bowed to Yeshua. "Forgive my intrusion, I have been coming to your temple for fourteen days straight in hopes of meeting this child of great promise."

"Your words are most kind and generous, fellow stranger," Yosef hid his caution behind politeness. "But I am afraid we have pressing matters to attend to right now."

"You are a crown prince from the far east," Yeshua said flatly.

"Son, hush now, alright?" Miryam, his mother put her arms protectively on Yeshua's shoulders. "It is best not to be impolite to strangers."

She flashed a forced smile in the stranger's direction as Yosef stepped closer towards his family. His focus did not depart from Ganesh's face.

"Fear not, mother," Yeshua said and turned an expressionless face upwards at his mother. "He is a crown prince from a kingdom in the Far East called 'India'."

Yeshua then turned his attention towards Prince Ganesh.

"Your father is King Rama," he said. "Your mother Queen Sangita, your younger sister, Suri and your younger brother, Gulam. Gulam is the youngest."

"How do you know this, son?" Yosef could barely contain his shock. "We have never heard of such a place."

"Do not concern yourself with the things I know, father," Yeshua spoke with unwavering firmness of tone, almost dismissively too. "But you must know that this prince is a goodly man and means us no harm."

"You are indeed a young master," Ganesh dropped to a knee and bowed his head low. "Alas, my journey is complete, and my purpose fulfilled."

His entire entourage of over forty people did the same. Yeshua's parents noticed them for the first time since meeting Prince Ganesh. Prince Ganesh then raised his head up.

"Sir, everything the young master says is true," Ganesh spoke to Yosef. "With your permission, I shall take him with me to my kingdom. Everything that is mine will be his. He will receive the best education and training we have to offer. His word will be second only to my father's and mine. This and much more, I promise to offer the young master, if you would allow me this honor."

Yosef turned to look at his wife. Their facial expressions underscored their fears, concerns and uncertainty about everything that was happening.

"Like I said," Yeshua reiterated to his parents. "The crown prince means us no harm and his word is true. My purpose lies beyond these lands and I must journey into the realm to unveil my true identity and purpose. You do not understand what I say now, but you know in your hearts that I speak the truth."

Young Yeshua then stepped away from his parents' protective arms around his shoulders, turned around and fixed a determined gaze on them.

"Father, mother," he addressed them with a demeanor that was a score of years his senior. "This I must do. This is what Creation has outlined for me."

Miryam swallowed nervously while Yosef scratched his beard.

"Ruth, the elderly woman down the street, now has both her legs back,"

Yosef said. "I have known her all my life and until recently, she had no legs."

"And Ezra is alive," Miryam chimed in. "He was dead for two days, my love. Two days."

"So many inexplicable events have been occurring," Yosef sighed in resignation. "And they all have one thing in common."

"Our son," Miryam took Yosef's hand and interlocked her fingers with his. "He is special, my love. We know that already."

She then turned a pair of loving but sad eyes towards Yeshua.

"But we never knew just how special he is," she continued. "We might never know, actually."

"I know you worry about me," Yeshua spoke via telepathy. *"But I assure you that Yahweh will protect and take care of me."*

He is doing that thing again, Yosef thought. *Speaking to us without moving his lips.*

"Telepathy, father," Yeshua continued via telepathy and smiled.

And he hears my thoughts, Yosef thought. *I cannot form words in silence as he does. I may never know how to.*

Yosef smiled back at his son before turning and meeting Miryam's gaze. She nodded slightly at him. He sighed and beckoned at Yeshua. As Yeshua returned to his parents, Yosef turned to address Prince Ganesh.

"Rise, Prince from the Far East," Yosef could not remember the name of the land whence the prince hailed.

Yosef did appreciate the prince's show of humility. Truly, the prince did seem like a goodly man. For one of such royalty to speak so humbly and take a knee and bow before a lowly carpenter like him, Yosef... This gesture alone spoke volumes on the prince's behalf.

Ganesh stood up and his entourage did the same.

"Return here the day after the Sabbath and you can take our son with you," he said.

Prince Ganesh's eyes beamed with unhidden joy and he bowed his head in gratitude.

"Thank you, sir," he said and raised his head. "I am honored beyond words. I shall return here as you command. I now bid you, your wife and the young Master a good day."

"Good day to you as well," Yosef replied.

And so, it came to pass that preparations were made for young Yeshua's departure. His parents and siblings wore their deep sadness and longing on their demeanors. On the day after the Sabbath, Ganesh was waiting for them at the temple with ten bushels of gold, a bushel of rubies and a box of the finest spices from India.

"Sir, please accept these humble gifts as a token of my appreciation for entrusting and honoring me thusly," Ganesh said. "I remember how three cycles ago, I saw the young master in a dream. In that dream, he asked me to seek him in this temple. Those three years seem like three days."

Ganesh let his gaze sweep across the temple. His features softened with joy, respect, reverence and deep relief for realizing a dream.

"I spoke about the dream to our seer," he continued. "He concurred that my dream was not just a dream. That, in fact, the young master had sent me a message. As such, I dedicated much time and effort to studying your language and once I was ready, I journeyed to these lands. You know the rest. And now, my joy is complete. Let not your hearts be burdened, I implore you. I give you my word that I will regularly send word to you on how your son fares."

Prince Ganesh bid his farewells to Miryam, Yosef and young Yeshua's siblings, pressed their hands and headed for his royal caravan. The tears flowed freely, hearts throbbed with sadness and longing and the stoic young master once again became as a child as he wept in his family's arms even more. It took much coaxing and some physical strength before Young Yeshua left his family behind to journey to the most prosperous kingdom in the Far East; India.

"That was a score-less-two years ago," Yeshua recalled as he sat on a rock that was near a dirt road. "It feels like everything happened only yesterday."

Three months ago, he returned to his homeland since his departure to India and word of his great wisdom and miraculous deeds were spreading throughout the lands like a wild fire through a wheat field. They called him different things; teacher, Messiah, demon, con man, magician, prophet, sage, healer and so on. The common folk loved him, the Jewish authorities dreaded him, and the Romans could not care less about his existence. When he returned, he stayed with his mother until he fashioned an abode for himself. A month later, he took a fair maiden as his wife. He had then chosen twelve men from various walks of life to become his apprentices. As he sat on the rock, he pretended not to notice two children sneaking up on him from behind and faked a yelp when they jumped out to scare him.

"Come here, you sneaky one," he laughed, swooping five-year old Dan off his feet and hoisting him up in the air. "You gave me a scare."

Dan shrieked with glee as he sailed through the air and landed in Yeshua's arms. Benjamin, his partner in crime, joined in the laughter and about a dozen more infants gathered around the five-foot-eight-inch tall Yeshua, each of them pleading to be tossed in the air in like manner. Yeshua would have done just that, but then he opted for a less physically taxing solution.

"How about I tell you all a story instead," he asked.

"Yes, yes, yes. Story time," they chanted.

"Let me see," Yeshua said and acted like he was trying to decide on which story to tell.

"Moreh Yeshua," Benjamin called out, sticking his right hand in the air.

"Yes, Benjamin," Yeshua replied.

"Could you please tell us a story that is about a king and his kingdom?"

"Hmmm… I could try," Yeshua caressed his neatly trimmed beard as he furrowed his dark, brown eyes. "Well, here it goes."

"Wait, Moreh," a little girl cried.

She stood up and made her way across her peers until she got to Yeshua. Then, she climbed unto Yeshua's lap and made herself comfortable. Yeshua chuckled.

"What is your name, child?" Yeshua asked.

"Esther."

"How old are you, Esther?"

"Four."

Yeshua kissed Esther on the crown of her head before Esther snuggled against him. He used clairsentience to sense the jealousy burning in many of her peers.

"Okay, there was once a king in a land far from here," Yeshua began. "He was well loved by his people and he had only child, a son, whom he loved so much. Peace and prosperity reigned in the land until a very bad famine struck, bringing pestilence and disease with it."

He smiled at how the children gazed at him with unflinching attention and unwavering focus.

"The king tried everything within his power, but there was nothing he could do about the situation," Yeshua continued. "Then one day, a magician came to the kingdom."

'I can rid your kingdom of this famine and disease, my king,' said the evil-looking magician with dirty teeth and yellow skin. 'For a small price, of course.'

'Name it,' said the king in desperation.

'You must offer your son as a sacrifice,' the magician replied with a toothy grin. 'Only then will your kingdom be saved.'

"With those words, the magician left the king's palace. The king's heart was broken, and he was struck with grief.

'How can I sacrifice my own son? He asked himself. 'But if I do not, many of my people will die.'

"The crown prince heard the magician's demands. He also knew his father was in a very tough situation. So, at night, he snuck out of the palace and went to hide in the streets until the morning. He waited when the marketplace was busiest before he ran to the town center and called out to the magician.

'I am here,' said the courageous prince. 'Take me and safe my father's people and his kingdom.'

"And, in a puff of smoke," Yeshua gestured theatrically with his hands. "The magician appeared at the town center."

'Wise decision, child,' the magician sneered and started meandering his way towards the prince.

"But suddenly," Yeshua's eyes popped in excitement. "All the children in the kingdom gathered and formed a wall around the crown prince."

'You will have to get through us, first,' Yeshua puffed his chest as he spoke.

'You brats,' glared the magician in anger. 'I will destroy you all, along with the kingdom. After all, that was my plan all along.'

'That is good to know,' the king called out from behind the magician, who had not noticed the king and his guards as they approached the town center.

"Word had spread to the king about what his son was about to do.

'My king, I…' stammered the magician.

'Seize him,' commanded the king. 'Take him to the dungeon where he will remain until his execution.'

'My king,' the magician cried as soldiers moved to seize him. 'May I make you an offer.'

'Speak,' the king commanded.

'I will remove the curse of famine, pestilence and disease in exchange for my life,' the magician offered.

'Very well,' the king agreed. 'Do so immediately.'

"And with words of magic, the magician removed the curse from the land and everyone was saved," Yeshua continued. "The king banished the magician from the kingdom, the young prince grew up to become a great and wise king, and peace and prosperity reigned for eternity. The end."

A round of applause and shouts of contentment followed the conclusion of the story.

"So, what is the lesson from the story, Moreh?" asked a little girl.

"The lesson is that you, my little friends, have hearts of purity, strength, and love. You are our future and you remind us, the older ones that, even in our darkest hour, when all seems to be lost, there is always hope and all we need is the courage to take that step and make the change."

The children's faces lit up with pride for they had learned a great lesson. The children may not have understood the full meaning of Yeshua 's words, but their hearts soared with empowerment and happiness. Yeshua sensed more questions were to follow, but alas, he had other matters to attend to. Yehuda, one of his apprentices had just arrived.

"Apologies, children," Yeshua said as he lifted Esther off his lap and set her on the ground. "Story time is over. I have matters to attend to."

Faces long and shoulders slumped from disappointment, the children left, but not before thanking Moreh Yeshua for his beautiful story.

"You asked to see me, Master?" Yehuda said.

Yehuda wore a pair of wooden sandals and a light brown robe that was tied to at the waist. He was an inch taller than Yeshua was and had dark eyes. He had black hair, just like Yeshua, but his beard was longer and not-so-neat. Yehuda was determined, fearless, poised, intuitive and loyal. On the other hand, he was secretive, controlling, perfectionist, resentful and more jealous than most. He was also the group's treasurer.

"Yes, brother. Come. Walk with me," said Yeshua.

Sometimes, Yeshua addressed his apprentices by their names. Other times, he addressed them as 'brother.'

"Do you believe in destiny?" he asked Yehuda as they started walking.

"Honestly, Master, I do not," Yehuda replied.

"And why is that, brother?" the master asked.

"You see, Master," Yehuda said, "I agree with the notion that Yahweh has a plan for us. But at the same time, I cannot understand why He would allow certain things to happen. Like the Romans ruling over us when we are supposed to be His chosen people. I do not know the role death, famine, wickedness, and everything else, have to play in our realm. As such, I think that there is no such thing as purpose; universal, subjective or both. I believe that there is cause and effect; that there is action and reaction. Believe me, I have pondered upon these things without success, Master."

The Master listened as Yehuda spoke his mind. He had a deep appreciation for his apprentice's philosophy. When they arrived at the top of the hill, Yeshua sat on a boulder and gestured for Yehuda to sit next to him. Dusk slowly approached. Yeshua sat in silence for a few moments with his eyes closed, as if he was basking in the gentle warmth of the setting Solara, while taking slow, steady inhalations and exhalations. He then opened his eyes and, without looking at Yehuda, he started speaking.

"Everything has a purpose," Yeshua said. "Nothing ever just happens. One's ignorance of the reason for certain occurrences ought not be either an affirmation or preclusion of the absence or nonexistence of purpose. There is always the big painting and a portion of a painting, while it may provide some insight, does not explain the entire painting. But if you can appreciate the entire painting, then maybe you can appreciate purpose. Do you understand my words, Yehuda?"

"Yes, Master. I understand," Yehuda replied.

"I chose you as one of my apprentices," the Master continued. "It was no coincidence. A random act of circumstances did not just culminate in our paths crossing. There was, and is, a purpose for it. Everything in Creation has a purpose. The stones you walk on, the grass in the fields, the birds in the air, things seen and unseen, birth, death, sickness, health, joy, sorrow, happiness, sadness, everything that exists, existed and will exist has a purpose.

"Your purpose, Yehuda will be a huge burden for you to bear. It is for this cause that, I am preparing you now. You will know much loneliness as you journey through this life, to say the least. You will be vilified, hated, cursed and banished. You will go down in the history of humanity as a vile, conniving person. You will see the dark and live in the dark. You will walk alone, mostly; without friends or family. But, alas, this will not be so forever, for you will be hailed in glory and honor. Your name will be restored, and you will play a significant role in protecting and saving humanity. Right now, you are confused and even afraid. I understand. As I said, I chose you for a reason. But for you to walk this path, it must be of your free will."

Yehuda's lips parted in shock as his master spoke words most unwelcome. He rubbed his temples as if he could rub himself back to a reality before that present moment.

This was not the life I had envisioned for myself when I was but a youth, he thought.

Given his personality, Yehuda always saw himself as a wealthy businessman, with the most beautiful woman by his side as his wife to bear him beautiful children, regardless of their genders. He wanted to be a great, wealthy father and husband. But now, Master was telling him about a future that was an aberration from his vision.

No. This must be a dream.

And as the thoughts raced through his mind, he felt his master's reassuring hand on his shoulder.

"Brother," said Yeshua. "Be not afraid. I will always be with you, even if you may not perceive my presence. Your purpose is one that extends beyond Earth Realm. I understand that this may be a terrible burden to bear, but though the world will turn its back on you, I will never leave you nor forsake you. You are the toughest and bravest of all my apprentices. This is part of why I chose you. If you decide to choose a different path for yourself, I will understand, and I will bear you no ill-will, nor will I be disappointed in you. So, Yehuda, I ask you: will you accept this path?"

Yehuda wanted to scream and run away.

This is my chance, my opportunity, he thought. *I can just walk away and choose* my *destiny*, my *path*.

His mind raced in a thousand different directions and his heart throbbed with the feelings of ten thousand conflicting emotions at the same time. But alas, he knew the right decision to make did not necessarily have to be the one he wanted.

"Master," Yehuda turned to face his mentor. "When you asked me to join you, I pledged my loyalty to you. I trust you are of the Most High and that what you say is true. I believe that you will never forsake me nor abandon me. My heart is heavy, my mind is weak, and I do not know what I am getting into. But I have faith in you, Master. So, yes, I will take upon this yoke. If it will be for the good of this realm and beyond, then so be it. I accept this path."

"I knew you would," Yeshua smiled and clapped Yehuda on the back. "Thank you very much. I am also glad to hear that you pledged your loyalty to me. Do you know why?"

"No, Master," replied Yehuda.

"Because, brother," Yeshua said as he stood up from the boulder. "*YOU* are going to betray me."

CHAPTER THREE

C. E. 1938

ADOLF HITLER. EVIL incarnate. Hatred personified. The Devil in the flesh. One of The Beasts described in the Book of the Apocalypse and the list goes on. He epitomized megalomania, psychopathy and sociopathy. Hundreds of millions murdered in his name, for his agenda. But what was his agenda? To rid the human species of races that were not pure, not Aryan? Was that his endgame? Was his quest for a pure and superior species merely a front, a smokescreen? Worse, was he just a pawn for something much more evil and nefarious?

Once, when Adolf was sixteen years of age, his uncle, together with the wife and fourteen-year-old cousin, Rosa, had come to visit them. Rosa was his favorite cousin because a year prior, he had confessed his deep fascination and desire for her; feelings which she admitted she also had for him. Adolf's family owned a small cottage about half a kilometer from a small forest near the river. Many teenagers and even young adults found convenient shelters to fulfill their sexual drives and Adolf and Rosa were no different. It almost seemed like the stars were blessing their infatuation with each other. But Adolf was not one to subscribe to the whims of any form of religion, be it one that was championed by a god, God or Mother Nature. Nothing held more importance beyond their teenage curiosity and fascination with their fiery libidos; not even the rumors of wild beasts lurking around and the occasional discovery of mauled animal carcasses in the forest. All they needed was a blanket, some privacy and the rest was history.

Today, I will go all the way with Rosa, Adolf promised himself. *All we do is fondle and play with each other and I want more. I want all of her.*

He wanted to give her his virginity and he wanted her to reciprocate. Prior to Rosa's arrival, he had found the perfect spot in the woods to seal the deal; already cleared, sheltered and ready to be used.

Thank the skies for a rainless day in spring, he thought.

Adolf was ready and hoped she was as well.

Well, if she's not, I'll just have to convince her, he gave himself a confidence boost. *I mean, I love her, and I think she loves me too. Yet, she hesitates. But why? Aren't lovers supposed to go all the way? At least, that's what the boys at school say.*

"Papa, we're off to the woods," Adolf called out to his father shortly after Rosa's family had settled in.

"You two be careful out there now. I hear the mosquitoes have teeth this time of the year," said Adolf's aunt with a smile.

"We'll return the favor, mama," Rosa replied. "Besides, I'm in the mood for some mosquito pudding right about now."

"Oh dear," cried Adolf's mother amidst fits of laughter from everyone. "Save some for us."

And more laughter erupted from everyone.

"Yes, mama," replied Adolf, holding open the door for Rosa.

When she walked past him, he closed the door behind himself.

"Those two are the best of friends," said Rosa's mother.

"Yes, they are," concurred Adolf's father, sipping on his cup of tea. "I'm glad they have such a great relationship."

Half an hour later, Adolf and Rosa pounced on each other like two starving souls would at an all-you-can-eat buffet. They worked their lips, hands and tongues all over each other's body until they moaned and convulsed with sweet satisfaction from climaxes. After a quick clean, the incestuous lovers crawled into each other's arms and closed their eyes. They basked in the warm glow of each other's love until Adolf broke the silence.

"My love," he spoke softly into the crown of her head.

"Yes, my love," she replied with half-closed eyes.

"I think it's time for us to start having sex, don't you think?"

Rosa recoiled from his chest and glared at Adolf as if he had called her fat and ugly.

"Are you serious?" she asked.

"Yes, I am," he replied with false bravado and propped himself on his elbows. "Come on now, we both know it's bound to happen. I know I'm ready. What's holding you back?"

He kept his crossed left fingers out of her sight.

"First of all," she said sarcastically. "Imagine that I miss my period and it turns out that baby Adolf is growing inside of me. What do we tell our parents? 'Hey mama, papa, I'm with child and my darling cousin is the father.' How does that sound to you, huh? Did you even consider that, you selfish buffoon."

Her face was reddening with anger.

"No," replied Adolf as his false bravado gave birth to embarrassment. "I never thought of that and I didn't mean to sound selfish. I just... You know, I hear when two people love each other..." he broke off and turned his back to her.

His eyes welled up with tears of embarrassment and shame.

"I'm sorry," he muttered. "Please, forget I even-"

"Oh, my love," Rosa reached for his shoulder. "I'm sorry I got upset. I'm just scared, I think. I've always wanted to go all the way with you too, but I'm afraid. Here. Come."

Adult let her pull him towards her. He felt her lips on his and managed a weak smile.

"There," she grinned and then stood up.

Rosa slowly took off her blouse and let it drop by her left ankle. Adolf sat on the blanket, mouth agape and groin growling with greed. He made to get up, but she stuck her right index finger out to him and waved it from side to side, shaking her head at the same time.

"No, no, no, *mein herr*," she commanded. "You'll have to work for it. You will go on a treasure hunt and when you find all my clothes, there will be treasure waiting for you."

Rosa giggled with sweet mischief. Adolf's eyebrows creased in frustration at first before his eyes widened with excitement. Satisfied with his reaction, Rosa turned around and started heading into the woods as she unhooked her bra. Adolf's breathing became heavier with the anticipation of a dream finally about to come true. He stood up after Rosa disappeared into the woods.

"I'm coming now," Adolf called out.

He picked up her blouse and then her brassiere a few feet away. Next came her skirt.

That leaves her socks, sandals and panties, he smiled at the thought.

He ventured further into the forest and found a sock and, about thirteen meters further, he found her other sock. He scanned around and tried to work on her possible path from there.

Maybe she doubled back to our spot? He wondered. *For that, she'll need her sandals.*

As such, he walked another twenty meters or so to the left, searching for her panties along the way. Nothing. He searched to the right.

"Found it," he cried out in victory as he scooped up his find and sniffed it.

The crotch area was still damp from her juices, the scent of which made him ravenous with lust. Talk about an aphrodisiac. He started doubling back towards what he thought was their spot when something caught his attention about half a stone's throw to his left.

Though the paralyzing fear that gripped his motor functions had nothing to do with the gore in front of him, it had everything to do with the reason for the gore. A creature that looked like a giant hound with hairy shoulders and forearms was jamming its head repeatedly into the bloody carcass of a deer. Its muscles were stretched taut underneath its black, leathery skin. Its back was unnaturally arched upwards and its spine pushed so hard against its skin that it seemed as it if was trying to break free from its protoplasmic confines. It growled as it feasted and Adolf remained motionless as he watched with fascination and fear. Suddenly, the creature pulled its head away from what remained of the deer and stared directly into Adolf with eyes that glowed white with evil.

Blood and chunks of venison dangled from its snout. Slowly, the creature parted its jaws slightly and let loose an evil growl that grew louder by the second and drowned the last of Adolf's adrenaline. Adolf's knees buckled and he sank to the ground in surrender. Rosa's clothes fell in a lazy pile in front of him. He wanted desperately to move, to flee, to live; but his body would not respond to his will. He wanted to scream for his mother, but his lips would not move. Slowly, the hairs on the creature's shoulders stood on edge, its back arched further and its growl became louder and more menacing in a prelude to an attack. Adolf's final thoughts and only regret as he braced for an impending, gory death, was that he was going to die a virgin.

But then, the creatures pupils flashed in a very bright whiteness. It stood on its hind legs, raised its head to the sky and started spasming.

No… No… It's impossible, he thought. Either this must be a terrible nightmare, or I am losing my mind.

The beast growled and cringed erratically as if someone was striking it methodically on random areas of its body. It buried its face in its claws and the hairs on its shoulders began receding into its skin. Its dark skin slowly turned lighter in complexion. Its claws receded and its knees broke forward so that its legs could now only bend forward. It dropped to a knee. It removed its hands from its face, as its snout retreated into what now looked like a bloodied human face. A few chunks of venison fell to the ground while others remained stuck on its face. Long, black hair grew from its head and covered most of its face and neck. Adolf almost fainted at the realization of what just happened.

Less than half a minute ago, he was staring into the eyes of a creature from hell itself. But now, genuflecting in front of him, with long black hair streaming down her face and clumps of hair sticking to the blood on her mouth, cheeks and neck, was a human being, a female. When she stood up and parted the hairs from her face, Adolf gawked at her astounding beauty; flawless skin, ample, perky breasts that seemed to defy gravity, and a heavily toned 1.7m tall exquisitely proportional physique. She seemed completely oblivious to her nakedness. Despite his spine-chilling, bone-rattling fear, Adolf found himself having a reaction in his nether region.

Suddenly, a rush of adrenaline flooded Adolf's body and sent him into flight mode. Maybe because his subconscious associated this naked beauty before him to harmlessness. The creature was gone and now he had a chance to flee. He did not care. He snatched Rosa's clothes from the ground and made a run for it. However, as he turned to flee, something zipped past his left peripheral vision and he almost ran into the once-upon-a-time-savage-beast-now-exceedingly-beautiful-bloodied-black-haired lady. The sudden recoil to avoid a collision caused Adolf to fall on his butt. He still held on to Rosa's clothes.

"Thank thine lucky stars for on this day, they look upon thee with favor," the lady said as she knelt in front of Adolf and inched her face closer to his.

Adolf could smell the iron in the drying blood and the odor of a pieces of venison that still clung to her skin. Her breath stank as if a corpse was rotting in her mouth. He suppressed the urge to throw up all over her resplendent body.

"But should thou ever speak of this, then thine fate would be far worse than that of the game I just slew."

She then inched closer to Adolf's ear, sniffed around his neck and hair. When she realized that she had smeared some blood on his cheek, she smiled and licked the blood off his cheek. The gesture was part-bestial, part-erotic and Adolf wet his pants with the contents of his gonads.

"Now I have thine scent... *Adolf*," she continued, putting extra emphasis on his name.

Adolf gasped and his eyes widened in fear and shock.

How could she know my name? he wondered.

She then stood up and walked around Adolf. He heard a whizzing sound and the lady was gone as if she was never there in the first place. He did not even have the time to process what had just happened. Finally, he realized his opportunity and quickly stood up. He wanted to sprint away but the extreme fluctuations of the adrenaline in his body culminated in a huge emotional crash. He could barely even walk. So, he dragged himself towards his picnic spot where Rosa, wearing nothing but a mischievous grin and a pair of sandals, was waiting for him. She gasped a little when she saw his pale, haggard, exhausted expression.

"Oh my. What happened to you? I never knew you were so scared of my nakedness," she giggled.

Her giggling gave way to genuine concern when Adolf said nothing..

"My love.... What happened?"

Rosa stood up and walked towards Adolf.

"Remember the film we watched where one person was turning into an animal and killing people. Like the big bad wolf? Only this time it was much bigger and very beautiful. It was so real that I wet my pants. And no! This is not pee, I assure you. I know it sounds crazy, but then she said if I told anyone, she was going to kill me. And she spoke funny. Oh, yes, my love. There is a big, scary human-beast creature out there. And you should see what it did to a deer. You can come and see for yourself, only that she disappeared like a flash of lightning..."

This was what he wanted to tell her. Instead, he settled for something simpler.

"Get dressed, Rosa," he said flatly. "We're going home."

After that incident, Adolf was never the same person again. But that was not the reason for his psychosis. His psychosis began manifesting with him killing his neighbors' pets. Yes, people were superior to animals. And humans were not all the same. Aryans were of the highest supremacy. They were the chosen ones, fashioned from and by the gods themselves. Every other race was inferior and, therefore, had to be eliminated! And so, Adolf Hitler had started envisioning, from a very early age, a world in which he would purge humanity of any race that was not Aryan.

Decades later, he would become the Führer and the events in the forest with the strange creature would become buried in the deep recesses of his subconscious, despite the occasional nightmares. He never sought psychological help for fear of being labeled as handicapped and weak. He was Führer! He was god, damn it! And there were more pressing matters at hand. The country was heavily in debt, he needed to build an army and re-arm. *But I'll not burden myself as such tonight!* He said to himself as he lay naked on his bed, waiting for his niece to come join him by way of their secret passage. She was the best he ever had!

Suddenly, two silhouettes zipped into Adolf's chamber before his mind could fully comprehend what just happened. The two silhouettes stopped about ten feet from his bed. Adolf's rational mind finally registered and took over. The fear and panic were palpable. Adolf went for his luger.

"If you want to live, you better sit still and pay close attention, Adolf," a deep, reverberating voice said.

Adolf froze mid-reach before retracting his hand and letting it rest on his stomach. The two fast-moving intruders stared down at him. They both had black hair. The male was very muscular, stood at six feet, five inches tall and very handsome. The female was six feet tall, had a very toned body, with perfectly formed features and was incredibly beautiful. They were both naked and cared less.

"Who-" Adolf stammered.

His throat was dry. He swallowed and tried again.

"Who are you?" he asked barely above a whisper.

"I am Dreyko Pakola," replied the male. "And this is my sister, Danka."

Then their pupils glowed brightly at the same time, and Adolf remembered seeing the same glow in the woman's eyes in the forest many years ago. The only difference was that the glow in his unwelcome visitors' eyes was red, not white.

"No!" he cried. "This can't be! Not again! No! NOOO!"

Adolf retreated into the bed post and wished he could escape through the walls to safety.

"Be still now," the woman said firmly. "Or we will make you."

A whimpering Adolf cowered back on to the bed.

"We know you met one of ours many years ago," said Dreyko. "Her name is Anna, and she's more than five hundred years old."

He paused to let this piece of information hit Adolf.

"So, if we wanted you dead, you would have been dead already," Dreyko continued. "Now, pay close attention to what I have to say. I want to make you an offer."

The Führer was petrified and confused. Were these... things... not there to kill him? He swallowed, summoned some courage and squared his shaking shoulders.

"Alright," he said. "You have my complete attention."

"Good," said Dreyko

He pulled up a chair and sat on it. Danka did the same.

"How would you like to have an army of superhuman immortals?" Dreyko asked.

CHAPTER FOUR

30 C. E.

"WHEN WILL YOU be back, my love?" she asked from the kitchen.

"Before sunset," Shi'mon replied as he fastened the straps of his wooden sandals.

"Alright, your food will be cold by then," she said without breaking her concentration on her cooking. "So you will have to give me some time to heat it up for your when you return."

Her voice was music to his soul. Her care gave him new purpose. And her love was the breath in his lungs. Her name was Rania, and she was the song of his life. Shi'mon's smile shone from the inner sanctum of his soul.

***

Shi'mon had lost his father many years ago to a storm while his father was out fishing on the Sea of Galilee. His father, David, was a man of calm persona, with sharp wit and wisdom. He was a model family man, outgoing and his kindness knew no bounds. He was also a man who earned an honest coin as a fisherman who owned four large fishing boats and managed over a dozen employees. David was everything Shi'mon wanted to be and become while Ruth, Shi'mon's mother, was the perfect example of the kind of woman Shi'mon wanted his future wife to be: caring, loving, kind, tough with the hand but sweet with a kiss, hardworking and a magician in the kitchen. Shi'mon had a younger brother, Aaron. Sadly, she was barren after Aaron's birth, but that did not affect her relationship with her family. Aaron later co-ran their father's business with Shi'mon.

Shi'mon was only seven when he lost his father. The bright, sunny skies had suddenly blackened as if the clouds had mounted a coup to snuff out the sun. The winds went wild with the fury of Mother Nature herself, joining forces with the endless walls of rain that pummeled the earth in a drenching wetness that promised nothing but death and destruction to anyone trapped on the storm-tossed sea, with waves rising to over thirty feet of raging wet dealers of death and desolation. David and half his employees were a part of the over fifty boats stuck in the surging savagery of the sea. Everyone else had run for cover and prayed to Yahweh, or any of the gods they worshipped, for a miracle. The storm had lasted for no more than ten minutes, but ten minutes was more than enough time to drag every creature and everything on the surface into the cold, briny deep of drowning oblivion.

Shi'mon stood at the shore with hundreds of others, waiting for whatever remained of their loved ones to be washed ashore. The wailing, the pain in the air, the sorrow in the soil all dulled compared to the numbness of his heart. His mother's hands rested tightly on his shoulders. He heard her say something along the lines of 'Stay strong, my boy,' or, 'Your father might still be alive.' But none of that mattered. He glanced a few times in Aaron's direction, who held his hand in a gesture that could only imply immovable faith in his elder brother. Shi'mon later understood that Aaron was still too young to process the events of that day. Unfortunately for him, he, Shi'mon, did not have the luxury of his psyche being shielded from the quagmire of emotions that came with the pain of loss of someone one loved, worshipped and adored.

Families camped along the shore when nothing turned up at the shore a day after the storm. Then, the first set of corpses slowly floated towards the shore. Every corpse washed ashore was cause for closure and renewed cries of heart-rending pain, grief and sorrow. David's corpse arrived on the second day after the storm. The sound of his mother's scream and the sight of his father's lifeless form cast Shi'mon into a realm of darkness and hollowness so profound that Shi'mon became numb to everything. He became an empty, emotionless shell and that hollowness became filled with something Shi'mon had never felt before: rage. He raged at Yahweh, the Maker of everything, including the storm that took his father away from him and, by extension, Yahweh was his father's killer.

David was buried three days later, which happened to be on his birthday.

And Yahweh spits on my face again, Shi'mon thought.

As young as he was, Shi'mon knew he had to don a demeanor many years his senior. He was now the man of the house and, therefore, had a family to take care of. Luckily, David's assistant groomed Shi'mon in the affairs of the business until Shi'mon turned sixteen and took over the management of the entire fishing business. Aaron was still an apprentice. A year after he took over his father's business, Ruth passed away from a protracted illness. His rage against Yahweh burned with an even more fiery ferocity until he met Rania and his life had never been the same after that. Rania was his light, his life, his savior.

***

Shi'mon tiptoed behind his wife and startled her. Rania shrieked, turned around and smacked him in the arm. He roared with laughter borne out of childish mischief.

"You know I do not like that, my love," she stifled a giggle.

Shi'mon slipped his hands to the base of her belly and caressed the eleven-week-old bump. She turned as he took a knee and kissed her stomach. A joyous warmed leaked from Rania's heart into her being and tears of love and happiness streaked down her cheeks.

I am the luckiest woman in the realm, she thought.

"Have you chosen a name yet?" Shi'mon asked her.

"I thought we agreed that if it is a girl, we will name her after your mother?" Rania said.

"We did. And what if it is a boy?" he asked as he pressed his ear against her stomach as if he was listening to what the baby was saying.

"I will defer to your good judgment, my husband," Rania rolled her eyes.

"Enoch," he said.

"Last week it was Daniel. Then Benjamin, and now, Enoch?" she chuckled. "Make up your mind-"

"Wait," he beamed. "I think I hear something. I think the baby moved. I hear it moving."

"No, my love," Rania said, shaking her head at his cuteness. "That was not the baby. Babies do not start kicking until after twelve to sixteen weeks. At least that is what mother told me."

"Then what did I hear?" Shi'mon asked innocently.

"Air movements," she grinned. "So, you know what is coming."

"Oh no. May Yahweh help this poor child," he gasped covering his nose with his left hand and playfully backed away from her. "I do not want to be that child right now."

"Hey," she exclaimed and threw a napkin at him.

They both broke into laughter.

"Did Master say why he summoned you?" she asked.

"No," Shi'mon replied. "He just asked me to meet him by the pier. It must be important for him to summon me on such short notice. But, no cause for fear or worry. He probably just has a task for me. Anyway, I will let you know when I return."

"Just do not stay out too late, please," Rania implored.

"Of course," Shi'mon replied, kissing her on the lips.

"Alright," she sighed. "I am sorry if I am acting like Mother Hen. I do not mean it like that."

"Never be sorry for showing me love, alright?" Shi'mon cast a look of deep love and longing upon her.

"Alright," she said. "See you soon."

"See you soon," Shi'mon replied and left the house to meet Yeshua.

How did I get so lucky? he smiled as he shut the front door and his mind took a detour down memory street.

***

Marriage was the furthest thing on Shi'mon's mind after he lost his father and took over his father's business. The business and Aaron were all he cared about, until everything changed on that fateful day. He had just struck a deal with Josiah, his biggest customer and was about to prepare Josiah's order, when a middle-aged lady walked up to Josiah's fish booth to make a purchase. A young maiden accompanied this lady, who Shi'mon assumed was the lady's daughter. They had waited for Shi'mon and Josiah to conclude their business because they wanted fresher fish, he believed. Shi'mon noticed that the maiden kept smiling at him while the lady he assumed was the maiden's mother was bargaining with Josiah.

"Is something amusing you, miss?" he asked almost rudely.

"I am not sure, sir," said the young maiden, still smiling. "But I am certain that no matter how bad your day may be, it is not as bad as that poor fellow's over there."

She gestured with her head and averted her eyes to hide her embarrassment.

Shi'mon followed her gaze. A young man, probably a merchant, was unaware that a part of his cloak was ripped around his buttocks and was strolling casually around the marketplace. Some children tiptoed behind him with a piece of stick and poked at the exposed flesh of his buttocks. Laughter erupted, and the children scurried away as the man gave chase. Even Shi'mon chuckled a little.

"See," said the young maiden with an even brighter smile. "It is not so hard to smile, is it? How did that feel, sir?"

Until that moment, Shi'mon had not realized that he might have become so used to his pain that it constantly reflected on his face.

"It is by the work of your hands and the sweat of your brow that my mother and I will be cooking some good fish today," she continued without waiting for his reply. "So, I thank you very much for everything that you do for my mother, the community and… for me."

The young maiden could barely look at Shi'mon now.

"You are a good man, sir; you and everyone you work with," she added.

She raised her head to meet his gaze and her smile… Something about her smile caused something within Shi'mon to break apart, like a wall crumbling to pieces and light suddenly flooding into the dark chamber that used to be his personality. He recoiled slightly, unable to understand what was happening to him. However, he reverted to his old self and quickly rebuilt another wall of protection around the fortress of his psyche; only this time, the wall had several cracks in them. And the light of her smile, of her persona, shone through those cracks like a beacon of… hope and a promise of much more.

"I-," Shi'mon stammered.

He cleared his throat and then gave it another try.

"I thank you, *almah*," he said and smiled genuinely.

More of his new wall crumbled.

"Of course, sir," she said and bowed slightly. "Enjoy the rest of your day. May Yahweh continue to keep you strong."

With those words, she joined her mother and the two headed further into the market.

She is a very bold almah, he thought as he stared at her as if in a trance.

"She is not yet married, you know. And neither is she betrothed to anyone," Josiah said with a mischievous grin.

Shi'mon, being as impulsive as always, ran after her.

"Madam, madam," he called out. "Please, wait."

The fair maiden and her mother turned around to see Shi'mon coming to a quick stop in front of them.

"Forgive my rudeness, madam," he addressed the maiden's mother. "But I must speak with your… daughter. Please."

"She is my daughter, young man," the woman said with an air of authority and confidence. "You may speak with her."

"Thank you, madam," Shi'mon nodded and straightened his gait.

"I," he cleared his throat and squared his shoulders. "I forgot to ask your name, *almah*."

Her smiled dwarfed the brightness of Solara and all of existence was lost in that singular moment.

"Rania," she replied. "My name is Rania."

"I am honored to meet you, Rania," Shi'mon bowed slightly. "My name is Shi'mon, son of David and fisherman by trade."

"I am honored to meet you, Shi'mon," Rania grinned and kept her gaze trained on Shi'mon because she was avoiding making eye contact with her mother for so many reasons.

A year later, Shi'mon and Rania got married.

***

Yeshua saw Shi'mon appear from the right at the foot of the hill. He waved at Shi'mon and Shi'mon returned his wave. He watched with an expressionless face as Shi'mon took steady strides towards him. He remembered the day he met Shi'mon. Shi'mon had just pulled up to the shore and, together with Aaron and Shi'mon's men, they had started unloading the boats, a task which looked like it was going to be over quickly, given the terrible catch that day. He smiled slightly at Shi'mon's resolve, focus and charisma. Shi'mon appeared to be someone who commanded much respect from his employees, despite being much younger than many of them.

A natural leader, Yeshua nodded to himself and walked towards Shi'mon.

***

"Hello Shi'mon," his voice was friendly and kind as he greeted Shi'mon. "It appears you had some trouble with the catch today."

"Two days now, sir," Shi'mon replied with a slight scowl. "Frustrating."

"How about you cast your nets further east?" Yeshua offered. "I think you will have a better catch. I know you just came from there, but if you go further inwards, you will not regret it."

Yeshua observed Shi'mon's scowl morph from frustration to uncertainty, before softening in agreement.

"Load up, men," Shi'mon commanded. "We are going further east."

"But we just came from there, sir," complained an employee.

"Just do as I say, Abel," Shi'mon said and hopped into a boat.

"You heard him," Aaron barked. "Let us move it, men."

Two hours later, Shi'mon and his men returned to shore with all four boats teeming with so much fish the boats barely stayed afloat. Shi'mon was out of his boat before it embarked. He waded through the water and, when he arrived at the shore, he ran towards Yeshua and fell at Yeshua's feet.

"Sir, how did you know?" he asked in awe and respect.

Yeshua smiled.

"How would you like to be a fisher of men?" he asked Shi'mon.

"A moment, please, sir," Shi'mon said and stood up.

"Abel," he called out. "You are in charge until my return."

"Aye, sir," Abel affirmed. "Is everything alright, sir."

"Everything is fine," Shi'mon replied almost dismissively. "I will see you all upon my return."

He then returned his attention to Yeshua.

"Wherever you go, I go... Master."

Yeshua nodded.

"That is your brother, Aaron, correct?" he asked.

"Yes, Master," Shi'mon replied.

Shi'mon did not even wonder how Yeshua knew his name, Aaron's name or even that Andrew was his brother.

Maybe he already asked around, he surmised.

"Bid him join us," Yeshua said.

"Aaron," Shi'mon gestured for him to join them.

Aaron hurried over, greeted Yeshua with a polite nod and then turned to face his brother.

"What is it, brother?" he asked.

"My name is Yeshua," Yeshua replied. "And I want you and your brother to come follow me."

Aaron shifted his attention between his brother and this stranger who asked them to follow him.

"He told me where to fish, brother," Shi'mon said. "I feel it within my spirit that he is a master of our time."

"Where you go, I go, brother," Aaron replied.

And from that day onwards, Shi'mon and Aaron became two of Yeshua's apprentices.

***

"Peace and goodwill unto you, Master," Shi'mon greeted and sat next to Yeshua.

"Peace and goodwill unto you, brother," Yeshua replied. "How fares Rania? Are you two still undecided on what name to give your baby girl?"

"So, it *IS* going to be a girl," exclaimed Shi'mon. "That settles the name dispute then." he chuckled. "We will call her Ruth, after my mother."

"That is a very beautiful name," replied the Master. "She-," he cut himself off as if realizing what he might say may not be welcome.

He sighed and shrugged.

"She will be a very beautiful child, and her beauty will surely come from her mother." The Master grinned broadly.

"Hey," Shi'mon exclaimed, and considered punching Yeshua for his joke. "What are you trying to say, Master?"

"I am just saying," the Master continued, "that it would be better if she does not get any of her looks from you."

Both men roared with laughter. When the laughter died, Shi'mon dove straight to business.

"So, Master, you asked to see me. Is everything alright?"

"Yes, all is well. I just wanted to discuss something with you." Yeshua had Shi'mon's full attention. "Do you recall the day I asked you and your brothers what the people think I am and do you remember your answer?"

"Yes, Master, I do."

"And do you remember what I said after that?"

"Yes, I do, Master."

"I have my reasons for calling you *Cephas*. You are a man of great impulse and strength, as well as intuition. The day I first called you and Aaron, you followed me without the slightest hesitation or reservation. You did not know who I was or whence I came. Yet, you were willing to follow me. I saw how you led your men. Leadership comes naturally to you. And in the short time I have known you, your progress has been tremendous. I see how your eyes light up at the mention of Rania and how you get serious when it is time for business. I truly admire your courage and passion. No other apprentice of mine's leadership skills match yours and it is for this reason that I want you to be the leader of your brothers-in-apprenticeship."

Shi'mon could not contain his happy surprise.

"Master," he stuttered. "I overflow with honor and gratitude."

Yeshua placed a hand on his shoulder and gave it a good squeeze.

"I trust you will be a great leader," he said and withdrew his hand from Shi'mon's shoulder. "Alas, this is not the only reason why I asked you to come today. One of you will betray me."

Shi'mon's joyous expression disappeared behind a scowl of justified anger.

"I will personally see to it that he pays dearly for even thinking such vile thoughts, Master," Shi'mon promised.

"Be that as it may, brother," Yeshua remained calm as he spoke. "Be aware that the time will come when you will betray me. On that day, you will deny me not once, not twice but three times and a rooster will crow to remind you of my words."

"I beg of you, Master," Shi'mon said. "Do not speak as if you have been possessed by an evil spirit. I will never leave you nor forsake you, Master. I will be with you till the very end, and you know that."

"Which brings me to the other side of you, Shi'mon," continued the Master calmly. "Your arrogance and stubbornness are your weakest points."

"But, Master-"

"AND confrontational," added Yeshua, holding up a finger. "You see, brother, my words are neither a reprimand nor a plot to hurt your feelings. I only bring this to your attention now because you denying me will be most vital to the fate of this realm."

He gave Shi'mon a moment to think about this.

"You see, everything, and I mean EVERYTHING, good or evil, has a purpose. The time will come when you will need both your 'good' and 'bad' traits. They will serve a purpose. If you want to change, do so only because you want to, not because you think I asked you to. I only ask you to understand that these traits exist for a reason and rather than fight them, accept them. You will have no teacher or master greater than yourself. I am but an aide in your path to self-awareness. Do not fight yourself, do not resist yourself and certainly, do not get attached to yourself."

"I do not understand, Master," Shi'mon said quietly.

"I know, brother," Yeshua nodded with a smile of encouragement. "But in due time, you will. That is part of the reason why I am here; to teach you, guide you and to prepare you for what you will go through for a long time. The fate of this realm and beyond will depend on what you do now and what you will do soon. You are a part of the whole painting, but I cannot help you fulfill this purpose unless you accept it of your own free will."

He paused to allow Shi'mon a moment to absorb his words. Then he placed his right hand on Shi'mon's left shoulder and asked calmly but firmly.

"Shi'mon Cephas, will you accept this path?"

Despite the uncertainty that plagued his conscious mind, Shi'mon felt deep in his soul what he had to say.

"Yes, Master," he finally said. "I accept."

The Master smiled and squeezed his left shoulder.

"I knew I could count on you, brother. Thank you. And now, just so you know, before you embark on this journey, the time will also come when you will have to lose something really important to you."

Shi'mon whipped a horrified look at the Master.

"No," Shi'mon gasped. "Not my Rania. Not our child. No."

"Calm down, brother," Yeshua chuckled. "You are so dramatic. I was not referring to your family."

Shi'mon let out a sigh of relief.

"What will I have to lose then?" Shi'mon asked.

Yeshua grinned before saying, "Your soul."

CHAPTER FIVE

C. E. 1938

"RAIN, RAIN. GO away," sang the stranger as he trudged through the went onslaught towards London's best kept secret: *The Bottomless Pint Tavern.* "Who the deuce came up with this piece of rubbish in the name of a rhyme?"

March... the month that heralded the end of winter and the start of spring. His black overcoat covered his black shirt tucked into a black pair of fitted jeans and a black belt that he wore just because. His black hat added to the eerie aura he radiated as he trudged through the raging wetness like a solid, black shadow with the full moon smothered behind pitch black clouds.

Just another night, he thought as he reached for the door knob of the bar. *Just another night.*

He opened the door and stepped in. A few heads turned in his direction out of habit. Using the power of will, he scanned the tavern using clairsentience by widening his aura to merge with the esoteric signatures of everyone he wanted to get an auric read and feel of.

No abominations.

A black pair of heavy boots thudded against the wooden floor with each step he took towards an empty stool at the bar. He slipped atop the stool and removed his hat and set it on the bar.

"A double of your strongest stuff, please," he said to the bartender.

The bartender nodded curtly and fished a half-empty bottle of whiskey from the counter. He slid a glass in front of the stranger and poured a double before striding over to the next customer. No one at the bar seemed to notice that the stranger was bone dry despite the torrential downpour outside. He downed his drink in one gulp and nodded in satisfaction as the blessed nectar burned its way down his gullet and spread its alcoholic heat along his stomach walls.

Humans, he thought. *Getting worse by the decade.*

He signaled to the bartender and tapped twice on his glass with his left hand as he reached into his overcoat with his right hand. The bartender poured another double-shot and swiped at the coins the stranger splayed on the bar.

"Keep the change."

The stranger scanned the bar again using clairsentience. Again, he detected no 'abomination' and, as such, clairaudience was not needed. He had no interest in listening to the idle chats of every horny, lonely, drunken, unhappy human in this somber, dank excuse of a bar. Be that as it was, making an honest coin was just that, an honest coin. Unless, *The Bottomless Pint* was a front for something else. Why else would she pick this as a meeting spot? Coincidence?

Doesn't matter, he surmised. *The outcome of tonight will be the same. Just like every other attempt in the past centuries.*

"What a waste," said a young lady in her late 20's in a Scottish accent.

The stranger glanced in her direction. She placed her right hand on his right shoulder and let it slide slowly across his back and down his left arm. She had short brown hair, a voluptuous physique and her green eyes danced with drunken delight. On heels, the not-so-dazzling damsel was about 1.7m tall. Her smile revealed white, well-shaped teeth.

"Oh dear, you feel a lot stronger than you look," she cooed, and waggled her eyebrows at him. "Would you like some company? *I* could use some company."

"Thanks," the stranger replied curtly and sipped his drink. "But I'm good."

"Say, how about you be a good bloke and buy me a drink, aye?" she winked and pressed her bosom against his arm.

"I'm waiting for someone, miss," he said.

"I'm sure your companion won't mind if the three of us had a party, would she? Or *he*?" she added with an inflection.

"As appealing as that sounds, this is one party you don't want to be a part of," the man said and took another swig.

"Why not?" she whined and made a sad face. "I'm in the mood for a party."

"Let's see what she has to say," he said, gesturing to his right.

The front door of the tavern creaked open. The drunk dame turned her attention towards the door as a lady walked into the tavern. Her calf-high boots thudded across the floor as she strode confidently towards the bar. She wore a pair of black, tight-fitting jeans and a black sleeveless blouse underneath a black leather jacket. Long, black hair flowed down to her scapulae. Everything about this lady, from her outfit, her athletic physique, to angular facial features, deep, blue eyes which accentuated her do-not-mess-with-me look, screamed 'not a local'. She, too, was as dry as the Arabian Desert, despite the torrential downpour she just emerged from. But no one noticed. Instead, the cacophony of chats in the tavern died for a second as heads turned in her direction and jaws dropped in awe and desire. She was glad clairaudience was not one of her talents. She could only imagine the vile thoughts and desires dancing around the minds of many of these foolish buffoons. A few catcalls erupted around the tavern as she sat on an empty stool next to the stranger. She shook her head at the bartender, who was already making his way towards her.

"Friend of yours?" she asked the stranger, referring to the drunken damsel

"Not your problem," the stranger replied and turned to face the Scotswoman.

"My name is Amanda," said the Scotswoman.

"Say, Amanda, why don't you go home now? When this private party is over, maybe you and I could have a party of our own?" the stranger offered, faking a seductive smile.

The hairs on her arms and on the back of her neck rose, goosebumps prickled all over her skin and an icy chill spread down her spine. Amanda swallowed and blinked nervously several times.

"O- ok," Amanda stammered.

She turned around to leave and then stopped.

"But how will you find me?" she asked.

"I know where you live, Amanda," the stranger replied and gazed deep into her eyes as he turned towards Amanda and held her gaze.

An overwhelming feeling of calm and peace took over Amanda's soul and she grinned sheepishly. Nothing mattered. All was right with the world. Life was perfect, life was sweet and life was beautiful. This feeling was far better than the best high she had ever had.

"Okay," she spoke as if in a trance. "See you later, stranger."

A few seconds later, Amanda left the tavern and walked into the storming night, with neither a memory of where she had just come from nor what had just transpired in the last few minutes. All she could think of was going home and getting some good amount of sleep.

"So, how do you want to do this?" he asked the woman sitting next to him in a cold tone.

"There's a park about 3km from here," she replied with equal iciness in her tone of voice.

"How many of you this time?" he asked nonchalantly.

"48," she replied.

"Twelve more from the last time," he said and nodded at the bartender.

The bartender refilled the stranger's glass. He gestured towards the lady and, again, the lady shook her head.

"How many are dogs this time?" he turned to face her.

He could feel her red, hot anger using clairsentience and her pupils flashed.

"Stop calling us that," she growled each word through clenched fangs only loudly enough for him to hear.

Without warning, he smoothly grabbed her by the back of her neck and kissed her hard on the lips. At first, her body stiffened in resistance and protest. But when she realized his intent, she gave in and kissed him back, fiercely and not necessarily because she wanted to. Their unexpected behavior made a few heads turn, and a few whistles erupted from various corners in the bar.

"This is not you," he said calmly, as he let her go and downed his drink in one swig. "You shouldn't let your anger get to you like that, especially in public."

"I'm sorry," she said. "Thank you... for stopping me."

"It's alright," he sighed,

A few heartbeats later, he tossed a coin on the bar and met her gaze.

"Tonight the end begins?"

"Tonight, both sides win," she slid off her seat and headed for the door.

"Sasha," he called out to her.

She stopped without turning to face him. She knew what he was going to say next even before he said it.

"I told you I don't blame you anymore," she said. "See you soon."

Sasha walked out of the tavern and disappeared into the night.

He gave Sasha a six-minute head start before stepping out into the dimly lit streets of London. It no longer poured, but the last of the rain clouds made it a mission to blanket out the moon. The stranger contemplated his options as he walked along the wet streets.

To run or to teleport.

He chose to run; not that he needed to, but more like to remind himself of whatever iota of humanity was left in him. Even what he called 'running' was more like a zip that was so fast that the normal human eye might observe the motion as a blur. He sighed audibly. Despite its perks, soullessness sucked.

They increased the number of guests for the party this time.

Interesting! He thought as he zipped towards his destination.

Nothing was different about tonight for the London, though. Under the cover of darkness, with blokes brawling, fancy ladies purveying erotic pleasures to paying participants in dark corners, beggars and homeless people reaching out for coin, the pickpocketing and purse snatching, nothing was out of the ordinary. At least, THEY were human. At least THEY still had their souls, even though a good number of them lived as if they had none.

It was interesting how words came to pass, especially words spoken by someone special. Over the centuries, new enemies were spawned with every enemy he beheaded. His arch nemesis had even gone as far as to set up a special task force with orders to, *'locate and subdue him by every means necessary.'* After all, he was the most wanted man in the underworld; a reputation that made him feel both good and bad at the same time. His arch nemesis wanted him alive to savor the pleasure of looking at him in the eye before keeping his promise. Vengeance was the word of a lifetime and in their line of work, a lifetime had translated to two millennia.

However, the other group of enemies had a different set of orders. Their leaders, The Twins, just wanted some of his blood. His blood, in their opinion, held the key to the next phase of their evolution. And he did not have to be alive for these creatures to see their mission through. Hence, the many 'parties' over the centuries to obtain the elixir that was his blood; the elixir that would set them free from the confines of their inherent nature.

I love parties, he smiled with savage gusto. *The more soulless creatures the merrier.*

The soulless ones had tried, and the soulless ones had failed. Tonight, in a few minutes, the stranger intended to make a repeat of history.

He arrived at the party location. As if by some dark poetry of the night, the clouds parted to let the moonlight wash across the park. Not that he needed any help from the full moon. He could see everything around him as clearly as if it was daytime, thanks to his ability to enhance his vision by sparking the ethers within his eyes as he deemed necessary.

No fun in that, he returned his vision to normal nocturnal levels.

Forty-eight pairs of eyes glowed randomly between the dark spaces and thickets about 40m away and low growls emanated from many nonhuman throats. A dark silhouette zipped past him to his left and another to his right. The stranger turned on his clairaudience by sparking the ethers around his ears so that his ears now acted like an organic receiver of thoughtforms. He listened to the chaos of their raging thoughts.

It's him.

This is my chance.

I shall kill him. Then maybe Sasha will promote me.

I'll have some of his blood for myself.

I wonder if what they say is true.

He's a lot shorter than I expected.

He doesn't look intimidating at all.

I hate my life.

Maybe I can bear his offspring.

I hate The Twins.

Maybe Sasha will see that I am worthy of her if I kill this man.

Lupers. Creatures with lycanthropic propensities, who can exist as humans and canine creatures. Chupers maintained their human form. Lupers and chupers had the same fatal weaknesses; silver and ultraviolet light. Decapitation ended their existences and was more satisfying. They fed on the blood and flesh of humans and animals. These creatures were soulless, nocturnal with crystal clear night vision, and collectively called The Bright Eyes.

Sasha walked into the open to face the stranger. She was a luper, but she maintained her human form for the moment. He nodded imperceptibly at her. Her rise among the Bright Eyes to squadron leader had been quick and more than impressive. She held his gaze. The stranger sparked the ethers. Two veils of mist formed in his hands and coalesced into double-edged daggers, with seven-inch, silver blades each. He wanted a close-range fight instead of using other, less personal and less satisfying options. Close-range fights gave him an intense rush and for every Bright Eye he beheaded, he felt a tinge closer to redemption and to reclaiming his soul. True or not, this notion was motivation enough for him.

"Squad," Sasha called out. "Attack."

A chuper and a luper zipped towards him; one from the left and another from the right, while another pair came for him within a heartbeat, one from the front and another from behind. The second pair of Bright eyes assumed the stranger would leap in the air to avoid the attack from the first pair and launched a preemptive aerial assault. Big mistake. The stranger zipped diagonally to his right instead. He braked suddenly, spun around in a semi-revolution as he bent his knees, transferring the kinetic energy of his zip to potential energy with the tightening of his leg and core muscles. At full transfer, he converted the potential energy to kinetic energy and leaped into the air. The two Bright Eyes in the air were still making their way down when the stranger sliced with his silver-blade daggers. Their heads parted from their bodies and the Bright Eyes slowly glided to the ground as piles of ash. The stranger landed on the ground and zipped towards the first pair of Bright Eyes who attacked him. He braked and stared defiantly at Sasha and her squad as the other pair of Bright Eyes settled on cold, wet ground as two piles of ash. The entire sequence had lasted about two heartbeats. Four down, forty-four more to go.

Sasha howled again, and Bright Eyes emerged from every direction as she, herself, morphed into a luper. The stranger zipped, leaped and lashed, twisted, turned, shifted, and sliced. Heads and headless bodies turned to ash on their way to the ground.

Twenty-one, twenty-two, twenty-three, he counted.

His heart pumped with pure adrenaline infused with charged chi and his muscles throbbed with excitement, making him faster than the Bright Eyes were. His ego soared with exhilaration and his fury burned white hot. Why? He knew no matter how many Bright Eyes he killed, he would never have his soul back, and that fury fueled his fight. He moved faster than the Bright Eyes could keep up. He went for the trees in gravity-defying leaps. Seven Bright Eyes chased after him in a disorganized fashion.

He landed on the closest tree and did his kinetic-to-potential-to-kinetic energy transaction once again and dashed for the seven Bright Eyes. He decapitated the first six in three moves and plunged both daggers right through the heart of the seventh. The momentum of his body accelerated the luper towards the ground, but not before he rendered the luper headless. He absorbed his landing with a forward roll as the luper turned to ash and dove into the last of the Bright Eyes. Six seconds later, all fourteen of the remaining Bright Eyes had turned to ash, except for Sasha and a chuper whose legs the stranger had amputated. The chuper grimaced and winced in excruciating pain from his amputated legs. He dragged himself to the base of a tree. The stranger made his daggers vanish as he loomed over the chuper.

"What *ARE* you?" the chuper gasped in pain. "Why spare me?"

"What makes you think I'm sparing you?" the stranger asked.

The chuper's eyes saucered with fright as he tried to heal himself. He failed. He could not regrow limbs but he could join the amputated portions of his legs to their respective stumps and heal his legs. Unfortunately, finding those leg portions was not going to happen.

Sasha returned to her human form and walked past the stranger and towards the chuper. The glow of the moonlight bounced on her naked, toned body, accentuating every curve of her resplendent feminine form. But then, she always looked beautiful ever since they met each other more than half a millennium ago. The stranger squared his shoulders and steeled his composure.

Business first.

Sasha knelt close to the chuper, and in that moment, the chuper understood what was really going on.

"No. How dare you. You filthy bitch. You damned dog," he screamed and spat in her face.

Sasha darted sideways at zip speed, and the chuper's spittle flew past her.

"What he is, is not important," she replied

"Then who is he?" the chuper glared at her.

"His name is Yehuda," she replied and towered over the chuper. "But you can also call him Judas Iscariot."

And then, Sasha slapped off the chuper's head… literally.

CHAPTER SIX

1922 C.E.

GÜNTER'S STORY WAS no different from those of his peers at the time. Orphaned from the First World War and living on the streets, he considered himself lucky to serve as an altar boy in the only Catholic church in a small village south of Stuttgart. One day, he made the headlines in his community when he beat up his parish priest to near-death after the priest tried to molest him sexually. The villagers were largely in support of young Günter and demanded justice. Unfortunately, the only judge in the village had a different notion of justice. After all, his secret life involved sharing the priest's taste in young boys. Birds of the same feather. After a sham of a trial, the judge ruled in the priest's favor and Günter was sentenced to a decade in prison for attempted murder.

Whilst in prison, Günter's knack for survival quickly caught the attention of a gang leader named Tomas, who took young Günter under his stewardship. Without any family or friends, Tomas and his gang became Günter's family. One day, three years later, a prison guard bangs against Günter's cell.

"You have a visitor," the guard said.

"Who the hell wants to see me?" Günter asked.

"A priest," the guard replied as he selected a key from his key ring.

"A priest?" Günter scoffed. "Tell him to go screw himself."

"Do I look like your errand boy?" the guard opened Günter's cell and fixed a hard stare at Günter, daring him to try anything stupid.

Günter rolled his eyes and slid off his bed. He was 1.75m tall, fit and strong from all the workouts in prison. He believed he could handle the barrel-chested guard and his two colleagues, despite their advantages in height and physical strength. However, such a move would only earn him time in the infirmary, followed by solitary confinement. He sighed, brushed his fingers through his thick, blond hair and walked past the guards, who followed closely behind him.

On second thought, I won't mind going into solitary for killing a priest, he grinned evilly. *I'm here because of a damned priest and they're all the same.*

"Behave yourself now, convict," said the barrel-chested guard as they walked into the visitor's room.

"I can't promise that," Günter teased.

He met the priest's gaze and his smile vanished from his face like a candle flame snuffed out in a pitch-black room. His stay in prison had exposed him to all kinds of criminals and the looks in their eyes. He had seen it all: rapists, thieves, killers, conmen, the innocent, the hateful, the weak, the strong, and the list goes on. He had walked among them and none of them scared him anymore. But this priest… his eyes reflected a dark emptiness and emotionlessness unlike anything he had ever seen before. Staring into this priest's eyes felt like staring into bottomless pit that promised unending pain and suffering to the unlucky soul that fell into them. The room suddenly felt as cold as a winter chill, despite the summer heat that burned outside. Günter swallowed and steeled his resolve.

You don't scare me, he thought as he raised his chin in mock defiance.

"Hello Herr Günter," said the priest warmly, gesturing at an empty seat in front of him. "How are you doing today?"

I'm not falling for that, Günter smiled wryly.

"Hello, *priest,*" Günter sneered and slid into the seat in front of the priest.

"Your sentiments for the clergy is understandable," said the priest.

"You don't say," Günter retorted with unhidden exasperation. "So, to what do I owe this honor? I mean, a priest comes to visit me in prison. This calls for celebration," he gestured mockingly around the room. "Someone get us some champagne."

"Would you like some champagne?" asked the priest.

"Of course," Günter snickered. "It will probably be piss in a bottle anyway, knowing these fools here."

"Well, Herr Günter. There's only one way to find out," replied the priest

He gestured with his right hand, without taking his eyes off Günter. A guard rushed into the room.

"Bring Herr Günter a bottle of your Steiff White," he said without looking at the guard. "And some food as well."

Günter's guards acknowledge the order and vanish from the room.

"Ha," Günter laughed derisively.

"How about some crab meat and fried rice, with a few slices of lamb?" asked the priest confidently.

Günter's narrowed his eyes in suspicion.

Who was this man? How did he know about my favorite meal?

"Tell me, Herr Günter, do you like it here?" asked the priest, as he relaxed in his chair. "Do the constant fights and having to watch over your shoulder all the time turn you on?"

Günter opened his mouth to say something, but the priest cut him off.

"Anyway, I see you are a man who hates evil and will stand up to it, even if it is the last thing you do. I, actually WE, could use a man of your motivation and potential."

The door opened, and two guards came into the room; one carried a tray of the most deliciously smelling food Günter had ever seen, and the other carried a tray with a bottle of Steiff White and a shiny champagne glass. The guards placed the culinary delight in front of Günter, popped the champagne bottle open, poured Günter a glass and hurried out of the room.

"Eat your fill, Herr Günter," prompted the priest.

When Günter hesitated, the priest reached out and took a fork-full of crab meat and rice and stuffed it in his mouth before he emptied the glass of champagne and refilled it.

"See," he said and let out a generous burp before relaxing in his seat again. "I assure you, I'm not trying to poison you. Go on. Eat, *mein herr.*"

Günter waited for just a heartbeat before going ravenous on the food, which disappeared within minutes. He washed everything down with the rest of the champagne, drinking it directly from the bottle.

"Did you enjoy your food, Herr Günter?" the priest asked.

"Trick question?" Günter wiped his mouth with the back of his left hand.

Günter eyed the cutlery in front of him; metal cutlery. He could not suppress the smile of mischief that slowly crept over his face as he fantasized burying the knife in the priest's throat several time.

Patience.

"I'm glad you enjoyed it," the priest said and paused for a moment as if sizing Günter.

When he spoke again, his tone was sterner and almost icy.

"Do you know why I'm here, young man?" he asked.

Gone were the 'Herr Günter' and smile. The 'mystery' that was the priest was out and this 'mystery' made icicles grow on Günter's spine.

Who the hell is this man, if at all he's a priest?

"No," Günter cowered slightly.

"I'll make it simple," continued the priest.

He leaned forward, rested his elbows on the table and interlocked his fingers at the same time, a gesture which made Günter sink a little deeper into his seat.

"I want you to work for me," he said.

Günter's eyes widened as his shock overrode his fear.

"You want me to become a priest?" Günter shook his head as if he was in a bad dream.

Years of pent-up anger, frustration and hatred buried in his subconscious erupted like a geyser.

"Do you realize that I'm here because of a damned priest?" Günter exploded in unhinged anger. "Because of what a damned priest tried to do to me? And where was the church when I was being burned at the stake, huh?"

The priest remained calm like a hill in a hurricane.

"You must be a special kind of wizard to have survived the Inquisition," the priest said sarcastically. "I see you know your history. Good. There may still be some brains in that thick skull of yours. Not bad for a brute like you. Not bad at all," the priest added with a smirk.

Two things turned Günter into a savage, thanks to prison life: attacks from behind and disrespect. This priest was guilty of the latter and, therefore, needed to be taught a lesson. But before his sudden rage overrode his sense of reason and turned him into a primal, feral beast, Günter made two mistakes before he lunged across the table for the priest. Firstly, he announced his intention with a maniacal snarl and secondly, he assumed the priest was nothing more than just an ordinary priest. Günter's snarl was replaced by a look of confusion when he realized the priest was no longer sitting on the chair. He saw the priest stand up and stand aside, making room for him to complete his trajectory.

But how? he wondered before he crashed into the chair and landed on the concrete floor in a clumsy heap. *How could he move so… fast?*

His elbows and forearms absorbed most of his fall. He winced and gritted his teeth to distract himself from the pain as he quickly stood up and pulled back his right hand in a prelude to a punch. But as he did, his mind could not process in time the fact that something opaque was suddenly barely inches from his face. By the time he realized it was the priest's head, excruciating pain tore through his left wrist and spread along his left arm. He screamed and forgot about his intent to punch the priest as he tried to yank his left arm away from the priest's vice grip around his left wrist. Something brushed against his torso as his left arm went up and created an arch. It was the priest stepping through the arch of his left arm and with that motion, Günter's left wrist, elbow and shoulder locked in unnatural positions and burned with pain he had never felt before. Günter stood on his toes to alleviate some of the pressure on his joints and instantly regretted it. Another level of sharp, ripping pain seared through his body as the priest yanked some more at his wrist. Günter never thought he could scream so loud as he dropped hard to a knee. Despite the suffering, he would not beg for mercy.

"Now," the priest asked calmly. "Are you ready to talk?"

When Günter did not reply, the priest twisted again and Günter screamed.

"I have all the time in the world."

"Alright," Günter said through clenched teeth. "I'm ready. Just let go of my arm."

"Only if you give me your word you won't try to do something foolish."

"You have my word," Günter replied with resignation and shame.

Sweet relief flooded Günter's body as the priest let go of his wrist. He flexed and massaged his left shoulder, elbow and wrist, while shooting and angry stare at the priest. The priest returned his chair to its original position and sat down. Günter walked over to his and did the same. He glanced towards the guards, who were doing everything in their power to suppress a laugh.

I'll get them later, he promised himself.

"I am a man of the cloth," the priest said. "But I am no ordinary man of the cloth. You will never find me at the altar but wherever certain unique services are required, I, and those like me, will be there."

Günter frowned in confusion.

"The organization I work for is known only to a handful of humans outside our organization. So, this is your recruitment. I want you to join us."

Günter was silent for a moment.

"If I accept this offer, what's in it for me?" he asked.

"Read that," said the priest, pointing a manila envelope on a table across the room.

Günter noticed the envelop for the first time since their meeting. He walked up to the table, picked up the envelope and cracked the seal. He cautiously pulled out the contents, sparing a suspicious glance at the priest. He then returned to his seat and started flipping through the pages he removed from the envelope. After reading through the first two pages, his heart sank.

"A report on your altercation a few months ago," the priest said. "I believe you recognize the name of the judge to preside over your future case?"

"He's recommending eight more years for me," Günter's voice was heavy with despair and disbelief. "But I'm supposed to be out in three months."

"You bludgeoned an inmate to near-death and broke his spine, Günter," the priest rebutted emotionlessly. "He is now wheelchair-bound for the rest of his life and all because he 'disrespected you' by calling you a 'priest lover.' I believe you deserve those eight years and more."

Günter wanted to say something but the words died in his throat.

"You and I both know," the priest continued, leaning forward, "that your anger issues will keep you locked in here for a very, very long time. Join us, and in exchange, I offer you freedom from here," he waved his hands around the room. "But if you prefer this paradise, then I'm afraid I have wasted your time and mine."

"Who are you really, priest?" Günter asked weakly.

Deep down, he knew this priest was not bluffing.

"The key to your freedom," the priest replied, glancing at his expensive-looking watch. "Three seconds."

"I'll join you," Günter replied immediately.

"Good," said the priest. "Training starts tomorrow."

The priest stood up and walked towards the coat hanger by the door. He reached for his black overcoat, slid it on and held open the metallic door that led out of the visitor's room.

"I don't have all day now," the priest said.

It took a split moment before Günter realized what was going on and as soon as he did, he scrambled from the table and hurled himself towards the door. The priest chuckled and shut the door behind them.

"If I'll be working with you-" Günter started saying.

"Who said anything about us working together?" the priest said.

Both men laughed.

"Okay, if I am going to be working for your group, or order, or whatever you call it, may I at least know the name of my liberator?"

"Aaron. But you will call me Andrew," replied the priest, without looking at Günter. "You're not worthy of calling me by my real name."

Andrew smiled.

CHAPTER SEVEN

COMPLETING THE CYCLE

THE ORDER OF the Rock, the O.R., was Earth Realm's most never-existing secret. Based in Vatican City, but without any religious or political affiliations, the O.R's primary objective was to protect Earth Realm and humanity from all paranormal and supernatural attacks from within and beyond the realm. Only the pope and maybe two or three other high-ranking officials in the Vatican, as well as eight of the leaders of the realm's most powerful countries, knew of its existence. Even more secretive was the head of the O.R.

Nine years since leaving prison, Fr. Günter became a Jesuit priest, meaning he was one of the less than 2% of candidates who made it through an arduous training process that would bring the realm's most elite special forces to their knees. For the first time in as long as he could remember, Günter was always bursting with zest for life and purpose. A deep sense of accomplishment throbbed in his being. Sometimes, regret filled his heart for not having the chance to say a final farewell to his prison family.

"I wonder how many of them are even still alive," he murmured to himself occasionally. "I wish them well, but I never want that life again for me."

The surreal nature of that ride away from prison in the black luxury vehicle with the tinted windows was forever inscribed in his memory. Even as they drove away, he still expected Fr. Andrew to reveal that everything was one sick prank. Günter shook his head and chuckled at the memory. They had arrived at a remote location that looked like a military training camp.

"Clean up and put this on," someone had commanded and tossed a white tee shirt, a pair of white pants and underpants in his direction a few minutes after Fr. Andrew had dropped him off and left without saying a word.

"Five minutes."

Prison life had helped him perfect the art of speed showering and he was done in three minutes.

"Follow me," someone else ordered and spun around on his heels.

Günter kept a constant pace behind this person's perfectly spaced strides until they arrived at a door.

"Your bed is No. 53," he said, gesturing for Günter to step into the dorm.

Twenty pairs of eyes turned in his direction. Every pair of eyes bore a different expression ranging from hollowness, frightened, angry to deadly excitement. He squared his shoulders and made his way to his bed.

Within a few days, he learned why he was there. The common denominator among them, the recruits, was that they were all orphaned, had no families, so no one either missed or would miss them, and had something they would never want to go back to. As such, each recruit regarded the opportunity of being in this secret facility as a shot at having a second chance at life. Thus, the recruits endured the inhumane training sessions that stretched their bodies, minds and psyches beyond any limit they had ever envisioned for themselves. Many died, those who lived and failed were 'transferred' to another facility and were never seen again. Günter, and those like him who made it through the training sessions, graduated to become Priests in the Order of Jesuits.

Günter's worst nightmare during training were the psychiatric sessions which involved simulating situations of past trauma. He would have gladly taken an extra week of training in Antarctica or the Arabian Desert. For heaven's sake, he would have gladly faced a lion or two if he had to. Unfortunately, he had to be stripped of all emotion, including his fear and anger broiled from the memory of his past. Many times, he almost broke down and quit, until the pressure became too much for his psyche to handle and as he neared that tipping point between failure and success, Günter found a way to bury this nightmare in the far recesses of his subconscious. In that moment, a huge part of his humanity died. He raised two eyes filled with a void that reflected the vacuum in the space where his heart used to be at his supervisor and, with slow, steady nods, his supervisor saw the birth of a true, heartless soldier who was ready and willing to do anything in the name of the Church of their Lord and Savior, Jesus Christ.

Günter's first missions included investigating claims of supernatural and paranormal sightings around the world. Easy job. Two years later, he became an external auditor and enforcer. Catholic parishes around the realm suspected of misappropriation of alms received an unexpected visit from him. He became so adept at his job that his peers nicknamed him 'The Cleaner.' Then, the moment for his first kill arrived. Günter was summoned to their headquarters in Germany. He arrived the following day and knocked on the door of his commanding officer's office.

"Fr. Johan," he greeted.

"Come in, Günter," Fr. Johan gestured towards the empty seat on the opposite side of his desk. "For you," he added and slid a manila envelope across the desk towards Günter as Günter sat down.

Günter picked up the envelope from the table, opened it and pulled out the only item in it; the picture of someone he was familiar with. His face flushed with anger and the veins around his temple popped as red-hot blood rushed to his head.

"Heinrich has ignored our warnings about his indiscretions for too long now," Fr. Johan spoke with icy dispassion. "Can you facilitate his fatality?"

Günter resisted every urge to say "With utmost pleasure." If he did, he would have been pulled out of the mission for his inability to not make this mission personal, especially his first kill.

"I can, Father," he replied almost dismissively.

He met Fr. Johan's penetrating gaze with an outward calm that neutralized the storm of rage that brewed within his being.

"Very well," Fr. Johan shrugged. "You have seventy-two hours."

"I may need less than twenty-four, Father," Günter offered.

"As long as you get the job done within 72," Fr. Johan spoke curtly.

"Aye, Father."

"Dismissed."

Ten hours later, Günter knocked on Fr. Heinrich's front door. The train ride to Stuttgart, followed by the drive to the village was uneventful, save for the myriad of thoughts that raced endlessly in Günter's head. However, his focus on the mission was razor sharp. A boy, no more than twelve years of age, opened it slightly. Like a kindred spirit, Günter sensed this poor child's suffering and clenched his fists in white-knuckled fury.

"Where is he?" Günter asked calmly.

The boy turned and pointed towards a corridor to the left.

"Go home and never come here again," Günter hissed.

The boy stepped past Günter and dashed away. Günter walked into the house and locked the door behind him. His rubber-soled shoes remained soundless as he took slow steps towards his target's bedroom.

"Who was it, boy?" Fr. Heinrich called out from his bedroom.

That 'boy' has a name, Günter fumed in his head.

"I am a soldier of Christ," he murmured to himself mantra-style. "And this is the Devil's lair."

He stood in front of the pedophile priest's bedroom and gently pushed the door open. He trained hateful eyes, filled with cold disdain at the pedophile priest who lay on his bed wearing nothing but his underwear. The picture in the envelope was far too generous to the child molester. He looked a lot older than Günter expected him to be. Startled, the priest sat ram-rod stiff and glared in defiance at the intruder.

"Who the hell are you and what are you doing here?" Fr. Heinrich demanded.

Günter remained silent as he clenched and unclenched his fists. Fr. Heinrich narrowed his eyes and stared more closely at Günter until, suddenly, his eyes bulged in recognition. He turned as pale as his stained white sheets and the cold claws of the dread of an impending horror seized his soul. He opened his mouth to speak but the words died in his throat.

"I take it you remember me?" asked Günter icily.

Fr. Heinrich tried to reply and failed. He swallowed hard and nodded.

"Good. Do you know why I'm here?" Günter asked.

Heinrich shook his head. A strange calm settled over Günter as he shed the personality of an angry, molested child and donned that of a Jesuit Priest.

"You have ignored several warnings from the Vatican to cease and desist your indiscretions. As such, by order of the church, I am to terminate you permanently. Do you understand what I'm saying?"

Fr. Heinrich trembled visibly from the sudden cold radiating from Günter and the fear of his certain end.

"Please," he whimpered. "I can stop. I will stop."

"It doesn't matter if you understand, does it?" Günter turned and headed for the closet.

The arrangement of everything was the same since he was here last. With a sigh, he shut out the fury that funneled upward from the pit of his stomach.

"Personally," he continued emotionlessly. "I'd prefer to make this last a very long time. To make you suffer. To hear you scream in pain and beg. To make you pay for what you tried to do to me and for what you have done to all those little boys. Every victim of yours."

"Please, Günter," Fr. Heinrich begged. "Please. I need help. I can stop if you help me."

"You don't get to say my name," Günter spoke with a chilling calmness.

He stopped about two meters away from Heinrich and breathed in deeply to quell the quagmire of vengeful emotions that brewed in him once again.

"You and I know that you will never stop and besides, I have my orders," he took another step towards Heinrich folding the towel twice along its length into a rectangle.

"Please," Fr. Heinrich's voice almost sounded like a low-pitched shrill. "Don't kill me. I don't want to die. I beg of you."

"Embrace your death, Fr. Heinrich," Günter said. "Enjoy this gift of mercy bestowed upon you."

"This will be a lot easier for you if you don't resist," Günter's features softened in an eerie calmness as his heart froze colder than an ice cube

In a smooth motion, Günter positioned himself behind Heinrich and held him in a chokehold with the towel acting as a cushion along Heinrich's neck. He flexed his biceps, cutting off blood flow to Heinrich's brain and oxygen to his heart. The pedophile kicked and clawed for four seconds before his body went limp. Günter held on for six more minutes, starving Fr. Heinrich's brain of oxygen and ensuring that the priest was actually dead. During the entire period of asphyxiation, he stared blankly into the nothingness he was not focused on, the nothingness that was a projection of his soul. He then relaxed his shoulders and biceps and Heinrich slipped to the side in a dead heap. Günter then slid off the bed, laid the priest on his back, placed the towel above the priest's heart and smashed his right fist into the towel with every bit of anger, hatred, loathing and fury he could summon. The force of the blow guaranteed Heinrich's heart would never beat again and the towel cushioned the blow enough to not leave any bruises. Günter unfolded the towel and laid it next to the priest.

Cause of death: cardiac arrest, as he was getting ready to take a shower.

Günter exited Heinrich's room, walked out of the house, closed the door behind him and breathed in deeply, but no relief followed. No weight came off his shoulders, no closure; nothing.

"But why?" Günter gritted his teeth. "Why am I still angry?"

And then, an evil smile spread across his face as he found his answer.

"Good thing I still have eleven hours to go," he said to himself as he headed for his car.

Hassler, the judge who shared in Fr. Heinrich's distasteful appetite for young boys, the same judge who handed Günter the unfair sentence many years ago, lived about twenty-five kilometers from the parish. Günter parked his car a block away from Hassler's house. He sat in wondering contemplation for a moment, wrestling with his conscience passing judgement on him. On the one hand, the priest in him demanded that he stuck to his mission and return to Berlin at once; but the child in him, the one who had gone through such a travesty, craved for justice and closure. In his moment of contemplation, Günter found his answer.

My Lord and my God put me on this path for a reason, he thought. *If I am a loyal soldier for his church, then I must uphold my oath and bring justice for this transgression on me and many others. It is my sacred duty and I can see the handiwork of God in this. His purpose is perfect and divine. Therefore, what I am about to do is also perfect and divine.*

Günter waited until late at night when, he believed, the judge's grandchildren and wife were asleep. He walked stealthily along the stone steps leading to the kitchen window, which had a direct line of sight to the judge's TV. The judge's attention was fully focused on some program about a young, charismatic leader of Germany's most prominent political party, the Nazi Party. Günter picked the lock on the kitchen door and slithered into the living room like a shadow. He towered behind the unsuspecting judge.

"Hello Judge," he spat.

Judge Hassler bolted upright from the chair and was about to speak with his eyes caught the glimmer of Günter's eight-inch blade. He instantly aged ten more years from the fright that sucked the life out of him as Günter raised his left index finger to his lips.

"Make a sound and your wife and grandchildren will bleed to death before your very eyes," Günter promised.

Judge Hassler whimpered and stiffened in absolute obedience.

Günter motioned towards the kitchen.

"Please, don't hurt my family," the judge pleaded quietly, taking a seat and facing Günter. "Don't hurt my babies. I'll do anything. I'll give you anything."

"How many sons and grandsons have you violated?" asked Günter coldly.

Morbid dread and fearful guilt petrified Hassler to speechlessness. Günter leaned forward and glared at the judge, who backed away slightly.

"I asked you a question."

Hassler swallowed and stifled a sneeze.

"I… I don't know," he confessed.

"Do you know who I am?" Günter asked.

Judge Hassler shook his head vigorously.

"I am Günter, the one you sentenced to 10 years in prison to protect your now dead friend, Fr. Heinrich," Günter replied calmly.

The judge furrowed his eyebrows as he searched through his memory until his eyes saucered in utter disbelief when he finally remembered.

"I am here to permanently put an end to you and your perversion. I am here to complete the cycle and fulfill the divine will of God," Günter hissed.

He stood up and walked behind the judge, who was still too paralyzed by fear to even move a finger.

"Please… please," tears of fear streamed down the judge's cheeks.

Günter leaned close to the judge's ear and whispered icily.

"I'm sending you to burn in the fires of hell. This will be your punishment for eternity."

Günter snapped the judge's neck in one quick motion and caught the judge's limp body before it slumped to the floor. He then bashed the judge's left temple against the side of the table before finally letting his limp body hit the floor.

Günter took a glass and filled it with water. Then, he spilled a tiny bit of the water a meter from the dead man's feet before walking along the corpse and letting the glass drop from his hand about two meters from the dead judge's outstretched right hand. The glass shattered on impact and water spilled in every direction. Satisfied with his work, Günter left the dead judge's house through the backdoor of the kitchen. He headed for his car he parked a block down the street.

Cause of death: trauma to the temple, due to an accidental slip and fall. Not uncommon for men his age, anyway.

The weight came off Günter's shoulder as he headed in steady strides towards his car. The peace flowed into his being. He smiled with sweet satisfaction as he slid into the driver's seat and revved the engine of his car.

Mission accomplished.

Two weeks later, he was summoned by Fr. Johan.

"Once again congratulations on Berlin. How do you feel?" asked the supervisor.

"Thank you, sir. I feel good, actually," replied Günter.

"Excellent. I asked to see you because I have a proposition for you."

"Of course, sir," Günter replied and leaned forward.

"Have you ever heard of the Order of the Rock?"

CHAPTER EIGHT

C. E. 1938

HE WATCHED THE waves wash along the shore in rhythmic patterns. After all this time, this basic gift of nature still remained one of the few things that brought him some peace. He took a deep breath, held it for a few seconds and then let it out slowly. The next few days promised nothing akin to peace or serenity. But what was new? This moment would be his only moment of peace for the next few days or even months. The realm was replete with filth and someone had to do the thankless job of keeping it clean and safe.

Uneasy is the head wearing the crown, he thought.

He stripped himself from the window and walked towards the king-sized bed in his 30x40 feet master bedroom, designed and decorated to exude a feeling of a medieval bourgeois. He slid on a freshly pressed black cassock over a black, freshly pressed shirt, tucked in a freshly pressed pair of black pants and slid his socked feet in a pair of polished, black shoes. The realm stank of filth, iniquity and more and someone had a to do the thankless job of addressing these situations. Thus, ass the leader of the O.R, and the most powerful man in the underworld, his plate was always full; not that he could not handle it. The next few days would be interesting, He had a great white shark to fry.

The sound of a gentle knock on the door reached his ears.

"Come in," Father Supreme said, putting on his watch.

The door cracked open and a priest's head popped through the crack.

"Father Supreme, your car is here," the priest said.

"Thank you, Marcelo," Father Supreme replied, heading for the door.

Marcelo opened the door wider and stood aside for Father Supreme. Marcelo closed the door behind Father Supreme.

"Is Antonio here?" Father Supreme took the stairs to the foyer.

"Yes, Father Supreme," answered Marcelo, staying two steps in front. "He's in the car. Would you like me to fetch your briefcase?"

"Not today, Marcelo. Thank you," replied Father Supreme, as he headed for the car.

Marcelo nodded and held open the main door for his boss. Father Supreme descended another flight of stairs. Another priest held open the door to the bulletproof, black car with tinted windows for Father Supreme. He made sure that Father Supreme was comfortable in the back seat before closing the door and riding in the front passenger seat. Fr. Antonio, second-in-command and next in line as the leader of the O.R, was also in the back seat. He handed Father Supreme a folder.

"Good morning, Your Supremacy," Fr. Antonio greeted.

"Morning Antonio."

He opened the folder and studied the blurred photos of a man within the vicinity of what looked like a park. A few seconds later, he closed the folder and returned it to Antonio.

"Did you verify the intel?"

"Verified and confirmed, your Supremacy," replied Fr. Antonio.

"So, it was him in London?" his supremacy spoke, more to himself than to Antonio.

"Yes, sir. He did a good job keeping it quiet and clean, and our men stayed out of sight, just like you ordered," continued Antonio.

"Apparently, not out-of-sight enough, since he sent us a message through one of our operatives," Father Supreme said.

"Apologies, your supremacy," Antonio cowered slightly at his boss's subtle reprimand.

He cleared his throat nervously. Father Supreme idly tapped on his left knee with his index finger as the car navigated the streets of Rome. The ring on his left ring finger bore a big, green crystal on it.

"How interesting," Father Supreme spoke as if to himself. "The most wanted man in the underworld wants to meet with the most powerful man in the underworld."

Father Supreme stared blankly through the tinted window. The car kept a steady pace, winding through the narrow streets of Rome towards the Vatican. A few minutes later, Father Supreme broke the silence.

"I see we have a new driver," he spoke softly.

"His name is Günter, your supremacy," said Antonio. "He's the one I told you about."

"Ah, yes," exclaimed his supremacy. "That was some stunt you pulled back there in Berlin, young man. I'm not sure I, myself, could've done a better job."

"His supremacy is too generous," Günter almost stuttered with excitement. "Thank you kindly, sir. I only seek to fight evil and protect the church and the innocent in every way I can."

"And your actions are a greater compliment to you, young man," Father Supreme said.

"Thank you so much, sir," Günter beamed, not fully understanding what his boss meant. "Without wanting to be rude, sir, I just wanted to say I'm honored beyond words to be assigned to your personal service. Thank you very much for this opportunity."

"Oh, that's nothing, Günter," Father Supreme said, almost smiling. "You keep up the great work, and much more awaits you in this order."

"I won't let you down, boss," Günter pledged.

"If I doubted that for a second you would not be here, young man," his supremacy spoke softly.

As they drove on, Günter gripped the steering wheel a little tighter to force himself to concentrate on the road. His recruitment into the O.R was a huge promotion. He had gone through much training to build strength and speed. At first, he wondered why he had to improve on his speed until his first exposure to a chuper and a luper. These Bright Eyes were held in separate cages in their training camp, and after watching some video footage of these creatures, he finally understood the need to build speed and strength. Günter knew of demons and ghosts, but The Bright Eyes were supposed to be myths, existing only in fiction. Apparently not Anyway, the Bright Eyes were just another face of evil. And he was proud to be a servant of the Lord Jesus Christ and fighter of evil.

BREAKING BONDS

"Sit down, Günter," an older O.R. priest gestured at a chair in front of him.

He was in his mid-50's perhaps, with a strong Icelandic accent, clean shaven, balding black hair and a slightly long face. Günter slid into the chair while the priest perused through a folder in front of him.

"Barely two years with us and you already have four successful missions," he said without even looking in Günter's direction. "Indonesia, Egypt, Mexico and Tibet. Quite impressive."

"Thank you, sir," Günter replied.

The priest closed the folder, leaned back in his seat and met Günter's gaze.

"We have another mission for you," he reached into his top drawer and retrieved another folder. "Berlin," he said, slipping the folder towards Günter.

"I know you just came back from -,"

"I'll do it, Father" Günter replied with military firmness.

A half smile crept over the supervisor's face.

"Are you at least interested in hearing about the mission?" he chuckled.

"Apologies, Father," Günter said. "I didn't mean to sound rude."

"It is quite alright, Günter," the priest said. "We received viable intel that the Nazis are trying to breed and weaponize the Bright Eyes in one of their facilities in Berlin. Your mission will be to infiltrate and destroy this facility along with every Bright Eye housed therein, both the seasoned and just recently converted. This will be a team operation."

"Aye, sir," Günter nodded sharply.

"Good," the priest leaned forward. "Your team is waiting for you in Room 6. You will receive further briefing from Fr. Scott. You leave in 7 days. Dismissed."

"Aye, sir."

Günter stood up and nodded curtly.

A week later, Günter and his team arrived in Berlin during the day as tourists. At night, they set out on their mission and everything was going smoothly until the intel on the security of the facility proved incomplete. As such, Günter's team mates were either ambushed or killed. Those who were still alive quickly bit down on their cyanide pills. However, Günter's was faulty and before he could pull it out with his fingers and try to crush it another way, a sharp pain radiated from the base of his skull followed by total blackness.

Consciousness slowly returned through hazy vision and throbbing pain in his head. He squeezed his eyelids together as the lights in this…place felt like a series of grenades were going off inside his head. A few seconds later, he opened his eyes and appraised his surroundings as far as his line of sight could allow, given that his forearms, arms, head and ankles were strapped tightly against a chair that felt metallic against his naked flesh. Günter winced from the throbbing pain at the base of his skull.

"Damn Nazis," he cursed.

"Hello, father," a shrill, masculine voice said through an intercom. "Welcome to Hell."

The door opened and two riffle-carrying Nazi soldiers of average build and height, but looking fit and strong, walked into the room. A third person, dressed in a white lab coat, followed behind them, pushing a small, wheeled table in front of him. He was no taller than 1.6m, completely bald and a little chubby around the waist. A rush of adrenaline flooded Günter's system, temporarily numbing the pain and haziness in his head. The white-coat wearing person pulled to a stop next to Günter, ensuring that Günter could see the contents of the table: a rolled-up tool bag, a pair of empty syringes and some tiny bottles of clear liquid. He adjusted his glasses made with cheap, black, plastic frames and forced a grin. Günter knew what was coming. Years of training had prepared him for a situation like this and he was ready. He started reciting the rosary, focusing on the sorrowful mysteries. He wanted to draw strength from the passion of Christ, from the last supper to the crucifixion.

"Ah," the man wearing the lab coat scoffed in a distinctive German accent and wagged a finger at Günter. "You are reciting the Rosary, ya? Hoping for Our Lady of Sorrows to give you strength?" he paused as if waiting for an answer.

"The second sorrowful mystery -," Günter continued reciting.

"The scourging at the pillar, ya," the man with the lab coat interjected. "My dear priest, you will experience something far worse than scourging if you don't shut your mouth."

His sudden outburst elicited a smile of victory from Günter.

"Score one for me," Günter muttered and then continued. "Hail Mary, full of grace the Lord is with thee…"

The man in the lab coat signaled to one of the guards. The guard stepped forward and punched Günter's left jaw and then followed the punch with a left punch into Günter's solar plexus.

This soldier is very good, Günter thought as his vision darkened from the pain and white specks danced before his eyes.

Another punch followed the other two; this time, in the solar plexus. Günter coughed several times and wanted to keel over but could not, since he was still strapped into the chair of torture. Instead, he squeezed his eyes shut as if to will the pain away.

"Alright," said the man in the lab coat, clapping his hands once and rubbing them vigorously for a few seconds. "Let us begin. Oh, I'm sorry, where are my manners? I'm Dr. Herman Klaus, lead doctor at the Führer's Division of Paranormal and Mythological Phenomena. Here is what will happen. I will ask you questions, and you will answer me truthfully. Only then will you not suffer any, uh, mistreatment. Yes, mistreatment. But if you do not answer me truthfully…."

He left his sentence unfinished.

"Do you understand me, soldier?"

Günter leveled a defiant gaze at Dr. Klaus. He smiled exposing bloodied teeth and a torn, lower lip.

"What I understand, you Nazi bastard, is that if you don't kill me now, I will make your death very slow and very painful."

"Ah. Spoken like a true soldier," said Dr. Klaus sarcastically.

He then walked to the table and pulled out a tiny, razor-sharp scalpel that was no more than an inch long.

"Be careful with that, doctor," Günter said. "I might use it to cut off that tiny pecker of yours."

"I would love to see you try… Fr. Günter," Dr. Klaus said.

Günter narrowed his eyes in surprise and anger.

"How did you know my name?" he demanded.

"Let's begin with me telling you about this little object, Father?" replied Dr. Klaus. "This," he said, holding up the scalpel between his left thumb, middle and index fingers, "was a gift from the Chinese when I visited them two years ago. They call it *The Ghost Blade*. Do you know why they call it *The Ghost Blade*, Fr. Günter?" he asked, raising an eyebrow at Günter.

"How did you know my name?" Günter insisted.

"You see," continued the doctor, ignoring Günter's question, "the Chinese call it 'Ghost Blade' because they could use this blade to make a thousand tiny but extremely painful cuts into the human flesh. Death from excessive blood loss is an unpleasant way to go."

He inched closer towards Günter.

"I'll ask you one more time," Günter spoke through clenched teeth, "HOW… DO… YOU…"

Excruciating pain exploded along Günter's upper abs as Klaus swiped the blade in a semi arc across Günter's stomach. A thin line of blood traced the slash in his abs. He had been cut several times before, but the pain from all those cuts did not compare to that which he felt just now and his scream was commensurate to the new level of pain he experienced just now.

"There," said Dr. Klaus. "That's a great sound from a soldier of Christ."

"HOW DO YOU KNOW MY NAME?" Günter yelled and panted from the pain.

"Why are you here?" asked the doctor in an icy tone of voice.

"To give you a piece of what's down here, you bastard," Günter gestured with his eyes towards his nether region.

"You mean this?" said the doctor pointing at Günter's phallus.

Suddenly, Dr. Klaus grabbed Günter's phallus with his left hand and brandished the ghost blade in his right hand.

"This thing, you mean? How generous of you," he sliced.

Günter let out a heart-rending scream and nearly passed out; more from the thought of losing his manhood than from the pain he felt.

"THE LORD IS MY SHEPHERD. I SHALL NOT WANT," Günter screamed.

"Oh, come on now, Günter. You're so sentimental," Dr. Klaus teased. "Take another look at your precious cock."

Günter did and noticed that it was still in place, but a trickle of blood was a testament of the ghost blade's kiss. He could barely contain his relief.

"See?" said the doctor. "I can be nice when I want to be."

"You still didn't tell me how you knew my name," Günter said.

"You are not being cooperative despite my generosity," said Dr. Klaus and drove a much longer and larger knife that Günter was unaware he had in his right hand. The blade sank two inches deep into the muscles of Günter's left thigh.

Another cry of renewed pain erupted from Günter's throat.

"EVEN THOUGH I WALK," Günter shouted and gasped, trying to catch his breath.

"THROUGH THE VALLEY OF THE SHADOW OF DEATH, I SHALL FEAR NO EVIL. AHHHHHHHH."

Günter screamed as the doctor slowly twisted the knife in his thigh clockwise.

"FOR YOU- ARE- WITH- ME," Günter enunciated each word and spat a thick spittle of blood at Dr. Klaus' face.

"You think you're tough," Dr. Klaus hissed, digging for a handkerchief and mopping his face.

He gestured towards the soldiers.

"Soften him up, boys," he instructed. "Break no bones. We will resume tomorrow."

The soldiers were experts at their job, true purveyors of physical pain. They executed their orders to the last, physically brutal letter with precision and sadism. Several minutes later, they left Günter alone in the torture chamber in a bloodied, beaten and battered pile of human brawn and no broken bones. Günter lost track of time.

A janitor walked into the chamber and started cleaning the blood, spittle, and sweat from the floor. Then, after stealing quick glances over his shoulders, he quietly shut the door and approached Günter. He dropped to one knee, unzipped his overall, pulled out a bottle of water and pressed it against Günter's lips.

"Drink, father," he spoke with a sense of urgency.

The janitor's accent was not German, but Günter could not place it. Günter tried to purse his swollen lips. But they hurt.

"N- No," Günter managed to say in a low husky voice.

"Come on now, father," the janitor insisted, and glanced nervously over his shoulders. "Please drink. You must. See."

Günter forced his left eye open, the one that was not fully swollen shut, and saw the janitor take a few gulps from the bottle.

"See?" the janitor said and brought the bottle back to Günter's lips.

Günter resigned and opened his mouth slightly. The janitor poured some of the heavenly nectar slowly into Günter's slightly open mouth.

"Thank you," Günter said weakly after he emptied the bottle.

"I must go now," replied the janitor. "But I will be back tomorrow during my shift. Stay strong, Father."

The janitor walked out of the room and into the corridor, idly whistling a tune to himself.

"Wait," Günter called out weakly. "Who are you?"

The janitor was already gone.

Time was an alien concept for Günter in the solitude of the torture chamber. A soft tap on his shoulder made him realize he had fallen asleep at some point. When he opened his one eye, he saw a beautiful, busty blond woman crouched in front of him. Her face was barely inches away from his, as if she was trying to study him. He could smell her perfume. She stood up and adjusted her tight-fitting blouse that was loose at the top to reveal ample cleavage, and a very short skirt that barely covered her buttocks. She stood unmoving, as if appraising him. Günter's only open eye raked over her physique and, even in his sleepy, painful, and delusional stupor, his heart raced at the sight of her curvaceous glory.

She nodded slightly, maintaining an expressionless face. She then turned around and bent over, straight-legged, to pick up a tray of food from the floor behind her. She wore no underwear and even in his pathetic state, his carnal nature sprang to life as if sucking from some omnipresent spring of energy. She stood up, turned around, walked towards him with the tray of food in hand, and knelt close to him. She gently placed the tray on his left lap, the one with the knife wound. She held the tray in her left hand and, whether it was intentional or not, the tip of his manhood found its way in between her index and middle finger. His manhood began to expand. He winced as the sealed cut from the ghost blade on his phallus reopened. But the pain was not intense enough to curb his expansion.

The lady proceeded to feeding Günter with her right hand. The food was delicious and tasted like pudding with ground meat. He realized after a few mouthfuls that he had not even resisted eating the food like he resisted drinking the water from the janitor. Shame for being so sloppy crept in. The lady would occasionally adjust her left hand under the tray for whatever reason and the gesture would provide a further stroking motion to the tip of his manhood.

Günter appreciated the pleasant distraction, at least until he finished eating his food. Some strength and vitality returned to his body. The lady stood up, turned around as if to leave and then stopped. She bent over and set the tray on the floor, once again revealing the nakedness underneath her short skirt. She then stood up with her back to him. He could tell she was unbuttoning her blouse.

This must be a dream; a good dream, though, he thought.

She turned around to face him as she undid the last button and opened her blouse. A white, perfectly fitting brassiere provided ample support for a pair of wonderfully sculpted breasts. His phallic reaction was complete. She took two steps towards him, her high heels clanging on the metallic floor, sending echoes across the deathly quiet torture chamber. And then, without warning, she lashed out with her right foot and plunged the pointed tip of the heel of her right shoe directly into his extension. White, hot pain jolted Günter to the reality of the situation. He whimpered and stifled a scream until, finally, he retched a mixture of food, blood and bile.

"You filthy Catholic pig," she exclaimed and lashed out on a different spot on his phallus with the heel of her shoe.

This time, she tore off some flesh. Günter nearly slipped into unconsciousness from the pain and did not hear the door open. She spat on him and stepped aside, buttoning up her blouse. Dr. Klaus walked around Günter's seat of torture and stood behind Günter. He leaned close to Günter's left ear, as his captive whimpered in pain.

"One way or another," he hissed, "we will break you. You can hold on for as long as you choose to. But you will break, priest. Just like the rest of them."

So there are more of us here? Günter wondered.

Dr. Klaus stood up and started heading towards the door.

"Why…" Günter murmured. "Why not just kill me?"

"Why kill you-" replied the doctor, holding the door for the lady to walk out. She planted a deep kiss on his lips before walking past him.

"When we can use you." he added and closed the door after him.

The lights went out, and Günter was, once again, left alone with nothing but a thread of his sanity and will.

CHAPTER NINE

TURNED

GÜNTER MADE ONE more left turn before pulling up at the south entrance to the Vatican. Two priests stood guard. Günter rolled down the window and nodded at one of the guards, who signaled to another guard by the main entrance. This guard opened the gate, and the first guard waved them in. Günter nodded briskly, rolled up his window and drove slowly through the gate. He then parked below a short flight of stairs. The other priest riding in the front passenger seat stepped out of the car and mounted the stairs. He spoke quickly with another priest and returned to the car.

"All clear, your supremacy," he said, opening the door for his boss.

"Thank you, Lucius," replied Father Supreme.

Father Supreme exited the car and mounted the stairs. Fr. Antonio followed his boss as they walked into the most secluded part of the Vatican. Like a reflex action, they walked along the hallways they had walked a countless number of times and took an elevator six levels down to an even more secret portion of the building. A priest greeted them and led them into their conference room. Father Supreme sat on his chair, and Fr. Antonio took a seat to his left as always.

"So, what did our agent say exactly?" asked Father Supreme.

The 18x12x10 feet conference room, with mostly oakwood furniture, a 40" television monitor concrete floor and ceiling, no windows and no rugs offered more privacy than the car did.

"'Tell your boss we must meet. The situation has changed and something big is about to happen. The Bright Eyes are creating a new and upgraded version of themselves.' Those were his exact words, your supremacy," replied Fr. Antonio. "I wonder how he came up with this intel."

"Did he say where and when?" Father Supreme ignored Antonio's question.

"No, Father," replied Antonio. "He said you would know what to do."

"I see," Father Supreme said flatly, and silence ensued.

Fr. Antonio hesitated for a moment and then spoke.

"Your supremacy."

"Yes?"

"Why do you think he said you would know what to do?" asked Antonio. "This is absurd."

"Indeed, Antonio," replied his supremacy. "I'll have to find out for myself soon."

"But Father," Antonio objected. "You can't be serious."

Antonio realized what he had just inadvertently done.

"I deeply apologize, your supremacy," he added quickly. "I did not mean anything by that."

"It's alright, Antonio," Father Supreme said. "I know you meant well."

He paused for a moment. A pensive mood filled the sealed-off room.

"Besides, if anything were to happen to me, I know the Order would be in great hands."

He winked at Antonio, a gesture which caused Antonio to recoil slightly with surprise before his features relaxed with relief.

"You honor me greatly, your supremacy," Antonio said.

"Dismissed."

"Aye, your supremacy," Antonio stood up. "I'll keep you apprised, sir."

"Good," Father Supreme nodded slowly, twice.

With a stiff bow, Fr. Antonio exited the room leaving Father Supreme by himself. He reached under the table and pressed a button. Multiple locks went into motion and turned the room into a fortress that was impervious to any form of electromagnetism and telecommunication. He clasped his hands, placed his elbows on the table and rested his chin on his clasped hands. Seconds later, he sighed and leaned back in his chair. He closed his eyes and slowed down his breath to five per minute. And then, his mind went blank.

His mind was in a state of thoughtlessness and in that state of mind, devoid of all thought, a ray of light sparked into existence and grew into an all-engulfing luminescence. In a whoosh, the luminescence was sucked into an oblivion and it disappeared, leaving nothing but the semblance of a presence in its stead. Then, the image of a face coalesced out of many tiny specks that appeared in the slate of nothingness of his mind, starting as a silhouette until it became a real-life, three-dimensional image of a person's face. The entire process lasted less than a thousandth of a second. He opened his eyes and frowned.

"I see you got my message," Yehuda said.

Even via their telepathic link, the most powerful man in the underworld could sense the impish grin of the most wanted man in the underworld.

Günter leaned against the hood of the car with his back to the entrance of the building. He was lost in thought as he idly flipped a rare coin in his left hand repeatedly. The coin was a souvenir from Fr. Wilson, his psychiatrist during his period of training with the Jesuits.

I wonder what those two could be discussing in there, he thought, referring to Father Supreme and Fr. Antonio.

He thought he had found closure after killing Judge Hassler and Fr. Heinrich.

But closure is overrated. My subconscious can attest to that.

He flipped the coin again and caught it with the back of his left hand. He peeled the coin from the back of his left hand with his right hand. Gently, he traced the scar on the back of his left hand with his right index finger, triggering a barrage of memories of a not-so-distant past to come flooding back in.

***

Günter later learned he had been in the Nazi torture chamber for eight days. He was tortured and given just enough nourishment to keep him alive. His favorite moments were when his bonds came off. Unfortunately, he was too weak and his limbs were already too numb from prolonged insufficient blood flow to them that he just collapsed and lay on the floor. The millions of pins and needles that pricked his flesh as blood circulation returned to his limbs were a welcome discomfort and did not compare to the psychological and physical torment he suffered at the hands of these vile, hell-bound, distasteful breed of humans. After a while, he stopped caring about sores that broke out on his buttocks and the back of his thighs after marinating in his urine and feces for such long periods of time. The hosing down helped, but that was as far as it went with sanitation. Despite the hell he faced, Günter fought the good fight of faith with hymns, prayers and declarations of his commitment to God and the church.

One day, Dr. Klaus came to the torture chamber by himself and took a knee in front of Günter.

"Are you still a soldier for God?" he asked calmly.

"I'll show you if you'd let me," Günter whispered.

"Well," Dr. Klaus sighed heavily as he stood up and straightened his lab coat. "I believe we have wasted too much time on you already. Time to say goodbye. Here, meet the priest who will preside over your last rites."

"You talk too much, *herr dokter,*" Günter scoffed

Dr. Klaus smirked and clapped twice. A man came into the torture chamber wearing a white cassock and holding a bible and rosary in his right hand. Dr. Klaus grinned when he saw the confusion on Günter's face.

"What's up your sleeves?" Günter sneered at the fake priest.

"Patience," Dr. Klaus replied.

"Before you kill me, at least tell me how you know my name," Günter spat.

Dr. Klaus ignored him and stepped to the side. The fake priest tossed the bible and rosary to the floor before lifting the hem of his cassock. He took his time to undo his belt, trouser button, and zipper, while directing an impish grin towards Günter. He let gravity pull his trousers down as he reached for his underwear and pulled it down to his ankles. An evil chuckle erupted from his throat when he saw Günter turn white with horror. Next, he unbuttoned his cassock, stripped it from his torso and let it slide to the floor. He stepped out of the pile of clothing that had gathered around his ankles. He followed Günter's gaze to his nether region.

"Impressive, isn't it?" he asked rhetorically.

Four soldiers entered the torture chamber and flanked the fake priest.

"Seize him," ordered Dr. Klaus.

"No. No. NOOO," Günter cried as two men grabbed his hands and the other two grabbed his legs.

They undid his binds adeptly and Günter tried to fight with every morsel of energy he thought he had left. But even with the sudden adrenaline rush that gave him strength he thought he never had, he remained powerless against four, strong and fit German soldiers. He was half-dragged, half-lifted to a table in the corner, kicking and screaming all the way. Two of the soldiers tried to push his head forward to bend him over the table, but he resisted. Big mistake. A soldier let go of his head and punched him in the solar plexus while the other punched him straight in the face. White, hot pain radiated across his body and the chamber spun around violently in his vision.

Günter retched, but the concentrated bile only made it halfway up his gullet, leaving a burning, acidic appraisal along its path. His face, stomach and ribs crashed harshly on the table, and the two soldiers who punched him pulled his arms down over the table using their body weight. The other pair of soldiers held each of Günter's legs against their bodies and pinned them to the floor. He was clearly not their first because they executed their acts with passion, precision, prejudice. He could not move. He could not fight. He was exposed and he was helpless against the situation.

"Please, stop," he cried and begged, though he recognized the pointlessness of his plea.

The trauma from being molested many years ago played harshly on his psyche, like a healing wound reopened without warning and made worse than it was before. Back then, he could fight, back then he fought and back then, he won. But now was different. He could not fight, and sadly, even if he could fight, he could not win. Back then, he held his head up with pride. But now, he was held down. Back then, he was angry and his anger had fueled him with unimaginable strength and courage. But now, his features slumped in a sad summation of self-loathe and self-pity and his anger in that moment summed to naught.

"Where is your God, Günter?" Dr. Klaus whispered in his ear. "Where is your Christ? Why can't he save you now?"

"Please," Günter begged, tears streaming down his eyes. "I beg of you, don't do this."

"Will you join us?" Klaus asked as he stood up straight.

Günter stayed silent, torn between his sense of duty and need for sanity.

"It doesn't have to be like this Günter," Klaus yelled. "Can't you see you're just a pawn to them? Where is the rescue team? Where is your God or Christ to come save you? You're nothing but trash to them; worse than toilet paper. They use you to wipe the crap out of their anuses and flush you down the toilet."

"Please," Günter could barely speak.

Günter's mental strength buckled and his psyche quaked. His breaking point loomed nigh.

Maybe he's right, he thought. *Where is the rescue team? Maybe I'm nothing but trash to them. But they did train me to know the mission was more important and that I was expendable.*

Even with this awareness, the flame of hope burned dimmer still.

"I'll ask you one last time," the doctor yelled. "WILL YOU JOIN US?"

Where are you, my Lord? he prayed. *My God, why don't you save me? I have been your loyal soldier all these years.*

Faith was his last weapon in his arsenal.

"The Lord… is my… Shepherd, I shall… not want," Günter began weakly reciting.

"So be it," said the doctor and snapped his fingers at the half-naked man. "He's all yours, Abelard."

Klaus crouched in front of Günter and stared directly into Günter's eyes.

"I want to savor this moment," Klaus snarled. "I want to feast on every bit of displeasure you're about to suffer."

Günter felt a cold liquid slide down the crack of his butt before he felt a finger applying the liquid on his anal orifice. He instinctively tried to squeeze his butt cheeks tight to no avail.

"Easy now, tough guy," said Abelard. "Everyone always puts up a fight, but they never win. You will be no different."

Abelard continued applying the liquid as he and the other soldiers exploded in derisive laughter.

"They say it's less painful if you don't fight it," he added. "Until they feel my hardness violating their insides."

More derisive laughter and more shattering of his spirit.

"And the pleasure will be all mine," he added and grabbed Günter's buttocks.

Günter sobbed and whimpering in desperation and resignation. Even God was failing him, it seemed.

"Relax," Abelard squeezed Günter's buttocks. "I'm about to enjoy myself."

Another round of laughter snuffed out the last flicker of hope that burned in him. The walls around his psyche, the final stronghold to his sanity and strength, came down in a pile of dust. He relived his worst nightmares and deepest fears a thousand-fold in a flash. Day turned to night, strength to weakness, anger to calmness and resistance to a soothing surrender. In that moment, his past and his concept of the future died, as well as his beliefs and ideologies. Most of all, his purpose for life died as well. A brand-new slate lay in front of him, beckoning him to write a new path for himself. He answered to the call and initiated a rebirth. Not the fake kind the church claims happens when water is sprinkled over one's head and a priest says a few words. His rebirth was true and transformational. In that instant, he was a man torn down and rebuilt, a man who had just gone through his own crucifixion, just like the one he once called his Lord and Savior. And, like the one he once called his Lord and Savior, he had resurrected as a new person with a new mind, a new heart, and a new purpose.

"Yes," he whispered.

Dr. Klaus held up a hand for Abelard to halt.

"What did you say?" the doctor asked.

"Yes," Günter repeated. "I will join you."

The doctor inched his face closer to Günter's. He lifted Günter's chin so that he could look at Günter in the eye. He saw what he was looking for. These were not the same eyes of the soldier who was captured more than a week ago. These were the eyes of someone who had been broken down and reborn into a new world, a world he was yet to discover.

"Let him go," Klaus ordered the soldiers.

"But *Herr Dokter*, are you sure you want us to-" a soldier protested.

"I said let him go… now," Klaus barked again.

The soldiers obliged and stood a few paces away from the table. Klaus was still on one knee in front of Günter.

"Give me your pistol," Klaus stretched out a hand towards one of the soldiers without taking his eyes off Günter.

"*Dokter-*" said the soldier.

"Damn you, soldier, I will not repeat myself," Klaus yelled.

The soldier unstrapped his holster, removed his weapon and handed it over to Klaus. Klaus took the Luger, checked the magazine and handed it to Günter, who was still hanging off the table. Günter looked from Klaus, to the gun and back to Klaus. Klaus took Günter's left hand, placed the gun in it and stood up. Günter held the gun in his left hand, with a finger on the trigger. Then, after a few seconds, he spun the gun to hold it by the barrel and made to return it to Klaus. But he was too weak to even lift his arm. Klaus took the gun from him and returned it to the soldier.

"Clean him up and take him to the infirmary," Klaus instructed and left the chamber.

Günter was taken to a bathroom and two nurses gave him a warm bath. He was then clothed, fed and his wounds and injuries were tended to. Four days later, his strength began to return. He was now one of them; not just a sympathizer but a full-blown Nazi. Why they had gone through all the trouble to convert him still eluded him. He did not care anymore, anyway. On the fifth day, he was lying on the bed, resting but not sleeping, when one of the nurses knocked on his door.

"You have a visitor," she smiled and held the door open.

Günter smiled back. She was his favorite nurse because she did provide other forms of healing that he was sure were outside of her professional mandate.

"Thank you," he heard his visitor say to the nurse.

Günter bolted upright from the bed. He winced from his sudden movement. He thought he recognized that voice.

But how? He wondered. *They say he was dead.*

His visitor walked in and Günter gasped in shock and awe.

"Hello Günter," said Fr. Aaron, who preferred to be called Andrew. "Congratulations on joining us."

And then, his eyes glowed.

***

Günter pushed himself from the car and rubbed his temples. He still had the coin in his right hand. He paced slowly along the car to improve blood flow to his lower limbs and glanced at his watch.

Father Supreme and confidant should be coming out any moment from now, he thought.

He resumed flipping the coin. Father Supreme was, no doubt, an enigma. Fr. Andrew, and Dr. Klaus had tasked him with a mission. Günter was 'the best of his kind,' Fr. Andrew had said, and he had no intentions of disappointing Fr.

Andrew.

He turned around in time to see one of the priests by the entrance to the building making his way towards him. The priest stopped mid-step when he caught Günter's eye and gave a thumbs-up. Günter returned the gesture and straightened his gait as he faced the entrance to the Vatican. Father Supreme descended the stairs without returning the salutes from the priests guarding the entrance. Günter opened the door for his supremacy to smoothly slide into the back seat. He closed the door and quickly walked back to the driver's seat.

"Where to, Father?" Günter asked.

Silence lingered for a moment.

"To the base."

"Aye, Father." Günter replied and started the car.

Günter wrestled with the idea that this could be a perfect opportunity to execute his orders, since he was alone in the car with the target. He was confident he could take on his boss. The man, Günter assumed, must be rusty after being away from the field for so long. They were both about the same height and build. But Günter thought it was going to be an unfair fight. And by unfair Günter meant it would be a cake walk for him.

Günter also entertained the possibility that the situation could also be a trap. Four of them came to the building, and only two of them were heading to the base. Panic started welling up inside of him, but he forced himself to *calm down.*

This can't be a trap, he surmised. *They wouldn't use someone as important as Father Supreme to lure flush him out. The O.R. had much more efficient ways of dealing with traitors. So, my cover is still intact.*

"Sir, may I ask you something please?" Günter asked timidly.

Good show, by the way, he thought.

"Speak, son," replied his boss.

"Is everything alright?" Günter asked.

And who does he think he is, calling me 'son'? The man does not even look like he is past forty-five and he calls me 'son'? How disrespectful!

"Why do you ask?" his boss asked calmly.

"Sir, the four of us went to the Vatican, and now it's just the two of us leaving. Plus, you want me to take you straight to the base," Günter proceeded cautiously. "It just aroused my curiosity, and that's why I asked. I mean no disrespect, sir, and if I'm speaking out of terms, then I deeply apologize."

"Good observation, Günter," his supremacy said after a few heartbeats and Günter was certain he detected a hint of warmth in his boss' voice. "I could not have expected any less from one of our best."

"Thank you, sir," Günter pretended to beam with pride.

"That is why you and I are going on this mission," his boss added.

Günter almost lost control of the wheel.

"Sir," he said.

But his throat felt dry and he could barely contain his excitement.

And opportunity comes a-calling, he thought to himself.

"Yes?" his boss prompted.

"I cannot find the words, sir," Günter said and meant it.

He was going on a mission with the most powerful man in the underworld. Finally. Talk about the perfect scenario. He would go on a mission with his boss, finish the task and his boss would be caught in an unfortunate and tragic accident. Word on the underworld streets was that his supremacy had never failed in any mission and had never lost a soldier under his command during a mission. Except for that one time that he lost someone very dear to him.

"I would choose no other, Günter," he said.

"Thank you so much, sir," Günter replied. "So, what are we taking out, your supremacy?" he asked. "Sinisters?"

"No," replied his boss.

Günter did not know the basics of the mission, but he thought he might have an idea. He would have to adapt. He would let his boss and their enemy wear each other out before jumping in for the kill?

Yes. That was it. He rejoiced in his mind and suppressed a smile. I will become an even bigger hero in the order and who knows, many years down the line, I can even become Father Supreme, especially with the Nazis on my side. We know they're going to win any war that breaks out and rule the world. They're too strong and they will want one of theirs to rule an organization as powerful as the O.R...

They hit the long country road towards Milan where the base was located. A small jet, fully equipped to take on the latest military jets and could fly at top speed, was already prepped and waiting for them. Father Supreme issued some orders to the base commander, who most likely thought Father Supreme was a cardinal from the Vatican in need of some discrete services from the O.R. Fifteen minutes later, Günter and his boss boarded the private jet and took off for France.

CHAPTER TEN

AMBUSHED

THE FLIGHT TO France was smooth. They landed in a small village in Cote d'Or located in the Bourgogne region. The full moon hid behind thick clouds, but the pilot was good at his job. Günter and Father Supreme now wore black, bulletproof, long-sleeved tee shirts, combat pants and sleeveless jackets. Their enemies did not use projectile weaponry, but the bulletproof gear served as extra protection from mauling. Günter packed some toys in his bag but noticed that his boss had no weapons on him.

This mission is getting stranger by the minute, he thought as he heaved his backpack over his shoulders.

The plane taxied to a stop.

"Refuel in Paris," Father Supreme spoke to the pilot as he opened the door to jump out of the jet. "We will meet you there in an hour."

"Yes, Sir," affirmed the pilot.

Such confidence, Günter thought.

Günter wondered how they could get from Cote D'Or to Paris in two hours, even by car. They were over a hundred kilometers from Paris.

He won't be making it to Paris, anyway, he shrugged.

The jet was airborne within two minutes as Günter and Father Supreme blended with the near-pitch blackness of the night, devoid of any sign of life or habitation for as far as the eyes and ears could fathom in such darkness. A few, small trees remained motionless in the gently breeze, but the rest of the area was covered with grass that was about thirty-five centimeters tall.

"This way," ordered his boss.

Günter followed him into the field, away from the road, and towards a small cluster of trees. They walked for close to six minutes before his boss suddenly stopped. Günter nearly bumped into him. Father Supreme scanned the area with his eyes and cocked an ear in the air as if listening to something in the wind.

"He's here, isn't he, sir?" whispered Günter.

"Get ready," his boss ordered. "They're here."

"They?" Günter asked in a whisper and realized what his boss meant.

Günter dropped his back pack to the ground, opened it and dug in. He pulled out two silver pistols fully loaded with silver-nitrate-tipped bullets and stuffed the guns in separate hip holsters. He retrieved four more clips, each containing two dozen silver-nitrate-tipped bullets and stuck them to pouches in his belt. Upon impact, the bullet tips explode, releasing its contents into the victim. Holy water was useless against the Bright Eyes. Günter then took out two daggers, each with silver six-inch blades and strapped each knife to each of his outer thighs.

A knife in the back or a bullet to the brain, he pondered. *How shall I kill him?*

He was safe from the Bright Eyes. They had orders not to harm him. If it came to it, he may have to kill a few of them to protect his cover; a tiny price to pay for such an invaluable trophy to be procured and Fr. Andrew had agreed.

Father Supreme looked at the phosphorescent hands of his watch.

"Now," he said, leaning against the base of a tree, "we wait."

Günter joined him and sat facing the other direction. While they waited, Günter's mind drifted back to the day Fr. Andrew had joined him in his room at the Nazi camp.

***

"Fr. Andrew?" Günter exclaimed. "But… How come? I thought you were-"

"Dead?" Fr. Andrew asked.

"Yes," Günter spoke almost to himself. "I actually wept for you."

"I did die," Fr. Andrew said. "I did fall off a cliff, but that wasn't all."

He took another step into the room and Günter backed away from him. Fr. Andrew raised his hand, to indicate that he meant no harm, and sat on a chair across from Günter. His smile never left his face.

"But you're a Bright Eye," Günter tightened his jaw

Instinctively, his training kicked in and he switched to kill mode.

Maybe this whole thing was a charade, he thought. *This is just another phase of my torture.*

"Before you try anything stupid," Fr. Andrew said, "remember I designed most of the O.R's training techniques to kill… us."

He paused to let the implications of his statement sink in.

"My death was not an accident,' he continued. "I work with the Nazis now and we have a mission for you if you can spare me a moment of your time?"

This is recruitment all over again, Günter fumed. *These Nazis are sick in the head.*

"I assure you, Günter," Fr. Andrew continued. "This is not an act. Let me ask you something. Have I ever lied to you? If I wanted to torture you, wouldn't it be a lot easier to turn you into the one thing you absolutely hate: a Bright Eye?"

Günter's features softened and he unclenched his fists.

"You do know how to find your way to a man's mind, don't you Father," Günter smiled.

Günter still had a lot of respect for Fr. Andrew, Bright Eye or not. The man practically was his savior.

"Better than the alternative, right?" Fr. Andrew said.

"What alternative would that be, Father?" Günter asked, a cloud of puzzlement hanging over his face.

"Forget I said that," Fr. Andrew replied.

"As you wish," Günter replied. "It's good to see you again, Father."

"It's good to see you too, Günter," Fr. Andrew replied.

Günter slid off the bed and met Fr. Andrew half way. The two men hugged each other for several seconds.

"So, what do you mean by your death was not an accident, Father?" Günter asked finally.

"You know how Father Supreme and I used to go on missions together sometimes, right?" he asked.

"Yes, I do," replied Günter.

"So, we went on this mission. We had some intel that the lair of the sinisters' leader had been located; somewhere not too far from Stonehenge of all places. Don't even remember anymore. Four of us went to check it out, but we were ambushed on the way by ten Bright Eyes. Easy number for the four of us to handle, right? We did take care of them, but here's what happened. During the fight, your boss and I stood at the edge of the cliff together. The plan was to lure the last of them to the cliff's edge and let gravity do the rest. Besides, it was soon going to be sunrise. Do you know what he did at the very last second?"

Günter detected a glint of anger in Fr. Andrew's eyes.

"He pushed you off?" Günter asked nonchalantly.

"That would've been too obvious," Fr. Andrew replied. "A luper leaped for him. But instead of just stepping off the luper's path, he synced with the luper's momentum. That is, he caught the luper by the neck, dropped to the ground but not before placing his leg on the luper's hip. He knew I was behind him. So, as he flung the luper backward. I was too slow to react and the luper's body crashed into mine. A chuper was attacking me at the same time. The three of us fell off the edge of the cliff. The last thing I remembered before I blacked out was sharp fangs piercing my neck and a deep sense of loss."

He paused to calm himself before he continued.

"I won't bore you with the details of my transformation. But I will say I have never felt more alive and stronger."

Fr. Andrew's eyes flashed. Günter had to admit, now that he was not afraid anymore, it was amazing seeing his recruiter's eyes flash like that.

"My God," Günter exclaimed, staring hypnotically at Fr. Andrew.

"And now, the kiss of death," said Fr. Andrew snapping playfully at Günter.

A thousand reactions flared at once throughout Günter's body and Fr. Andrew erupted in laughter.

"I just meant now I bite you and turn you into a Bright Eye," his said.

"I like your new sense of humor, Father," Günter said without meaning it.

"Come," Fr. Andrew motioned to Günter. "Time to brief you on your mission."

Günter got up from the bed and followed his former recruiter. They made a left turn and walked along a corridor that had labs on each side and a few people, most likely scientists, who seemed to be engaged in various kinds of experiments. They then made a right turn and stepped into an elevator. Fr. Andrew hit the B5 button, and the elevator jerked to life, making a slow but steady descent.

"We're working with the Nazis to build an army of Bright Eyes," Andrew explained.

"But you can't survive in daylight," interjected Günter. "So, does that mean you'll be fighting the war only at night?"

"It is true that daylight is our biggest weakness and we could fight the war only at night," answered Fr. Andrew. "But there is an even greater problem. Our numbers can't exceed a hundred and forty-four; that is, seventy-two lupers and seventy-two chupers. For every Bright Eye that dies, a new Bright Eye can be spawned. But once the threshold is reached, no Bright Eye can be spawned."

"Unbelievable," Günter said. "It sounds like some kind of control by nature to keep the population of Bright Eyes in check. Imagine if there were no threshold whatsoever and they, uh you, could just turn people at random! Then the human race could easily be wiped out."

Fr. Andrew smiled and did not reply. The elevator chimed to a stop. Both men stepped out, and Fr. Andrew made a sharp left turn before taking a right turn along another corridor with Günter in tow.

"I knew I didn't recruit you for just your prickly personality," Fr. Andrew said, and both men laughed.

"I feel special, Father," Günter managed to say amidst fits of laughter.

"You're welcome," Fr. Andrew joked. "So yes, it appears as if it is a control mechanism from Mother Nature to keep our numbers in check. We are stronger and faster than humans, and we stand a small chance against a small army. But if a large-scale attack is launched against us, our chances of survival are next to none. Therefore, it is imperative that we address our numbers problem and later, we will address our weakness to daylight. Or we could do both at the same time."

He stopped outside a door and pressed a red button. The doors parted, and both men walked into what looked like a balcony with a large glass partition. About twenty feet below, there was a room about twenty feet wide and forty feet long, with men and women dressed in white slacks idling around. Some were sitting, others either standing or pacing up and down and talking among themselves. Günter stared at them.

"Who are these?" he asked.

"Test subjects," Fr. Andrew replied. "There's a lead scientist who works with The Twins. Says he can find a solution to our major problems."

"So, The Twins really do exist, huh?" Günter asked rhetorically.

"We must have our origins, don't we?" Fr. Andrew replied.

The ease with which Fr. Andrew used 'we' when he spoke of the Bright Eyes fascinated Günter.

He does have a new family, Günter thought.

"And what is this solution this scientist speaks of?" Günter asked.

"I'm not exactly sure on the details," Fr. Andrew replied. "But I do know this is where you come in."

"What am I supposed to do?" Günter asked.

"To obtain a sample of Father Supreme's blood and bring it here.".

Günter whipped a face drained of all color by dread in Fr. Andrew's direction. "Are you serious?" he half-yelled. "How am I supposed to even get close to him? Let alone stick a needle in him without him realizing it."

"There are many other ways to obtain his blood," Andrew replied calmly.

Günter understood that Father Supreme did not necessarily have to be alive for the mission to be successful. A fleeting feeling of guilt touched his soul. He stared into Fr. Andrew's eyes, his recruiter, his savior, his friend. A moment of sadness seeped into his being. Fr. Andrew was a chuper and Father Supreme was to blame. Sadness sleuthed into a cold fury that burned with a steady flame within the pit of his stomach. In that moment, he declared himself judge, jury and when he turned to face the test subjects in the room below, he also declared himself executioner. Father Supreme had to pay for what he had done to his friend.

"So, what's the plan, brother?" Günter asked.

***

"Get ready," Father Supreme's voice sliced through his reverie like an alarm clock on an early Monday morning.

Günter immediately crouched. Father Supreme was already crouching and staring in the darkness.

Look at him, acting like he can see in the dark, Günter scoffed.

Bodiless pairs of eyes twinkled at random in the blackness of the night. Günter unclasped both holsters, withdrew both guns and cocked each hammer. Something was eerie about the way Father Supreme had spoken to him. His boss' voice did not sound 'normal', as in his boss' voice did not register in his ear.

I heard his voice more in my head than in my ears, he frowned. *But how? Maybe I only imagined it.*

But if this was not an imagination, was that why the Bright Eyes wanted Father Supreme's blood? Because Father Supreme was a telepath?

Focus.

"They have picked up our scents. They know where we are," said his boss a-matter-of-factly. "That is why they are in attack formation."

He can see in the dark, Günter exclaimed in his mind. *Jesus Christ, who is this man?*

He swept his right index finger in a tight arc in front of them. Günter's eyes had adjusted to the darkness as moonlight started seeping through parting clouds.

"I count twenty-eight of them," Günter said.

"Forty, actually," corrected his boss.

"How can you tell, sir?" Günter asked, perplexed.

"From their auras," his boss replied

Father Supreme stood up and walked towards the creatures.

Günter courageously followed not knowing how to respond to what his boss had just said.

A telepath, a clairvoyant and he can see clearly in the dark, Günter pondered. *This mission just got a lot more interesting. I'm going to be so famous for killing such a rare person. I'm going to be famous for saving the Bright Eyes.*

Father Supreme stopped at about fifty meters away from the creatures. Günter stood by his boss' side.

"So," Father Supreme spoke aloud, "which one of you abominations will be the first to die tonight?"

A chorus of low growls from lupers and high-pitched clattering of teeth from chupers simmered into the night as the clouds parted even further, letting the full glow of the moon to bathe the field with its blessing of light. A Bright Eye stepped forward with the demeanor of a leader. It was Andrew.

"Hello, brother,"

"Andrew?" Father Supreme's voice quavered slightly from shock. "I... I thought you perished."

"Wasn't that what you wanted?" Andrew scowled. "You thought you'd get rid of me, but," he gestured around, "I found a new family and a new purpose. Don't you just love how I look?" he added and his eyes glowed.

"You're... an *ABOMINATION*," Father Supreme screamed.

"Always the self-righteous egomaniac," Andrew shot back. "You were so damn insecure about everything. You even feared I wanted your throne."

Andrew's voice was filled with anger as he spoke. He took a step towards Father Supreme.

"I gave you everything," Andrew lashed out. "My loyalty, my dedication, my love. I would have laid my life for you. And this is how you repay me? By sending me over a cliff?"

"I'm sorry," Father Supreme said almost to himself. "I'm truly sorry."

Günter could not believe his stoic boss was on the brink of tears.

"Well, I'm not sorry for what I'm about to do to you," Andrew said. "I am an abomination, yes. Even better, I will be your worst nightmare. Blood for blood. Life for life."

He turned around to walk into the group of Bright Eyes.

"ATTACK."

A chuper and a luper each zipped from both ends of the group. Two pairs of attackers converged onto Father Supreme at a forty-five-degree angle from either side, cutting down the grass as they zipped for a kill. Günter rolled backwards twice to separate himself from Father Supreme. He crouched and aimed his pistols, ready to fire. But when he witnessed the spectacle that unfolded in front of him, the guns felts like ship anvils and his hands dropped to the side. Shadows whizzed around in blurring speeds and his problem was that he could not tell which whizzing shadows were the Bright Eyes and which was Father Supreme.

Father Supreme dashed to the left at a slight angle, evading past an extended paw of a luper. The claw of its index finger trimmed off some hair strands close to his left temple. He caught the luper's left hind leg as he planted his right foot on the ground, coiling his hips as he executed a backward cross step with his left leg. The kinetic energy from his dashing move became potential energy. Father Supreme then transferred this potential energy in his coiled hips to kinetic energy as he swung the luper in a full circle and crashed its body into the spine of the chuper that was attacking from the left. The two Bright Eyes landed on the ground in a confused heap.

The other pair of attackers from the right flank flew over him, not expecting that he was going to duck while they were in mid-flight towards him. He plunged his fists into the backs of the spines of the two abominations on the ground. The two creatures turned to ash as he crushed their hearts in his hand. The other pair of attackers was returning for another assault.

Too slow, Father Supreme scoffed.

He lunged at them and drove a hand into the chests of each Bright Eye. He seized their hearts in his hands and crushed them as if they were ping pong balls. Their bodies turned to ash before they hit the ground. The entire sequence lasted just over 0.80milliseconds.

He spun around to face the rest of the Bright Eyes. Eight more Bright Eyes zipped in the same formation, four on each side this time. Three more zipped directly towards him. He opened his right hand and sparked the ethers. A razor-sharp sword with a three-foot long, double-edged, silver blade formed in his right hand. He whizzed to his right, and four bodies turned to ash. In three more moves, the other seven attackers met a similar end.

Günter stood up, shoulders slumped in resignation.

Night vision, telepathy, clairvoyance, super speed and who knows what else, Günter sighed. *How do I even begin to sneak up on someone like him who clearly isn't human but looks human?*

Eight seconds later, every Bright Eye was dead, except for Fr. Andrew. He took slow, careful steps towards Father Supreme and stopped three meters away from his former boss. The two men stared each other down with soul-burning hatred. Then, to Günter's utter shock, Father Supreme dismissed his sword as the two men burst into laughter and hugged each other in a tight embrace.

"So, how do you plan on killing me now, Günter?" his boss asked as he let go of Andrew.

Günter's instinct for survival overrode his shock and he raised his weapons to fire. But something pushed his hands upwards and he fired in the air instead. He did not even have the luxury of appreciating the extreme discomfort and pain that radiated across his body as something jabbed into his solar plexus and throat with insane precision. Two hands grabbed his wrists and twisted them sharply upwards, forcing him to let go of his guns and locking in his wrists, elbow, shoulder and spine. A yelp of pain escaped his throat while his body involuntarily sank to its knees to alleviate some of the pain in his joints. But the pain only intensified.

"Your grenades are duds," Father Supreme said as Günter's attacker let go of Günter's wrists and walked towards them.

"What-" Günter coughed, gasped and winced.

His voice was hoarse, and his wrists felt like hot coals. And his logical mind still could not make sense of the speed with which the other person had disarmed and neutralized him.

"What's going on?" he asked.

"I was not betrayed," Andrew replied. "I chose to become one of them and go undercover."

Günter sat up. The realization that these may be his last moments seemed to grant him some strength and clarity of mind.

"Always so clever," Günter managed to say with a slight chuckle. "So, I was just a pawn to you, *brother?*" he said with a sneer.

"No, you weren't a pawn," Andrew replied. "The moment you turned, *you* betrayed the Order. For all intents and purposes, *you* betrayed *me. You* betrayed *us*, and *you* became our enemy. Infiltrating the Bright Eyes was my idea. He," he said gesturing towards Father Supreme, "was strongly against it at first. But like you once told me, Günter, I do have a way with words."

Even in the dark, Günter knew Andrew was smiling.

"You turning on us was the perfect opportunity for me to seal my position even deeper with them. When opportunity beckons, I seize it."

"How noble of you," Günter stood up and wiped the dirt off his knees, as if it mattered. "Before I die, may I, at least, know your names?" he asked gesturing at both Father Supreme and the third party that disarmed him.

"Oh, I'm sorry," Andrew said smacking himself in the forehead. "Where are my manners? To the right is your assailant," he announced gesturing at the third party. "He is known as the most wanted man in the underworld. His name is Yehuda, also known as Judas Iscariot."

Günter's jaw dropped in shock.

"Yes, he actually is Judas Iscariot, the one who betrayed Jesus-"

"And he will pay in blood for that," Father Supreme hissed between clenched teeth.

"Brother. That was very, very rude of you," Andrew wagged a finger at Father Supreme and grinned. "Can't you see I was introducing Günter to the family?"

"Anyway, Günter, we are three of the Apostles you have read about in the bible. My real name is Aaron, like I told you already. But Andrew will do, just because a bunch of idiots decided to edit history and call it a bible. Pathetic job, they did. Still with me so far?"

Günter shook himself back to reality.

"So, if he's Judas," Günter said, "you're Andrew, and you two," he gestured at both Andrew and Father Supreme, "are brothers, then that means…"

His eyes widened in something beyond shock, awe and surprise.

"Oh, my God."

"I knew I recruited you for more than your prickly personality," Andrew said and laughed out loud.

But Günter did not join him in the laughter.

"Yes, this is Shi'mon, popularly known as Simon Peter, the one who was crucified upside-down on the spot where St. Peter's Basilica now stands. The first pope of the Roman Catholic Church, the rock upon which Jesus was going to build his church, and so on and so forth. Sounds familiar?"

Andrew rolled his eyes with each sentence.

Günter's head pounded from too much information and he slumped to the ground in resignation. Too many questions raced through his mind but he knew he would never have answers for them. He felt a wisp of air past him but he paid it no mind. He met the gazes of Aaron and Shi'mon and felt the looming presence of Yehuda to his right.

"Now I know why they wanted his blood," Günter said to himself.

"And now you die," Yehuda said

Yehuda sparked the ethers. A gun formed in his right hand. He raised it to Günter's head and pulled the trigger.

CHAPTER ELEVEN

THE TWINS

"STATUS UPDATE?" DREYKO demanded as he walked with Danka in steady strides down a hallway.

"The subjects are ready your highnesses and at least one of the samples should be here in three hours or less," Dr. Klaus replied, keeping a steady pace behind The Twins.

Dreyko and Danka stopped outside their suite on the top floor of the Nazi facility in Berlin, where Günter had been held captive. Dr. Klaus walked past The Twins, ensuring no physical contact with them. He entered a four-digit code and the door slid open. He reached inside and flipped on the switch to reveal a large, plush suite. The floor was covered in a single burgundy-and-black Persian rug, with a pair of white glowing eyes at the center. A king-sized bed with blood-red, silk sheets, and no blanket, sat at the far left-hand corner. The Bright Eyes were impervious to the elements and hence, they had no need for covers, quilts, blankets and so on. The bed frame was built with reinforced steel because The Twins had a habit of breaking wooden bed frames, no matter how strong the wood was.

Blood-red silk curtains draped over the windows and several paintings of Danka and Dreyko decorated the dark, grey walls of the suite. An oak wood dining section for two was on the right-hand side of the suite and a blood-red sofa was placed against the wall on the right, about four feet from the door. The Twins desired no other pieces of furniture. Too much furniture tended to cause prolonged moments of separation, which was something they did not want. A door to the left separated the suite from the bathroom. It was closed. Dr. Klaus stepped back for The Twins to walk into the suite. Dreyko stopped a meter from the door. Danka walked further into the suite and appraised it.

"The Scientist?" Dreyko asked.

"He's in the main lab, your highness," Klaus replied, and swiped beads of stress sweat from his temples with the lapels of his lab coat.

"Is - Is everything according to your expectations so far, your highnesses?" Dr. Klaus stammered.

"It is missing the blond woman," Danka said.

Klaus' heart sank, but he dared not show it. The blond woman, Katya, the one who partook in Günter's torture, was his girlfriend. Klaus did not know if The Twins wanted to feast on her or get freaky with her.

"Of course, your highnesses," he swallowed nervously. "Will that be all?"

"For now," Dreyko replied as he walked to the window.

"Thank you, your highnesses," Klaus said and made to leave.

Klaus made sure not to ignore Danka. Dreyko was the devil himself. But compared to his sister, he was an angel.

"The door code is 8646," he added as he entered it.

The doors slid shut, allowing The Twins some privacy. Dreyko glanced at the clock on the wall.

Almost midnight. He stared blankly into the night. His sister came to him and wrapped her arms around his strong, broad shoulders from behind.

"We're almost there, sister," he caressed her arm while keeping his blank stare ahead. "If The Scientist succeeds, then not only will we be able to spawn our kind beyond the threshold, but we will also be able to walk in daylight again…" his voice trailed off, "like the humans."

"Indeed, my love," Danka whispered in his ear. "No more acting from the shadows. No more hiding from sunlight. We will expand our numbers and create the world in our image."

She took his shoulders and gently turned him around until his face was barely inches away from hers.

"We will be their gods, and they will be our subjects."

"Indeed, sister," Dreyko agreed. "And this fool, this Hitler, thinks he will rule the world and create a pure, superior race."

The Twins chuckled and shook their heads in a rare moment of humor.

"His ambition is cute, even adorable," Danka rolled her eyes. "If The Scientist succeeds, then no race will be purer or more superior than ours is."

Danka kissed him softly on the lips. But when she made to withdraw herself, he grabbed her by the waist, pressed her body against his and kissed her passionately. She surrendered to his brute strength and returned his passion. A few beeps tore into the suite, and the doors slid open to reveal Katya wearing nothing but lingerie.

"You asked to see me, your highnesses?" she asked, her facial expression and indication of her ignorance of their intentions.

"Come," Danka commanded as she peeled away from Dreyko.

Katya stepped into the suite, entered the code and the doors slid shut. She continued walking towards The Twins until she stopped about a meter away from Danka. Danka reached out and grabbed Katya by the throat with just enough force to simulate a blood choke. As Katya gradually slipped into unconsciousness, Danka planted a rough kiss on her mouth and forced an unnaturally long tongue down Katya's throat, initiating an air choke. Katya clawed at Danka's arm until she started turning blue from lack of oxygen. Only then did Danka withdraw her tongue and release her hold on Katya's neck. Katya stumbled to the floor, coughing vigorously and sucking in huge, lungfuls of air. Katya felt a breeze and heard a whizz before realizing that her lingerie was gone, as if by a magic trick. She looked up just in time to see Dreyko towering over her and dropping her torn lingerie to the floor. She blinked and before she knew it, her back was slammed against the wall and her legs spread eagled.

Dreyko filled Katya's accommodation with bestial savagery. His roughness elicited a gasp of joyous enjoyment and her initial dryness turned into a drenching wetness almost instantly. She dug her long fingernails into Dreyko's back and clawed until she drew blood. Katya moaned with unimaginable pleasure that was spawned out of a feeling of being trapped between raw fear and surreal ecstasy. Then, her eyes rolled into the back of her head and her body slumped in sweet surrender as every nerve ending in her body went afire with something she had never experience before with any human. Dreyko went ravenous in her, pumping over fifteen times the normal human speed. She recalled Dr. Klaus telling her about how fear was an aphrodisiac to them.

And Dreyko is feasting on mine now.

She wanted to say something. To beg him not to stop. To call him daddy, master, lord, god, anything. But she feared for her life and the more she feared, the more Dreyko ravaged her and the more she sank deeper and deeper into a dimension of pleasure she never knew existed.

Danka saw fresh blood trail down her brother's back as Katya clawed and her body became awash with intense sexual arousal. Her fingers turned to claws as she zipped towards Dreyko. Danka dug her claws into his sides before her canines turned to fangs. She growled and bit into Dreyko's neck. A shrill, ear-splitting cry emanated from Dreyko's throat as he clattered his teeth at near super-sonic speed. Then, their eyes flashed bright, blood red and a terrifying threesome began.

Katya was convinced beyond a doubt that her end had come and, with that acceptance, she released insane amounts of adrenaline into her system, causing nuclear-level aphrodisiac reactions within The Twins. They were a tireless trio. Katya was unsure how she survived but was proud of herself for keeping up with their stamina, especially since The Twins were... superhuman. Cursed or not, she desperately wanted to be like them. She wanted to be as strong and as fast as they were. She would do anything, trade everything, to be just like them, regardless of their weakness for sunlight and silver. Too bad she was nothing more than a pet to them... for now, hopefully. She was their plaything, sandwiched in a sexual parody of sheer savage gusto as they toyed with her everywhere: on the floor, the wall, the bed, the table and the sofa. Talk about copulation on the ceiling.

This was Katya's version of heaven, having every orifice of her body filled up by Dreyko's savagery. At times, Danka was in the middle, and Danka pleased her like no woman ever had before. Katya had to admit, Danka was a pro. Perhaps such expertise in exhibiting such extraordinary eroticism could only be achieved after a millennium of practice. Katya did her best to match Danka in a hip gyration contest when they both straddled Dreyko; one gyrating on his pelvis and the other gyrating on his face. She considered herself a pro, after many years of being a fancy lady. But even with her years of practice, she was never going to gyrate her hips at the blurring speeds of a Bright Eye. Two hours later, she was dismissed. Her lingerie was nowhere to be found, but she was glad to at least still be alive when she entered the code to shut the door to the suite.

Danka cuddled against her brother and The Twins lay on the bed in silence for a few minutes. Dreyko slowly caressed his sister's long, black hair, a gesture she always loved. They were born on the same day. Dreyko was the crown prince, and his birth sister had died at birth. On that same night, a maiden in a nearby village had also died giving birth to her only daughter. Her husband had died a few months prior due to an illness. A soldier had then brought the baby to the palace. The queen named her Danka and adopted her into the royal family. As such, Dreyko and Danka were siblings by adoption, not by birth.

***

The royal family was a strange one. After giving birth to Dreyko, the queen's mental condition had taken a turn for the worse, and she was confined to her private quarters during the day. But at night, she returned to a normal state of mind. As for the twins, they started exhibiting unusual strength and speed at puberty compared to their peers. One day, at age sixteen, they ran after a deer, caught up with it and snapped its neck with their bare hands just for fun. The king was deeply concerned.

"Do not burden yourself, Sire," the palace doctors would say. "The palace cuisine is the best in the kingdom."

Even the king did not seem to age.

"Palace cuisine, Sire," the doctors said. "Palace cuisine."

However, the king thought he knew better.

On their eighteenth birthday, the king threw a banquet. The rich and royal from within the kingdom and beyond attended the banquet and brought gifts for the twins. A guest brought a rare wolf in a cage. Covered in near-pristine white fur and it stood at four feet tall on its legs, the wolf was an exotic, scary-looking and impressive beast. Another guest brought in a huge, white bat with a wingspan of five feet. Danka laid claim on the wolf and Dreyko laid claim on the bat, despite their parents' protests.

A week later, Danka was feeding the wolf in its cage and instead of tossing the creature its food, she unwisely decided to hold on to the piece of meat with her bare hand as she fed her pet. She turned around to bid her brother come witness her bravery. The wolf gnawed hard at her hand, almost biting it completely off.

Dreyko heard Danka scream. He dashed to her rescue and forgot to lock up the bat in its cage. He realized his mistake too late as the uncaged, flying mammal ferociously attacked him. During the struggle, the bat dug its fangs deep into Dreyko's neck, barely missing the jugular. Dreyko's fury numbed his pain. He ripped the creature from his neck, slammed it to the ground and crushed its head under his boot.

Danka and Dreyko were rushed the palace infirmary and the palace doctor attended to them immediately. The king came to see them and was relieved to know that they would be alright. That night, Danka insisted on sleeping in her brother's bed. She was too traumatized by the events of the afternoon to sleep in her chamber alone, or so she claimed. The physicians had done a great job with saving her hand but not her mind. She sought solace in her brother's arms as he gently caressed her head.

"I love you, brother," Danka said a few moments after she had joined him in his quarters.

"I love you too, sister," Dreyko replied. "I am sorry I did protect you."

"It was not your fault," she reassured him. "No one saw this coming."

"If only I had-," Dreyko started saying, but Danka sat up and took his face in her hands.

"No brother, please do not do this to yourself," she smiled weakly at him. "It was an accident and see," she showed him her bandaged hand, "I still have my hand, right?"

"But what if -" he started.

"The only thing that matters," she cut him off, "is that the worst did not happen. I am right here, right now."

Her eyes softened, and her face relaxed

"With you, Dreyko, my brother…"

Her lips parted slightly, and her head inclined at an angle.

"My love."

Danka closed her eyes and kissed Dreyko on the lips. Dreyko wanted to push Danka away and scold her for even thinking the unthinkable.

What was she doing?

But when he grabbed her by the shoulders, his resolve melted away faster than cheese on a hot knife. For years, he had wrestled with his feelings for his sister. His fantasies, desires and longing for her were killing him on the inside like a torturous plague. And here she was. In his arms. Her body against his, her hands on his face, her soft lips on his. Nothing else could have been more perfect than this moment.

Dreyko did not hold back. He returned the kiss. It was their first time and their first time together. Their pent-up lust for each other erupted like an angry volcano. Their garments disappeared quickly and they united their naked bodies in an intense frenzy of erotic ecstasy. That night, they declared and sealed their hidden love for each other with their abominable union. That night, the bites from the wolf and the bat transformed the dormant to the dominant. That night, the sleeping monster of evil was birthed within them in all its dark glory. Their souls merged as one, and in the moment of the joint, first-time climax, their carnality attained a purity that was aligned irrevocably to the dark side of their humanity. In that moment of joint, first-time climax, their dark sides intertwined in an etheric explosion that consumed their very essence as humans and erased their souls. In that moment of joint, first-time climax, Danka and Dreyko Pakola became two soulless creatures.

The siblings lay on the bed, spent and satisfied. Deep down, they knew something significant had just happened to them. They could neither understand nor explain it at the moment. It would take six years for them to understand the metamorphosis they underwent that fateful night. But in the meantime, they basked in each other's warmth and love. And if anyone ever attempted to tear them asunder, a certain death would be their only portion.

Three years later, their mother hanged herself. The king was distraught with grief, and as a family, they mourned their wife and mother. Three years after the queen's suicide, the king went on a hunting trip, and his horse lost its footing on the hill. He went down with his horse into the rapids, which flowed into a waterfall. After more than two months of intense searching, his body was never found. And so, at age twenty-four, Dreyko Pakola was crowned king and he decreed that Danka his queen, for no other woman in the kingdom was worthy of the status.

***

"Brother," Danka called softly, realizing that Dreyko had drifted off to memory lane.

"What is it, sister?" Dreyko asked, still caressing her hair.

"Do you trust The Scientist?" Danka asked.

"The only person I trust is you," Dreyko replied. "But The Scientist is resourceful. Once he is done synthesizing a…" he could not say the word.

"Cure?" Danka offered and sat up on the bed, locking eyes with him. "I know you hate that word, but it is just a word. We do not need a 'cure,' per se. We just need…"

She searched for a suitable word.

"An upgrade. Yes, we just need an upgrade, right?"

"You always know the right things to say, sister," he smiled. "Alright, once he is done with synthesizing our… upgrade, we will get rid of him, and Hitler will follow."

"Let Hitler do all the heavy lifting, The Scientist the light lifting," she smiled, "and then we will just waltz in and bask in our new glory."

"I love it when you talk about the future like that," he said grabbing her by her hair and forcing her head down on his hard extension.

She gladly obliged. He pulled her head back after two minutes, forced her on her stomach and took her from behind. As always, she offered no resistance.

"And I will ravage you like the dog you are, you filthy, stinking bitch."

She moaned and climaxed just from him talking dirty to her. And just as he was about to explode inside of her, the alarms went off all over the building. He exploded, anyway. The door slid open, and The Scientist stepped in. When he saw them in that position, he averted his gaze.

"Forgive me, your highnesses," he spoke quickly, keeping his eyes away from them, "but there has been a breach."

And how did he get here so quickly? Danka wondered.

"And you cannot handle it yourself?!" Dreyko hissed.

"No, your highnesses," replied The Scientist. "It's not just any kind of breach." He swallowed. "It's them… *BOTH* of them."

"Who?" Dreyko barked.

The Scientist leveled his gaze at them and said, "Shi'mon and Yehuda."

***

"You can come up with a story for Günter's death?" Shi'mon asked Andrew.

"Sure," replied his brother. "He made a move on you, and you took him out. Simple. I had warned them already about your superior fighting skills."

Andrew smiled and rolled his eyes.

"And how did you survive?" Shi'mon asked, ignoring Andrew's sarcasm.

"It wasn't easy, but I made it only because I've dealt with you before,"

Andrew answered. "Most I could do was cut you on your bicep."

"So, you're returning without any sample of his blood?" Yehuda asked.

"Unfortunately, no," replied Andrew, turning to face Yehuda. "I know they won't be pleased but oh well."

"I'm sure they won't," Yehuda concurred.

"And I suppose you already have a strategy on your end?" Shi'mon asked Yehuda with a heavy dose of contempt.

"As a matter of fact, I do," replied Yehuda, choosing to ignore the negative vibe coming from Shi'mon. "I have a luper undercover. Her name is Sasha. She was the one who told me about the London ambush. Her kind is aware that she and I had some history together and they believe that they could use her against me but, to my – to our – advantage, she's still loyal to me."

"And what would you know about loyalty, traitor," Shi'mon barked.

"In your perfect judgment," rebutted Yehuda, "I may be a traitor, but I'm not the one who denied Master three times to save his skin. So much for being a leader, I guess? The Mighty St. Peter, leader of the twelve apostles of Jesus Christ, and the First Pope of the Roman Catholic Church."

Yehuda sneered, turned around and spat on the ground.

"The most powerful man in the underworld?" he added. "More like the biggest coward and hypocrite. Your fakeness is second to none. You hide behind the very false laurels on which you ride. You're a pathetic excuse for a leader and the only thing your-so-perfect-self is so perfect at is casting the first rock at the sinner. After all, you're only living up to your reputation, right? 'The rock upon whom I will build my church'."

Shi'mon's eyes flashed brightly in anger and he made to attack Yehuda, but Andrew caught him at the hip and forced him to stop.

"Enough," Andrew barked at Shi'mon, sparing a moment to glare at Yehuda. "We have more pressing matters at hand right now, brothers."

"He's not my brother," Shi'mon fumed.

"And, as usual, your emotions are devoid of intelligence," Yehuda added calmly, infuriating Shi'mon even more.

"Shut up, Yehuda," Andrew ordered. "Just shut up."

Yehuda raised both hands and took a step backwards.

"After two thousand years," Andrew shook his head in disappointment and disbelief and sighed.

"We have to come up with a strategy for tonight," Andrew said.

He turned his attention to Yehuda.

"You said you're working on something with Sasha, correct?"

"I did," replied Yehuda. "She's heading to the facility with a blood sample."

"By Yahweh," Shi'mon exclaimed and threw his hands up in frustration.

"How could you give her a sample of your blood? And is she just going to waltz into the facility and be like, 'Here's a sample of his blood. I extracted it myself'? You just signed her death sentence."

"If you took half a second to pay attention to what I was saying, perhaps you would have realized that I said 'a blood sample' and not 'MY blood sample,'" Yehuda replied without missing a beat. "The blood sample she has was obtained from the hospital."

Yehuda paused to let Shi'mon wallow in the stupidity of his outburst.

"Here's her story: during the attack I was wounded, and she saw her opportunity to rip off a piece of my jacket which had my blood on it."

Yehuda showed them the area on his jacket that had been snatched off. It looked authentic.

"The blood sample is human," Yehuda continued. "By the time they realize the blood sample is useless, it will already be too late."

"Good plan, brother," Andrew admitted. "I like it."

Yehuda nodded his thanks.

"We should get going," Yehuda said, glancing at his watch. "Sasha should be at the facility within half-an-hour."

"Will she zip her way there?" Andrew asked.

"Let's just say she hopped on a late flight to Berlin," replied Yehuda. "Like she was actually ON the plane right before it took off and because it is dark, no one noticed."

"She sounds like a slick one," Andrew said with admiration.

"That's my Sasha," Yehuda concurred with pride.

"Let's go," Shi'mon commanded. "Time to bring down that facility."

The three brothers formed a triangle, closed their eyes and merged their minds. Andrew visualized the Nazi facility for them since he was the only one among the three of them to have been there. As their minds became one, the space around them seemed to vanish and, with the speed of thought, beyond any temporal and spatial constraints, the etheric constitution of the three men disintegrated and dissipated almost everywhere and nowhere at the same time. Then, a non-spatial portal formed and connected their current physical location to their visualized location. As soon as the connection was made, their dissipated, individual etheric constitution traversed through the non-spatial portal and reconstituted at the visualized location. The non-spatial portal vanished and the spatial and temporal constraints that existed prior returned. The three apprentices of Yeshua appeared in their physical forms once again. To the irrational, they had vanished from a field in Cote d'Or in France and reappeared in Berlin. And if Günter were still alive, he would have marveled at the fact that he had just witnessed a teleportation.

CHAPTER TWELVE

THE ASSAULT

SHI'MON, ANDREW AND Yehuda emerged from teleportation about a kilometer from the Nazi facility in Berlin.

"Now, we wait for Sasha," Yehuda said.

"She better hurry," Shi'mon said. "Sunrise approaches."

Eight, eternal, hostility-charged minutes later, a naked Sasha crept up the three men and crouched next to Yehuda. She clutched the piece of garment from Yehuda's jacket in her right hand.

"Sasha," Yehuda said and turned towards Sasha. "Meet my brothers, Aaron and Shi'mon. We had the same Master. Aaron goes by Andrew, though. Don't ask me why."

"Please to meet you officially, Sasha," Andrew said and offered a hand, but Sasha hugged him instead.

"He is not my brother," Shi'mon spat via telepathy.

"I don't have time for this, brother," Andrew scolded Shi'mon in like manner.

"Neither do I," Yehuda scowled at Shi'mon as Sasha hugged Shi'mon.

"It's an honor to meet you two, officially," Sasha said with a kind smile. "Yehuda told me about you all a long time ago. It's comforting to know that I have an ally in there," she added, nodding at Andrew.

"Likewise," Andrew said.

Shi'mon remained silent, despite his appreciation for their good fortune.

"Unfortunately, we have to get moving. You two can catch up later," Yehuda said and turned his attention towards Sasha. "We'll give you a ten-minute head-start and then Andrew will come in later. His mission was the same as yours, and neither The Twins nor The Scientist have made any connection between Andrew and Shi'mon yet, safe for their work history."

"Affirmative," Sasha replied, like a true soldier. "See you later, partner," she winked at Andrew.

"Aye, partner," Andrew replied with a wink of his own.

Sasha turned to zip away, but Yehuda caught her left arm. She hesitated and kept her eyes on the ground.

"Be careful, please," Yehuda said.

His tone of voice was heavy with concern and much more. But she still had her wall around her. Why? She had no idea. Her psychological protection against Yehuda was illogical and uncalled for. Yet, she clung to every justification for the wall she fabricated. Sasha sighed, turned around and kissed him on the lips before zipping away without saying a word.

"Never too busy for some romance, huh, traitor?" Shi'mon smirked.

"Maybe if you weren't spending so much of your time basking in your new-found glory, you could have had a love life yourself," replied Yehuda and he instantly regretted his words.

"I'm sorry," he apologized.

"You two can kill each other later," Andrew scolded. "Do I have to remind you that we are on a mission? For Master's sake, act like 2,000-year-old men."

Shi'mon and Yehuda averted their eyes to the ground like two scolded school boys. Andrew then turned around and faced the facility.

"I was wondering," Andrew said. "Why did she catch a flight when it would have been a lot faster if she just zipped her way here?"

"'Cause the three of us were running behind," Yehuda replied pridefully.

"I like her even more now," Andrew hi-fived Yehuda. "Good catch, brother."

Yehuda grinned and Shi'mon rolled his eyes. When it was time for Andrew to go, he turned around and winked at his brothers, who nodded sharply at him.

"I'll see you two later," Andrew said with a broad grin. "Assuming you two don't kill each other while I'm gone."

They all laughed a little. Andrew hugged each of them separately and whizzed towards the facility. Five minutes of resentment-and-hatred-charged silence later, Yehuda and Shi'mon stood up.

"Ready?" Shi'mon asked.

"Right behind you, brother," Yehuda replied.

Shi'mon hesitated at the mention of 'brother' but he decided to let it slide for now.

"Let's take this place down," said Shi'mon.

Sasha halted in front of the gate and whistled at one of the guards. He saw her, naked and bloodied, and understood she was one of the creatures in the facility. The soldiers had been given strict orders not to interfere with the affairs of the Bright Eyes; unless, of course, they wanted to end up as dinner. The soldier ran and opened the gate for Sasha.

"Shirt," she demanded, gesturing at his shirt.

The guard readily complied. He moved to drape his shirt over Sasha's body, but the shirt vanished from his hands along with Sasha. She went to her suite in the facility to kill some time and gather her thoughts. Nine minutes later, she zipped into The Scientist's lab, as if the lab was hers. The elevators were too slow for her. The Scientist, however, did not take his eyes off the microscope; nor did he even flinch from her sudden intrusion.

"So," he said, still peering down into the microscope, "I take it you're the only one who survived?"

Sasha did not reply.

Instead, she stretched out her arm that held out the bloodied piece of cloth. The Scientist took the piece of cloth from her hand and stood up straight. He had thick black hair, a beard that was neat and evenly trimmed to about half an inch, and unless one had known him for a while, he could easily have passed for someone in his late 30's. But he prided himself on being more than half-a-century old. Saying his age like this made him sound as cool as a Bright Eye. He was of average build with dangerously seductive eyes to which Sasha was immune. He studied the bloodied cloth, holding it with latex-gloved hands and gave a slight nod of approval after a few moments.

"You did it," The Scientist finally said.

"At too high a cost," Sasha hissed.

"A small price to pay for the greater good," he rebutted without taking his attention away from the piece of bloodied cloth.

"To you, this may just be an experiment, a game," Sasha glared at him, faking all the anger she could fake. "But to us, this is about surviving."

"And that is exactly what I'm trying to do, Sasha," he barked at her. "You think I enjoy watching your kind get slaughtered? Everything I do is to try to help *you* out. To erase *your* weaknesses and give *you* more joy and peace."

The Scientist paused and breathed in deeply to calm his nerves.

"Wouldn't you love to walk in the sun once again?" he asked.

He placed the piece of cloth on the table and took a step towards Sasha as she looked away.

"No, stop," Sasha held out a hand and backed away from him.

The Scientist took her in his arms and held her close.

"You could lose the thirst," he continued. "Become human again."

The Scientist gently stripped her from his bosom and looked deeply into her eyes.

"We could finally be together, Sasha. You and I, we could-"

"Ahem," Andrew cleared his throat. "Am I interrupting something?"

Thank goodness, Sasha exclaimed in her head and relaxed her body. *Thought I was going to have to slap that huge head of his off his neck. Such childish infatuation.*

But that would have spelt her instant death because The Scientist was under the protection of The Twins.

"No, you're not, Andrew," replied The Scientist and released Sasha. "I take it you're also the sole survivor?"

"Your predictions on his actions were correct," Andrew ignored The Scientist's innuendo. "He was too guilt-ridden to kill me, though I'm a Bright Eye. Still, despite his weakened frame of mind, I couldn't kill him."

Andrew then walked into the lab.

"Not for sentimental reasons though. He's just too good."

"I see," said The Scientist. "Well, Sasha was successful."

He picked up the bloodied piece of cloth from the table and held it up.

"She brought us a present. I can work with this for now and-"

A deafening explosion cut him off and warning alarms went off throughout the building. The phone in the lab started ringing. He got to the phone in three long strides and he snatched it off the receiver. After a few seconds, all the color drained from his face as he slammed down the phone and dashed for the elevator.

"What's going on?" Sasha asked, putting on a perfect show of ignorance.

"Two men just breached the facility moving at 'incredible speed,'" The Scientist said. "The guards are being taken out one-by-one."

"They're here," said Andrew.

"I must inform The Twins," said The Scientist stepping into the elevator. "Only they can stop these two."

The elevator doors closed and began its ascent.

"They're on their own now," Andrew said quietly.

"I know they're your brothers, Andrew," she whispered. "But if you interfere, then we will compromise our positions."

"I know," Andrew agreed. "I guess we'll have to fight them twice in one night huh…" he smiled weakly.

"And no pretense this time," she smiled back.

"Agreed," he replied and then sighed. "Let's go hunting then."

Sasha and Andrew zipped away from the lab and headed towards the sounds of ensuing chaos.

***

The Nazi guards stood no chance against Shi'mon and Yehuda. Heads rolled and lifeless bodies fell as the two men whooshed around the facility leaving nothing but death and destruction in their dance. They left a guard with barely enough strength to sound the alarm. They wanted The Twins to know they were coming. Andrew had told them about the prisoners, or test subjects, being held up five floors underground in some special chamber. Only one guard remained after their assault on the facility. The guard peed himself when Shi'mon lifted him off the ground as if the guard was weightless.

"Where are the prisoners?" Shi'mon asked sternly.

The guard shook his head rapidly.

"Sorry, *mein herr*," he managed to say after Shi'mon eased his grip on the guard's neck just enough for him to talk, but still holding the guard off the ground. "No, understand."

Shi'mon asked in German.

"Room 44, fifth floor down," the guard replied. "Three turns to the right and one to the left."

"Same thing Andrew told us," Yehuda said via telepathy.

Shi'mon dropped the guard to the floor.

"Go," he commanded.

The guard scurried away and bounded up the stairs two at a time.

"Think he's going to inform The Twins?" Yehuda asked.

"I am counting on it," Shi'mon said.

The two, mortal enemies whizzed away towards Room 44. The prisoners had to be sent to safety before their dance of death with The Twins.

***

The Twins, naked and uncleaned from their moment of intimacy, stormed past The Scientist, burning with crimson-red fury. Who did these humans think they were, jeopardizing their operation and threatening their survival? They were about to make a turn down the stairs when a terrified guard came bounding up the stairs. He smelled of urine, and the crotch area of his pants was wet.

"Your highnesses," he called out in German

Danka made to shove him over the stair railing.

"I know where they are heading to," he said.

Two pairs of red, feral eyes zoomed in on him.

"What did you say?" Dreyko demanded.

"I… I know where they are going, your highnesses," he stammered. "To the prisoners."

"And how do you know this?" asked Dreyko.

The guard's shoulders slumped with the realization of his inevitability dawning on him. He never saw Dreyko move, but he felt his body come of the floor and two sharp objects dig into his neck. Within seconds, he blacked out before he sank into the bottomless pit of death.

Dreyko tossed the guard's corpse over the railing. It looked as dry as a 4,000-year-old mummy. The corpse shattered upon impact with the floor.

"Go to Switzerland at once," Dreyko commanded without looking at The Scientist. "We will meet you there."

"Aye, your highnesses," affirmed The Scientist before The Twins zipped away.

***

"Hurry," Shi'mon yelled in German and English at the prisoners.

Yehuda held open a door and ran esoteric scans on each prisoner to ascertain they were still human by tapping into their esoteric signatures. Once he confirmed a prisoner was still human, he directed them towards their escape route.

"There are two elevators and each can hold about 12 of you or more," he spoke in German and English. "Take them to the ground level and head east. Do not stop until you find human help."

A few prisoners expressed their gratitude as they hurried away to freedom.

"Yehuda," Shi'mon called out to him and gestured upward.

The last prisoner left the chamber. Yehuda shut the door and looked up.

The Twins stood at the window. Danka grinned evilly and Dreyko took a step back. His sister followed suit. Dreyko started clattering his teeth, and a very high-frequency sound emanated from his throat. Within seconds, the glass partition started moving in a slow, wavy manner as the glass molecules began resonating to the frequency of the sound from Dreyko's clattering teeth. At full resonance, the glass partition shattered into a million china pieces and a wall of millions of tiny shards of glass plunged towards Shi'mon and Yehuda. Using their power of thought, Shi'mon and Yehuda held the shards of glass in the air for a few seconds using telekinesis. Then, they let the shards of glass slowly descend until they gently settled on the floor. The Twins leaped through the open space and landed at about twelve meters away from Shi'mon and Yehuda. Both parties had a brief stare-down, until Yehuda broke the silence.

"So," Yehuda said, "is it really true that you two can't get your hands off each other?"

He chuckled and continued.

"I'm curious; how do you two do it?" Yehuda asked Danka rhetorically. "Like does he hang upside down, you just turn into the dog that you are and then it's sick Kama Sutra time?"

"The one with the big mouth is mine," Danka said.

"Time to teach them a lesson," Dreyko said

And then The Twins began their transformation.

Dreyko's feet expanded and became larger. His toe-nails extended into four inches of curving claws and his calves grew to three times its regular size with larger and more pronounced musculature. The same changes happened to his thighs. His stomach and lower ribcage caved as if succumbing to an internal suction force. His arms extended past his knees and his fingers doubled in length, with each finger culminating in a sharp, four-inch claw. The rest of his ribs pressed against his thin, white, leathery skin, giving him the look of a badly starved prehistoric creature. His lips peeled back into a circular formation, exposing sharp fangs and elongated canines; two pointing down and two pointing up. With a snap, his lower and upper jaw came apart and rearranged themselves into what looked like a snout. His nose melted into that snout-like feature of his face. His ears quadrupled in size and lined up along the sides of his head. With a shrill, bestial cry, Dreyko fell on his hands and knees and arched his back. His shoulder blades pressed hard against his skin and his skin stretched in resistance. Once, twice and on the third attempt, Dreyko's shrill reached a crescendo, followed by the ripping of his skin and two, huge, six-foot-long wings bursting out from his scapulae.

Meanwhile, Danka's body was jerking in erratic patterns with every loud snap of her of her skeletal structure breaking down and reconstructing itself. Her feet and calves slowly shrank to half their original sizes. Her knees snapped and cracked as they rearranged themselves to bend backwards and her thighs doubled in size with more pronounced and defined musculature. Her stomach and lower ribs underwent the same changes as Dreyko's and her fingers ended in sharp, three-inch claws. Her feet and toenails underwent the same changes as her hands and fingers. Her lower jaw broke apart and realigned itself into a snout. Her top three vertebrae came apart and realigned themselves so that she appeared to have a longer neck. Then, she fell to the floor on her hands and knees at the same time as her brother and millions of long, thick, white hairs slowly burst out of her entire body.

Dreyko and Danka slowly rose from the floor and stood on their hind legs. Danka was completely covered in pure, white fur and stood at eight feet tall. As bone-chilling as the sight of her was, she exuded an eerie, hypnotic beauty; a remarkably stunning, wolf-like creature standing on its hind legs. Dreyko was also about eight feet tall, but his was a grotesque, spine-numbing, abhorring sight to see. He had the face of a rodent and when he spread his wings, he looked like a cross between a prehistoric bat and a Neanderthal. In a warmup fashion that summoned a gag reflex, Dreyko flapped his wings once and completely covered up his body after the second flap, before spreading them out and letting them hang idly in the air. He then let out a very high-frequency, ear-drum shattering shrill, and his sister roared, instead of howl. The combination of their bestial cry echoed along the hallways of the facility for a few seconds. Shi'mon and Yehuda opened their right fists and sparked the ethers. Pale, blue light coalesced in them to form swords with four-foot long silver blades. A few seconds of glaring passed between the two parties before they charged at each other.

Danka zipped towards Yehuda. He sidestepped out of her line of zip, but he forgot that she was eight feet tall. As such, he did not properly distance himself from Danka. Her outstretched paw slapped him dead on the chest with enough force to break his ribcage and send him crashing into a wall 20ft away. Despite the excruciating pain from broken bones tearing through his skin and into his internal organs, Yehuda did not let go of his sword. He shook his head to clear the vision that was hazed up from that slap in the chest, only to find Danka lunging straight at him again, jaws open, aiming for his neck, and going for the kill. On instinct, Yehuda shot both his feet in the air just in time to divert her trajectory past him. She crashed headlong into the wall behind him, breaking off pieces of tile and concrete from the wall. But Danka quickly shook off the impact as she rose to her feet and towered over Yehuda. Yehuda summoned his chi and moved it along his body. Bones reformed, internal organs and torn flesh were healed as if nothing ever happened. He stood up and met Danka's glare of nuclear anger and bared fangs with a mischievous grin.

"Is that all you've got, bitch?" he taunted.

"No," Danka growled evilly. "I was just sizing you up."

She roared and attacked again. Yehuda sidestepped again to the right. This time, he turned his entire body a hundred and eighty degrees to the left and brought down his sword hard and fast, slicing right through a part of Danka's left scapula and shoulder. Her entire left arm and part of her left shoulder became detached from her body, hit the ground and burst into flames. A sickening howl of pain erupted from Danka's throat. The momentum of her charge sent her rolling several times on the floor until a wall violently stopped her. She reached for the exposed stump of her left shoulder and arm with her right hand. Her howling and whimpering were erratic heavy and heavy with pain. After a tighter grip on his sword, Yehuda started walking slowly towards her to finish her off.

Shi'mon did not wait for Dreyko to attack. He zipped towards Dreyko and swung his sword at Dreyko's neck. It traced a fiery, light-blue arc in the air. Just like Yehuda, Shi'mon also underestimated Dreyko. Dreyko leaped in the air at zip speed, spread out his wings so that he paused for less than a second in midair, before folding his wings and accelerating downwards at the same speed of zip as if he was impervious to gravity. He landed behind Shi'mon as Shi'mon's sword sliced through nothing but air. Before Shi'mon could execute an evasive forward roll, the claws of Dreyko's right hand dug into the flesh of his shoulder and breast. Shi'mon felt his body coming off the flow and sailing helplessly through the air to the right, until cracks appeared in erratic patterns on the wall where his body impacted.

But before Shi'mon's body hit the ground, Dreyko whizzed towards him and planted an uppercut into his solar plexus. The sheer, brute force of Dreyko's punch sent Shi'mon's body flying fifteen feet in the air. Shi'mon let go of his sword, which evaporated in a pale blue smoke when it clanged on the floor. He never had the time to process the excruciating pain that radiated across his body from Dreyko's punch. Dreyko zipped upwards, spread his wings and waited for Shi'mon's body to reach maximum height. Then, he folded his wings, zipped downwards and rammed his hands together into Shi'mon's back. Shi'mon hit the floor so hard that the concrete cracked around his body in zigzag patterns. The entire assault lasted less than three seconds. Shi'mon's entire skeleton was broken and his internal organs suffered severe trauma. He needed about four seconds to heal himself, which would be three seconds too late. Shi'mon turned over and lay on his back in time to see Dreyko gliding towards him, with red glowing eyes burning with the fury and excitement of an impending kill.

Shi'mon's crash caught Yehuda's attention. He turned around and saw Dreyko floating towards Shi'mon for the kill. He dropped his sword and kept both fists opened. His sword disappeared in a wisp of pale, blue smoke as he sparked the ethers into two pistols with silver bullets. Yehuda fired over eighteen shots in rapid succession at Dreyko. The wall behind Dreyko was riddled with bullet holes from all the bullets Yehuda fired, none of which hit Dreyko.

He's faster than the average Bright Eye, Yehuda thought.

Dreyko's attention shifted from Yehuda to his sister on the ground. His eyes flashed in crimson red fury. An eardrum-splitting shrill of rage left his vocal cords and reverberated across the facility. He whooshed towards Yehuda, right arm pulled back in preparation for a right hook. Yehuda tossed his guns to the ground and whizzed towards Dreyko. He leaped in the air and connected his left knee with Dreyko's chin as his guns puffed away.

The impact lifted Dreyko's body off the ground and slowed Yehuda's upward momentum, giving Yehuda the split-second he needed to connect a solid, right hook with Dreyko's left temple, or what looked like his temple. Dreyko spread out his wings to slow down his acceleration towards the concrete floor, but he was a fraction of a second too late. He slammed with the full force of Yehuda's punch into the concrete floor. Yehuda floated towards the floor, summoned his sword and prepared to zip in for a decapitation. He raised the sword above his head. But just as he was about to zip in for a kill, he heard Danka roar. He glanced in her direction and saw her zipping towards him, fangs bared in a feral glare and both paws outstretched.

Shi'mon watched Yehuda save his life which bought him the few seconds he needed to heal himself. Out of the corner of his eye, he saw blood trickle out of Danka's exposed stump. But the blood did not hit the floor. Instead, it gathered around her freshly exposed stump and started forming bone, tissue, and flesh. Before his very eyes, Danka regrew her missing limb within seconds, and she completed the regeneration of her butchered arm and shoulder with pristine, white fur. Then, wasting no time, she zipped towards Yehuda, who was about to kill Dreyko. Shi'mon's instincts kicked in, and he zipped perpendicular to her line of zip and crashed his shoulder into her lower ribs.

The force of his momentum lifted Danka off the floor and rammed her into the wall. As she recoiled from the impact, she flung her left paw in a wide arc towards Shi'mon's face. Shi'mon ducked as he caught Danka's left arm in his bent left arm. He slid behind Danka until he wrapped his right arm around her neck and connected his right arm with his left arm, catching Danka in a reverse choke hold. In a swift motion, he jerked his arms upwards. Danka's neck broke with a loud snap and Shi'mon let her limp body crumble to the floor.

Danka's attack temporarily distracted Yehuda, and when Shi'mon came to his rescue, Dreyko healed himself. Dreyko bolted off the floor and drove a solid stump kick into Yehuda's chest. Yehuda crashed to the floor. Dreyko whooshed up in the air and accelerated back downwards with the intent of crushing Yehuda's skull against the floor. Yehuda rolled away just in time. The impact of Dreyko's feet on the floor caused the floor to crack in irregular patterns around his feet. Dreyko heard a snap and whipped his head around to see his sister's limp body slump to the floor.

Shi'mon met Dreyko's bright, red orbs fuming with anger and extreme aggravation. He walked towards Yehuda. Each apprentice summoned a sword and took combat stance. Dreyko took a step back, and his bat-like mouth stretched in a grotesque smile. To their surprise, Yehuda and Shi'mon saw Danka rise from the floor and walk towards her brother. She flexed her shoulders, planted a deep, gross kiss on Dreyko's snout. The Twins turned to face their enemies again.

"Forgot they are Bright Eyes," Shi'mon said. "Snapping their necks does not kill them."

Yehuda did not say anything, though he could think of many smart remarks he could throw in Shi'mon's direction.

"And now, you die," Dreyko hissed.

"Your highnesses, we must leave now," Andrew called out to them. "Sunrise is nigh."

The facility was starting to fall apart from all the impacts from the multiple explosions Shi'mon and Yehuda had set off. Chunks of concrete fell to the floor from the ceiling and gas pipes ruptured as more explosions rocked the building.

"Your highnesses, please," Andrew implored.

"We must go, your highnesses," Sasha pleaded as well.

Reluctantly, The Twins relaxed their features.

"We will meet again," Dreyko promised.

"No fooling around next time," Danka added.

"Looking forward to it," Shi'mon said.

"Just make sure you have a bath beforehand next time," Yehuda said to Danka and furrowed his nose. "You're a stinking pet."

Danka snorted, or so Yehuda thought. The Twins zipped away. Andrew and Sasha paused for the briefest moment to nod their goodbyes at Shi'mon and Yehuda before they followed their bosses. Shi'mon turned around to face Yehuda, and the two arch enemies stared at each other, unfazed by their crumbling surroundings.

"Thanks for saving my life," Shi'mon said finally.

"Thanks for saving mine," Yehuda said in turn. "We'll get them next time, brother."

Another explosion shook the building.

"Yes, we will," Shi'mon said, sparking the ethers into a grenade and walking towards a gas pipe.

He ripped it open with one hand, and flammable gas started hissing out.

"Until then," he said, pulling the pin from the grenade and tossing it into the torn gas pipe.

"I'll be in touch," Yehuda said.

Both men teleported away to their respective locations as the grenade went off. At the end of the chain reaction of explosions, the Nazi facility had been reduced to dust, smoke and a pile of rubble.

THE END OF PART ONE

PART TWO

A PART OF AKASHA

"YOU HAVE HEARD of me. You feel like you have met me before. Rest assured, you are not the only one who feels like that when they come here. But that's not important. You have been here before, though not in this current form and not within your current timeline. I do admire your courage and bravery. Not many in Creation dare to venture in this part of Akasha. For this, you have my respect and I bid you good fortune during your stay here.

"I know you have many questions, and I have all the answers you seek. But I will not give them to you. Why spoil the fun? Why make it easy for you? You made the choice. You abandoned your form in Earth Realm and came here. So, it is your responsibility to find your way out of here. I suppose you already know that if you fail, not only will you die in Earth Realm, but you will also die the true death, and your existence will be erased even from the walls of Akasha; that was just a small reminder.

"I can see the fire in your eyes; the fearlessness, the resilience, the strength and the confidence. Here, you will need all those and more. Whatever you think you have heard, whatever you think you know, whatever you expect, will all sum up to naught. In this part of the Realm-Dimension of Akasha, your darkest hours and your greatest weaknesses are multiplied a thousand-fold and more. Alas, I have spoken too much. So, accept my best wishes, and welcome to the Shadow of the Soul..."

"Thank you, Priya," said Melchizedek.

CHAPTER THIRTEEN

BUCHAREST

"AMERICAN, HUH," SAID the customs officer.

"Yes," Jake replied and fought the urge to roll his eyes.

No need for sarcasm now, he reminded himself.

"Business or pleasure, Mr. Fellows?" she asked.

"Pleasure," Jake replied, stealing a glance at her ample bosom.

She flipped through his passport.

"You travel a lot, Mr. Fellows.".

"Yes, I do," Jake concurred.

She stamped his passport.

"Someday, I wish I can travel the world like you, Mr. Fellows."

She smiled and returned his passport.

"Enjoy your stay in Romania."

"Thank you, miss," Jake replied and smiled back.

She was nice, Jake thought.

The *Myth Huntsmen* headed for the baggage claim. All of their equipment arrived without any damages. Normally, they would hail a cab to their hotel, but after corresponding for a few months with the man who sent them the video, they had decided to take him up on his offer to be their designated driver. He also insisted that it was only fair that he be a part of the expedition because it was his discovery after all. After much debate and deliberation, the team had agreed, and the necessary legal papers had been drafted and signed. The man was going to accompany them during their investigation, but he would not be entitled to any financial compensation whatsoever.

"I don't care about the money," the man had said via Skype. "I just want to get to the bottom of this situation."

The team met him at the terminal. He was a well-groomed, middle-aged man, dressed in a nicely ironed dark-blue shirt tucked in a pair of gray pants, holding a hand-written sign that read *MYTH HUNTERS: TEAM JAKE*. He matched the picture on Duke's phone.

"Sure he watches the show?" Blades asked rhetorically.

"Let's consider this a typo," Duke offered as everyone tried to stifle a snicker.

"Hello, everyone," the man said. "I'm Petrov."

"Hello Petrov," Jake shook his hand. "Pleased to finally meet you. I'm Jake."

Jake introduced Petrov to his team before they headed to Petrov's minivan. The drive to their hotel was thirty-six minutes of uneventfulness in light traffic.

"You must come with some good luck because it is unusual for traffic to be this light close to rush hour on a workday," Petrov said.

They arrived at their hotel.

"I'll pick you guys up at 6," Petrov said. "I'll take you to one of my favorite spots for dinner."

Jake and his friends had two hours to rest of and get ready for dinner. Petrov was on time and they went to a restaurant called *'The Fountain of Plenty'* when translated into English. The service was great, and the food was even better. The team opted to eat something local. While the men wolfed down tons of food, Blades stuck with a salad and breadsticks. Three bottles of white Romanian wine later, the boys slumped in their chairs from gastronomical satisfaction and a little wine intoxication.

"I think there's a problem with the tab," Petrov furrowed his eyebrows.

"Don't worry about it," Jake handed the waiter his business credit card. "It's all part of the business expense."

"As you wish," Petrov shrugged. "Don't worry about tipping too."

"Too late," Jake grinned.

That's the wine talking, Petrov kept his thoughts to himself.

Having Petrov as the designated driver turned out to be a great idea. They all made it to their rooms in one piece. Duke shared a room with Mark, Jake was with Paul, and Blades did not mind sharing a room with any of the guys. Besides, she considered herself as 'one of the guys.' Given her involvement with Jake, she shared a room with Sam. By the time she was getting ready to take a shower, Sam was already spread across his bed, passed out, with his mouth wide open. He still had his clothes and shoes on.

"So cute," Blades smiled.

Fifteen minutes later, she emerged from her refreshing shower. As she walked to her bed, a towel wrapped around her torso and another around her head to dry her hair, she considered paying Jake a visit in his room. A gentle knock startled her a little. She walked softly towards the door, caution guiding her every step and peered through the peephole. Jake. Her heart warmed with excitement and butterflies went wild in her tummy. Jake knocked on the door again. She opened the door.

Are those puppy eyes? she raised her eyebrows.

"May I come in?" Jake asked.

"I'm sorry," she apologized, realizing she was standing in the doorway doing nothing. "Please, come in."

"Sleeping like a baby," Jake said, gesturing towards Sam as he walked in.

"He was out before he hit the bed," she replied, and closed the door.

"So," Blades said, sitting on the bed. "What's up?"

Jake frowned and seemed to gather his thoughts.

"I'm not sure, but my Spidey senses are starting to tingle a little," he said. "I mean, am I the only one having this feeling?"

"Perhaps," Blades replied.

She unwrapped the towel from her head. Long, wet strands of black hair curled down her back and shoulders. Jake swallowed involuntarily.

"I mean," he continued. "We watched a video with two people getting torn to pieces, but not before they're both..." he fumbled for the right words.

"Drained?" Blades completed the sentence for him.

"Yes," he replied. "Drained. We concluded the video was genuine and STILL flew out here to check it out? Come on now, Eva, think about it. Something doesn't add up."

"You mean besides the fact that if we prove the video was real and have more concrete evidence, then we're gonna be talking about money like we've never dreamed of before?" Blades asked rhetorically.

Jake sighed.

"Yeah, maybe our greed smothered our sense of reason," Jake confessed.

"Know what really doesn't add up?" Blades asked.

"What's that?" Jake's facial features contorted with confusion.

"You called me Eva," she said in a soft whisper.

Their eyes met.

"I like it when *YOU* call me Eva."

"Screw this," Jake said and reached for her hand. "I've missed you so much."

"I've missed you too, Jake," Blades replied, taking his hand.

Jake inched closer and they kissed passionately. Her towel came off her torso and his clothes came off his body within seconds. A quarter of an hour later, the couple lay on Eva's bed. Sam had not even turned in his sleep yet.

"Gotta get back to my room, honey," he said.

Blades sat up on the bed and stared at him in disbelief.

"What did you just call me?" she asked.

"You heard me," Jake replied.

Blades smiled and lay back on his chest. Her heart soared with joy.

"This will be our last trip as a team, Eva," Jake said.

Now Blades bolted from the bed and could barely contain her shock.

"You can't be serious," she half-yelled and cupped her mouth when she remembered they were not the only ones in the room.

They froze. Sam turned in his sleep but did not wake up.

"Dead serious," Jake said and sat up from the bed. "We're now a couple, and I think it's time I retire and have a normal life, free from the camera. And I was hoping you'd join me."

Blades relaxed a little and seemed to give it some thought.

"I guess I'll join you," she said. "We're doing the right thing, aren't we?"

"We are," Jake smiled.

Jake left for his room a few twelve minutes later. The team was scheduled to meet their guide at 9 a.m. in the hotel lobby the following day. From there they would head out to camp somewhere near the location where the video was captured. Jake lay on his bed and stared at the ceiling. The feeling that something was amiss gnawed at his stomach. He replayed the video several times in his mind hoping to find something. In the end, he gave up and let sleep take over.

That night, he dreamed of living in the suburbs with Eva and their two children: a boy and a girl. He was watching the children playing in the backyard, while Eva was preparing lunch. Suddenly, the bright noon sky was smothered in pitch blackness. Naked, corpse-like women and men emerged from every corner and started making their way towards their house. The kids screamed and ran towards him. Eva came outside to join them.

"Go back to the house," Jake screamed at his family.

They ran for the house but could not get it. The door was locked from the inside. Intense panic ensued Suddenly, the naked, living corpses stopped their march, looked up to the black sky in unison, before closing their eyes and turning their faces towards Jake and his family. When they opened their eyes, Jake and his family stared into hundreds of brightly glowing eyes and the naked living-dead resumed their march towards them, with outstretched arms. Jake bolted from his bed, relief flooded his body at the realization that it was just a nightmare. He turned off his alarm.

Petrov was waiting for them at the hotel lobby. He wore a long pair of brown jeans, a gray polo shirt, brown face cap and a black pair of boots. He urged Duke to change his khaki pair of shorts and put on a long pair of pants.

"Bugs are the least of my problems, Petrov," Duke joked. "They don't like me anyway. Can't say the same for Sam."

"I think you're confusing me with Mark," Sam countered.

Jake sat in the front seat, mainly because he wanted to feel out their newest companion.

"It's a two-hour drive to the location," Petrov said. "I hope you'll all be sober by then."

"You should've seen me trying to get them out of bed," Jake added.

"Tell me about it, my friend," said Petrov. "Getting my ex-wife out of bed was always a struggle,"

Jake noticed the sadness in the guide's eyes.

"At first, it was cute, but later, it got old, you know."

"If you don't mind me asking" Jake said, "what caused your divorce?"

"Irreconcilable differences," Petrov replied. "She died seven years later."

His eyes seemed to tear up.

"My deepest sympathies to you," Jake offered.

"Thank you kindly, my friend," Petrov said.

They drove for another half an hour in silence. Jake enjoyed the city sights and sounds until they started driving towards the countryside. The scenery was so peaceful and serene, unlike the buzz of city and country life back home. For a moment, Jake had nothing on his mind as he absorbed everything: the farms, hills, livestock grazing in the fields, little children, girls and boys, playing soccer, seemingly oblivious to the cares of the world. They looked happy and content, despite their lack of riches. Jake smiled with healthy envy at how they could be so happy without the materialism and greed he was used to experiencing back in the US. This strengthened his resolve to quit the team even more.

"So, been meaning to ask," Jake said, still looking out the window, "what makes you so sure that the couple will show up at the exact spot again?"

"Because I have seen them around the same area before," the guide replied.

Jake and his team gasped.

"What do you mean?" Blades asked.

"The first time was purely by luck," he replied. "I was out at night with my camera because I wanted to take some pictures of night creatures. As I lay in the bushes, camera in night-vision mode and looking for something to shoot, I saw the naked couple."

Petrov slammed on the brakes and the car screeched to a hard stop.

"Jesus H. Christ," Mark exclaimed. "What was that about?"

"He didn't want to squash a bunny rabbit," Jake replied.

"Oh ok," Mark said less aggressively. "Good man."

Petrov shifted the car into gear and resumed driving.

"As I was saying," he continued. "I noticed the couple. I thought about calling out to them, but instinct held me back. I'm glad I listened to my instinct. So, I kept watching them. They were just standing there doing nothing. And then they both suddenly crouched, raised their noses and sniffed the air."

Petrov paused.

"What happened next?" Blades prompted.

The guide navigated the minivan around a few turns before continuing.

"A few seconds later," he said, "two deer came idling by. What happened next blew my mind."

"Please, continue," Jake prompted, and observed Petrov.

"Well," he hesitated. "They moved so fast that the deer barely had any time to react. In a few minutes, nothing was left of the animals but torn flesh, blood, and bone. It was a very… unusual sight to see."

Petrov cleared his throat and swallowed.

"I mean," he continued, "these were human beings draining animals of their blood and eating their flesh… RAW."

He took a few deep breaths to calm himself and tightened his grip on the steering wheel.

"I bet it was a sight to see," Jake interjected still keenly observing Petrov.

"And that was just the first time," continued their guide. "I saw them once more around the same area doing the same thing. The video I sent to you was from the third time I saw them. I went to collect hard evidence of what was going on, but instead…" the guide trailed off.

"The couple?" Jake asked. "I mean, didn't anyone notice them missing?"

"They must have been new here," the guide replied. "I asked around, but no one seemed to have noticed their absence."

"And the police?" Jake prompted.

"Did you really expect me to take this video to the police?" Petrov shook his head incredulously. "I would've been locked up and fined for 'making such a video.' Besides who would've believed me?"

"And that's why you tried to reach us," Blades interjected.

"Yes," he confirmed. "Because I hoped you would believe me. Perhaps, if you people gather evidence and make it public, then it would lend more credibility to everything that's going on here."

"Logical," Jake admitted.

"Thank you," Petrov relaxed his grip on the steering wheel. "I've only been able to see them at night; so, my guess is that they are creatures of the night," he added. "That's why I asked we set out during the day and camp in the area."

"Good thinking," Blades agreed.

"And thank God for silver knives and bullets," Mark added derisively. "And wooden stakes. Freaking amazing. We're about to gather evidence of real life-"

"Yeah, yeah, yeah," Jake smirked. "Let the man just get us there safely."

"And please don't tell me you brought a gun," Blades chimed in.

"Wait, what?" Petrov exclaimed.

"Ah, the stick in your butts," Mark replied with a smile. "Can't y'all just take a joke? Thought the alcohol was supposed to loosen y'all up a little."

Jake imagined Mark rolling his eyes.

"So, on to more fun topics now," Mark rubbed his hands in excitement and directed his attention towards Petrov. "How would you rate Romanian girls in bed, my friend?"

Another hour of driving later, they arrived at the intended site and hiked for two more kilometers. Hiking turned out to be a great cure for a hangover. The scenery was breathtaking. Hills and fields spread across the distance, the air smelled fresh and clean, and everything brought about a feeling of peace. The weather also cooperated. The temperatures were mild, and the winds were gentle. The temptation to take a swim in the gentle-flowing stream they walked along was strong. Heaven. Petrov tried to answer as many of the questions the team asked him as possible.

"How do we know you're telling the truth?" Mark joked.

"You don't," Petrov replied.

They found a great spot about two hundred yards from the woods where Petrov took the video. They mounted cameras at various positions and ran tests to ensure everything was working properly. The time was almost 2 pm when they sat down to eat some snacks. For added safety, the team kept watch from behind a group of boulders towards the east of the woods. If it came down to it, they would benefit from their strength in numbers and two cannibals will have nothing on them. Blades had her knives strapped to her thighs. Paul monitored the video feeds from the cameras, and Duke worked on the sound equipment and checked for any sudden spikes or anomalies. The rest of the team scanned the area with binoculars.

Jake stared blankly into the forest. His mind raced still in hopes of appeasing his gut feeling that something was amiss.

4:55 pm.

Most of the team relaxed on the grass, whiling the time away. Jake shifted his focus to rethink everything from Petrov's perspective as opposed to focusing on the video. A few minutes later, it struck him.

The camera.

During the drive, Petrov seemed terrified just from recalling the events of those nights. His driving had appeared to be a little unsteady during his narration and his grip on the steering wheel attested to Jake's observation. But in the video, he was calm, and the camera was *STEADY* in his hands. He was *NOT* afraid of these creatures, as if… The dire implications made Jake turn white with shock, anger and most of all fear.

"Oh crap," Paul exclaimed. "They're here already."

The same naked couple had come into the cameras' view and was slowing walking in the forest. Everyone but Jake and Petrov gathered around the computer. Jake was stared at Petrov in utter disbelief, and most diabolical grin spread across Petrov's face.

"Aren't they the most beautiful works of Creation your realm has ever seen?" Petrov said almost to himself.

"Hold up," Mark exclaimed. "Ain't they supposed to be nocturnal?"

"Who or WHAT are you?" Jake asked barely above a whisper.

"I go by many names," Petrov replied. "But in this realm, you can call me what most others have been calling me."

"And what is that?" Jake prompted.

The Myth Huntsmen looked back and forth between Jake, the images on the monitors and Petrov.

"The Scientist," Petrov replied. "'Petrov' is just a name I chose to interact with you and your team."

"Oh, screw me sideways," Paul exclaimed, pointing at the laptop.

Everyone, except Jake and The Scientist, turned to look at the laptop.

The naked couple was staring directly into one of the cameras. From that position, the couple seemed to be staring at the team. Jake's gaze remained glued to The Scientist. The naked couple then looked at each other and then suddenly disappeared from the camera's point of view.

"Lady, and gentlemen," The Scientist said, standing up from his crouching position. "I present to you Earth Realm's future rulers."

The naked couple appeared next to The Scientist, flanking him on both sides. They closed their eyes and relished the warmth of the sunlight on their bodies. When they opened their eyes, they glowed in a brightness that was noticeable during the day. The Bright Eyes were now daywalkers. In less than a minute, The Myth Huntsmen were eviscerated one-by-one. The last thing on Jake's mind before the painful, goring and vicious hands of death seized him was the regret for not quitting sooner.

CHAPTER FOURTEEN

HOMECOMING

YOUNG YESHUA, PRINCE Ganesh, and his entourage made it safely back to the palace. A servant had been dispatched to herald their arrival a few days prior and a second servant was dispatched a day before to reiterate this fact. As such, when the city gates opened to let them in, the streets throbbed and thronged with citizen celebrating the return of the crown prince. Prince Ganesh rode on a horse instead of staying in his royal carriage because he wanted his people to feel a connection with him as he wanted to feel with them. After all, he would one day be king and ruler over these people. The men hailed and sounded the trumpets, the older women spread fine cloths in front of the prince's horse, young maiden threw flowers at him, and children ran alongside the prince's horse. Some of the children tried to touch the sole of his royal shoes.

"All hail Ganesh, Crown Prince of India," they chanted repeatedly.

Prince Ganesh dismounted his horse without warning and opened his arms towards the excited children, eliciting the immediate protective charge of his guards. However, with a hand gesture, he bid them stand down. The guards obliged but remained on the alert. The children rushed in, many of them dirty and smelly from a life a poverty, and the prince hugged as many of them as he could, caring less of the outcome of his clean, royal robes. He just wanted to bond with his people. Their parents dropped on their knees to apologize for their children's behavior, but the crown prince motioned for them to rise. Finally, he peeled himself away from the cheering children, rose to his feet, and made to mount his horse when something to the right caught his attention.

A little girl, no more than nine years of age, slowly headed towards the royal carriage, unperturbed by the organized chaos on the streets. She held something in her closed fists over her chest. A guard stepped in to block the child. She stopped, but her focus remained razor sharp and aimed at Young Yeshua. Prince Ganesh motioned for the guard to stand down and let the girl pass. The guard obeyed and stepped out of her path. She took careful, but steady, steps towards Young Yeshua. Young Yeshua opened the door of the carriage but he did not step out of the carriage. The little girl stretched out both hands towards young Yeshua and spoke to him in Hindi. She opened her hands to reveal a small, black, uneven piece of rock about one-third the size of a mango. She gestured towards Young Yeshua, as if urging him to take the rock. Young Yeshua turned towards Prince Ganesh, eyes pleading for help.

"She said," the prince explained in Hebrew, "that if you truly are the one, this stone will glow brighter than the sun when you take it."

Young Yeshua nodded and reached for the stone. The moment he stretched out his hand, the stone glowed brighter than the afternoon sun, but without the blinding effect of the sun. Only Young Yeshua, Prince Ganesh and the girl witnessed this brilliance. To the rest of the crowd, a little girl had just handed the strange boy a piece of rock. Young Yeshua stared at the stone in his open, right palm for a few heartbeats before gently closing his fist around it. His entire body glowed with a golden aura that could only be seen by clairvoyants. Ganesh thought he sensed a surge of energy beaming from Young Yeshua.

The girl then spoke a few sentences to him.

"She said you are truly the one," Prince Ganesh translated, "Your path has been inscribed on the walls of Akasha. You will undo what has been done, you will right the wrongs perpetuated by The Anomaly throughout Creation."

He paused for the young girl to speak again. She never took her gaze away from the young master.

"She said," he continued after she finished speaking, "that your life will bring death and destruction; but your death will bring redemption and rebirth. Trust in Creation, and it will never let you down. This is your path; this is your purpose Yeshua the Nazarene."

"And she knows my name," Young Yeshua said in a monotone. "How do you say, 'What is your name?' in Hindi, your highness?" he asked Prince Ganesh.

"I go by many names, Young Master," replied the young girl in perfect Hebrew. "But for now, you can call me Priya, until such a time when you are ready to know my real name."

And with these words, she bowed to young Yeshua and Prince Ganesh before turning around and walked into the crowd. Prince Ganesh stared after her, stunned to speechlessness. But he quickly regained his composure and motioned for the caravan to continue towards the palace.

A guard closed the door to the royal carriage. Young Yeshua searched for Priya in the crowd to no avail. Her words kept replaying in his mind.

Who is she, really? he wondered. *There is something different about her.*

Meanwhile, Priya wormed her way through the crowd. She crouched behind a tall man to pick up a non-existing object from the ground just as Young Yeshua scanned around that section.

Humans... so predictable, she said to herself.

She stood up as a six-foot, broad-shouldered man in his late twenties, with neatly trimmed beard and wearing the clothes of a wealthy merchant.

Shape-shifting made easy, she shrugged.

The young man continued to expertly navigate his way through the crowd until he arrived at the city gate. He mounted his horse, which was not there a blink-of-an-eye ago because he had just sparked the horse into existence.

I could just teleport away, but... I'm bored, Priya sighed. *This realm is so...*

She left her thought hanging. She, in the shape-shifted body of a man, waved at one of the guards at the gate. The guard waved back at her.

Do you even know who waved at you? Priya thought.

She, now a he, rode away towards the open wilderness.

Like a speck of dust in the wind, no one noticed her, at least not consciously. She might as well have been a fleeting peripheral observation with no imprint on memory. As such, no one noticed her and her horse gradually fade into thin air as she rode away into the open, barren land. Even if they did, they would not remember because Priya had sparked the ethers to erase every esoteric imprint of her presence in this realm of existence. How could she achieve this?

Because, as a multidimensional entity, I can do just about anything.

Prince Ganesh made a brief stop at the outer quarters of the palace to change into cleaner robes. He loved his people but he had to honor his father, the king, by looking as regal as a crown prince is expected to look in the presence of a king. He then headed for the palace with Young Yeshua by his side. Court and palace officials lined up on either side of the aisle leading to the throne where King Rama and Queen Sangita, his wife, sat on their thrones. Queen Sangita sat to King Rama's left and their two other children, Prince Gulam and Princess Suri, sat to their mother's left. Suri was sixteen years old and would soon be betrothed to a prince from another royal family. Gulam had just turned fourteen and was already looking forward to the day when he would go on his March to Manhood, just like his older brother, his father and grandfather had all done.

When a prince turned eighteen years of age, he was sent to the outside world and given three years to find himself or discover his purpose in life because a prince could only become a successful ruler after experiencing an awakening. Ganesh was the crown prince and heir to the throne. Hence, the reason why the seat to the king's right was vacant and reserved for him. Three years ago, he left for his March to Manhood even though he had already discovered what his purpose was.

A thunderous applause erupted within the palace as Prince Ganesh walked in with Young Yeshua walking alongside him. Officials cheered, young maidens danced and threw flowers at their feet, guards moved in military choreography, clashing swords and shields ceremoniously, drums and trumpets sounded in rhythm, and more young maidens sang. Prince Ganesh's heart soared with genuine appreciation for the warm welcome. He waved and nodded his thanks at everyone as he slowly made his way towards his father's throne. He placed a protective right hand on Young Yeshua's right shoulder during the entire walk towards the stairs leading to the throne. When they were a few feet from the bottom of the stairs leading to his father's throne, Prince Ganesh bent down and whispered something into Young Yeshua's ear. Young Yeshua nodded.

Young Yeshua had never been in the presence of royalty and had never beheld such riches. The palace was the largest building he had ever seen; even larger than the temple back home. The walls, both inside and outside, shone from something white and shiny, which he later learned was called marble. Resplendent artwork adorned the walls and ceilings, officials in the palace wore expensive and magnificent garbs and jewelry, and the women, were exceedingly pleasing to the eyes. He noticed that the young maidens wore clothing on their legs like the men did and their bellies were exposed, revealing skin so smooth and bellies so flat. He swallowed at the sight of their exquisite physiques and hoped no one noticed his embarrassment.

And gold. So much gold.

Yahweh be praised, I have never seen so much gold in my life, he marveled. *Let alone in one building.*

The window frames had gold on them. The middle portion of the stairs leading to the king's throne was made of gold. The king's throne and all the seats next to him were made of pure, solid gold. The king's crown was a golden and glorious magnificent sight to see, with precious stone ornately and artistically placed on it. Of course, the king's crown had a remarkably distinguished design from the other crowns on his wife's and children's heads, but even those were breathtaking beauties to behold. A sword, with a handle and sheath made of pure gold, hung from the king's left hip and a golden ring with a diamond the size of the human eye protruding from it. Young Yeshua later learned that this was the royal heirloom worn only by the king.

The queen and the princess wore more jewelry on their bodies than Young

Yeshua had ever seen any woman wear in his young life. Golden jewelry extended from their noses to their ears, golden jewelry hung from their necks, they wore golden jewelry with precious stones embedded in them on their wrists and ankles, and even their long, beautiful garments seemed to have gold threads sewn into them in certain areas. The queen and princess had their long, black hairs pulled back in tight buns and fancy markings graced their hands.

I wonder how long it takes for them to get ready, he wondered.

Prince Ganesh advanced a few paces and stopped at the bottom of the stairs. The royal announcer approached from the left corner of the palace and climbed about halfway up the stairs. He raised both hands and a deathly quiet swept across the palace. He turned towards the king, dropped to one knee, extended both arms sideways and bowed his head as low as he possibly could. Then, he stood up.

"Oh, greatest and mightiest of kings," he said. "Your wisdom and love for your people is as boundless as the River Ganges itself. Your power and leadership are like unto none other before you. May your name be inscribed forever in the stars, but most especially in the hearts of your loyal subjects."

The royal announcer placed a closed, right fist to his chest and bowed towards the king. Everyone in the palace did the same.

"All hail the king," cried a soldier, most likely the general of the royal army given that his armor looked much different from those of the other soldiers.

"All hail the king. All hail the king," everyone chanted.

The royal announcer raised his hands again and again. Silence.

"Oh, great King Rama," continued the royal announcer, "Oh greatest of kings, spawned from Krishna's loins himself. We all are gathered here today to welcome back our most beloved crown prince amongst us."

He gestured and bowed in Prince Ganesh's direction.

"Three years ago, he embarked on his March to Manhood. Three years ago, a young prince journeyed into a world unknown to him, and three years later, a young man, a great prince, a true heir to the throne returns to us; an exact but much younger version of his father, our great king in every aspect-"

"No," the king bellowed, standing up with a broad smile hiding behind his thick, long beard. "Not an exact version. Never an exact version."

He walked towards his son. Ganesh dropped to one knee and bowed his head as low as he could. Young Yeshua did the same.

"Your majesty," the royal announcer stammered, with his head bowed low. "I deeply apologize. I did not mean to offend his majesty with my words-"

"Fear not, Dilip" the king assured him, as he continued his slow walk down the stairs towards his son. "My son will never be like me."

King Rama paused in front of Ganesh, whose head was still bowed low.

Murmurs of confusion washed over the palace.

"Rise, my son," said the king.

Ganesh rose to his feet. King Rama gathered Ganesh in a bear hug and whispered, "Welcome home, my son" in his ears.

Ganesh returned his father's hug. The king withdrew from Ganesh, held his son's face in his hands, kissed his son on both cheeks and took hold of his son's left hand. Father and son faced the guests in the palace.

"You say I am a great king: the greatest of our times," he bellowed. "I have been proud, honored and blessed to hold such high esteem among my people. Shiva be praised. After all, what is a kingdom without a people? What is a king without people who love him? Who am I without you?"

He raised Ganesh's left hand in the air with his right hand and held it there.

"Behold the man who will be far greater than I have ever been," he bellowed even louder. "Behold the man who will be much wiser than I have ever been. Behold the man whose legacy will dwarf mine for all eternity. Behold your future leader and king, my son, Ganesh."

A deafening applause ensued, the drumming and trumpet sounding resumed, and everyone chanted "Long live Ganesh," repeatedly.

King Rama and Ganesh took it all in. The royal announcer almost collapsed with relief when he realized the king did not take offence to his words. Young Yeshua was still on one knee, head bowed low.

"Who is your young friend," the king asked gesturing towards Yeshua.

"Father, may I present to you Yeshua, a Nazarene from the land of Israel," Ganesh replied.

Ganesh asked Yeshua to stand up in Hebrew. Young Yeshua did as told but lowered his eyes in respect to the king.

"Do not be afraid, my child," said the king. "You may gaze upon me."

Prince Ganesh translated before Young Yeshua raised his eyes towards the king. He said nothing. The silence in the palace was so intense you could hear a feather drop.

"He is a young master, father," Ganesh continued. "I had a dream about him, and I am convinced that, given our resources and training, he will grow and walk in his destiny."

"I trust your judgment, my son," replied the king, carefully studying the young master. "Besides, his aura glows brighter than any I have ever seen."

The king nodded and turned his gaze towards his son.

"You have done well, Ganesh. This young man is an old soul, a master of many lifetimes. He just needs a few… reminders and he will remember."

He patted Young Yeshua gently on the head and smiled.

"Thank you, father," Ganesh replied with a broad smile.

No one else in the palace heard their conversation just now. Ganesh translated his father's words for Yeshua.

"Please extend my most profound gratitude to his majesty for his kindness and generosity, my prince," Yeshua said to Ganesh.

Ganesh relayed the message, and the king nodded. As the king turned around and started walking back towards his throne, the royal announcer motioned for the festivities to resume. Ganesh followed behind his father until he made it to the last stair. From there, he rushed into his mother's open arms. His mother's love and joy touched the very core of his soul and he had to stifle a tear of joy.

Men do not cry in public, his father had told him repeatedly since his childhood.

His mother sized him and felt his face, shoulders and arms. Then, she kissed him on both cheeks and took him in her arms once again.

"I have missed you so much, my son," the queen said tearfully. "I thought these ceremonies would never end."

"Oh, mother, I have missed you too," he replied, kissing his mother on her forehead. "I see you are doing well. Father must be taking great care of you." He grinned mischievously. "After all, only the most beautiful woman in the kingdom is fit to be the wife of the king, no?"

Queen Sangita turned as red as a fully ripe tomato.

"You talk just like your father," she replied.

They laughed and hugged each other again.

Ganesh felt another pair of arms smother him from behind and he grinned.

"Oh how I have missed you, brother," Suri cried against his robes. "I thought all the gallantry would never end."

"I have missed you too, my dear sister," Ganesh replied.

He released his mother, turned around and took Suri in his arms. She buried her face against his chest. A brief moment of silence transpired between the siblings until Ganesh gently stripped her away and held her at arm's length.

"By Shiva. You are growing more and more beautiful by the day. And did Hina make this dress?" he asked, spinning her around.

Suri gladly complied and showed off the dress.

"Yes, she did," was her reply.

"She has the most gifted hands," Ganesh added.

Someone punched Ganesh on the right shoulder.

"What are you feeding him, mother?" Ganesh asked as he play-wrestled with Gulam.

"Oh, Ganesh," the queen raised her hands in the air in mock resignation. "There is not enough food in the kingdom to satisfy your brother. He eats a feast every day, and he keeps growing taller and stronger."

"You do not say, mother," agreed Ganesh, feeling his brother's arms. "I am not sure I can arm-wrestle him anymore."

"Would you like to give it a try, brother?" asked Gulam.

"Only after you tell me what your secret is, big man," he replied. "I have missed you so much, brother. We have much to catch up on."

He noticed Gulam blush slightly. He nodded his understanding, a sly grin forming on his face.

"How is Ada doing, by the way?" Ganesh asked.

"Brother," Gulam exclaimed and blushed even more.

"Alright, alright," Ganesh feigned resignation.

Young Yeshua remained a silent observer the entire time until Ganesh bid him come hither.

"Mother, Suri, Gulam," he took Young Yeshua by the shoulder. "This is Yeshua, a Nazarene from the land of Israel."

Ganesh gave them a compendium of how the young master ended up coming with him to India. The royal family listened with intense fascination and intrigue.

"Tell him any friend of yours is a friend of the family," Queen Sangita smiled.

Ganesh translated and Young Yeshua bowed his head in respect and spoke a few words.

"He said," Ganesh translated. "That he is honored and grateful beyond words for your hospitality and generosity and that he is your humble servant-"

"Tell him he is our guest, not our servant," Queen Sangita said.

Ganesh relayed the message and Young Yeshua said something back.

"I thank her majesty for her kindness," Ganesh said. "Please forgive me, I am not yet accustomed to your ways but I promise to do my utmost best."

"We will teach you," Suri beamed at Young Yeshua's cuteness.

"You may raise your head now, son," Queen Sangita said.

Ganesh translated and Young Yeshua raised his head but will not make eye contact with any member of the royal family, except with Ganesh.

"I shall take him to his quarters now, mother," Ganesh kissed his mother on the cheek. "I will see you all shortly."

Ganesh took Young Yeshua to his quarters where two naked, young maids stood next to a bathtub filled with water. Young Yeshua stiffened with hesitation and confusion.

"It is alright, young master," Ganesh explained. "Here, it is customary for the servants to bathe the rich and the royal. They perform this task with pride and honor, and they will feel insulted and disgraced if their master did not let them perform their duty."

Young Yeshua swallowed nervously and nodded his understanding.

"I will see you later," Ganesh headed for the door. "Rest assured that these maids will take proper care of you."

Ganesh closed the door behind him, leaving Young Yeshua feeling like an animal caged in with two predators. He trembled slightly from embarrassment as the young maidens stripped him bare. They spoke words he did not understand and he noticed how they gasped when they saw his phallus. He felt doubly embarrassed because he assumed the young maidens gasped at his reaction to seeing naked women for the first time. He later learned that the men in this part of the realm did not practice circumcision; hence why the maidens reacted as such when they saw he was circumcised. Once he was in the tub of warm water, his body relaxed and soft hands gently sponged him to sweet satisfaction.

A few hours later, Ganesh met the young master in his room, and the two of them joined the rest of the royal family for supper. Young Yeshua had never seen such a banquet before, and he retreated a little from being so overwhelmed. To make matters worse, he was also the center of attraction, after Ganesh. Word had already spread about 'the young master from the holy lands in the west'. He sat between Ganesh and Suri. Ganesh did his best to bring him up to speed with some of the customs and expected table manners, while Suri tried to put him at ease with constant smiles and friendliness. She even seemed a little overprotective of him.

Musicians played instruments and sang, young maidens danced, and guards kept a watchful eye the entire time. The food was delicious and Young Yeshua wolfed down the strange foods until he slouched in his seat.

"My prince," he burped. "I cannot eat anymore."

He burped again and again. Suri smiled at him.

"See the cooks there?" Ganesh gestured in the direction of a group of women grinning from ear to ear. "You give them much honor by burping because, in our kingdom, burping during or after a meal is a huge compliment to the cook."

Ganesh accompanied him to his quarters an hour later, where the same maids who had given him a bath earlier were waiting for him. They undressed him and eased him into his sleeping outfit.

I never had sleeping outfits before, Young Yeshua thought. *Talk less of one made of such smooth fabric.*

He slowly caressed his outfit. Ganesh strolled in with an elderly gentleman.

"Silk, young master," Ganesh smiled. "The fabric is made of silk."

"Silk," Young Yeshua reiterated. "I am only used to coarse wool fabric."

"This is Ramalesh, my father's seer," he introduced the elderly gentleman.

"He is here to give you an esoteric examination."

Ramalesh bowed, walked over to Young Yeshua.

"May I have your hands, please," he said and Ganesh translated.

Young Yeshua extended his hands towards Ramalesh. Ramalesh took Young Yeshua's hands in his and studied them. He then took a step back and gave the young master a slow, appraising look from head to toe. Next, he closed his eyes, and his facial features relaxed in total stillness. After a few heartbeats, he opened his eyes and bowed towards Young Yeshua. He then spoke to Ganesh, who nodded as the seer stepped out of the room.

"That will be all for tonight, girls," Ganesh spoke to the maids, who stood in a corner of the room, waiting for their next set of orders.

The maids bowed their heads and exited the room.

"The seer said the same thing my father said earlier," Ganesh said to the young master. "You are, indeed, an old soul: a master and enlightened one from lifetimes past. So, your training will be a lot easier than most because you may only require a few reminders and the memories will return."

"So, when do I start training?" Young Yeshua asked.

"Tomorrow morning," replied the crown prince.

He headed for the door.

"Tonight, you must rest. I understand you are overwhelmed by all this," he waved around the room.

"I am indeed overwhelmed, your highness," agreed the young master. "Do you know what my first lesson will entail?"

"I do," Ganesh replied. "To learn how to access the Realm-Dimension of Akasha."

CHAPTER FIFTEEN

PROFILE OF A PRIEST

NAME: PATRICK NGOLLE

DATE OF BIRTH: February 27th, 1982

PLACE OF BIRTH: Kumbo, NW Province, Cameroon.

FATHER: Constantine E. Ngolle, August 4th.

MOTHER: Bernadine K. Ngwa, November 4th, 1955.

O. R. MEMBER: July 3rd, 2000 to present.

O. R. STATUS: Protégé of Father Supreme.

CODE NAME: Ether

Despite his parents' separation when he was eight years old, Patrick had a great childhood. A baptized and confirmed Catholic, receiving his elementary and high school education in Catholic schools, Patrick later consider himself spiritual and not subscribe to any religion. He was also a stutterer, but the stuttering wore off as he grew older. Three major events changed his life forever.

The first occurred when Patrick was four years old. His father worked for the government at the time as an administrator in a little town called Mamfe, the capital city of Meme Division in the Southwest Province of Cameroon. One night, Patrick had to use the restroom. Everyone in the house was asleep. For a child of his age, he had no fear of the dark and he valued his independence, especially after learning how to use the restroom by himself. That night, after taking care of business, he decided to pay a visit to the refrigerator; the sirens of leftover chocolate cake serenaded his soul with sweet, savory seduction. Even better, the cake was within his reach when he opened the door. He scooped up a handful with his bare hand and took a bite of heaven. His buccal cavity came afire with glorious gusto.

So worth the butt-whooping I'll get in the morning, he thought.

As he munched away, eyes half-closed from pleasure, he thought he heard a noise behind the back door of the kitchen. Patrick ignored the sound and took another bite of heaven. He heard the sound again and his childlike innocence cloned itself into childlike curiosity. He closed the fridge, finished the last piece of cake in his hand and walked to the backdoor. He wiped his hands on his pajamas, smearing it with chocolate cake, pressed his ear against the door and listened. He heard the sound again but could not make it out.

I'd better go see what's making that noise, he decided.

However, the door knob was a little out of his reach and he looked around for a stool. He dragged the stool close to the door, climbed on top of it, turned the lock open before he opened the door. He climbed down from the stool and pulled the stool aside before opening the door much wider and poking his head outside. His eyes popped with childlike fascination at the sight in front of him. He opened the door all the way and stepped out into the mildly humid night.

A huge dog, which was taller than he was on its hind legs, stared unmoving at him. Patrick raised his left hand and ran his palm along its thick, pristine white fur. He giggled and raised a hand to touch the dog's snout. The dog bared its fangs before it started licking Patrick's hand. Patrick giggled some more before he closed his eyes and hugged the dog. They remained in that position for a few seconds until the dog gently detached itself from Patrick, took a step back and leveled a pair of glowing white eyes at Patrick.

"My name is Ashram," it spoke telepathically.

"Hey," Patrick exclaimed in like manner. *"You can talk. So cool."*

"Yes, Patrick," Ashram affirmed. *"I can and you must listen now, alright?"*

"Okay, Mr. Ashram."

"Good," Ashram said. *"I am the first-born of all the Hounds and our duty, amongst others, is to seek out unique creatures in every realm and dimension."*

"I don't understand, Mr. Ashram," Patrick said.

"In due time, you will," it assured Patrick. *"Alright?"*

"Alright," replied Patrick.

"For now, you must go back to sleep and this," Ashram gestured with his snout, *"will all seem like a dream to you. Go now, my little friend. Sleep peacefully."*

With these words, Ashram turned around and walked into the darkness of the night as his body disintegrated into thousands of tiny, sparkling dusts. Patrick stepped back into the kitchen, locked the door, walked back to the room and climbed back on his bed as if in a trance. To Patrick, what just happened felt like a dream. As the last specks of sparkling dusts disappeared into the night, the clocks and watches in the house resumed ticking. His home was no longer trapped in an etheric bubble in which time and space were frozen.

The second major event in his life occurred during the first term of his third year of secondary school at Sacred Heart College, Mankon, Bamenda, the capital city of the Northwest Province of Cameroon. Dry, ashy skin, with cracked lips and heels remained the most common fallouts of the harsh harmattan weather in mid-November. Patrick was returning to the dormitory from the refectory, after another bland but hunger-quenching lunch. Boarding school had its perks and good food was not one of them.

"Not those two again," he mumbled under his breath when he saw his least favorite people in the school walking towards him; Sir Chubby and Sir Twigs, names he believed fit the physical attributes of these two bullies.

Patrick wrinkled his nose in utter disdain for these two. When he was a few paces away from them, Sir Chubby reached out and grabbed him by the shirt and shoved him against the wall.

"I thought we told you to get us fish rolls from the square every day for lunch," spat Sir Chubby.

"And I thought I told you I don't run a charity," replied Patrick with defiance without skipping a beat.

A snarl spread across Sir Chubby's face. He released Patrick's shirt and threw a fist at Patrick's gut, but Patrick moved his hip to the left and Sir Chubby's fist crashed into the wall. A wail of pain erupted from Sir Chubby's lips and he cradled his hurting hand in the other. Sir Twigs, not wanting to look foolish in front of a younger student, cocked his left leg and aimed for Patrick's knee. Patrick read the move and extended his right foot forward. Sir Twigs banged his toes against the sole of Patrick's shoe. Patrick heard a snap, followed by a howl of pain from Sir Twigs before Sir Twigs fell to the ground and reached for his foot.

Definitely a broken toe, Patrick thought.

By this time, the air was abuzz with excitement from the gathering of many students, most of whom saw what happened to Sir Twigs. The senior prefect, Eric Mekong, happened to walk by and by an unwritten, unjust rule, the younger, smaller-framed Patrick was guilty of brutally assaulting two older, bigger-framed senior students. Severe punishment was in order, if not suspension or even dismissal. Patrick was about to be hauled away to the upper-sixth dormitory when a voice froze everyone in place.

"Let him go," said the priest, referring to Patrick. "I'll take care of him."

"But Father-" Eric started to protest.

"I saw everything, and, as I said, I will take care of him," the priest said. "Have some students take these two buffoons to the infirmary, will you?"

It was more of an order than a request.

"Yes, Father," Eric replied and did as he was told.

Patrick smiled wryly. The bullies would eventually recover from their injuries, but they would never recover from their broken egos. After all, the two of them got beaten up by a junior student. The crowd started to disappear. Patrick's back was still pressed against the wall. His classmates and friends cheered him on while the older students gave him death stares. He was torn between the pride that came with heroics like those he just pulled off and the terror that was the promise of vengeance from the senior students. He just earned the top spot on their 'Most Wanted' list. He shrugged and peeled himself away from the wall and was about to head to his dormitory when he heard a voice call out to him.

"Patrick," it was the priest who had just saved his butt.

Patrick was surprised the priest knew his name. He walked towards the priest.

"Yes, Father," Patrick replied.

"Where did you learn to fight like that?" asked the priest.

The priest radiated a certain aura of authority that made Patrick shudder involuntarily despite the dry heat of the afternoon.

"I watch too many action movies, Father," he replied in earnest.

The priest nodded slowly.

"Come to the chapel after your 3 pm studies," the priest turned around and started walking away. "I have something to show you."

"Yes, Father," Patrick replied.

When the priest was about ten meters away, Patrick sighed.

It looks like I'm in deep trouble even with the school authority now.

3 pm studies ended at 4:30 pm, and 4:30 to 6 pm was assigned to sports. But Patrick skipped sports to honor his summons.

It was not uncommon for a priest from another parish within the country or abroad to spend a year or two at the school teaching and partaking in communal services. The priest who summoned Patrick was one of such priests. Rumor had it he was from Italy. Patrick walked into the chapel, genuflected facing the crucifix and traced the sign of the cross across his torso. He then chose a corner in the chapel that kept him hidden from outside view. He forgot to dust off the pew before sitting down. He cursed out loud, forgetting he was in church.

"Where is this damned priest?" he muttered.

A heavy sigh of annoyance later, he knelt down and started reciting the Rosary.

"How ironic," the priest said, startling Patrick out of his skin. "A man of prayer trapped in the body of a man of violence."

"Tell that to St. Ignatius Loyola, Father," Patrick rebutted and sat down.

"Touché, young man," replied the priest amusedly.

"You asked to see me?" Patrick said with just a dash of teenage rudeness.

"Very well," said the priest. "Let's get down to business. But first, do you have any questions for me?"

"Are you really from Rome?" asked Patrick.

"I am."

"Do you see the Pope all the time?"

"No. Maybe once every two months."

"What?" Patrick exclaimed. "How come you don't see him every Sunday?"

"Do you know what purpose is?" the priest asked suddenly.

"No," Patrick frowned in confusion. "And how do you know my name?"

The priest stood up and walked through the pew that separated them before sitting next to Patrick. Patrick's rational mind tried to make sense out of what just happened, but his irrational mind screamed with curiosity and excitement.

"How did you do that?" Patrick asked with untamed excitement that echoed within the chapel.

"There are many things I would like to teach you, Patrick," the priest spoke with an emotionless monotone. "But first, you must be reminded of something you've forgotten."

The priest raised his hand towards Patrick's face.

"May I?"

Patrick hesitated for a moment.

What the hell is going on? he wondered. *Is he going to cast a spell on me or something?* Patrick tried to read the priest's body language. Nothing.

But then, if he wanted to hurt me, he rationalized. *I mean, he walked through a pew.*

Finally, Patrick nodded.

"Okay," said the priest.

The priest placed his right index finger between Patrick's eyebrows, above the bridge of his nose. In a flash, Patrick relived his encounter with Ashram on that fateful night in Mamfe. When he opened his eyes barely a second had passed, but Patrick no longer felt the same after that. Something alien but strangely familiar gnawed at the pit of his stomach. He felt it as strongly as the hard pew felt on his butt. Yet, that something existed just beyond his perception. A new sensation burned in Patrick's eyes as he met the priest's: awe.

"Who *are* you, Father?"

"My name is Shi'mon."

The final milestone in his life came after his final year of high school. He had just finished writing the final exams of the Government Certificate of Education (G. C. E) Advanced Levels Exams and was heading towards the main gate of the school campus with some of his friends to hail a taxi to take them home. The walk on the half-mile main drive was the best walk of his life. Finally, he was free; free from boarding school life and bursting with the excitement of experiencing life in the university.

He had many more meetings with Father Shi'mon after that day in the chapel. During those visits, Fr. Shi'mon told him about the Order of the Rock. He also received some basic self-defense training that proved particularly useful against bullies. At the end of that school year, Fr. Shi'mon returned to Rome and Patrick never saw or heard from him. Patrick waded through a temporary period of sadness until he let go of his attachment to Fr. Shi'mon. On his way to hail a taxi home, a black, luxury car drove through the gate and started making its way towards the school campus. It slowed to a stop when it came close to Patrick, and a tinted window rolled down to reveal a familiar face.

"Hello, Patrick," Father Shi'mon said.

"Fr, Shi'mon," Patrick exclaimed with delight.

He would have hugged the man if no car door separated the two of them. Fr. Shi'mon summoned a genuine smile. Patrick's friends recognized the priest and greeted him. When Fr. Shi'mon returned their greeting with a wave of his hand, Patrick saw his ring. He froze in shock and a much deeper sense of awe.

This whole time… he thought. *I never knew… I… I… Oh my God.*

"Nice ride, Father," Terence, Patrick's close friend said.

Fr. Shi'mon nodded his thanks. Patrick swallowed, still feeling too dumbfounded to say anything.

"Would you boys excuse us?" Shi'mon said to Patrick's friends.

They complied and continued to the main gate. Fr. Shi'mon turned his attention towards Patrick.

"So, have you decided?" he asked.

Given everything he remembered about his life, his encounter with Ashram and now Fr. Supreme, everything came full circle. He was being recruited by the very head of the O.R. himself. Patrick felt the resonance of everything in his being. As such, he dropped to one knee and bowed his head.

"I am at your service, until the end of my days, Father Supreme," Patrick replied without a moment's hesitation.

This was the first time he had ever addressed Shi'mon as 'Father Supreme'.

Father Supreme extended his right hand through the open window. Patrick took it and kissed his ring. To those watching, Patrick had just genuflected and kissed Fr. Shi'mon's hand. But to Patrick, the walk towards freedom had just taken an abrupt end. He now had work to do. He had much more to learn. And most of all, he had a destiny to fulfill, a destiny which still eluded him. Yet, his faith was immovable. His life had a purpose and that purpose would reveal itself to him eventually.

"Let's get you home, shall we?" Father Supreme said.

He stood up, walked to the other side of the car and got in. A decade later, Patrick earned the title of 'Protégé of Father Supreme' as well as the reputation of being the only O. R. priest who almost bested Father Supreme in hand-to-hand combat. He left Sacred Heart College, barely an adult and walked into a world that would later nickname him *Ether*, the best agent the O.R. had ever seen.

CHAPTER SIXTEEN

BIRTHING A BRIGHT EYE

"FALL TO THE right," ordered General Sarko.

His order somehow filtered through the chaotic clashes of weapon and landed on one his captain's ears.

"FALL TO THE RIGHT," reiterated the first captain to his troops.

General Sarko; the best general the Northern Kingdom had spawned in the last two centuries. At least, that was the claim. The year was 594 C. E. and the Kingdom of the North was at war with its allies consisting of the armies of the Southern Kingdom and two other nearby kingdoms. The enemy was about to execute their signature attack: the spear-clam. The attack involved the troops arranging themselves like the tip of a spear and charging head-on into the enemy. Usually, the enemy would concentrate on that formation. The spear-tip formation then fans out from the base and close in on the enemy like the shells of a clam. This move created a feeling of instant overwhelm. Up until this war, victory was always the outcome of this strategy. However, the army of Kingdom of the North was already familiar with this strategy.

So, while the first captain peeled to the right with half of the troops, the general peeled to the left with the other half, thereby creating a clear path down the middle for the enemy. This rearrangement trapped the soldiers who formed the tip of the spear and prevented them from executing the clam formation. The battle would have been over quickly had the enemy not outnumbered the army of the North by 2-to-1.

"Is there word of the princes, yet?" the general asked.

"They will be here soon, General," replied a soldier.

"Royal brats," he cursed out loud. "They had better hurry."

"General, they are here," another soldier cried with relief.

Princes Marlo and Merko charged down the hill and straight into the enemy with 600 soldiers, 300 of whom rode on horsebacks. They were twins and Marlo was the older. They had just celebrated their twenty-first birthday the previous week, and this was their third time in battle. The clangs of metal against metal and the war cries of thousands of men filled the air like a worthy sacrifice to the gods of violence, war and death. The twins were skilled with the sword, General Sarko's protégés. In less than a quarter of an hour, the scales of victory had tipped significantly in favor of the Northern Kingdom.

"Twenty-two," Merko called out to his brother.

"Twenty-five," Marlo called back.

"Liar," Merko cursed and smiled as he cut down an enemy.

Suddenly, he found himself surrounded by six enemy soldiers; two trained their spears towards him, and four held swords. Merko grinned with excitement and took off his helmet, freeing his peripheral vision.

"Finally, a real challenge," his eyes danced with sadistic zest.

He let his helmet drop to the ground and stared defiantly at the enemy.

"So," Merko said, "which of you wants to be the first to die?"

Two of them went for his neck from opposite directions with their swords.

They took the bait, Merko thought.

By removing his helmet, he not only freed his peripheral vision; he also presented his neck as a perfect target. So, when the two soldiers went for his neck, he crouched, spun to his left. Riding the momentum of his spin, he drove his sword underneath the helmet of the soldier to his left, where the soldier's head was unprotected, slicing through the soldier's brain until his sword struck the soldier's inner helmet above the crown of the soldier's head. The soldier was dead before Merko removed his sword. He pulled his right foot around his left ankle in a cross step, and his body continued to spin in the same direction. The other missed his target, but the momentum of his motion caused him to bend forward as his sword struck the ground. Before he could regain his stance, Merko brought the sword down to the back of the soldier's exposed and unprotected neck, separating the soldier's head from his body.

Two down, four to go, Merko said to himself.

From the corner of his eye, Merko noticed one of the soldiers cocking his spear. Instinctively, he leaned back just enough to feel the spear whizz past him to impale another of the six enemy soldiers behind him. In his position, he saw beneath the soldier's helmet where the neck was exposed. He thrust his sword into the soldier's neck for good measure, in case the soldier survived the impalement somehow. He pulled his sword out of the dying soldier's neck, straightened, pinned his sword into the ground and rolled forward, pulling out his dagger with his right hand at the same time. His move was so smooth and quick that the soldier who had just thrown his spear had no time to react. Merko held the back of the soldier's head and plunged his dagger below the soldier's mouth until the dagger struck the soldier's skull.

Merko instinctively spun around and used the soldier's dead body as a shield. He ignored the dead soldier's warm blood running down his right hand as the soldier's life gradually ebbed away. He glared at the last of the six soldiers. The soldier cocked his spear and desperately searched for an opening to attack. Suddenly, the soldier's body abruptly lurched forward, and his spear dropped to the ground as if it had become too heavy for him. With a grunt of shock and pain, the soldier fell face down. The wooden part of a spear extended from his spine.

"You are very welcome," Marlo winked and Merko.

"Damn you," Merko grinned.

He let the dead soldier's body slump to the ground. He wiped most of the dead soldier's blood off his dagger on the soldier's outfit before heading to pick up his helmet and sword from the ground. He put on his helmet and, with a maniacal war cry, he charged into the enemy.

Half an hour later, the North won the battle and last of the enemies began to flee for their lives, much to the anger and humiliation of the King of the South.

"Fetch my bow," he seethed through clenched teeth.

His squire quickly handed the bow. The king back-handed the squire, sending the teenager sprawling on the ground.

"Where is the arrow?" he yelled at the squire.

With a shaking hand, the squire pulled an arrow from his quiver.

"No, you imbecile," he barked. "*The* arrow."

The squire reached across his shoulder and unslung the sack he was carrying. He dropped to a knee, placed the sack on the ground and opened it. The sack contained one item wrapped in deer skin. He unwrapped the deer skin and picked up *the* arrow from its middle with extreme caution. The king snatched the arrow from squire's trembling hand and set it in his bow. He pulled as far back as he could and took careful aim.

"He assured me that victory would be mine," the king fumed. "Everything he asked of me, I did. Everything."

He relaxed his shoulders.

"I may lose the battle, but I will have my consolation prize," he snarled and narrowed his eyes as he focused on his target.

Which of these smug bastards shall I kill? he shrugged. *Any of them will do just fine.*

The king took a slow, deep breath and relaxed his shoulders some more. He closed his eyes for a few seconds until his mind went blank and a calm washed over his being. Then, he opened his eyes, made his decision and loosed the arrow. It tore through the air and glided towards its mark, as if guided by the hands of the gods themselves because the king was a master archer. He held his arms in draw position as he watched the arrow glide gloriously through the air..

Perfection, the king thought.

The arrow struck its mark. He lowered his arm and his being flooded with contemptuous pride and disdain.

The army of the Northern Kingdom sang and danced to songs of victory while the twins argued over who had the most kills between the two of them. Then an arrow tore through Merko's armor, chain mail and struck his breast, two inches above his heart. Marlo stared at his brother's chest as if he was in a horrible dream. He met his brother's gaze, whose facial expression revealed he was too shocked to accept the situation. Then, Merko's face contorted into a painful expression. His eyes rolled to the back of his head and he slumped to the ground. Marlo turned in the direction from whence the arrow came just in time to see the king of the Southern Kingdom lowering his arms. He returned his gaze towards his brother on the ground. Many soldiers rushed in to tend to him. His mind burned red with anger like he had never felt before and a wild, bestial cry of rage escaped his throat. His entire existence shrank to the singularity that the King of the Southern Kingdom embodied and that singularity had to die. As such, Marlo unsheathed his sword and bounded towards that singularity.

"Take twelve men and see the prince to the palace physician at once," General Sarko ordered his first captain.

"I swear on my life that it will be done, general," replied the first captain.

General Sarko unsheathed his sword and charged with Prince Marlo. The rest of the army followed their general and prince. Enemy bodies dropped dead in this final onslaught until none was left to kill. The king of the south drew his sword and charged at Prince Marlo.

"He assured me I would have the Queen of the North as my bride," he snarled and leaped off his carriage. "If I cannot have her, then she will be childless."

He was the last man standing in his army, but he would not run, he would not back down, and he would not surrender.

Not until those brats are dead, he raged in his mind.

Both men narrowed the space between them. Fury gave the king of the Southern Kingdom extra strength as he raised his sword to strike. However, Marlo accelerated and drove his right shoulder into the king's gut with so much force that it knocked the air out of the king's lungs as the king fell several meters behind. The impact from the fall caused him to lose his sword and helmet. He scrambled back to his feet, ready to attack. However, his vision blinded and white, hot pained burned into his head as Marlo's armored, clenched fist hammered into his right jaw, followed by a snap and a pop as his jaw broke and came apart from its joint. The sky whirled and the king of the Southern Kingdom faceplanted on the ground. He coughed, spitting out a mixture of saliva, blood and several teeth.

Marlo pounced on him like a starved vulture. The sound of metal against flesh fueled his hellish hate and maddening rage even more as he pummeled away at his enemy until his enemy's face was a mass of bloodied, battered flesh randomly attached to bones. Then, he picked up the king from the ground with both hands, lifted him above his head, as if the king was a sack of potatoes, and brought the king's spine to settle on his right thigh that was perfectly placed perpendicular to the ground. The ear-splitting snap of a breaking spine did nothing to quell his fuming soul. The king's body rested on his thigh like an open door. Marlo pushed the king off his knee and towered over the king. He looked for his sword and found it a few meters away. He walked towards his sword and picked it from the ground before returning to the king.

"You... you," the king struggled to speak as his body stiffened and twitched. "Two... weeks."

A wicked, toothless grin spread across his bloodied, battered face as he retched and convulsed.

"I do not have time for this nonsense," Marlo sneered.

He raised his sword and brought it down. The king's head rolled away from his body. Marlo stared at the headless body of the king for a few seconds before he sheathed his sword. Not that it mattered, but he thought it wise to add humiliation to the king's legacy as he reached underneath his armor around his pelvis, unfastened its binds and started urinating on the headless corpse of the King of the southern kingdom. His comrades cheered him on.

Marlo wasted no time. He immediately headed back to the palace. He rode his horse so fast that his horse almost gave up on him. He found Merko in Merko's chamber, lying on his bed with eyes closed and his chest rising and falling slowly. Their parents sat near Merko's bed in the room. Servants put their hands together in hope and prayer. The queen could not stop crying, but the king remained stoic.

Men do not cry in public, Marlo remembered his father telling him once. *Especially those with royal blood.*

"Did you kill him?" King Borash Pakola asked taking his eyes off Merko.

"Yes, father," Marlo replied. "General Sarko has it. I cleaved it myself."

"Excellent," said King Borash. "The madness is over."

He turned to face Marlo.

"You did very well, son."

"Thank you, father," replied Marlo almost dismissively.

He turned his attention towards the palace physician.

"How is he, Kano?" Marlo asked.

"Young sire," the physician said. "I am afraid his condition is dire. If you could please come this way," he bid Marlo to move closer.

Marlo moved from the foot of the bed to sit on the left side of the bed. His armor was stained with dirt and dried blood, but he did not care. Merko seemed to be in a peaceful, dreamless sleep but Marlo feared much worse was going on. He was about to take his brother's hand in his when Kano stopped him.

"No, young sire."

"Why not?" Marlo asked, his voice on the edge of anger.

"Do you see this?" Kano pointed at the arrow's point of entry.

A part of the broken arrow still stuck out from Merko's chest like a disgusting magician's trick. The flesh around the wound had taken up a black discoloration which radiated outward in the typical fashion of a powerful poison spreading fast

"Can you cure him?" Marlo's despair and desperation could not drown out the false hope in his tone of voice.

"Young sire," Kano stammered and swallowed nervously. "I am afraid this is beyond my skill. Your brother was struck with an arrow that had been coated in the deadliest poison known to man, called *kawasha*. I thought this poison did not exist, but the coloration and the spread are evidence of what I have read about this poison. It is forged by boiling together a mixture of the Egyptian cobra's venom, and some poisonous herbs from the lands in the far south, beyond the great waters. I do not recall the names of those herbs."

He shifted his weight from his left leg to his right leg. His 65-year-old frail frame was starting to weigh on his injured left ankle and his walking cane could only offer so much comfort for so much time.

"This poison causes a slow and painful death by internal organ decay, while one is in a state of wakeful death."

"So, what you are telling me," Marlo managed to say after a moment, "is that my brother's insides are already in the process of decay."

"I am afraid so, young sire."

"He is in excruciating pain."

"Yes, young sire."

"And you are saying there is nothing you or anyone can do about this?" Marlo yelled at the palace physician.

"Young sire," Kano cowered slightly. "I have looked after you and your brother ever since your births," his voice broke, and he fought back the tears in his eyes. "If I could, I would take your brother's place, without any hesitation."

Marlo realized he was unfair to the physician. His features softened a tinge.

"Apologies, Kano," he said. "I meant no ill."

"No need, young sire," Kano replied. "These are dark times for us all."

Kano mopped his eyes with the right sleeve of his robe. He could not hold back the tears any longer.

"I will see to it that he is cleaned and fed. I did not want you to touch him for I will not risk you getting poisoned from the sweat of his body."

Marlo's resolve shattered into a million pieces, but he maintain a stoic persona.

Men do not cry in public, especially those with royal blood.

He stifled the urge to scream, to punch a wall, to take his horse and command the army to decimate the rest of the Kingdom of the South. He wanted a miracle. He opened his mouth to say something but changed his mind because of the lump in his throat. Suddenly, he remembered something.

"Kano," he said, his voice heavy with hope. "Right before I beheaded him, Yushla said something about two weeks. Do you think this may have anything to do with the poison?"

"Yes, young sire," Kano affirmed. "Two weeks is how long it takes for the poison to finish consuming the victim's brain."

Kano hesitated for a second.

"Two weeks is how long the victim has to suffer before he or she dies."

Marlo's heart plummeted to the pit of his stomach, pulled down by the anvil of despair. He heaved his shoulders in a heavy sigh before nodding his thanks to Kano and hurrying out of Merko's chambers. His emotions were brimming over, threatening to explode at any moment. He needed some privacy, which he found in the palace garden. There, he took off the breast plate of his armor and sat on the ground.

"Leave me be," he commanded the servants who followed him to the garden. "I do not want to be disturbed. Is that clear?"

"Yes sire," they chorused their response and quickly departed from sight.

When Marlo was certain he was by himself, he exploded in a wail of pain so deep it could melt the snow off a mountain top. He wept for his best friend and brother, who had only a fortnight to live. He was so engrossed in his pain that he did not notice the middle-aged man carefully trying to catch his attention.

"Sire?" the man kept calling. "Sire?"

Marlo jerked his head up and drew his dagger.

"Show yourself," Marlo ordered.

The man emerged from the darkness, hands in the air. He dropped to a knee in front of Marlo and bowed his head.

"Apologies, sire. I did not mean to startle you," the man said. "I heard about your brother. I am sorry. May the gods keep him strong."

Marlo sheathed his dagger.

"Thank you," Marlo said. "And what are you doing here at this hour?"

"Sire," the man said. "After a long day of mending shoes and providing for one's family, one sometimes deserves some ale from the tavern; even it is but a minuscule reward for the toils of one's hands."

"True," Marlo replied dismissively. "Now, rise and go home to your family, mender of shoes."

"Sire," the man said, making no move to rise just yet. "If I may, I think there may be a remedy for your brother's malady."

Marlo's eyes blazed with a mixture of confusion, anger and hope.

"Speak," Marlo commanded.

"Sire," the man continued. "It may only be a legend, but at the same time, there is an aspect of truth to every legend."

"Do not waste my time, peasant," Marlo roared.

"Apologies, sire," the stranger said and cowered. "It is said that a man resides in the Caves of Callow, who suffered a curse of some kind; a curse that turned his blood into a panacea for all ailments. So, if you can find him, get some of his blood and feed it to your brother, then your brother just may be saved."

"The Caves of Callow are a seven-day ride away," Marlo said. "Even if this legend were true, it is nearly impossible to return in time to save my brother."

"Sire," said the man. "I mean no disrespect, but I know that if it were my family smitten thusly, I would go after the gods themselves if I had word that even the slightest possibility for a remedy exists for my smitten family."

Marlo furrowed his eyebrows in deep thought.

"Sire," the man pressed on. "If you decide to go, it must be now."

"How did you come about this piece of information?" asked Marlo.

"Sire, I may only be more than half a century old," replied the man. "But I know enough to last my children and their children's children a lifetime. Stories have been passed onto us for generations and I will continue in the light of my forefathers. That is all I have to say, sire."

Marlo made up his mind and rose to his feet.

"Thank you," Marlo straightened his gait. "I will heed to your words and ride out at once."

"May the gods ride with you, sire," the man bowed his head lower.

Only after Marlo had left did The Scientist rise to his feet and disappear into the darkness of the night. He was pleased with himself and with the unfolding of his plan so far.

CHAPTER SEVENTEEN

DEATH BY DESPERATION

"I MUST LEAVE at once for the Caves of Callow, father," Marlo said. "A peasant speaks of a man who abides there, who was afflicted by a curse that rendered turned his blood into a cure for all ailments.".

"I give you six of my finest soldiers, my son," his father said. "They will see you to a safe return. Hope may be slim, but we must seize whatever we can."

Marlo beat his chest once in affirmation and exited the king's chamber.

An hour later, he was galloping across the country on his way to the Caves of Callow with six of his father's best soldier's, handpicked by his father himself. They rode with unwavering focus and resolve. A half-moon peered from behind thin clouds providing extra illumination along their journey.

"Sire," called out one of the guards.

Marlo did not response. He just kept riding.

"Sire," the guard called out once more.

No response.

The guard kicked his horse, accelerated past Marlo and cut him off. Marlo's horse came to an abrupt stop and he glowered at the guard.

"You had better have a good reason for this insolence or else," Marlo barked, reaching for his sword, "your life will meet its end by my sword."

"If it comes to that, my lord," the guard replied, without the slightest hint of emotion, "then it will be as my lord wishes. But if we continue in this manner, then our course will be lost because these horses can only ride for so long without food, water and rest."

Marlo's features relaxed with the wisdom of the guard's words. He nodded.

"What is your name?"

"Pranko, my lord," he replied.

"Apologies, Pranko," Marlo said, without warmth.

"His highness need not apologize," Pranko replied still without emotion. "These are dark times for all of us. We share in your burden. Your family has been kind and generous to us and I speak for all of us here present that we are ready to lay down our lives to see this mission is accomplished, your highness."

Marlo stared at Pranko for a few seconds. His features softened even more as the weight of the physical exhaustion of the war and the emotional exhaustion of his brother's dire situation slowly pressed on his shoulders. He turned his horse around and regarded each of the five other guards as if he was just noticing them for the first time. He nodded briefly at each of them before turning around to face Pranko.

"You are their leader, correct?" Marlo asked Pranko.

"Yes, sire. Your father handpicked us himself and like I said," Pranko gestured at his men, "the six of us are ready to lay down our lives for you and the mission."

"Thank you, Pranko," Marlo said.

Marlo turned his horse around so that he could face the other guards. The exhaustion pressed harder on his shoulders and his legs wobbled slightly as if from a drunken stupor.

"Thank all of you. You are good men and I am lucky to embark on this mission with you."

The six soldiers beat their clenched right fists on their left breast plates three times in unison, symbolizing a pledge to accomplish a mission to the very end. Only death could prevent them from seeing that mission to completion.

"Your highness," Pranko said. "The horses could use a drink of water and some rest. And so do you, your highness."

"I do not-" Marlo started saying as he dismounted his horse.

However, he missed his step and landed awkwardly on the ground. He tried to get up but exhaustion, coupled with the crash that came from adrenaline wearing off, got the better of him and he faceplanted to the ground. The last thing he remembered before he slipped into unconsciousness was a pair of strong hands picking him up from the ground and swinging his right arm over the broad shoulder of someone who seemed to be bigger and taller in stature than he was.

"We will stand guard in pairs," Pranko said as he pulled Marlo's near-death weight to the base of a tree.

He gently laid Marlo on the ground.

"Nanko and I will take the first watch," he continued. "You two," he gestured at two of the soldiers, "tend to the horses and you two," he gestured at the other two soldiers, "you have the next watch."

The soldiers beat their chests once and dispersed to execute their orders.

"He has passed out already," Pranko said.

"I have never seen the prince like this," Nanko leaned against a tree and played with a tiny tree branch between his teeth.

"He acts as if he is possessed by a demon," agreed Pranko. "I pray that this nightmare ends soon before something worse happens."

"What could be worse than losing a loved one, my dear Pranko?" Nanko asked, finding a semi-comfortable spot on the ground to sit. "Losing a parent is one thing, almost understandable. We are expected to bury our parents. But when death looms over a sibling...."

"True, he is afraid," Pranko unsheathed his dagger.

He tossed it in the air and caught it.

"And dire times have strange ways of bringing out the worst in people."

He examined the knife, shrugged and sheathed it.

"Well, we must ensure the success of our mission then," Nanko replied, yawning and stretching at the same time, "You do not plan on getting any sleep tonight, do you?"

"You know me even better than you know the maiden down the road from your house, my good friend," Pranko replied.

The two soldiers managed a little laughter.

"What is her name again? I keep forgetting."

"That, my good friend will remain my secret," Nanko replied, nestling his head on his left arm and shoulder. "I do not trust you when it comes to women."

Both men broke into laughter once again.

They awoke at first light after an uneventful night and continued their journey, pushing their horses to the brink of death. On the third day, they arrived at a place called the Curve of Callow. It had a semblance to a caldera, but this natural structure was not an extinct volcano. It looked like Mother Nature used a bowl and scooped some land mass out of the ground, and the Curve of Callow was formed. The edges stretched across at approximately five hundred meters in diameter. An assessment of the majestic scenery that lay in front of them revealed the origins of the phrase 'Caves of Callow.' More than fifty caves punctuated the Curve in random patterns.

"Where do we begin?" Marlo growled with frustration.

Marlo was about to charge downhill when Pranko called out to him.

"Sire, I suggest we exercise caution and wisdom," Pranko said.

Marlo panted out of frustration, but Pranko proved to be a reliable voice of reason after everything. He sighed, turned around and face Pranko.

"Alright then," Marlo said. "What do you propose?"

"If I was a hermit," Pranko explained, "I would choose a cave in the eastern corner. It would be illuminated with as much direct evening sunlight as possible when the Sun sets in the west. I would also want to stay as far away from the valley floor as possible to avoid possible flooding of my cave. With these in mind, I say we start searching from the top eastern corner and make our way down."

"And we are at the southern corner," a soldier interjected.

"The eastern corner it is then," Marlo agreed and made to mount his horse.

"And when we find this person," Pranko asked, a worried look spreading across his face. "Do we just hold him down and um… 'obtain' his blood?"

"Yes," Marlo replied coldly. "We take it by any means necessary."

"Perhaps it would be wise to ask nicely," said a man Marlo and the soldiers were unaware of his presence.

Instinctively, Pranko and his soldiers drew their weapon and formed a barrier in front of Marlo.

"Identify yourself, stranger," Pranko demanded.

"My name is of no consequence," replied the stranger, hands clasped behind his back.

He wore a dark, brown, ankle-length robe and no shoes. A thick, black beard hid much of his face. His overgrown and unkempt hair gave him a grizzly look.

"If I wanted all of you dead, you certainly would have been dead already," the stranger added.

His eyes settled briefly on each of the soldiers before he spoke again.

"I know why you are here and no, you will not have it," he added.

"And if you know already why we are here, you also know that we will have what we came here for, with or without your consent," Marlo rebutted, pushing through the wall of guards to face the stranger.

"Be careful what you say, Marlo," the stranger warned.

Marlo froze for a moment, stunned by the stranger's words

"How did you know my name?" Marlo asked.

"And no, I did not make the poison that killed Merko," the stranger added.

Marlo's hands went limp and his heart sank.

If this man knows my name, why we are here and that Merlo was poisoned, then could he also be saying that Merlo is dead? Marlo wondered while his mind was torn between the logical conclusion from this syllogism and the prospect of being so close to the cure for his brother's affliction.

"No," he snarled and shook head.

"NO," he screamed.

Marlo drew his sword and pressed the tip against the stranger's chest.

Pranko and his soldiers took fight stance.

"Go home and bury your brother," said the stranger calmly. "There is nothing more you can do."

To Marlo utter shock, the stranger walked through his sword and through him, casting Marlo's vision in pitch blackness for a second as his body walked through Marlo's.

"By the gods," Marlo exclaimed and whipped around just in time to see the stranger walking through the soldiers, who gasped and fled to the side as if someone threw hot coals towards them.

"How...?" Marlo's shock prevented him from completing his sentence.

Marlo quickly realized that he could do nothing to physically hurt this stranger who had just done the impossible. He quickly sheathed his sword and ran after the stranger, who was making his way down the Curve. He overtook the stranger and fell at the stranger's feet.

"Please, sir," Marlo implored. "The man who told me about you said that your blood is an elixir of life."

Marlo coughed hard as if to catch his breath.

"If this is so, then please let me have some of it. It could bring my brother back to life."

"You do not know what you are asking for," replied the stranger. "There is a purpose for everything and everything happens for a reason. This is something you must understand."

"Then surely, sir, there is a reason why I am begging at your feet right now," Marlo rebutted.

A moment of silence passed with Marlo still clinging to the stranger's ankle.

"Please, sir," Marlo said. "I will do anything to save my brother."

"Rise, young man," the stranger said, finally.

Marlo rose to his feet.

"Are you willing to do anything to save your brother's life?"

"Yes, sir," Marlo replied without hesitation. "I am."

"I ask again; are you willing to do anything to save your brother's life?"

"Yes, sir, I am."

"Marlo Pakola, are you willing to do anything to save your brother's life?"

"YES, SIR, I AM," Marlo screamed, out of anger, impatience and frustration. "I will sell my soul if I have to."

His resolve shattered and tears of desperation flowed freely down his cheeks.

"Light begets light, darkness begets darkness," the stranger said as he reached out, grabbed Marlo by the throat and lifted him off his feet.

"Blessings beget blessings, curses beget curses."

The soldiers drew their swords but Marlo gestured at them to stay their hands. To Marlo's surprise, he was not choking. All he felt was the stranger's hand around his throat and his body suspending in midair. The stranger then let go of Marlo, and Marlo remained hovering in midair. The stranger then opened his right hand and a pale, blue light coalesced on his palm to form a dagger with a six-inch blade. He closed his fist around the hilt of the dagger and extended his left hand to the side.

"Life begets life, death begets death," he said and slit his left palm with the dagger in his right hand.

"Marlo Pakola, I claim your soul," he clenched his left fist. "So that your brother, Merko Pakola, may return from the realm of the dead," he added as his blood gathered on a large. circular leaf that was not there until a blink-of-an-eye ago, "and walk among the living yet again."

Marlo's body violently arched forward as if an unseen force grabbed him by the torso, squeezed and yanked him forward. A terrifying scream of unimaginable pain escaped from his lips. Then, his body tensed up and arched forward some more as if that invisible force tightened its grip and yanked some more. His face tilted towards the sky in the direction of the sun and, despite his resistance, he could not shut his eyes.

I am going to go blind, he screamed in his mind.

Yet, he did not go blind, a realization that made him relax and cease resisting. He stared directly into what appeared to be the eye of the sun as a sweet, serene calm washed over his being, keeping him in a trance-like state. He could neither blink nor look away. He completely let go and surrendered to that sweet, serene calm and in his surrender, every iota of his physical and psychical anatomy went ablaze with a fire that existed beyond the perception of a normal human eye. It burned without heat; it blazed without a flame. It consumed without destruction. The pain that came in its wake was unlike Marlo had ever felt or could describe and out of that pain came a feeling of exuberance, of ecstasy, of aliveness that Marlo had never, ever felt before.

Yes, he scream in his head. *Yes.*

Of power, of freedom, of… of… death?

Nooooo, he wanted to scream but his vocal chords tightened under the grip of an unseen force.

The force of suction beyond the physical, beyond his ability to describe, snapped him back to reality. A deep sense of loss tarried in the wake of that suction, giving rise to panic and confusion. He stripped his gaze from the sun and trained it on the stranger and what he saw made his jaw drop and his eyes nearly pop out of their sockets. A tiny wisp of brilliant, white mist was flowing from his mouth into the stranger's. He stole a glance towards the soldiers, who all cowered and shivered visibly from confusion and fear. He tried to close his mouth to no avail. The last wisp of brilliant, white mist flowed into the stranger's mouth. He closed it and opened his eyes. For a moment, Marlo thought the stranger's eyes shone as brightly as the mist did, but he could have been wrong.

Marlo felt his body slowly descending towards the ground. Even before his feet touched the ground, and he rested himself on all fours, with his head bowed low, he knew innately why he felt such a deep sense of loss.

"You do not know what you are asking for," the stranger had said.

But now, he knew. He had just sacrificed something he never thought was real until just now; he had just sacrificed his soul.

"What have you done to me?" Marlo asked the stranger weakly.

"The blood must be drunk by none other than your brother," the stranger said, ignoring Marlo's question and started walking towards the caves. "You hold no comprehension on the sacrifice you just made, Marlo," the stranger added. "I hope it was worth it."

He began slowly fading into thin air.

"Maybe one day, you will understand what just happened. But until then, stay on the path of the light."

He disappeared completely.

"Or be doomed for all eternity," a non-corporeal voice added.

Marlo crept on all fours towards the small pool of blood that had gathered on the huge leaf on the ground. He extended his left hand towards Pranko, who placed a small, leather container in his open palm with a trembling hand. Marlo uncapped the container and poured the stranger's blood in it. The blood still maintained its original viscosity despite its exposure to the elements. When he finished, he dropped the leaf and it vanished into thin air before touching the ground. He stood up and only then did he finally lift his eyes towards the soldiers. The guards all took a step back as if they had just beheld a terrifying creature.

"What is the matter?" Marlo asked.

He took a step towards them, and they all backed away.

"S… Sire," Pranko stammered. "Your … your eyes, sire."

"What about my eyes?" Marlo asked.

"They…" Pranko hesitated.

"What about my eyes?" Marlo asked with a mix of fear and irritation.

"Sire," Pranko steeled his resolve. "Your eyes are glowing."

Marlo recoiled at Pranko's words, but he quickly regained his composure.

"Hurry now," Marlo ordered, as he strode to his horse. "Every moment we waste spells doom for my brother."

He mounted his horse and started riding away. Despite the stranger's words he still hoped his brother was alive.

The soldiers looked at one another as if deciding whether or not to follow the prince who had just undergone something their logical minds could not grasp. who had just undergone the strangest of situations or not.

"We made a pledge," Pranko said. "And whatever creature or demon he has become, we must honor that pledge."

He mounted his horse. His soldiers shrugged, mounted their horses and the six of them rode after Marlo.

From a distance, the stranger watched them disappear into the horizon. Over five hundred years later, his burden felt as heavy as it did on that fateful day. He thought if he imbibed the soul of one who was willing, he would rid himself of his curse. But he was wrong. He was still the same soulless creature he had become over five hundred years ago. Frustration turned to anger; his anger turned to fury; fury at himself for his myopia, for his sin, for the unforgivable that happened five centuries ago. Yehuda let out a scream that could rend the non-existent heart of the Devil himself in twain and plunged his fist into the ground. And for the millionth time, the Curve of Callow rocked as if hit by an earthquake. When the quake was over, Yehuda collapsed on the floor of the cave and wept, yet again, for the millionth time.

At the first sight of a stream, Marlo jumped off his horse and knelt at the bank of the stream. In his reflection in the stream, he saw the brightness in his eyes that Pranko was talking about and did not understand how this could be. He vigorously washed his face over and over, as if the water would remove the brightness like dirt on a piece of fabric; a most futile attempt. Marlo collapsed on his back, squeezing his eyes shut as if that would douse away the brightness in his eyes. A thousand thoughts rushed through his mind, mainly centered on how to explain the brightness in his eyes to his parents. He was so engrossed in his mental quagmire that he was oblivious to the sounds of approaching horses.

"Sire," Pranko called out, his concern reverberating in his tone of voice. "Sire. Are you alright?"

Pranko tapped Marlo lightly on the cheek and Marlo opened his eyes. Pranko smiled and his eyes lit up with happiness.

"It is gone, sire."

"What do mean it is gone?" Marlo asked.

"Your eyes, sire," Pranko straightened. "They are back to normal."

Marlo rushed on all fours to the stream and he let out a heavy sigh of relief when he saw Pranko spoke the truth. He did not know why and neither did he care to know.

"This is good fortune," he said to himself and stood up.

He turned around and faced the soldiers. For a moment, he did not know what to say to them.

"So," Marlo began. "I am not sure what happened out there or what you saw," he half-lied, half-told the truth. "But I think it would be wise if no one else finds out about this."

"Do not burden yourself, sire," Pranko stepped forward. "I speak for all of us that, by the gods, we swear no one else will ever know about the events that transpired at the Curve of Callow. We are as baffled as you are, sire," he added. "But we will never tell a soul."

Marlo winced at the mention of 'soul' and hoped the soldiers did not notice.

"Thank you," Marlo replied. "Thank all of you."

He clasped the forearm of every soldier.

"We ride, sire," Pranko said. "At this pace, we may arrive two days earlier."

"Then let us make sure we are ahead of schedule," Marlo replied

Marlo mounted his horse and the soldiers mounted theirs. For the first time in days, Marlo smiled as they headed for the palace.

They did arrive two days ahead of schedule. However, when they reached the palace, the look on everyone's face bespoke of unwelcome tidings. His parents looked weary with grief and sorrow and the pain in the air seemed to have a life of its own. His mother even mumbled words to herself as if she had lost her mind. Marlo scanned the room for Kano and found him sitting in a far corner, with his head buried in his hands.

"What happened, doctor?" Marlo asked trying his best to contain his fury; at what, he was unsure of.

"I am sorry, young sire," Kano spoke as if to himself. "But it seems as if the arrow that struck your brother contained a variation of the poison."

"A variation?" Marlo asked.

"Yes, young sire," Kano replied. "Instead of the two-week period before the victim's life expires, this variation took your brother's life in three days." Kano's voice broke, but he found the strength to continue. "By the third day, his body had swollen to twice its size, and it was already completely…"

Kano hesitated. He could not find the confidence to continue.

"Go on, doctor," Marlo encouraged him.

"Young sire," Kano managed to say. "His body was already completely rotten from inside. Two of the maid servants attending to him got infected, and the young boy cleaning his room was also infected."

Kano cleared his throat. Marlo was speechless.

"Your father ordered his body be burned immediately. He also ordered that the two maids and young boy be put to death and that their bodies be burned as well, for fear that the entire kingdom may also become infected."

The tears fell from his eyes like miniature waterfalls. Marlo was too stunned to say anything. Finally, he walked over to his father and knelt beside his father. His father took his hand and squeezed it gently.

"His ashes are in a jar in my chambers, son," King Borash said. "That is the least I could do."

Marlo nodded, stood up and went to his chambers.

"I do not want to be disturbed for any reason," he commanded the guards.

He closed the door, stripped himself of his armor and sat on the floor. He had nothing else to give or feel. He wondered if the hollowness he felt for... everything was a biproduct of him losing his soul. He just sat on the floor, numb to life and everything else. The journey, for naught. The sacrifice, for naught and what did he have now? Neither a brother nor a soul. He reached for the container with the blood and held it in his hand. He sighed, threw his head back and closed his eyes.

When he opened his eyes again, night had settled upon the land. Suddenly, he bolted upright as an idea struck him.

If the blood is an elixir for everything, then perhaps the blood could restore my soul.

Marlo clutched the container in his hand and left his chambers. His guards immediately started walking behind him.

"No, I must be by myself," he said.

"But, sire," the guards protested.

"That was an order," he barked and continued marching on.

"Aye, sire."

He sat at the foot of a tree in the garden and stared at the container in the palm of his hand. He uncorked the container and was about to drink from it when he remembered the stranger's words.

"The blood must be drunk by none other than your brother."

The blood was special, indeed. It retained its original viscosity after all this time. Marlo sighed and steeled his resolve. He closed his eyes and emptied its contents into his mouth.

And so, it came to pass, that a young prince, full of life, energy and love, had lost his brother to an enemy's arrow in battle; that a young prince, with every prospect for good and lacking nothing, lost the one thing he could never replace, his soul; that a young prince, aligned with the light, was drawn to the dark because he drank the blood of one who was already soulless and cursed into darkness.

Light begets light; darkness begets darkness. Blessings beget blessings; curses beget curses. Life begets life; death begets death.

And it came to pass that Prince Marlo later ascended to the throne as King of the Northern Kingdom, upon the untimely death of his father, two years after his mother took her own life. It also came to pass that King Marlo Pakola took upon a fair maiden for a wife, who would bear him twins; Dreyko and Danka Pakola. Or so he thought. It came to pass that King Marlo's offspring would carry his soullessness in dormant form, tainted by the blood of one who was soulless, until it awakened on the night brother and sister bonded in an abominable union after an attack by a bat and a wolf. It came to pass that Dreyko would become the first chuper and Danka would become the first luper.

The Scientist smiled.

He was never supposed to interfere directly with other realms and dimensions, and in fact, he never did interfere directly. As a purveyor of purpose, bending the rules to his advantage was his forte. Well, not really 'bending', per se. It was more like circumventing the rules. All he did, in this instant and in every realm and dimension he visited, was supply enough purpose for the pawns in his play to do their jobs to the letter. And who could blame him?

It is in my nature, The Scribe grinned evilly.

King Yushla of the south suddenly felt lust for King Borash's queen; lust that was never there. And Yushla was never smart enough to forge such a poison, unless he had help from a magician he had never heard of before.

I sowed the seed of lust in his head and just when he needed a magician, I was very ready to lend my expertise, The Scribe shrugged. *This is too easy for me, but then again, Earth is a most primitive, but most important, realm. What an oxymoron.*

Part of the perks of being a multidimensional being was that he could assume multiple roles in multiple realms and dimensions within the vastness of the Dimension of Space, Time, Energy and Ether. And to the best of his knowledge, Akasha was the only other entity to possess similar abilities, aside from the others who did not care for the affairs of the creatures of Creation... luckily.

Imagine what they would have done to me if they cared, The Scribe sighed.

Merko was the elder and stronger twin, and heir to the throne. So, even as Marko mourned his brother, deep down, he was glad Merko was no longer in the picture because now he had become the sole heir to the throne. Marko was also convinced that the untimely death of his father was anything but untimely. As far as he was concerned, the gods themselves had chosen him to be king, though the purpose of his soullessness eluded him.

The power of purpose. Purveying purpose meant being in power and that power was absolute... almost. The Scribe, functioning as The Scientist in this Time-Space plan of Earth Realm's existence, was very pleased with himself, and with the unfolding of the plan so far.

CHAPTER EIGHTEEN

C. E. 13 – C. E. 18

"WHAT DO YOU know about the Akashic Records?" Ramalesh asked young Yeshua.

Prince Ganesh translated.

"I am not sure, Rama Sir," young Yeshua replied.

"I believe I asked you to just call me 'Rama', young master."

"I prefer to address one as elderly and wise as yourself with respect, sir."

"As you wish, young master," Ramalesh sighed.

Young Yeshua had become popular in the kingdom, especially to astrologers, mystics and yogis. They thronged the courts daily to behold the young master of promise, rumored to be an embodiment of Shiva, destined to be the greatest human being of the current age and humankind's next evolutionary leap lay in his hands. A yogi in the making. These wise men brought ancient manuscripts replete with prophecies about young Yeshua. While some of these prophecies foretold dark omens, most held a promise of redemption and the restoration of the glory of humankind; a new birth, a new beginning, a new people.

"I will help you remember what you know about the Akashic Records, young master," Rama said and sat at the table.

A priest brought in some jasmine tea in a marble tea pot, along with four marble tea cups, and set it on the table. A palace guard stepped forward, poured some of the tea for himself and drank it one gulp. He waited. Nothing happened.

"It is safe, your highness," he nodded at Prince Ganesh.

The priest poured some of the tea into the other three teacups.

"Protocol," Ganesh explained to Young Yeshua. "Nothing to worry about."

Young Yeshua nodded, almost timidly and did not take his cup just yet.

"Go on, young master," Ganesh encouraged him with a smile. "Besides, it is considered rude to not accept nourishment offered to one."

"Apologies, your highness," Young Yeshua said. "I mean no disrespect. I am just not familiar with this brew."

"All the more reason why you should learn about it first hand, young master," Ramalesh chimed in.

Young Yeshua reached for his cup and took a careful sip of his tea as everyone present looked on. His eyes popped with pleasant surprise and he emptied the cup in three gulps. Instantly, he stuck out his tongue and fanned it with his left hand, much to the amusement of everyone present.

"It is meant to be drunk in sips, young master," Ganesh chuckled. "Would you like some more."

Young Yeshua nodded and smacked his lips. With a grin of pride, the priest poured Young Yeshua another cup of tea and spoke a few words to him.

"He said that it is truly an honor to be in the presence of a yogi as yourself and that you enjoyed his special brew," Prince Ganesh translated.

"Please extend my gratitude for his most generous words, my prince," young Yeshua said. "The honor is mine."

Prince Ganesh translated.

Ramalesh observed the young master intensely on the physical and esoteric levels using clairvoyance. Young Yeshua's auric colors oscillated between white and gold, indicating the highest levels of purity. Even his halo matched the colors of his body's aura. However, what caught his attention the most was the bright, golden pulsation from in between his eyebrows, which was the final confirmation that this young lad sitting in front of him was truly the master of the present age, the one who held the key to the next evolutionary phase of humankind. Ramalesh nodded imperceptibly and sipped from his cup.

***

On the day Ramalesh was born, the village astrologer, as was the custom, came to his bedside and made a prophecy.

"This child will see beyond the stars," the astrologer's hoarse, raspy voice swept across the dimly lit room of the tiny thatch house his parents lived in. "Most of all, he will initiate the grand awakening of a mighty yogi of the ages."

"Thank you," said Rama's father.

His tone of voice was heavy with disappointment, a sentiment his wife shared. When the astrologer left the house, Rama's father kicked one of the only three clay pots they had in frustration and anger, breaking it to several pieces.

"Why could we not have a better prophecy?" he fumed. "Like, our son will one day become a wealthy merchant."

"Or work for one who will later pass on his business to our son," the wife joined in. "If he was a girl, at least we could have hoped to collect a good bride price for her. Who will take care of us now in our old age?"

"'See the stars' my foot," his father scoffed. "Since when did seeing the stars put food on the table?"

As Rama grew up, his parents did a phenomenal job at communicating their extreme disappointment in him for a bleak future that was yet to come. As such, in a bid to prove his parents wrong, he began to pursue a life of wealth and riches and liberate them from the mindless misery they called life. However, a yearning for something else, something more fulfilling, tugged at his being like a goat tugging at a rope around its neck.

There must be more to life than being Dogra's errand boy, he thought constantly. *Yes, he is a wealthy merchant and I can learn much from him. Still...*

One day, the king at the time was taking a stroll in the city. When his horse rode close to Dogra's stand, Rama had a vision so powerful he momentarily lost control of himself. Without thinking, he rushed towards the king, threw himself to the ground, and spoke words more blasphemous than taking the name of Shiva in vain.

"Your brother shall attempt to take your life in eight days, just before sunset, my king," Rama said. "You will be at your east balcony, drinking your favorite wine and wearing the robe the queen ordered for you in the last moon cycle. Your brother will say 'I should have killed you that day in the forest' right before he strikes with his sword."

Rama lost consciousness immediately after he said those words. He awoke later to find himself chained to a wall by the ankle in a dark, dank dungeon, dripping with sewage-smelling water and infested with mice. A tiny hole far up the stone wall provided the only form of illumination to his den of despair.

At least, I am still alive, he consoled himself.

He lost track of days. A guard would slide some food through a hole at the bottom of the metallic door every so often. The food consisted of molding bread and tasteless soup. His stomach rejected his first three meals, but when starvation swooped in and his need for survival surfaced even more, his system gladly took in the food, despite the reflexive resistance that came with it.

Then, one day, the door to his dungeon opened for the first time since he awoke from losing consciousness. Two guards stormed him and stripped him naked, while two other guards came in with buckets of water and poured on him. Rama had no strength to fight back and his body was grateful for the half-bath. Marinating in one's feces and urine was not the best of situations, but he found some satisfaction in the soldiers wrinkling their noses and cursing at the acrid stench that filled his cell, an odor his olfactory organs had already adapted to.

"His majesty summons you," a guard said as he toweled Rama before forcing a gown over Rama's head.

Rama was dragged in chains to the palace and cast in front of the king. Before he bowed to the ground he noticed the king's left arm wrapped in a bandage.

"How did you come about my brother's intention?" the king demanded.

"My king, I just saw it in my mind," Rama replied.

His head was still bowed to the ground but he could feel the kings' stare digging into his back.

"You lie," said the king.

"My king, if I lie, may Shiva strike me dead and may my parents suffer many afflictions for the rest of their lives," Rama replied.

A moment of silence filled the atmosphere.

"I had my suspicions about my brother," the king spoke less firmly. "I must admit, I did not want to believe your words. But my instincts begged to differ. Thanks to your warning, I am alive today, while my brother not."

Another moment of silence went by.

"Rise, peasant," commanded the king.

Rama staggered to his feet but kept his gaze to the floor.

"What is your name?"

"Ramalesh, my king," Rama replied. "Son of Vijay Agarwal."

"Ramalesh, son of Vijay Agarwal, from this day on, you will become a student of Vidya, my personal seer," the king declared. "And you shall serve within these palace walls until the end of your days."

And so it came to pass that Rama was sent to the temple, to become a steward of Vidya, the royal seer. Twenty-eight years later, Rama succeeded his mentor as royal seer upon his mentor's death; a title he still held.

***

"Man is a tripartite being," Rama began his lectures.

He set his teacup on his wooden desk and lean back in his chair.

"Man is spirit, having a soul and living in a body. The spirit is pure, unsullied and is the source of Creation. We call this the Creator or Brahma, although I prefer Shi'va. This is not to be confused with Shiva. 'Shi'va' means 'that which is not' and 'Shiva' is the Adiyogi, the first yogi. We will talk more about his later. The body is just a part of Creation. Creation is everything manifested and because Creation is an illusion, therefore the body is also an illusion. Are you with me so far, young master?"

Prince Ganesh translated as Ramalesh spoke.

"Yes, Rama Sir," young Yeshua replied.

"Good," Rama said. "Please interject as you wish, young master."

"Thank you, Rama Sir," young Yeshua replied.

"The spirit, the un-manifest, is the Creator," Rama leaned forward. "It is consciousness and truth in its purest form. The Creator precedes all of Creation and Creation is all that is manifested; from time, space, energy and beyond. The body is an illusion, but it is unaware that it is an illusion. It thinks it is real and that its reality is what it perceives with its physical senses. But even then, it plunges into a deep state of confusion in a desperate effort to know more about itself. It attempts to mimic the only truth there is, which it does not know yet, by creating an identity for itself. It is this false identity, this illusion, this ever-changing sense of self that we call the 'ego.' As such, the human being is the embodiment of the greatest truth and the biggest lie there is. Hence, every time you say 'I Am,' you are either professing an absolute truth or an absolute lie."

Rama paused for a moment to allow Ganesh to finish translating.

"What about the soul, Rama Sir?" asked the young master.

"The soul is like a middle-man or battleground between the truth and the lie. Well," Rama adjusted himself in his chair, "the term 'battleground' may not be the best fit because there is, in fact, no battle. There is no fight between 'good' and 'evil,' because 'good' and 'evil' are merely polarizations of consciousness, thanks to the discriminatory aspect of the human psyche. They are inventions of the human mind. Great for society but utterly useless in the grand scheme of Creation. Both are illusions."

"How do you mean, Rama Sir?" young Yeshua was a little confused for the first time.

"Let me show you something," Rama reached into a drawer in the table.

He pulled out a small, nicely cut, clear piece of crystal that was no bigger than an adult's big toe and walked towards the wall to his right. A tiny ray of light shone through a crack in the wooden window.

"Your highness, if I may, could you please take that kerchief," he pointed at a white kerchief on his table."

Ganesh obliged.

"Please stand over here," Ramalesh pointed to a spot on the marble floor about three meters to his left, "and hold the kerchief in front of your chest."

The prince did as he was told.

"Thank you, your highness. Now, if the young master could stand over here and face his highness, please," Rama pointed about two meters to his left.

Young Yeshua obliged.

"Now, you see the ray of sunlight on the cloth, right?" Rama asked.

"Yes, Rama Sir," said the lad.

"Now," Rama smiled. "Watch what happens when I do this."

Ramalesh placed the piece of crystal on the crack in the window. Various colors of light appeared on the cloth. The young master walked towards the prince and counted.

"There are seven colors," he said, more to himself than to anyone else.

"Correct, young master," Rama said, "Now when I change the angle of the crystal," he changed the angle of the crystal, "the colors disappear, and we have one color, right?"

"Yes, I see what you are saying, Rama Sir," the lad replied. "But I still do not see what this has to do with the purpose of the soul."

"In a moment, young master," Rama replied. "Please return to your seat, for now. You as well, your highness. Thank you very much for your help."

They all returned to their seats, and Ramalesh returned the piece of crystal in the drawer.

"So, back to the role of the soul," Rama began. "Consider the role of the crystal on the ray of light and the kerchief. If the light from the crack in the window represents consciousness, and the kerchief his highness held up represents the body, then the crystal represents the soul. The soul is like a cushion between the spirit and body, between the higher and the lower selves. Consciousness wants to manifest in the world of form. But because it has no form of its own, it uses a medium through which it manifests; the body. But the body is resistant. Consciousness is boundless while the human body wants to create boundaries. It is in their respective natures. Thus, the soul becomes the middle ground for this purpose; to serve as a helper in the transcendence of the human person from its ego-based self, to its true deific form.

"This is the only true evolutionary process of the human being and this is the only true victory there is; that is, the victory of new consciousness over old consciousness. The old consciousness, in this case, is the ego, because, due to amnesia, we only know what the ego has gathered over many lifetimes. The new consciousness is our true 'identity,' which is pure, unsullied consciousness. It is 'new' because, due to amnesia, we forgot who we really are. It is this victory and transcendence that is called 'enlightenment,' which is awakening to our true self, or self-realization."

"Your words are heavy with wisdom and truth, Rama Sir," young Yeshua nodded with profound gratitude. "So, if I understand correctly, the soul is not just a cushion but also a warehouse for all the accumulated lessons, memories and all that, from past and current lives?"

"You are correct, young master," Rama agreed. "As well as everything that make up your body."

"So, what about the notion of good and evil?" young Yeshua asked.

No 'Rama Sir,' Ramalesh remarked in thought. *Good.*

"Good-evil," Rama replied, "right-wrong, left-right, up-down and so forth are just opposites and only exist in an ego-based world. It is part of the ego's ploy to know itself. 'Good' is not necessarily good, and 'evil' is not necessarily evil. They just are. But, just like the piece of crystal split up the light to seven different colors, the human mind tends to polarize, analyze and dissect everything. All one has to do is align with consciousness itself, just like shifting the piece of crystal such that the ray of sunlight maintains its original status quo. This so because, so long as one is identified with what one is not, the ego will dominate.

"Now, would you say a knife is a good or a bad thing, young master?"

"It depends, Rama Sir," young Yeshua replied.

"You answer like many would. If I use a knife to cook food, it is deemed a good thing. If I use it to take a life, it is deemed a bad thing. So, the mind comes to play with analyses, justifications and all the like. Societal relevance. But a knife itself is neither good nor bad. It just is, just like everything else, and we imprint all these things on the soul over many lifetimes."

"And if one were to lose one's soul?" asked Yeshua.

Ramalesh's expression darkened for a moment before he replied.

"It depends," Rama said. "There are two basic outcomes. The first is that the person may retain his or her humanity but may find himself or herself completely aligned with the light or with the dark. The second is that the person may not retain his or her humanity. They become a new creature. In both instances though, the person would be capable of 'superhuman' feats, partially because of the limitlessness of the spirit having a 'direct' impact on the physical body, tearing down much of the body's boundaries."

Rama decided to end the topic at this point and young Yeshua did not press any further. Not wanting to let the pause last too long, he continued.

"The terms 'mind' and 'soul' can be substitutes for each other," Ramalesh said. "The mind is more associated with the human brain, and hence has a more 'physical' component attached to it. I say 'physical' because the mind itself is not localized. Those who are less 'spiritual' can appreciate using the word 'mind' more than using the term 'soul' because the word 'soul' has a more spiritual connotation attached to it. But they are both the same thing.

"You see," Rama shifted in his seat, "the Ancient Egyptians removed the brains of their pharaohs prior to mummification because they did not want their pharaohs to return to Earth Realm. If there is no brain, then there is no soul, and therefore, the pharaoh could not be reborn. Pharaohs were gods to the Ancient Egyptians, and hence, they had to return to the realms and dimensions whence they came and where they, and their ancestors, belong."

"Do you have manuscripts on Ancient Egyptians?" young Yeshua asked.

"No, I do not, young master," Rama replied.

"Have you been to Egypt?"

"No, I have not."

"Then how did you come to know all this?"

"Very observant, young master," Rama smiled. "Your question brings us to your main lesson for today; the Realm-Dimension of Akasha."

"I remember that word from yesterday," Yeshua said.

"Let us begin then," Rama adjusted himself in his seat.

"Every thought, word and action," Rama continued, "from the densest forms in the lowest dimensions to the finest, and most subliminal aspect of physicality, everything manifested, from the very beginning and the very end, create vibrations and these vibrations are recorded in the Realm-Dimension of Akasha. Akasha is the keeper of the records of Creation. Different religions have different names for this realm-dimension. Akasha is Creation's ethereal repository of knowledge. You asked how I learned about Ancient Egyptian mummification rituals. There is your answer, young master."

"I feel like I have heard of this before, but I do not recall," the young master said, furrowing his eyebrows as he tried to remember.

"These are your memories from past lives, young master," Rama interjected. "You have even accessed the Akashic Records involuntarily before; but starting today, you will learn how to consciously access these records. This will accelerate your learning. I will only serve as a guide during this period."

Young Yeshua nodded and furrowed his eyebrows in thought. Rama waited for more questions. Young Yeshua nodded again and met his gaze.

"So, what would my first lesson in Akasha entail?" young Yeshua asked.

"I think the most logical step would be for the young master to learn Hindi," Rama replied with a pleasant smile. "That way, his highness could attend to matters of the kingdom and you could communicate more easily with our people. Your highness?"

"I agree, Rama," Prince Ganesh replied. "However, let it be known that I am greatly enjoying the company of the young master. It is an honor that I would prefer not to let go of."

"Of course, your highness," Rama agreed. "And after his lessons on Akasha, I would like to proceed with training him on the chakras and the Kundalini or Serpent Power."

"I am your humble student, Sir," young Yeshua replied.

"Such humility in greatness," Rama remarked. "The honor is all mine, young master. I have waited my entire life for this moment."

Ramalesh stood up and gestured.

"Please, this way, your highness, young master."

The lad from Israel and the crown prince followed the seer into the inner chambers of the temple.

And so, it came to pass that the young Jewish boy, who followed an Indian prince to India, began his journey down memory lane to unlock the powers that lay within him. He learned and adapted quickly. Most of all, he never lost his essence. Young Yeshua grew up strong and so did his popularity among his peers and across India. He studied and trained in the mornings, he played in the afternoons, and he meditated at night. In less than half a decade, Young Yeshua had mastered what took other people decades or even lifetimes to master. Prince Ganesh remained most protective of the young master as an elder brother would a younger brother.

The young master became particularly intrigued by the story of Siddhartha Gautama and his teachings. The man was unique to his time, and indeed he was an awakened one. But he also learned that Siddhartha Gautama had learned from Shiva, the first yogi, during his sojourn in the jungle in search of himself. Gautama had learned only a minuscule aspect of the 114 from Shiva. But even that minuscule aspect was enough for him to bring humanity to such an awakening. As such, while Young Yeshua deeply appreciated Gautama's teachings, he sat at the feet of Shiva, while in the Realm-Dimension of Akasha, and learned in the ways of the first yogi. As such, it came to pass that Young Yeshua became the youngest living yogi of his time.

The more he learned while in the Realm-Dimension of Akasha, the more the memories from past lives returned, and the pieces of the puzzle that constituted his destiny became clearer.

On the morning of his eighteenth birthday, while he was selecting a garb for a feast in his honor, Prince Ganesh came into his room, wearing a haggard and a pain expression on his face.

"Is everything alright, your highness?" Yeshua stiffened with concern.

"There is a man here who would like to see you," the prince replied.

"Oh. Do you know who he is?" the tension in his body eased up.

"He says his name is Bai-Ming and he is a monk from the Wu-Feng Monastery in the far eastern lands of China."

And with these words, the prince quickly turned around and stormed away. He did not want Yeshua to see him cry.

CHAPTER NINETEEN

BOOT CAMP, C.E. 32

"MASTER, WHAT DID you do to me?" Shi'mon's face contorted in a painful grimace as he clutched his stomach and writhed on the ground.

"You are so dramatic when hungry," Yeshua shook his head.

Yeshua sat at a table he had just sparked from the ethers. He hovered midair with his chair and table. A meal of finely seasoned fish and baked bread lay in front of him. He spared another glance in Shi'mon's direction.

"Are you enjoying the aroma?" Yeshua smacked his lips.

"This is cheating, Master," Shi'mon complained. "How do you expect me to concentrate in this state?"

"Not my problem," Yeshua replied, licked his fingers and smacked his lips. "So delicious. You are welcome to join me."

For this training session, Yeshua and Shi'mon had teleported to a private location on the coast of the Sea of Galilee that anyone hardly visited. Two years since his return to Israel and started an apprenticeship, his apprentices had shown progress with self-defense, teleportation, telekinesis, telepathy, clairvoyance, clairaudience and clairsentience. The more difficult lessons like experiencing the flow of the kundalini and going through conscious death required certain special preparation, and sometimes psychic surgery, before training.

"Today, you will learn how to spark the ethers and consciously manipulate your chi," Yeshua said.

"I am not paying attention, Master," Shi'mon scoffed and grimaced.

"As expected," Yeshua shrugged. "What you are experiencing now is hunger that can literally make someone go insane."

"Master, please," Shi'mon begged. "I'm dying."

"And yet I hear you loud and clear," Yeshua leaned back in his seat.

"Master..." Shi'mon begged. "I can't. I just can't."

"Wrong words."

Yeshua had yelled at him, and the other apprentices, many times before. Yet, something about the sternness in his mentor's voice this time caused a shift in his energies and temporarily diverted his focus away from his mind-blasting hunger.

What is Master insinuating? Shi'mon pondered.

He dug into his memory. Once, he, the other apprentices and Yeshua were on a boat at sea when the quiet evening suddenly turned into a dark, drenching deadly storminess. Yeshua was asleep despite the waves rising over twelve feet and the boat along with its occupants danced wildly at the mercy of the waves. They faced death from the briny brutality. Shi'mon fought his way towards his mentor and shook him violently.

"Master," he called out as Yeshua arose from his slumber. "Do you not care that we perish?"

With the calm of a sleeping child, Yeshua stood up and raised his right hand without saying a word. The storm died off quicker than it began.

In another instance, for some reason unknown to Shi'mon, he and the other apprentices had suddenly found themselves in the middle of the sea. No matter how hard the paddled and rowed, the boat did not budge.

"Look," Yaakov pointed ahead.

The figure of a male person was walking towards them... on water.

"It is a ghost," Tau'ma declared.

"No, it looks like Master," Aaron countered.

"It is I, brothers," Yeshua spoke to them via telepathy as he approached.

"If it really is you, Master, bid me come hither," Shi'mon said via telepathy to everyone's hearing.

"As you wish."

Shi'mon leaped from the boat and landed on the water, which felt solid to his feet. He took several steps towards his mentor, ignoring the gasps of awe from his brothers-in-apprenticeship. However, fear wiggled its way into his heart and he began sinking.

"Master," he called out in panic. "Help."

Yeshua was still about thirty meters away from him but he appeared in front of him as if by a magic trick. Shi'mon felt his body slowly ascend out of the water as if an unseen hand was lifting him up.

"Never doubt yourself," Yeshua commanded.

Shi'mon sighed as he exited memory lane.

I see what Master wants me to do, he said to himself. *Master wants me to take charge but I don't know how and I will do what must be done.*

He raised his eyes towards Yeshua.

"Master," he said weakly, "I do not know what to do."

Shi'mon immediately felt some of his strength return to his body. He pushed himself up to his knees and gazed upon Yeshua.

"Please, show me," he pleaded.

"I will show you, brother." Yeshua replied.

Yeshua hovered higher and waved at an empty space on the opposite side of the table.

"Sit."

Shi'mon nodded with firm resolution. He stood up and took a step as if he was about to mount a flight of stairs. His foot went through empty space. He tried again and failed. A bubble of frustration expanded in his chest, but then he recalled how the master had calmed the storm. He closed his eyes and took in a deep breath. He visualized himself at sea in the middle of a terrifying storm. He gently blew into the storm and the storm subsided as quickly as it started. The bubble of frustration in his chest popped and calmness draped over his psyche. He opened his eyes and, for the first time since training that day, he grinned at his master.

"Thank you for the invitation," Shi'mon said.

Using the power of thought, Shi'mon connected his etheric body with Earth Realm's gravitational force, thereby temporarily offsetting a part of his sense of individuality. Earth Realm's gravitational force could now bend to his will and he used that force to levitate off the ground and hover in space at the table opposite his master. He sparked the ethers into a chair and slid unto it.

"I am not hungry anymore," Shi'mon said as he sparked the ethers into food.

"Well done, brother," Yeshua said. "And now, for the bigger lesson."

"What is it, master?" Shi'mon remained calm and confident.

"What will you do every time Rania cooks for you?" Yeshua asked.

Shi'mon cursed out loud and both men started laughing.

C. E. 19 – C. E. 24

Young Yeshua's eventual departure from India was a given, though this fact never really registered in the minds of those who had grown attached to him until Bai-Ming and his group showed up at the palace. As such, his birthday, a day meant for festivities and joy, turned into one of farewell and sadness. Still, the king bid his guests tarry a few days more before they returned to China.

"His majesty is most generous," Bai-Ming accepted the invitation on behalf of his entourage.

Bai-Ming was proficient in speaking Hindi and served as translator between his brothers from the monastery and their hosts.

"A year ago at the temple," Bai-Ming said later during the feast. "I sat in meditation on a rock. Suddenly, I was thrust into a dimension of existence that was alien to me. The world around me disappeared, and I floated in nothingness. The meaning of the situation eluded me. Yet, I felt a calmness and serenity unlike I have ever felt. Then, specks of light began forming in my vision. They grew brighter and coalesced into a message:

"A NEW AGE IS NIGH. GO AND FETCH GRANDMASTER WONG FROM THE LANDS OF INDIA."

"The message then disintegrated into many specks of light before fading away. The nothingness also vanished. I emerged from this state to find many concerned and curious pairs of eyes staring down at me. Grandmaster Chang was also present. I thought no more than a minute had passed. But I was informed that I had been in that state for three days."

"I have had similar experiences during some of my trips to Akasha," Yeshua said.

"It was a first for me, grandmaster," Bai-Ming said. "I was confused when I awoke. Grandmaster Chang explained the meaning of the vision to me and told me that I had been tasked with finding the reincarnation of Grandmaster Wong."

"Hence, why you addressed me as 'Grandmaster Wong' when you first laid eyes on me?" asked Yeshua rhetorically.

"It was that and the glow, grandmaster," Bai-Ming explained. "The glow is so intense around you."

"The glow?" Rama asked.

"Oh, I am sorry, sir," Bai-Ming turned his attention towards the seer. "I meant that grandmaster here has the glow of the Buddha. You see, Grandmaster Chang personally gave me an accelerated tutelage on many things that would take most people lifetimes to learn. I underwent special esoteric surgeries for this reason."

Bai-Ming sipped from his cup of jasmine tea. He smacked his lips with savory delight.

"So, within the space of one year, I was trained on how to access the Realm of Records," Bai-Ming continued. "I believe you call it 'Akasha.' That is how I learned your language and many other things so quickly. Right now, I am adept at harnessing my chi, telepathy, clairvoyance, clairaudience, and teleportation."

Rama nodded slowly but said nothing as he gave Bai-Ming an esoteric scan. Bai-Ming had just passed his test without realizing he was being tested. The fact that Bai-Ming mentioned the glow of Yogi Yeshua's aura bespoke of Bai-Ming's genuineness. Bai-Ming turned to face young Yeshua.

"It is an honor to be in your presence, grandmaster," the monk said reverently.

"Please, brother," Yeshua said. "Could you not refer to me as 'grandmaster', since you already have one? I feel like it is disrespectful to Grandmaster Chang. I know you mean well, but could you please grant me this request?"

"As you wish, grand- I mean, master," Bai-Ming bowed slightly.

The festivities continued. Over the past six years, Ganesh and Yeshua had forged a strong bond that was beyond friendship. They were now siblings by adoption. As such, Ganesh's heart was heavy with sorrow.

"We are vegetarians because eating vegetables creates less of a karmic bind," Bai-Ming explained. "We hope you do not feel offended, your majesty."

"Of course not," King Rama said. "We are well accustomed to this lifestyle."

A week later, Yogi Yeshua was ready to depart with the monks. He bid his farewell to the royal family and to the friends he had made during his stay in India. Sadness at his departure smothered everyone everywhere.

"I will ride with you, at least until the end of our kingdom," Ganesh declared.

"My heart leaps with gladness to hear you say this, my prince," Yeshua said. "But do not burden yourself with all the supplies you have prepared for us. We will not need them."

Ganesh noticed for the first time that the monks themselves neither had horses nor supplies with them.

How could they have made such a long journey then? On foot? He wondered.

They arrived at the border. Yeshua, the monks, and Ganesh dismounted their horses. Ganesh pressed the hand of each monk and gave them his blessings. Then, he faced Yogi Yeshua. Both men's eyes brimmed with tears.

"I hope our paths will cross again," Ganesh spoke with a lump in his throat.

"They certainly will, brother," Yeshua assured him.

He extended his hand. Ganesh pressed it, and then both men crashed into each other in a tight embrace. The tears flowed freely and the two men burned with deep sadness.

"May the stars continue to look out for you, brother," Ganesh whispered.

"And you as well, brother," Yogi Yeshua replied.

They removed themselves from each other. Ganesh mounted his horse while Yogi Yeshua joined the monks. The monks sat on the ground in a square formation. Yogi Yeshua sat in the middle. The five of them closed their eyes and took three slow breaths. The monks then locked hands with one another and bowed their heads. All five men then took in one long, deep breath. Ganesh observed the situation without comprehension. He thought they were practicing an alien prayer ritual. But when the five men vanished from his sight in the blink of an eye, it all finally made sense to him. Teleportation was a lot more fascinating than he had expected.

***

Yeshua and the monks appeared in the main hall of the temple. Every monk in the monastery was present and waiting. The monks lined up on either side of the aisle leading to the altar. The temple was built with solid, polished wood that seemed to have withstood the test of time and the elements. The ceiling tapered upwards from four directions to a focal point in the center. A massive wooden column stood at each of the four corners of the temple. Symbols on the walls, holding meanings that eluded Yeshua for the moment, graced the walls of the temple. Unlike the palace in India, this temple was the very epitome of art without the splendor and décor of the wealthy.

Grandmaster Chang donned a red and orange garment wrapped around his body with his arms exposed, just like every other monk in the temple. A prayer bead rested in his left hand and he held a wooden staff in his right hand. His chair held nothing majestic or spectacular about it. A giant statue of the Buddha sitting cross-legged perched on a large table behind him. The statue was the only object in the temple that was covered in gold. Bai-Ming led Yeshua down the aisle to the bottom of the stairs that led up to the grandmaster's chair. Bai-Ming bowed his head and greeted the grandmaster. Yeshua followed suit. He had learned how to speak Mandarin within two days of Bai-Ming's arrival in India.

The grandmaster returned their greeting with a nod and stood up. His frail, five-foot form was a stark contrast to the strength of his gait as he walked. The wooden staff in his right hand looked like an emblem and a symbol of his authority and not a walking cane. His gaze remained razor sharp and focused on Yeshua. Five stairs away from Yeshua, Grandmaster Chang pointed his staff towards Yeshua. The bells of the temple gonged in unison of their own accord.

"He has the glow of the Buddha," Grandmaster Chang spoke in a raspy voice. "And his vibrations are almost in tune with that of The Sound."

Grandmaster Chang descended two more steps.

"Almost," he added. "Not there yet."

Grandmaster Chang then bowed slowly in Yogi Yeshua's direction, and every monk did the same.

"Welcome, young master," he said. "It is, indeed, an honor to have you in our midst, once again. I have longed for this day for a very long time."

Grandmaster Chang then turned around and started his ascent up the stairs to his chair before Yeshua could express his gratitude.

"Bai-Ming will be your personal attendant," he added.

"Thank you, Grandmaster." Yeshua replied. "The honor is all mine."

A senior monk who stood to the grandmaster's right stepped forward. He looked younger than Grandmaster Chang but much older than most of the other monks.

"Welcome once again, young master," he said and turned his attention towards Bai-Ming. "You may take him to his quarters now."

Bai-Ming bowed his head but as soon as they turned to leave, every monk in the temple suddenly crowded around Yeshua, Bai-Ming, and the three other monks. A cacophony of words erupted as every monk tried to gain access to Yeshua. The sound of a struck gong echoed across the temple, forcing the monks to cease their sudden congregation around Yeshua, Bai-Ming and the others.

"Please do not overwhelm the young master now," said the senior monk. "He will be with us for a while, and I am sure you will get the opportunity to meet and spend some time with him. But he must get settled in first."

The monks stepped away, clearing a path for Yeshua and Bai-Ming to leave the temple.

"Are you feeling alright, master?" Bai-Ming asked as they started walking down the half-a-mile path towards their living quarters.

"Yes, I am, brother," Yeshua replied.

Bai-Ming's heart glided at Yeshua referring to him as 'brother'.

"Apologies for my brothers' behavior earlier," Bai-Ming said. "They are just very excited. Your reputation precedes you."

"No need for apologies," Yeshua replied with a smile.

Moments later, Yeshua spoke.

"I miss my family a lot," he said. "This is part of the sacrifice I must make to resonate with my purpose."

"You will see them again, master," Bai-Ming assured him.

"I know," Yeshua agreed. "Still, my heart aches with longing for them."

They arrived at Yeshua's living quarters, which was a stark contrast to his chamber in India. The bed was small, barely large enough for his frame, with two thin mattresses stacked on top of each other. Yeshua deduced doubling his mattress was their definition of giving him special treatment. His eyes swept across the rest of the room that was no larger than fifteen-by-twenty feet and devoid of any furniture and naked maidens to give him baths. However, to say his living area was pristine was an understatement of epic proportion.

"Unless I am mistaken, master," Bai-Ming spoke after Yeshua had studied his new abode for a few moments, "you do not require food or drink. Correct?"

"Correct, brother. Thank you," Yeshua replied. "I am fine for now. I would like to know when I begin training, though."

"Grandmaster says tomorrow at first light," Bai-Ming replied.

"You must have enormous respect for grandmaster," Yeshua remarked. "The tone of your voice changes to underscore your sentiment towards him."

"He is like a father to me, master," Bai-Ming explained. "He pulled me away from the streets and gave me a new life and a new purpose in this brotherhood. I owe him my life."

Bai-Ming paused and smiled.

"If master pleases, one day I will share my story with him."

"Of course, brother," Yeshua replied. "I would love to know everything about you; without having to steal a glance at the Book of Remembrance."

Both men laughed heartily. Yeshua extended his right hand towards Bai-Ming and Bai-Ming looked at him quizzically.

"Where I come from," Yeshua explained, "men clasp forearms as a symbol of agreement, good fortune, and so on. But right here, right now, I extend my hand as a symbol of our growing brotherhood."

Bai-Ming grinned, nodded and extended his right hand in like manner. Both men clasped forearms. Yeshua placed his free left hand on Bai-Ming's right shoulder and squeezed gently.

"Thank you… brother," he said.

"The honor is all mine… master," Bai-Ming replied.

Yeshua shook his head in resignation.

He will never call me 'brother', Yeshua concluded.

"One more thing," Yeshua said suddenly remembering something.

"Anything, master," Bai-Ming replied.

"Well, now that I am one of you," he said, smiling mischievously, "when do I get to shave my head like everyone else?"

Bai-Ming grinned mischievously and dug into the front pouch of his garment. He brandished a razor.

"I think," Yeshua said, sparking the ethers into a wooden stool, "that you and I are going to be really good friends."

"Master," Bai-Ming said. "If you continue such profuse flattery, my ego will grow too big for this room to handle."

Both men laughed out loud as Bai-Ming began working the razor on Yeshua's head.

CHAPTER TWENTY

STICKS AND STONES, C. E. 32

"HUNGRY YET?" YESHUA asked.

"I just replenished, master," Yehuda replied confidently.

"Good," Yeshua nodded. "I am pleased with your progress thus far."

"Only because I have a great teacher," Yehuda replied.

"Walk with me," Yeshua said.

A few minutes of silence went by as they walked. They stopped at a boulder that was a little over half as high of the ground as they were tall. "Are you ready for your next lessons?" Yeshua asked.

"Yes, mast- AHHHHH."

Yehuda screamed as unexpected pain ripped through his body from his leg. He fell on the ground and made to reach for his right leg but every move he made fired up the pain even more. He glanced at the leg: a compound fracture of the tibia. Jagged edges of broken bones stuck out of torn flesh in a gruesome, picturesque poetry. Bile, gastric acid and the food he just filled his stomach with burned their way up his gullet and exited his mouth.

"First time seeing a fracture?" Yeshua asked with nonchalance.

"Yes," Yehuda grunted.

"Me too," Yeshua heaved his body and sat on the boulder. "Well then, let the training begin."

Yehuda stared at the master in total disbelief.

How can he be so cold? he wondered. *Can't he see I'm suffering? With just a thought he can make all this go away but there he is... Sitting there doing nothing.*

Yehuda grunted and groaned in agony.

And how did my leg... he continued to wonder but he had his answer before he finished his thought.

For a tiny moment, his anger overrode his pain and he glared at his mentor. *He did it. He did it.*

"If I had my way-" Yehuda started to say but stopped.

Yehuda looked around, teeth clattering, body shivering uncontrollably like a feather in the wind. A beautiful, cold-beyond-measure whiteness stretched as far as the eyes could see. With every whistle of the wind, the cold burned his skin. For a moment, the uncannily freezing temperatures numbed the pain in his leg for which he shivered his gratitude. Curiosity made him scoop some of the white substance on the ground in his stiffening palm. His fingers slowly darkened from frost bite. He closed his fist around it. It clumped in his hand. He opened his fist, with painful difficulty, and dropped the clump to the white ground. Yehuda tried to speak but realized his lips were frozen shut.

"Where are we, master?" Yehuda asked telepathically.

"This is a land in the very far south," Yeshua explained audibly. "Here, it is so cold that an unprotected human can die within minutes. What you see around you," he waved his hand around as he spoke, "is just hardened water. Sometimes, they form gigantic structures and sometimes, they form the fluffy substances you now sit on."

A field of warm surrounded Yehuda. His body lost its rigidity and he relaxed.

Master's doing, he surmised.

"I have never seen anything this beautiful," Yehuda marveled out loud.

"And now your training," Yeshua said.

The excruciating pain in his leg returned and Yehuda's scream was lost in the harsh, howling winds of the white desert.

"Get yourself out of this situation," Yeshua commanded.

Yehuda always considered himself a fighter. As such, even as his life slowly froze away he refused to give up. He pushed himself to sit upright, screaming in pain as he did. He then scooped up handfuls of the white substance and pressed it over the area of his leg where the jagged, broken bones stuck out. Relief was only temporary but welcome, nonetheless. Next, Yehuda sparked the ethers into two splints and some rope. He placed the splints on either side of his broken leg and tied them in place with the rope using telekinesis. Still, his life slowly ebbed away.

What now? he asked himself as he collapsed into the cold, white fluffiness.

A moment, which felt like an eternity, went by. He made up his mind.

"I do not know what else to do, Master."

"What do you mean, Yehuda?" the Master asked.

Yehuda pondered on the master's question.

"I do not know how to heal myself, and I do not know how to be a master over the

elements. Please teach me."

Suddenly, Yehuda felt a surge of energy infuse his body. Strength, vitality and, above all, warmth returned to his body. The fracture and their environment remained unchanged, though. He knew it was his master's doing.

"I will show you then, brother," Yeshua replied.

THE LIFE FORCE

Bai-Ming was waiting outside of Yehuda's chamber at first light. They walked towards the western section of the monastery, at the foot of the mountain. On the way, they passed several groups of monks performing synchronized routines: some used weapons like long staffs and swords while others did not. Some monks sat in rock-stiff poses. Some stood on one leg, others on their heads and a monk balanced his entire body on his left index finger.

"This is fascinating," Yeshua exclaimed.

"We call this 'kung-fu'," Bai-Ming explained. "It is a form of martial arts. We practice it for self-defense and to condition the mind and body. It is one of the many paths that one could use for inner peace. I can tell you more about that later. The other brothers you noticed in the strange positions are just meditating. Different paths, same destination."

"Destination..." Yeshua repeated.

"Do you have a different opinion, master?" Bai-Ming asked. "I always thought of life as a journey to a destination, which is ultimately enlightenment and liberation from the cycle of birth, death, and rebirth?"

"True, in some sense," Yeshua agreed. "This present life may be considered a journey and the total of all our experiences could also be classified as a path. But to speak of enlightenment as a destination is a contradiction itself. Think about it; does the term 'destination' itself not imply a starting and an ending point?"

"It does," Bai-Ming agreed, still unclear as to the point Yeshua was driving at.

"So, if enlightenment is a destination, then how can we talk of boundlessness and oneness with the Creator, who has no beginning or end?" Yeshua asked.

"I think I see what you are saying," Bai-Ming conceded.

"We need consistency in thought, word, and deed," Yeshua continued as they walked on. "I think it would be better to regard enlightenment as an awakening to who one is, or self-realization, instead of regarding it as a destination. And that awakening can only take place in the now because past and future are illusions."

"That makes a lot of sense," Bai-Ming seemed to have an epiphany. "Thank you very much, master."

"You are welcome, brother," Yeshua replied.

"Do you get attacked often?" Yeshua asked, wanting to change the subject for no reason. "I could not imagine a peaceful group like yours having enemies."

"No, we do not," Bai-Ming replied. "But unfortunately, I cannot say the same for other monasteries. Some of them have lost their way."

Bai-Ming sighed.

"So, it is not uncommon to hear of monasteries having rivalries with other monasteries, all in the name of pride. What a pity. We prefer not to meddle in such affairs. We just focus on our awakening."

"Because we are the way, the truth and the life," Yeshua added. "*Self*-realization or enlightenment is solely one's responsibility, not anyone else's."

"Indeed, we are, master," Bai-Ming concurred.

They arrived at the infirmary. Two monks groaned on wooden tables from their severe injuries after falling off the side of the mountain. One had a compound fracture in his left arm and the other had a crushed vertebra, just above his shoulder. He was paralyzed from the neck down. Grandmaster Chang regarded both monks with an expressionless gaze.

"Greetings, grandmaster," Bai-Ming and Yeshua greeted him.

"Greetings to you two," he returned their greeting and met Yeshua's gaze. "I hope you enjoyed a good night's rest, young master."

"I did, grandmaster, thank you," Yeshua replied. "Brother Bai-Ming saw to my accommodations."

"Right to the haircut, I see," the grandmaster said with a slight smile that was almost concealed by his long, white beard.

"Everyone, leave us," Grandmaster Chang spoke calmly but firmly.

The monks obeyed, leaving Grandmaster Chang and Yeshua alone with the injured monks. He approached the monk with the fractured arm.

"Your lesson will be on the chi," he said. "Do you know anything about it?"

"I am not sure, grandmaster," Yeshua replied.

"Chi," Grandmaster Chang began, "is the life force in everything, and yes, I mean everything. Everything is from the Source, is one with the Source and, hence, everything carries the Source within itself. Chi is like an extension of the Source. Therefore, it is described as the 'life force' of everything. Most people have only unconsciously accessed their chi. But if anyone can access their chi consciously at any time, then the possibilities will be endless."

He reached out to the monk with the broken arm and touched his arm. He closed his eyes and slowly breathed in and out three times. Suddenly, the monk's arm straightened out, and the fracture became whole. The monk sat up and massaged the area on his arm that used to be fractured. He stared in disbelief at his grandmaster before he fell to his knees and bowed at the grandmaster's feet.

"Thank you, grandmaster, thank you," he said repeatedly.

"Go now," Grandmaster Chang said. "You have duties to attend to."

The monk stood up, bowed once before bolting out of the infirmary.

"So, if I can gain mastery over this life force," Yeshua spoke as if nothing had just happened, "I can heal the sick, revitalize the body and even-"

"Raise the dead?" the grandmaster finished Yeshua's question as he walked towards the other monk, who was paralyzed from the neck down, and placed his hand on the monk's head.

"Yes, you can," Grandmaster Chang replied. "You can even rejuvenate the human form over and over. In our tradition, the chi is like a well that never runs dry, and anyone can always drink from it. This is the true panacea for all ailments, the real elixir of life, and a fountain of eternal youth."

Grandmaster Chang removed his hand from the monk's forehead and motioned to Yeshua. Yeshua stepped forward and placed his right hand on the monk's forehead.

"Do not fear, brother," he said. "Healing will be yours shortly."

Then, he closed his eyes.

Yeshua visualized himself as a being of light and colors. He held on to this image and filtered out the colors until only a white brilliance remained as his body. This body lost some of its brilliance and became transparent. He focused on his heart region and chose this as the source of his chi. He imagined chi pulsating from this region as beams of light. The pulsating beams grew bigger and brighter as it spread out and filled up his body of light, causing his body to lose its transparency. He became an embodiment of chi. Yeshua then shifted his focus to his right hand, and he imagined his right hand pulsating with chi.

Every cell of his physical body burst with surging energy as his chi throbbed across his body. His body vibrated with an aliveness unlike anything he had ever felt before and, for a split second, he fell into his ego. When he realized this, he quickly opened his eyes to end his vision and regarded the monk, fear written over his face regarding possibly hurting the monk at an etheric level instead of healing him. However, the paralyzed monk's body glowed with a brightness that further lit up the somber infirmary. The monk sat up, brought his hands in front of his face and examined his entire body, a look of awe and excitement gracing his features. Gone was his paralysis. Yeshua opened his right hand towards the monk. The brilliance of the monk's body gradually faded as he reduced the intensity of the monk's activated chi. The monk regarded Yeshua, mouth agape, before he fell at Yeshua's feet.

"You have duties to attend to," Grandmaster Chang said.

"Yes, grandmaster," the monk replied and scurried away.

Grandmaster Chang turned a hard stare towards Yeshua and Yeshua cowered.

"We have some fine-tuning to do," Grandmaster Chang said.

"I am your humble student, grandmaster," Yeshua replied.

***

"Now, apply the same to your leg," Yeshua encouraged Yehuda.

The full blast of the white, hot pain of the fracture slapped Yehuda in the face once again. He gritted his teeth to fight the pain, tried to focus and failed.

"Visualize," Yeshua commanded.

Yehuda growled in frustration.

"Pain is only an illusion," Yeshua spoke more firmly. "Suffering is a choice. You are the one in charge, not the pain. Seize it. Own it. Take dominion over this situation."

And as the master pressed on, the apprentice had his epiphany.

In the eye of the storm is stillness. In the center of the spinning wheel is stillness. The waves may rage, but the bottom of the sea is still. Greater is what lies within you than what lies outside of you. If you find yourself outside the stillness, then you will find yourself outside of peace. You are the immovable mountain in the onslaught of the wind. Be the one with the dominion. Be the stillness and not the storm.

Yehuda had never understood the master's words then. But now, in his hour of desperation, the master's words finally made sense to him. He closed his eyes and breathed in and out as slowly as he could. He shifted his focus from the pain in his leg to his breathing. The pain subsided with his shift in focus. The slower he breathed, the more the pain subsided. Using clairvoyance, he perceived his aura changing colors from red to faint yellow. Then, he opened his eyes and gazed upon his fractured leg. The pain was completely gone.

First step, Yehuda said to himself.

"Excellent," Yeshua said. "Now, heal your leg."

Yehuda nodded and closed his eyes again. He visualized himself as a human silhouette on a white piece of cloth. He then mentally cut out that silhouette from the piece of cloth and gave it a three-dimensional form.

This form is dark and needs light, he thought.

Yehuda visualized an oil lamp in the heart region of the silhouette. He summoned a flame and lit the lamp, which burned with a bright white flame. The light from the flame increased in intensity, spreading from the heart region to light up the entire body. Every cell in his body burst with a surge of energy

174

and an aliveness like he had never felt before.

So, this is what supercharged chi feels like, he thought. *I never would've understood it no matter how many times or how hard Master explained. This is something that can only be understood experientially.*

He opened his eyes.

Stay focused now, he reminded himself.

Yehuda brought his right hand to eye level and focused on it. Suddenly, a non-consuming, heatless, white flame burst forth from his hand.

I choose to manifest this chi energy as a flame, he said to himself.

He turned his right palm towards his fractured leg. The flame slowly extended from his hand to the leg. It encompassed the fractured area, fusing the broken tibia to one piece and putting the flesh back together. Yehuda breathed in and out slowly. This time, he reduced the intensity of his chi. The flame around his hand and leg gradually died down with the decrease in his chi's intensity. He closed and opened his right, non-flaming fist and glanced at his leg. His leg looked like it had never as much as received a scratch in his life.

A sudden assault of a killer-freeze washed over Yehuda. He cringed from the onslaught and shivered uncontrollably.

"You removed the protection field, master," he said via telepathy.

"You know what you must do," Yeshua replied in like manner.

Once again, Yehuda supercharged his chi. The winds howled the white substance into a near-blinding whiteout. Yet, he remained impervious to these harsh, inhumane elements. He stood up and flexed his shoulders and neck.

"I am the eye of the storm, the center of the spinning wheel," he muttered.

Yeshua watched with pride as a perfect circle of about two meters in diameter melted into water and seeped into the ground. He switched to clairvoyance and saw a bubble of supercharged chi energy forming and growing around Yehuda as intense heat. He smiled and fondly recalled his days with Grandmaster Chang on the mountain and how they boiled water for tea using their supercharged chi.

"Well done, brother," said Yeshua. "You will keep practicing, yes?"

"Yes, master," Yehuda beamed with excitement. "Thank you very much."

Yeshua teleported them back to the same boulder on the same hill where Yehuda had his fracture.

"No one noticed our sudden appearance, Master," Yehuda observed.

"And no one noticed we were ever here in the first place," Yeshua added.

"How?" Yehuda asked.

"Another lesson for another time," Yeshua replied

***

Yeshua stayed at the monastery for six years. He lived as one of them and learned their ways. He performed the chores they performed, he shared in their meals and even went out with them to nearby towns to teach and perform community services. The locals treated him as one of theirs, though he was a foreigner. Over the years, he became more adept at many things, including martial arts. The concept of martial arts was alien to him at first. But once he started learning, he did not stop. He blamed Master Chu, the *gung fu* instructor, for his love of the art.

"*Gung fu*," Master Chu said, "simply refers to any skill that has been perfected over time with training, patience, and purpose. For us at the monastery, martial arts is not just for self-defense. You see, young master, *gung fu* also means 'an achievement,' as well as 'man.' So, it the grand scheme of things, *gung fu* simply means 'an achievement of man'. And what is the ultimate achievement of man? Enlightenment. Therefore, young master, we practice *gung fu* as another path towards enlightenment."

"What about Tai Chi, master?" Yeshua asked.

"Oh, that," Master Chu exclaimed, excitement beaming from his eyes.

"Tai chi is about the flow of energy. Meeting resistance with resistance will only cause more resistance. The yin and the yang must coexist. Hence, in tai chi, resistance meets non-resistance."

"So, by extension," Yeshua interjected, "tai chi is simply offering the attacker no resistance? Like turning the other cheek if one slaps you? And if they want to take something by force, like your coat, you let them have it?"

"Very insightful, young master," Master Chu agreed. 'Through tai chi, we learn non-resistance and non-attachment."

On the eve of Yeshua's departure from the monastery, Grandmaster Chang summoned him. They went to a hall south of the monastery, 30x10x15 cubic feet. It contained twelve life-sized statues of monks perched in Buddha poses. Six statues lined either side of the hall.

"These, young master," Grandmaster Chang said, "are the mummies of our greatest grandmasters. Not every grandmaster gets mummified; just the great ones, those who became enlightened."

Yeshua nodded with awe, respect and reverence. He walked along the statues on the left until he stopped at the sixth one and stared unblinkingly at the statue.

"You recognize yourself, young master," the grandmaster's raspy voice peeled through the silence.

Yeshua remained silent. Grandmaster Chang walked and stood next to him.

"Grandmaster Wong," Yeshua whispered.

"It is truly an honor to be in the presence of two incarnations of the same grandmaster at the same time," Grandmaster Chang said reverently. "Yes, young master, you are his incarnation. It was your consciousness, as well as his, which knows no time or space, that chose Bai-Ming to seek you out in India. Perhaps that is why you felt so much at home right from your first day here."

Yeshua said nothing. The ethereal connection between his present and past incarnations took a lifeform and energy of its own. He stretched his left hand towards the statue, which glowed into a golden brightness that lit up the entire hall. Yeshua smiled and Grandmaster Chang bowed his bald head. He retracted his hand and the brightness dimmed until it disappeared. Moments later, both men began their return walk towards the temple.

"Thank you very much for bringing me here and showing me all of this, grandmaster," Yeshua said gratefully.

"The honor is mine, young master," Grandmaster Chang replied.

The following day at sunset, all the monks gathered to bid the young master farewell. He pressed many hands and gave many hugs. The main temple thronged with the combined feeling of sadness for his departure. Yeshua had made great friends, had found another family and had learned so much. Bai-Ming seemed to be the saddest of them all. Yeshua hugged him the longest.

"You have been a true brother to me," Yeshua whispered into his ear.

"As you have been to me," Bai-Ming replied, fighting the lump in his throat.

"Our paths will cross again," Yeshua said and removed himself from their hug. "This I promise you."

"I look forward to that day, master," Bai-Ming forced a smile.

Yeshua turned to face Grandmaster Chang. He dropped to a knee and bowed his head.

"May the blessings of the Buddha follow you to the end of your days and beyond, young master," Grandmaster Chang bowed his head. "Farewell to you."

"Thank you, grandmaster," Yeshua stood up. "Farewell."

He turned around and faced the rest of the monks.

"Farewell, brothers," he said.

"Farewell, master," they chorused.

Yeshua disappeared from their sight.

While in mid-teleportation, Yeshua hovered for a moment over the Pyramids of Giza. They never ceased to take his breath away, even when he viewed them from the Akashic Records. A blink-of-an-eye later, he appeared within the temple walls of a monastery in Heliopolis. Eight men wearing brown robes of priests bowed their heads towards him in welcome. A ninth priest, who looked like their leader, wore a black robe with a white belt around his waist. A golden necklace hung from his neck. A pendant designed like the sun, with rays of light streaming from it, hung from the necklace. He stepped forward and dropped to a knee in front of Yeshua. Yeshua appraised his surroundings and nodded his approval.

"Not much has changed since I left," Yeshua said.

The priest smiled and rose to his feet.

"Welcome to the Monastery of Melchizedek, master," he said. "I am Salemwalek, head priest and your direct descendant by more than forty-nine generations. So, forgive me, for I am not sure how to address you. After all, you named this monastery, and rightfully so, after yourself."

"I know, Salem," Yeshua replied.

Yeshua walked towards his much older descendant and hugged him.

"I remember."

CHAPTER TWENTY-ONE

C. E. 33

NISAN 13TH, PASSOVER time. Israel was abuzz with preparations for this yearly feast. Yeshua waited for Shi'mon by the boats. At the ninth hour, the skies promised no rain, despite the winds blowing from the east indicating the contrary. Rainfall was the least of Yeshua's worries, though; if he had any worries, that is. The end of his sojourn here on Earth Realm in his current form drew close. A glimpse into the future revealed that, in a few hours, the same people who hailed him as king less than a week ago were going to condemn him as a criminal.

"All part of the plan," he muttered.

Shi'mon joined him a few minutes later, face contorted in a scowl and lips pursed behind his thick beard.

"Is everything alright, brother?" Yeshua asked.

"Just Rania, master," Shi'mon replied.

"Is that all?" Yeshua asked further.

"I don't follow, master," Shi'mon said and avoided making eye contact with his mentor.

"You know what I mean," Yeshua said.

"I am not sure, master," Shi'mon admitted with a sigh of resignation. "I am just angry and frustrated."

"Those are carefully chosen words," Yeshua said. "Is there something on your mind you would like to share with me?"

"You can read my mind, master," Shi'mon replied with a tone of sarcasm.

"I only read your mind if you want me to, brother," Yeshua assured him. "And if you chose not to share, then so be it."

He waited for Shi'mon's reply. But, sensing Shi'mon's discomfort, he decided to abandon the subject.

"Anyway, do you know why we are here?" Yeshua asked.

"No, master," Shi'mon replied, exhaling with gratitude.

"I just wanted us to sit here and enjoy the breeze and the birds," Yeshua smiled and waved his hands elegantly over the waters.

"I never took you for a poet, master," Shi'mon managed a smile.

"Well," Yeshua's tone of voice turned serious. "I thought we could do a recap of your progress over the past three years. I have taught you so much and there is more I can teach you; but you are not ready yet, and certain things are best learned from experience. Soullessness is a good example. I could give you an idea of what to expect, if you'd like."

Yeshua noticed Shi'mon's features tense up a little and he understood why.

"It is not too late to change your mind, brother," Yeshua continued. "I will not be disappointed if you do and I will not judge you."

Clairvoyance revealed that Shi'mon's aura was a mélange of constantly changing colors. The Master nodded slightly.

"I would be lying if I said I am not afraid, master," Shi'mon said. "But, like you taught me, everything happens for a reason and everything has a purpose. You have introduced me to my purpose, and I have been your apprentice for this reason. Though I may not understand the burden I must bear in the future, I am deeply honored to be your apprentice, no matter the cost to me. For humanity's sake and for the sake of the realm, I gladly accept my path."

"And I give you my word, you will not walk alone, brother," Yeshua promised. "Trials and tribulations will abound and, just like everyone else, you will have your moments of weakness."

Yeshua crouched and ran his fingers in the water with an absent-mindedness that confused Shi'mon.

"This is my advice to you," he spoke firmly. "When the time comes, and you find yourself in dark times, remind yourself that the mission comes first. No matter what you feel, no matter what you want, remember, the mission comes first. And what is your mission?"

"To protect Earth Realm and humanity at all cost," Shi'mon replied.

Yeshua stood and faced Shi'mon.

"Good," Yeshua said. "Now, I know how you feel towards Yehuda."

Shi'mon stiffened, and the veins in his temple stood out.

"He did something terrible, master," Shi'mon hissed with hatred.

"Well, whatever you think he has done," Yeshua spoke calmly, "he will do something much worse. If you think you hate him right now, then wait until you see what he will do shortly."

Shi'mon turned pale with shock.

Does Master know what Yehuda did and cares not? he wondered. *Or is he in denial? I hope it is the latter because, if it is the former, then my faith in Master stands on weak ground.*

"If only you knew, master," Shi'mon sighed.

"I can tell you what I do know, brother," Yeshua said. "How loyal would you say you are to me?" he asked.

"To the death, master," Shi'mon replied without any hesitation.

"And I believe you," Yeshua said. "However, I also know tomorrow after we eat the Passover meal together, you will deny me. And to remind you of what I have just told you, the rooster will crow after the third time you deny me."

Shi'mon stared blankly at Yeshua for a moment before he burst into fits of side-clutching laughter.

"Forgive me, Master," he said amidst fits of laughter. "I never thought I would hear such madness from your lips. This is the second time you are telling me this. The first time, I passed it for a joke. But when you said it again just now, I do not know why but I could not help myself."

Shi'mon dabbed at his eyes that welled up with tears of laughter.

"I am glad tomorrow is only a few hours away. I will look at you in the face and remind you of this very moment."

Shi'mon roared with laughter, eliciting a kind smile from Yeshua.

"I am pleased to see you in such a good mood, brother," Yeshua chuckled.

"Forgive me, Master," Shi'mon wiped tears of laughter from his eyes and laughed some more.

"Anyway, I pray I am wrong," Yeshua replied.

Then, as if to cry for the master, droplets of rain fell from the skies as master and apprentice chose to walk, rather than teleport, to their respective homes.

***

"I would like to speak with the high priest," said Yehuda to the guard at the entrance to the temple.

A cauldron of raging emotions boiled in his heart. After the long talk with the master a few hours earlier, he had decided this was his best option.

"Do you not know what time of the year it is?" the guard frowned at him.

"Yes, sir, I am aware," Yehuda replied with impatience.

Three years ago, he would not have dared such boldness at a temple guard, or any guard for that matter. But today, he would spit in the face of Caesar himself, if he had to.

"Then you must know, peasant," the guard sneered at the word 'peasant', "that the high priest is very indisposed."

"It is a matter of utmost importance," Yehuda gritted his teeth, trying hard to control his temper.

"Be gone now, peasant," the guard ordered. "Do you not have a feast to prepare for?"

"Please do not make me do this," Yehuda admonished.

The guard shot an incredulous look at Yehuda before he broke into laughter.

"You are even more stupid than you look," the guard spat with spite. "And just what do you think you can do?"

Yehuda closed his eyes and bowed his head. He wrestled with a few options.

Option #1: turn around and walk away.

But I must have audience with the High Priest.

Option #2: teleport into the temple and speak directly to the High Priest.

Such a grand entrance will only incite trouble, for obvious reasons.

Option #3: physically neutralize the guard and everyone who got in his way.

It will cause a ruckus and erase my chance of having an audience with the High Priest.

Yehuda made up his mind, lifted his head up and stared at the guard.

"Look into my eyes," Yehuda commanded.

Yehuda's sudden change of tone made the guard do as he was commanded. The guard's features softened, his arms fell to the side and his spear clanged on the stony stairs at the entrance.

Sorry, Master, Yehuda thought. *I know you forbade us from using our training for now. But these are desperate times.*

"From now on you will do exactly as I say," Yehuda commanded. "Your thoughts, words and deeds, your will, are all under my control."

Yehuda breathed in deeply to calm his raging emotions, while the guard stared blankly ahead.

"Now, you will take me to the high priest."

Nefiki, the high priest, sat in council with a few priests and temple officials but they were not discussing anything about the Passover.

"Some call him a prophet," one priest said.

"Others call him the Messiah, son of Yahweh," another added.

"But how can he be the Messiah when we still are under Roman rule?" asked another priest. "Where is his army? Where is his glory?"

"We know he is no Messiah and he certainly is no son of Yahweh."

"Yahweh was no carpenter."

"He is a blasphemer and a demon."

"Then how else could he perform those great works of healing?"

"Like I said… demon."

Nods of agreement followed.

"Surely, he is gaining a strong following."

"And that is why, fellow brothers," Nefiki finally spoke up, and everyone fell silent, "we must put this blasphemy and outrage to an end. This man, Yeshua, must be stopped."

"Can any of us even identify this man? I mean, we have heard of him, but I do not think any of us knows what he looks like, right?"

"I can assist you with that," Yehuda's voice startled everyone in the room.

They had not heard him coming in.

"How did you get in here?" Nefiki asked. "Leave at once, before I summon the guards."

"I would suggest you seize an opportunity while it is available," Yehuda said, stepping further into the room. "Like I said, I can identify this man, Yeshua."

"You speak as if you know this blasphemer personally," said one priest.

"I am an apprentice of his," Yehuda replied. "My name is Yehuda, and I have walked with Yeshua, of whom you seek, for three years now."

"And how do we know we can trust you?" Nefiki asked, eyeing Yehuda with suspicion. "Surely, anyone who is ready to betray his master cannot be trusted."

"You do not, High Priest," Yehuda replied flatly. "Besides, you falsely assume this arrangement would be based on trust."

Murmurs filled the room as the priests and high priest weighed their options.

"What will you gain from betraying your master?" Nefiki asked Yehuda.

The murmuring ceased.

"That is no concern of yours," Yehuda replied with impatience. "You focus on your end of our arrangement and I will focus on mine. This is a one-time deal; you can either take it or leave it."

More murmuring ensued as the priests deliberated on their options. Yehuda considered using clairaudience to eavesdrop on their thoughts but changed his mind. Finally, Nefiki raised his right hand and silence followed.

"Alright, stranger," Nefiki said. "We will take your offer. What is your fee?"

"Forty pieces of silver," Yehuda replied.

"Twenty," Nefiki counteroffered.

Yehuda turned around to walk away.

"Thirty," Nefiki called out. "That is the most we can offer."

Yehuda paused in mid-step and pretended to consider the offer. He could care less for any payment, but he had to make a case for this brood of vipers who called themselves priests.

"Tomorrow, after the Passover meal, I will meet you here and take you to him," Yehuda replied without turning around to face the priests. "When you have him in your custody, you can pay me then."

Yehuda then turned around and faced them.

"And please, for your sake, do not double-cross me," he warned.

He turned around to walk away.

"And if we do?" asked a priest.

As soon as he asked the question, he screamed in pain and crashed to the floor in a fetal position. Yehuda heard him writhing on the floor as he screamed and begged for the pain to end.

"Like I said, do not double-cross me," Yehuda reiterated.

He released his telekinetic squeeze on the priest's intestines before he walked away and faded into the shadows of the temple.

**

The twelve apprentices of Yeshua engaged in conversations at the dinner table while waiting for their master. The Passover meal included a lamb shank, bitter herbs, non-bitter herbs, eggs, a mixture of nuts, apple and wine, amongst other food items. Each of these food types held symbolic importance to this feast. Yehuda and Shi'mon sat at opposite ends of the dinner table. To keep the peace during the feast, they had come to a temporary truce.

"But you will answer for your acts," Shi'mon had promised.

"Ok, father," Yehuda had replied with spiteful contempt.

Yeshua walked in with his wife, Miryam of Magdala. She glowed more than normal and appeared to have gained some weight. The apprentices did not expect Yeshua to bring her along and had reserved space for him alone, but that quickly changed as they rearranged their seating to accommodate her. She sat at her husband's right-hand. Some of the apprentices grumbled their disappointment at Yeshua for bringing his wife, when he asked them to leave their wives at home.

"My brothers," said Yeshua. "Thank you all for accepting to eat this Passover with me. My sincere apologies for asking you to leave your families behind and please convey my apologies and gratitude to them for their understanding."

"It is our honor, master," Yochanan said.

"Speak for yourself," Nathanael joked. "You're neither a husband nor father."

"And whose fault is that?" Yochanan asked, grinning.

"Pay him no mind, Nathanael," Mattityahu said. "He cannot understand. But we all know why he takes such long baths."

"Ha," Yochanan mocked as everyone else burst out laughing.

Miryam bowed her head to hide her embarrassment. She stifled her laughter.

"Brothers, we have a lady in our midst," Yeshua said between chuckles.

"Your problem, Master," Mattityahu replied. "You brought her."

After the laughter subsided and Yochanan no longer blushed too much from embarrassment, Yeshua resumed speaking.

"So, as I was saying," he said. 'Thank you all for coming to dine with me. I asked that we have this Passover meal just us, master and apprentices and that is why I brought my wife, Miryam. She, too, has been my apprentice all along."

Every apprentice gasped with genuine surprise, including Yehuda.

"She has, in fact, received the same amount of training you all have," he continued. "So, please welcome her, not as my wife, but as one of us. She is my wife, but Shi'mon is your leader, and as such, Shi'mon is also her leader."

Shi'mon stared daggers in Yehuda's direction but Yehuda ignored him.

"You two better behave yourselves," Yeshua scolded Shi'mon and Yehuda via telepathy. *"At least, for tonight."*

Both men seemed to relax.

"Just like each of you," Yeshua continued, "she has a mission and purpose. Eventually, you will understand. You will all understand the grand purpose."

"I think I speak for all of us, master," Shi'mon chimed in. "That we are honored to have Miryam as one of us. So, dear sister, welcome."

Everyone welcomed Miryam.

"Thank you all… my brothers," she hesitated.

A round of applause followed her words.

"Good," Yeshua said. "I can now share some wonderful news with you all. Miryam is with child-"

No one paid any attention to what he said after that. Slaps on the back, hugs and kisses on Miryam's cheeks, as well as congratulatory messages followed Yeshua's announcement. Yeshua smiled and Miryam beamed with pride. Her words of gratitude were drowned in her brothers' celebration.

"Long overdue, master," Nathanael exclaimed.

"Why do you say that, brother?" Yeshua chuckled.

He had a fair expectation of the response to follow.

A few of the apprentices tried to motion Nathanael not to speak, but they were too late.

"Well, master," Nathanael cleared his throat which suddenly felt parched. "Some of us worried that perhaps you were not able to… you know…" he trailed off. "I mean, after three years of marriage, you two still had no children. So, we were wondering if you were not doing your job or if you were unable to."

Nathaniel lowered his head in embarrassment.

"But then," Tau'ma interjected. "You walked on water and even brought Lazarus back from the dead. So, we were baffled. If you could do all these things, then how come you two did not have children after three years of marriage?"

Yeshua roared with laughter, much to everyone's relief that he did not take their words the wrong way.

"Brothers," Yeshua said amidst fits of laughter. "We did not have any children until now for a reason. But I hope your worries have been addressed?"

"They sure have," Nathanael said. "You see, Yoch," he turned his attention towards Yochanan. "Even Master is a busy man. I would suggest you take some lessons from him, especially since you are the youngest of us."

A round of laugher erupted across the room. Even Miryam joined in.

"Let us begin with the feast, brothers," Yeshua said.

They said prayers and began feasting. For a moment, nothing but quiet chats and cutlery tapping against cutlery filled the room. Yeshua observed them.

They still do not fully understand the task ahead, he thought. *Yet, they follow me with unwavering faith. My family..*

"Brothers and wife, there is something I must tell you," Yeshua said.

A deathly silence swept across the room. Yeshua took a sip of wine and placed the cup on the table.

"This is my last meal with you in the flesh," he said

Immediately, a chorus of gasps and exclamations erupted. Miryam turned pale and placed her hand on her belly. She opened her mouth to speak, but no words could come out of her mouth.

"What do you mean, master?" Tau'ma asked.

The others joined in chorus. Only Yehuda and Shi'mon seemed oblivious to what was going on. Both men were too involved in a death-staring competition with each other. Yeshua raised his hand for silence.

"Tonight, one of you will betray me," Yeshua explained.

Another round of ruckus broke out. Again, he raised his left hand for silence. He sipped some more wine and placed the cup on the table.

"As I was saying," Yeshua continued. "This is my last meal with you in this form. One of you will betray me. I will be arrested, tortured and killed. This is how it is meant to be. It will be a huge burden for this person to carry. It may be easy for you all, because you do not see the grand plan, but I implore you all not to judge him."

"I cannot guarantee that, master," Shi'mon countered.

"Then maybe you should consider this as a test of your leadership, Shi'mon," Yeshua replied.

Shi'mon noticed that the master called him by his first name and recognized it was as close to a public reprimand as it could get.

"Yes, master," Shi'mon replied sourly. "I will do my best."

If looks could kill, Yehuda would have been chopped to pieces and dumped into Gehenna as Shi'mon glared at him.

"When I am gone," Yeshua continued, "you will be in a state of fear and confusion. But take heart for I will only depart from you in this present form.

You must stay true to what I have taught you and most of all, stay true to one another. This is my final commandment to you all; that you love one another as I have loved you. You must be a beacon of light for the realm. This is the birth of a new age, and the Cosmic Clock is winding down to another Great Reset. I would stay and walk with you a while longer, but alas, I must leave you in this form. I have pressing matters to address within Creation."

Tears were already streaming down Miryam's eyes, and the other apprentices' shoulders slumped with deep sadness. Miryam lay on her husband's chest as he spoke and sobbed silently. She was, after all, the apprentice whom Yeshua loved the most. He put a comforting arm around her shoulder. For a moment, even Shi'mon's anger at Yehuda gave way to sympathy, and Yehuda's heart was rent in twain. Yehuda bowed his head slightly as he considered changing his mind about betraying his master; but his purpose beckoned like a siren's call. He steeled his resolve.

If I am to be vilified, hated, and despised for all eternity, then so be it. I shall play his part in preserving humanity.

Yehuda turned his attention towards Shi'mon. He did not need clairsentience to feel Shi'mon's hatred towards him. He turned towards Miryam sobbing on Yeshua's chest. He met his master's gaze and saw the encouraging smile on his master's face. He closed his eyes, took in a deep breath and strengthened his resolve even more.

"Who will betray you tonight, master?" Yoch asked.

"I will not say his name," Yeshua replied.

The apprentices eyed one another suspiciously.

"I hope for his sake," Shi'mon said. "That I never find out."

He then turned his attention towards Yehuda.

"I may have to make him pay."

"I have no doubt that your pride will lead you straight to that," Yehuda replied, leaning forward and looking straight in Shi'mon's eyes. "And I also have no doubt that he would love to see you try."

"I am looking forward to it," Shi'mon added and smiled wickedly behind his beard.

"I trust you are, *brother*," Yehuda sneered at the word 'brother.'

The other apprentices stared at Shi'mon and Yehuda in confusion.

"The one who will betray me," Yeshua interjected to defuse the situation, "will dip his bread in the bowl at the same time with me. But please, brothers, let this news not burden our hearts thus. Tonight, we celebrate the Passover, no? So, let us make great use of this meal before us."

Yeshua's attempt to bring to happiness to the sour and sad atmosphere in the room was feeble. Nonetheless, everyone obliged.

The dining resumed with less gusto than that before Yeshua broke the news to them and conversations came in whispers. The apprentices avoided eating anything near their master because they feared being the betrayer. However, the bowl containing the bread on Yehuda's side of the table ran out of bread. So, he walked to the center to get some more. He broke off a piece and remembered he forgot his soup bowl on his side of the table.

I shall just dip my bread in this soup bowl here before I return to my seat, he decided.

For some reason, his empty seat distracted him as he reached to dip his piece of bread in the soup bowl in front of him. His hand collided with another hand. He turned his head around and realized his hand was in the same soup bowl as Yeshua's. Yeshua smiled weakly, and Yehuda's heart broke into too many pieces to count. Only Miryam, Yochanan, and Shi'mon noticed what just happened. Miryam and Yochanan froze in shock while Shi'mon glared daggers at Yehuda.

I swear on my honor that Yehuda must die, Shi'mon promised himself.

"It is okay, brother," Yeshua reassured Yehuda telepathically. *"Fulfill your purpose. Do what you must."*

And without saying a word, Yehuda left the room and ran into the night to meet with High Priest Nefiki and his crew to finalize his betrayal of the master.

CHAPTER TWENTY-TWO

EGYPT, 25 – 30 C. E.

YESHUA ROUSED FROM slumber and stretched his muscles.

I am here, he studied his surroundings. *Good. My one-week, nonstop meditation yoga successfully sent my soul here. Salem and the others must be tending to my physical body back at the temple.*

***

Yeshua took the first week after his arrival at the Temple of Melchizedek to adjust his esoteric energies to resonate with those of the temple. The temple still buzzed with strong esoteric energies that Melchizedek, a past incarnation of his, had left behind over 3,000 years after his 'departure', which many mistook for his death. On the second week, though, Yeshua received an unconscious telepathic message from his mother.

"Where are you my son? Your father is dead and you are not here to bury him."

His clairsentience picked up her sorrow, grief and pain. His heart shattered to splinters. He wrestled with his painful emotions and thoughts.

Could I have saved him? Of course, I could have. There are few things that I cannot do.

If it was his time, would I have prevented it?

Is his death part of my training? A test?

Why did he die now, while I am still away from home, and while I am about to complete my training?

Why am I feeling this way? Who is feeling this way?

Like a leave in a storm, his mind went on a rampage with these questions and more, while his heart throbbed to the frequency of too many emotions to process consciously at the same time… until alas, he found his peace and clarity of mind. Yeshua then separated his astral form from his body and projected it to his father's house to attend his father's funeral. His physical presence would have been the reason for too much distraction on such a solemn day of mourning. Plus, the hour was not yet perfect for his return to them in physical form. Extended family, friends and well-wishers gathered at the funeral, many of whom he recognized. His siblings had all grown up and had little children of their own. They did their best to comfort their mother and grandmother, who lay on the floor in a helpless, grieving and sorrowful mess.

I miss them so much, he said to himself. *I have been away for too long.*

Yeshua wept.

He wept for himself but mostly for them; for their ignorance of the grandeur of Creation. For the blanket of blissful darkness draped over their awareness.

They mourn for their father and grandfather, as if life ends at death. If only they knew that death is only the beginning; that death is liberating, that death is but a doorway to something much, much bigger than life on Earth Realm for, in death, the boundaries of the physical form are broken and that which is beyond the physical is set free.

Suddenly, his mother sat up and narrowed her eyes with intense concentration in his general direction. Then, her eyes swept around the room, as if searching for something.

"What is it, grandmother?" asked a little boy.

Miryam, Yeshua's mother, kissed the little boy on the forehead and took his fluffy cheek in her left hand.

"Nothing, my child," she sniveled. "I... I just..."

Again, she broke down and fell to the floor and wept.

"Where are you, Yeshua?" she sobbed. "Your father is dead. Where are you to bury your father?"

Yeshua's astral form glided towards his mother and lay next to her on the floor. He took her in his arms, fully aware that she could not feel his astral form with her physical body.

"Right here, mother," he said telepathically. *"Right here."*

He knew she could not hear him. Yet, as if guided by a bond between mother and son too strong to break and which transcended three-dimensional physicality, she reached with her left hand and placed it on her right shoulder, where his astral hand settled. Her sobs subsided, and she closed her eyes.

"I know you are here, my son," she said. "Somehow, I feel your presence and it gives me great joy and comfort. I love you so much, with all that I have and with all that I am."

"I love you too, mother," Yeshua said telepathically as tears of joy and peace raced down his cheeks. His tears left wet marks on the floor behind his mother's occiput that the normal human eye could see.

***

Yeshua examined his immediate environment, which vibrated at a frequency much higher than that of Earth Realm's. The floors, walls, and ceiling seemed to be forged from a seamless and flawless piece of white marble. Even the bed seemed to be a part of this single structure. He ran his hands along his garments. They reminded him of his robes in India, only this one felt much softer and smoother to the touch. He had never seen fabric so... he lacked a good word to describe it. He dug his fingers three times into the mattress.

So plush and comfortable.

Yeshua closed his eyes and fell backwards into the bed, relishing in the feel of the mattress hugging and caressing his body.

"Pleased to see you are making yourself comfortable.".

The voice was feminine and omni-directional. Yeshua remained unmoved and unperturbed by the voice.

"I am pleased as well," Yeshua stared blankly at the ceiling.

"Do you know where you are, Yeshua?" asked the feminine voice.

Yeshua's ethereal body tingled to the seduction in the voice.

"No, I do not," he propped himself on his elbows. "But I have a feeling you will be telling me very soon."

His soul resonated to the presence of a familiar esoteric signature. About 30ft away from him, the silhouette of a woman began manifesting and walking slowly towards him. The more it manifested and looked human, the more Yeshua appreciated perfection in the flesh, from the shape of her toes, her knees, hips, core, bosom, neck and finally her face. A piece of pure, white cloth barely covered her ample breasts and pubic region. Straight, pitch-black hair draped over her shoulders. Yeshua understood why her esoteric signature felt familiar to him.

"Priya," he uttered.

"You remember," Priya smiled.

A fitted, white gown appeared and covered her body, accentuating her curves as she walked towards him. Yeshua cleared his throat and straightened his gait.

"I am actually glad you remember me," Priya added.

Her dimples deepened, her cheekbones elevated slightly, her lips thickened as the spread in a radiant smile to reveal glistening, perfectly-shaped, white teeth. Her big, black eyes danced with warmth and... yearning? Yeshua cleared his throat again and tried to speak but failed.

She... she's changing her form to my vision of a perfect woman, he thought.

He cleared his throat again; this time, he fidgeted from nervousness. Then, he crossed his legs to stop himself from fidgeting.

But why am I nervous? he wondered. *I should not be nervous.*

"You have grown into quite the man yourself, Yeshua," Priya added.

She stopped walking and turned around. Her gown pressed against her skin and accentuated the crease in her lower back and buttocks.

She's wearing nothing underneath, he observed.

Suddenly, her gown became transparent. Yeshua swallowed with discomfort. He uncrossed and crossed his legs. A table, with a pitcher of water and a cup on top of it, emerged from the floor in front of Priya. Priya poured some water into the cup, turned back around and slowly walked towards Yeshua. She stopped about three feet away from him.

Yeshua's eyes glued to her pelvic region. Slowly, she placed the cup of water between his face and his line of sight to her pelvis. Yeshua, realizing how much he had been caught in the moment, jerked a glowering face towards her. Heart racing, face feeling warm with unnecessary anger, he glared at her.

How dare her, he raged in his mind. *Who does she think she is? I will have her. I must have her.*

"I heard you clear your throat several times and thought you might be thirsty," Priya said and pushed the cup a little closer to his face.

Yeshua's right hand felt as if a mountain was chained to it as he reached out to take the cup from Priya. He took a sip, then a gulp before emptying the contents of the cup. He wiped his lips with his left sleeve and returned the empty cup back to Priya.

"Thank you," said Yeshua.

"You are very welcome," Priya replied, spinning on her heels to return the cup to the table. "I am glad you have your voice back."

Yeshua cleared his throat again.

"Yes, it is great to have my voice back," Yeshua agreed, not knowing what else to say.

She's playing with me, he fumed. *She thinks she is wise, but I will show her who I am.*

"So," Priya said.

A chair formed from the floor to accommodate her, while the table and its contents disappeared into the floor.

"You have not answered my question."

"Which one?" Yeshua asked, a little confused.

His chest rose and fell with impatience and frustration and he clenched and unclenched his fist repeatedly.

"I asked you if you know where you are," she replied.

"Oh," Yeshua shook his head as if to clear his mind. "No, I do not."

What is happening to me? Why am I feeling all these emotions and desires like I have never felt before? he wondered.

"Then let me enlighten you, my very confused friend," Priya relaxed in her chair and crossed her legs.

As she did, her gown looked a lot shorter than Yeshua remembered and more of her toned legs and flawless skin became exposed... up to her mid-thigh. Yeshua leaned forward and clasped his hands over his knee, more an attempt to hide his bulging phallus than for any other reason.

"You have my complete attention," Yeshua said.

"I know, Yeshua," Priya said.

She grinned and winked at him, her head inclining with seductive mischief. Yeshua tightened his grasp on his knee and clenched his jaw.

Fight it, he encouraged himself. *Fight it. Can't you see, she's just toying with your feelings and making a fool of you.*

"You are in the Realm-Dimension of Akasha," Priya said. "But, this is the part of Akasha that you have not yet accessed in your current existence. It looks different from what you are used to, does it not?"

"Indeed," Yeshua agreed. "It does not even feel like Akasha."

"Actually," Priya explained. "This part of Akasha is not alien to you. You have just been avoiding this place, unconsciously. And in case you did not know already, Akasha is neither a realm nor a dimension. It exists on its own for various reasons. As the keeper of the records of Creation, it must remain objective and non-polarized. As such, Akasha is the truest reflection of both the illusionary and truth aspects of Creation, and ultimately you."

"I see," Yeshua said. "But what exactly is *this* part of Akasha?" he asked.

"Welcome, Yeshua," she uncrossed her legs and crossed them again, "to the Shadow of the Soul. Here, you will face your worse fears, your greatest weaknesses, your strongest desires and, most of all, true death. So far, you have not yet experienced your polarity on Earth Realm at the subconscious level. But here, in the Shadow of the Soul, you will experience your polarity at its purest, unadulterated and unhindered form."

"That explains the insanely strong urges I have been feeling ever since I awoke here," Yeshua muttered.

Priya roared with derisive laughter, much to Yeshua's discontent and displeasure. The pressure cap to the containment of his fury shook violently in a prelude to an explosive ejection.

"Urges?" Priya said in between fits of laughter. "Oh Yeshua, you have not even yet begun to experience these 'urges' of which you speak. Everything you think you are experiencing right now will multiply a thousand-fold."

She roared with more laughter and Yeshua's fury riled within its containment.

"But why?" Yeshua glared spears and daggers at Priya. "Why do I have to go through this?"

"What you call 'this,'" Priya explained, "is *YOU*. These are *YOUR* urges, *YOUR* feelings, *YOUR* emotions, *YOUR* everything. This is the shadow of *YOUR* soul. Thus, it is *YOUR* problem. So, *YOU* figure it out."

She rose from the chair, which disappeared into the floor and her short gown draped over her ankles once again. Yeshua lowered his eyes to the floor, emotional and mental exhaustion weighing heavily on his psyche.

Fight.

He raised his eyes until Priya's feet came into view. As if controlled by an unseen force, he continued raising his eyes. Priya's gown shortened with his rising line of vision.

Fight. You must fight.

But the power of the unseen force of desire dominated his will. Her ankles became exposed, followed by her calves, knees, thighs, and… her pelvis. His gaze rested on her exposed womanhood and lingered there for a moment. His breathing was erratic, his heart raced, and his loins boiled in anticipation of what was to come.

How am I even breathing? Heart pumping? he wondered. *This is my soul. It doesn't have a heart, or lungs for that matter.*

Yeshua tried to peel his eyes away from her womanhood, but he could not.

Memories of the flesh, imprinted on my soul, he answered his own questions.

His shoulders heaved up and down and he gripped the edge of the bed.

Fight. Avert your gaze.

But Yeshua could not; not because something prevented him. He could not, did not, avert his gaze because… he wanted Priya, all of her, like he had never desired anything in his life. His soul's features relaxed in submission and surrender. His eyes continued their slow ascent. Her tummy, ribs, perfect breasts all became exposed, and finally, Priya, his prize, was completely naked.

She took a step towards him and stopped. Yeshua stood up from the bed and walked towards her. His gown evaporated from his body when he was about two feet away from her. He looked in her eyes as hers dug into his. He welcomed her into the innermost parts of his soul as sweet, seductive surrender serenaded his soul. Then, with bestial savagery, he snatched her off the ground and threw her on the bed. He cast himself on top of her, hardened and ready to seal his soul to her service for all eternity. But, she stopped him with a hand to his chest.

"Not yet," she said.

Yeshua roared with rage and punched the mattress close to her face.

"What do you want, Yeshua?" Priya asked calmly.

"Just stop talking, will you," Yeshua yelled and slapped her hand away.

Priya used the momentum of his slap to roll his body in the opposite direction. In a smooth motion, Priya flipped him on to his back and straddled him. His hardness pressed against her lower lips, sending pangs of unfulfilled, pent-up, sexual desires through his soul. She placed her right hand on his chest and her left hand on the bed beside his right temple. She leaned forward, her breasts pressing against his chest and whispered in his right ear.

"What do you want?"

"You," Yeshua replied with desperation and helplessness. "I want you, Priya. I want you so badly. I will die if I don't have you."

"Patience, Yeshua," Priya said and slowly faded into thin air. "You must face yourself first."

Yeshua lay on the bed, alone, naked, extremely confused and unthinkably horny. He propped himself on his elbows and looked around the room like a caged, frantic animal.

"Oh, I forgot to tell you," Priya's omnidirectional voice tore through the air. "On Earth Realm, you are very dead. If you don't find your way out of here, you would have failed; not just yourself, but humanity."

Yeshua squeezed his eyes shut to soothe his soul. It seemed to work.

"If you fail, you die the true death," Priya added. "And your existence will be erased from Creation for all eternity."

Yeshua heaved his shoulders and sat at the edge of the bed.

"Once again," Priya's bodiless voice said, "Welcome to the Shadow of the Soul."

***

Back in Egypt, Salemwalek entered the chamber that was once his but was now occupied by his ancestor-in-the-flesh. Yeshua's lifeless body lay on the bed. Brother Muzek tended to it. Other priests came in and left; most of them doing the same thing; staring and wondering what was going on with the master.

"It has been a full moon cycle now, Master," Brother Muzek said.

"Yes, brother," Salemwalek said. "He is experiencing true death."

"True death?" Brother Muzek asked, mopping Yeshua's forehead with a wet cloth, more so out of habit than out of necessity. "I have never heard of this."

"Yes, brother," Salem replied. "True death is a state through which one must pass to conquer death itself, because death is the last enemy of the physical man."

Salemwalek pulled up a chair and sat near his ancestor's body.

"So, when we die," Brother Muzek asked, "is it a false death?"

"It is an illusion," Salem replied. "So yes, it is false; false because during death, we merely abandon the flesh and move on to the next phase of existence. But true death is different. If you crush a seed, it is simply destroyed, right?"

"Agreed, master," Muzek said.

Other priests gathered to listen to Salemwalek's teaching.

"What happens when you plant a seed?" Salem continued. "It grows to become a plant, obviously. But what happens before it grows to become a plant?"

"It dies?" Muzek replied with uncertainty.

"Exactly. It dies," Salem agreed. "Before that seed can grow into a plant, it must first die. Only in death can it unleash its potential to become a plant. Same with us. Only in death, which comes with an intense shift in consciousness, can we be reborn.

"True death is death of both the body and soul. That is, your physical body dies as you all can see," he gestured towards Yeshua lying on the bed, "and the soul also dies. And with that, you are simply erased from Creation because all that is left is the spirit and it returns to the Source. You can die a true death by entering a realm of existence which holds the darkest aspects of your being; your worst fears, nightmares, even your greatest desires and most of all death. However, entering this state must be a conscious decision; it is virtually impossible to get into this state by accident. Some people also call it conscious death but mistake it for the ability to simulate illusionary death. Anyone, with sufficient practice, can simulate illusionary death. I am yet to meet in the flesh, other than the master, anyone who has ever experienced true death."

"So, there are those who attempted true death, master?" one priest asked.

"Yes," Salem replied. "But this requires a very high level of self-awareness. Only a few have tried, and even fewer have succeeded."

"His body is still perfectly preserved after all this time," Muzek remarked. "Remarkable. Master, do you know how long it could take to return from this state?"

"The only person I know of was in this state for six years," Salemwalek replied. "The decay of the body usually indicates failure."

"The one you know of, who experienced true death and lived, who was he?" asked another priest.

"Him," Salem pointed at Yeshua. "In a past incarnation as Melchizedek, the founder of our monastery."

CHAPTER TWENTY-THREE

SHADOW OF THE SOUL

"HELLO, MY SON."

Yeshua froze at the sound of the familiar voice. He turned around slowly as if turning any faster would spoil everything.

"Father?" he managed to say. "Is that really you?"

"Yes, it is I, son," Yosef grinned and opened his arms.

Yeshua teleported into his father's loving embrace.

"Yahweh be praised. You have grown so big and strong, son," Yosef stripped Yeshua from his embrace and appraised him, while tears of joy streamed down his face. "What have they been feeding you?"

The two men laughed a little.

"I have missed you so much, father," Yeshua wiped the tears from his eyes.

Yeshua rubbed his left palm on his gown, just to make sure he was actually wearing one. His shoulders relaxed.

Embarrassment averted, he said to himself.

For a moment, he had forgotten he was still in the Shadow of the Soul. He bowed his head slightly at the realization.

"Let us sit, father," Yeshua said.

Two chairs emerged from the floor to accommodate them.

"I was at your funeral," he spoke the words like an accusation.

"I know, my son," Yosef replied. "I saw you there and what you tried to do for your mother and siblings."

"But I never saw you, father," Yeshua's voice quavered. "Maybe I could have saved you if I was there. You would have still been alive had I not been away on this... mission or whatever this is."

Yeshua broke down and wept bitterly as guilt unrestrained guided his thoughts and shame unsullied smothered his soul.

"Yes, son, maybe you could have prevented my death," Yosef moved his chair closer towards Yeshua's using telekinesis. "Maybe you could have changed everything. Maybe the family could have been whole."

"But I was not there," Yeshua exclaimed with guilt-filled frustration. "I have been successful in everything but keeping my own family whole. I failed you, father. I failed you."

"No, son, you have not failed me," Yosef took Yeshua's hand in his and gave it a squeeze of reassurance. "You can never, ever fail me. In fact, there may be another way out of this."

"Out of what?" Yeshua sniveled.

"Out of your feeling of failure, my son. It may not be wise for you to despair when you have come so close."

"You speak in riddles, father," Yeshua scowled as guilt morphed to confusion and shame to skepticism.

"My son, what I mean is this," Yosef shifted forward and sat at the edge of his seat. "I am dead on Earth Realm, but not here. See?"

He squeezed Yeshua's hand again.

"You feel me, do you not? So, you see, you have not failed me."

"But you ARE dead, father and so am I. On Earth Realm, we are both dead."

"True, son," Yosef insisted. "But not here. So, all is not lost. Besides, here we can have everything we want; ANYTHING we want. There is no sickness, no poverty, no disease, no pain or anguish or anything you do NOT want. We can create OUR own heaven here, my son. You and I… TOGETHER."

Yosef let the words resonate for a moment.

"Here, there is no guilt. Here there is no failure," he added.

Yeshua pondered on his father's words. Yosef's logic was hard to ignore, but he sensed major treachery afoot.

Why? he pondered. *Why is he insisting on 'here'? Besides, if I knew father well….*

He had his moment of clarity. He knelt in front of his father and took his father's hands in his.

"You are right," Yeshua said. "That in here I can create whatever I want. I can have everything and anything I want. You are correct that you and I can be here together and create our own heaven, that in here, there is no guilt or failure."

He stood up and let go of his father's hand.

"But this is the Shadow of the Soul, and you are not my father," Yeshua added more sternly. "You are my feelings of guilt and failure made manifest. You are an illusion. I may be dead on Earth Realm, but I chose this test, and I will succeed."

He took a step away from the illusion that was his father.

"You are not my enemy. You are a part of me and I am a part of you. But you are an anchor trying to hold me back and I must let you go so I can move on."

"No, wait," the illusion called out. "You cannot just toss me aside like that. You must see that I am very important to you and I AM your father. Can you not see that?"

But the illusion of his father slowly faded before his eyes, even as it tried to hold on and continue pleading for recognition, until it disappeared entirely. Yeshua closed his eyes and heaved a sigh. Then, a voice called out from nowhere and startled him.

"I am very proud of you, son," said a voice that was identical to his father's. This time, Yeshua felt a connection and bond, the kind that can only exist between a parent and a child, which nothing, not even death, can break.

"Thank you... father," Yeshua replied.

The bright, marble whiteness of the room rolled away to nothingness. Yeshua floated in a dark void, with no sense of space or gravity. He braced himself for the next test.

Priya was not exaggerating about the experiences in the Shadow of the Soul, he thought.

"Good job passing that first test," a familiar voice sounded in the darkness.

"Who are you?" Yeshua demanded. "Show yourself."

"I think you know very well who I am," the voice replied coyly. "Denial is useless. Perhaps you wonder how this could be?"

"Cease this trickery and show yourself," Yeshua ordered.

"Your wish is my command," the voice replied.

A form manifested in front of Yeshua. It was masculine, five-feet-eight-inches tall, with a neatly trimmed beard, broad shoulders and long, dark, brown hair that curled slightly above his shoulders. His big, brown eyes stared directly into Yeshua's eyes and a mischievous smile formed on his face.

"After all, I am you, and you are me," the voice that was an exact replica of Yeshua's said.

Yeshua's jaw dropped slightly as he stared at the spitting image of himself.
Shadow of the Soul.

Yeshua straightened his shoulders.

"Well, we both know that someone is taking a test right now," said the other Yeshua. "And I ask, which means you are asking as well, why is this test taking my form?"

He cocked an eyebrow, but Yeshua said nothing.

"Silence..." the other Yeshua continued with just a dash of overconfidence.

"Good strategy."

He started slowly pacing around Yeshua, hands clasped behind his back.

"Do you know who I represent?" he asked.

"My dark side," Yeshua replied flatly.

"So, you can speak after all," the other Yeshua taunted. "Good answer, though. Yes, I am your dark side in all its sweet, dark glory."

He stopped in front of Yeshua and gestured at the nothingness around them.

"You see all this? This is what everything looks and feels like when you can tap into omnipotence. When you have the power of the Creator in the palm of your hand. What I want to do is create. I want to fill this void and design everything to MY taste, MY desire."

He took a deep breath, held it for a heartbeat or two, before letting it out slowly. Then, he placed his right index finger on Yeshua's chest.

"And I want you to join me," he added.

"And then what?" Yeshua asked.

"And then all of humanity will be better ready for the next evolutionary leap at the Great Reset," the other Yeshua replied, spinning around and spreading his arms in the air.

"Indeed," Yeshua agreed. "But I am not to interfere with Earth Realm and the humans directly."

"Who said anything about direct interference?" the other Yeshua asked. "After all, there is a fine line between leadership and direct interference, right?"

"And how do you propose I do that?" Yeshua asked.

"Do you not know already?" the other Yeshua asked rhetorically.

"By becoming the ruler of Earth Realm and its creatures," Yeshua scoffed.

"Is that not a most logical path?" the other Yeshua beamed with excitement. "Look at their history. They are a violent and ignorant race. Left on their own, they will self-destruct, and you know that. Unless, of course, you have no problem with that..."

The other Yeshua left the statement hanging. Yeshua leveled an expressionless gaze at him.

"Think about it," the other Yeshua vibrated with fiery passion. "Your training has made you omnipotent, omniscient and all-loving. In their eyes, you will be more than a king... You will be a god."

The other Yeshua took Yeshua by the shoulders.

"What better king could there be but you? You will use your might, wisdom, and love to rule and usher Earth Realm through the cosmic countdown. In this way, you will be achieving your purpose. You will become the greatest ruler ever. Earth Realm and the humans survive the Cosmic Countdown and the

Great Reset. Everybody wins."

"And what about those who reject my authority?" Yeshua asked.

"What do you do with weeds in a garden?" the other Yeshua rebutted.

Ruling over the humans does sound like the easiest route to take, Yeshua paced back and forth as the other Yeshua's words seduced their way into his psyche. I have awakened my abilities and I have what it takes to bring Earth Realm under my rule, for the good of everyone. Resistance is guaranteed, but, for the sake of the greater good, the resistance must be dealt with.

The more he considered the other Yeshua's words, the more the idea of becoming Earth Realm's ruler burned from mere hot coals to a raging fire. Yet, in the furthest recess of his soul's psyche, a tiny voice of reason cried out for an alternative path.

But why? he asked himself. *Why the conflict?*

Yeshua paused, raised his eyes to meet the other Yeshua, who smiled with much delight. He stared unblinking, unthinking at the other Yeshua for an unknown length of time until the light of an epiphany shone within his soul.

This is the Shadow of the Soul, he surmised. *Therefore, nothing good can come from my dark side.*

"You forget one thing," he said.

"What is that?" the other Yeshua asked.

"Free will," he replied. "My purpose includes undoing the works of The Anomaly, not to bend the free will of the humans to suit mine. Granted, I am awakened to my true self. But just because the humans of Earth Realm are not yet awakened to theirs does not give me the right to lord over them. I will assist, but I will not interfere. I will not violate the rules like The Anomaly has done already. I have faith in the creatures of Earth Realm. They will survive the Cosmic Countdown and Great Reset, and they will do so of their own free will.

"And as for you, my dark side," Yeshua approached the other Yeshua, who retreated, "You are not my enemy. You are just a part of my ego in its purest form, and you are only doing what is in your nature. I am not my light side either. But both sides abide in me, and I unite you two. I accept and take you two in with me, as one."

Yeshua extended his hand towards his other self, and the other Yeshua backed away from him again.

"No," it cried. "I want to be by myself, to be me. I do not want anything to do with you. Leave me alone."

It turned around to flee but ran straight into Yeshua.

"What are you afraid of?" Yeshua asked calmly. "You have nowhere else to go. Look around you."

He gestured around.

"You are in the shadow of *MY* soul. Not yours."

Yeshua extended his right hand towards his other self again. The other Yeshua hesitated for a moment before he extended his right hand as well. The moment their fingers touched, the other Yeshua disintegrated and disappeared into Yeshua so quickly as if it was never there in the first place. Yeshua closed his eyes and breathed in deeply.

Second test… passed.

When he opened his eyes again, he was not alone.

"Well done, Yeshua," Priya said as her naked form walked towards him. "How about we celebrate, just you and I?"

Yeshua's clothes evaporated from his body.

"You have earned it," she pressed her naked body against his and leaned forward with her lips so close to his ear.

"Now," her lips gently brushed his ear, sending waves of desire and ravenous lust throughout his soul. "Show me how badly you want me."

Two bodies fell into the oblivion that surrounded them as they locked lips in an untamed passionate kiss. Two bodies pressed against each other in a wild frenzy of pure carnality. Two bodies fell… and fell… and fell… deeper… and deeper… and deeper into nothingness.

Finally… my prize, Yeshua rejoiced.

Yeshua had longed for this moment from the very first time he laid eyes on her when he awoke… here.

Where was here again?

Doesn't matter.

Everything had narrowed down to this singular, unsullied, raw desire and now, this desire was about to become a reality. Priya wrapped her legs around his waist, granting him access. A hardened Yeshua felt her nether parts rub against him. The last of his resolve evaporated into non-existence and he surrendered to her irresistible invitation. The two continued falling, deeper… and deeper… and deeper into the dark oblivion that surrounded them… here. The fall was beyond the simple act of falling. The fall initiated a transmutation of his soul, like a slow poison from a painless sting from a scorpion. His eyes remained closed and his clairsentience ignored the slow disintegration of the etheric constituency of his soul, blinded by his succumbing to the seduction of something deep within his being that could only be made manifest by his lust for Priya. It serenaded him, sang to him like a siren and slowly swallowed his soul in its shadow.

"Take me…" Priya's voice begged him via telepathy.

Yeshua adjusted his hips in a prelude to a penetration; a prelude to claiming his prize and sealing his soul to hers… to its shadow… to *his* shadow, in this….

Where am I? a tiny voice cried in desperation within his soul.

"I am all yours... your well-deserved reward... Take me..."

What is happening? the voice cried out with greater urgency within his soul.

"Take me, my love... Take me... Let us become one for all eternity..."

Yeshua opened his eyes as his memory returned.

Shadow of the soul.

Summoning willpower and strength he never knew he had, he ripped himself from Priya, ceasing their fall.

"Why did you do that," Priya glared with maniacal rage and lunged for him.

He rolled to the side, and she flew past him.

"This is not right," he exclaimed.

The etheric constituency of his soul slowly returned as the light of realization burned brighter within him.

"I know this is a test, but I am not sure what it is."

"Then why fight it," she hissed and hovered towards him, but her movement repelled him like a magnet.

"Did I not tell you that you could have me in due time? And you passed the first two tests. So here I am. Congratulations."

"Then why does it feel different from the first time I saw you?" Yeshua asked, rising to his feet. "Why do *you* feel different?"

"I do not know, and I do not care," Priya spat with impatience. "You are the one with the feelings. So, YOU should have the answer."

She folded her hands over her full, voluptuous breasts and pouted.

"All I know is that I have wanted this for the longest time as well and now that I can finally have my way..."

She turned her back towards him.

"I thought we could have something together, Yeshua," she sniveled. "I've waited for you for too long to remember. But now..."

To his greatest surprise, she buried her face in her hands and started crying.

"I ache on the inside," she sobbed. "I'm torn apart by your rejection."

Yeshua's features soften with empathy. He hovered towards her, but she glided away from his approach.

"Stay away from me," Priya barked.

"I am sorry, Priya," he said. "I just do not know the meaning of this."

"Have you considered the possibility that there may not be *any* meaning to this at all?" her voice was heavy with hurt and pain.

Yeshua sighed.

"Perhaps you are right, Priya," he said after a moment of thought. "Perhaps, I just have to accept the situation the way it is."

Yeshua sat down in a Buddha pose and bowed his head in contemplation.

His clairsentience indicated that Priya was gradually coming towards him. He opened his eyes and saw her crawling on her hands and knees towards him, her beautiful breasts remaining perfectly in place and not hanging downward, thanks to the absence of gravity.

"Then take me, Yeshua," her eyes burned with seduction. "I can be yours, and you can be mine... forever."

Yeshua reached for her, took her face in his hands and kissed her on the lips..

"I accept you," he said.

Priya grinned and gently pushed him on his back before she straddled him. She returned his gentle kiss, and they both enjoyed the warmth and comfort of each other's body.

"I accept you," Yeshua continued between kisses, "because you are not Priya. You represent the feminine side of me, and hence you are an illusion. You balance and compliment my masculine side."

Priya, or Yeshua's feminine side made manifest, struggled to break free from him, but he held her fast.

"I accept you because in accepting you, I accept me," he continued. "And in accepting this aspect of me, I become complete."

The illusion that was Priya continued to wrestle against him. Yeshua kissed her again and, this time, he poured all that he had and all that he was into the kiss. His kiss broke down the walls of individuality between him and her, causing the illusion that was Priya's body to go limp with surrender, initiating a union between the male and the female. Yeshua and Priya bonded and merged together in a union that was beyond the carnality of sexuality. As the two became one, the illusion that took the form of Priya dissipated and became absorbed into Yeshua. For the first time in his current existence, Yeshua experienced a wholeness he had never felt before as he completely let go and accepted the illusion.

Third test... passed.

He floated within the dark oblivion that surrounded him. As he savored the moment, tens of thousands of specks of light appeared in front of him and began to coalesce into a form. The form started with a pair of big, green crystalline eyes and then the broad head of a cobra complimented the eyes before the rest of the serpent's body slithered into a twenty-foot long form.

Kundalini, the Serpent of Consciousness, Yeshua said with reverence and stood up.

It hissed and slithered its golden form towards Yeshua and stopped six feet from where Yeshua was standing. It then fanned its head and brought its eyes to less than a foot from Yeshua's face. Its ethereal, cosmic energy washed over and into Yeshua, causing a transmutation of Yeshua's soul into a form that

Yeshua never imagined possible. The energy felt like supercharged chi magnified a trillion-fold and this sensation had nothing to do with the effects of being within the Shadow of the Soul. Yeshua closed his eyes and surrendered himself to this creature of Creation, unique in every aspect beyond conception and powerful beyond his sphere of awareness. This was as close to omnipotence as he had ever experienced and he was ready for whatever this multidimensional entity had in store for him.

Kundalini retracted its head and lowered it towards Yeshua's feet. From there, the Serpent of Consciousness proceeded to slowly wrap itself three and a half times around Yeshua's body, starting from his feet, past his pelvis and up to his shoulders and neck area. Then, the Serpent of Consciousness briefly rested its head on the crown of Yeshua's head before it slowly pulled its head upwards and fanned it. It opened its mouth and a pair of long, curved and sharp upper golden fangs slowly slid out. Suddenly, Kundalini plunged its golden fangs into the crown of Yeshua's head. Blinding beams of white light shot out from Yeshua's mouth, ears, nose and eyes. Yet, Yeshua felt no pain. However, a surge of energy, far greater than the tinge he experienced from Kundalini earlier, coursed through his body, and a sense of omnipresence, omnipotence, and omniscience followed.

Knowing beyond knowing… Awareness beyond awareness… Yeshua had now become a multidimensional being, and could now access, at-will, the Dimensions of Space, Time, Energy and Ether.

It is done, Kundalini declared across Creation via telepathy.

CHAPTER TWENTY-FOUR

MULTIDIMENSIONAL BEING

YESHUA PERCEIVED AND experienced the states of Creation, the four major dimensions, in a never-ending spark of instantaneity.

TIME

As a human, he could glimpse into the future and remember some of his past lives, mainly by taking a peek into the Akashic Records. At times, he caught a glimpse into the Dimension of Time, which proved no better than peeking into the Akashic Records. However, as a multidimensional being, everything changed.

Linear time, a tiny aspect of the Dimension of Time, stretched within his being in three sections: past, present and future. It flowed from past to future in a cause-effect fashion. Most creatures in Creation lived within the present while a few creatures in much higher realms and dimensions of existence could live within the past and present, given their level of evolution. Keyword: could.

The flow of linear time varies from one dimension to another, Yeshua thought. *The higher the dimension, the slower linear time flowed, relative to that of lower dimensions.*

Yeshua nodded.

So, if a creature from a higher dimension could find a way to exist within a lower dimension as one of the creatures in that lower dimension, linear time would move much faster for them in that lower dimension, relative to their home dimension.

Yeshua smiled.

Therefore, a creature could 'buy time' by falling to a dimension of much lower vibrational frequency than theirs.

In a blink, he searched through the Akashic Records to find proof of his logic.

No record of any creature falling… None in all of creation.

He made a mental note of that.

The Cosmic Clock slowly ticked towards the end of another perfect cycle.

A perfect cycle, he nodded. *The only measurement of time Creation cares for. All other cycles are relative and only hold importance to the creatures who are subject to those cycles. Creation has seen six perfect cycles so far. This is the seventh and its completion is nigh.*

SPACE

Creation pulsed as a single entity, despite its many components. All was one and he was a part of that one. His sense of self, his individualism, existed only as a notion; a role he had to play, a role that just became more apparent than he had ever imagined. He was everywhere and nowhere in the same instant.

Omnipresence… Yeshua thought. *So, I can be wherever and whenever I want. I can even exist in multiple locations and points in linear time simultaneously. Shapeshifting, among other things, will be so much easier now.*

Yeshua's being pulsed with an intense energy of realization.

This is how The Anomaly has been doing it, his thoughts beamed within his being. *I knew he was a very powerful entity, a bringer of chaos. But I am starting to realize that he is a lot much than just a bringer of chaos.*

ENERGY

The vibrations of creations resonated with his new esoteric energy in a sweet harmony. Yeshua closed what he believed were his eyes and savored the feeling. He let the resonance continue until, suddenly, the resonance hit a crescendo and forced him out of his state of serenity.

What just happened? he asked himself.

The energy responsible for the crescendo in the resonance hit his being even harder, causing Yeshua to hold on to his sense of individuality out of his human survival instinct. As such, he began to exit the state of omnipresence. However, he quickly let go of his human survival instinct and returned to omnipresence.

Kundalini, he frowned. *I will have words with you later.*

Suddenly, unimaginable, indescribable pain flared throughout his being. Yeshua wanted to scream, but not a single sound could escape his lips, or what he thought were his lips. Even his thoughts seemed to be smothered.

I made you into a multidimensional being, a voice he recognized innately as Kundalini's said via telepathy. *Do not mistake my generosity for anything else.*

The pain vanished and Yeshua learned his lesson. He regarded what he considered was his form and noticed the change. His form now existed in its most fundamental state, its etheric state.

ETHER

So, this is what the ethers are, Yeshua perceived the ethers within its dimension.

A smile spread across what he believed were his lips.

Kundalini did this, Yeshua concluded. *The flaring pain, the sense of disintegration and being torn apart. That was him, teaching me a lesson and ushering me into this fourth state of Creation, the Dimension of Ether.*

A subtle, but irresistible force, pulled him closer to something. A sphere of 'being' hovered by itself within an oblivion of nothingness and darkness. However, neither was the nothingness the absence of something nor the darkness the absence of light. The nothingness was a no-thingness, a presence unto itself, and the 'darkness' was the field from which light and dark were created. The 'darkness' was the precursor of the ethers.

If I tell Rama I beheld kaala, *he is going to be so jealous,* Yeshua thought fondly.

The sphere of being remained the same, despite it being as small as an ether and as large as creation at the same instant. Yeshua bowed what he thought was his head in reverence.

I thank Creation for this moment, he thought. *I am blessed to behold the Core of Creation in its true form.*

Suddenly, the ethers that constituted Yeshua's being came apart as if by an unseen force. He no longer experienced each state of Creation as separate. He experienced all four of them as one and at once. His being riled from the overload. In an instant, he was Creation and Creation was him. Images, names, aspects of time, energies, locations and so much more flashed repeatedly across his being and left many imprints. He wanted to scream, to alleviate the sensations pulsing through his being that he had never experienced and which no language could explain.

Names… he wondered. *Why all these names?*

Lithilia, Michael, Lunok, Patrick, Eliel, Yehuda, Mikum, Melchizedek, Emok, Shi'mon, Beelzebub, Fazim, Luceefa and many more flashed across his being.

Paradins, Shemsus, Guardians, Annakis, Hounds of Creation, Yeshua saw these creatures and many more across Creation. *A lion? What do these mean?*

Yeshua stilled his thoughts and immediately, everything became still. He waited… waited… and waited… in absolute stillness. Slowly, the ethers sparked what appeared to be an innumerable number of manuscripts within his perception. He vibrated his etheric constitution to omnipresence and perused through every manuscript.

The Dark Fires, Chaos' Call, The Siren's Song, Devorah the Deluge, Yeshua called out the titles as he perused through them. *What are these?*

When he came to The Soulless Ones, his being flared with realization, horror and anger.

This is what The Scribe is doing in various sections of Creation, he fumed. *These are the pieces of his plan for chaos.*

Yeshua flared even more with anger, unknowingly causing massive shifts in the vibrational energies of trillions of realms and dimensions.

I thought he only wanted to bring chaos on Earth Realm, he raged. *But now I see he wants to undo Creation using the vibration of chaos.*

He dismissed the manuscripts.

I must alert the other multidimensional beings, he thought. *We cannot let The Scribe see his intention to fruition.*

Yeshua increased his vibrational frequency to the highest possible in Creation. In so doing, he could perceive the other multidimensional beings in Creation. He tried to resonate with the first, but he could not get through. A force and energy, much stronger than what he could handle, pushed him away. He tried the second and received the same treatment. He considered reaching out to Kundalini but he remembered Kundalini's stern warning and changed his mind.

Frustration and anger boiled within his being threatening to explode in rage of multidimensional proportions when suddenly, his clairsentience indicated a creature with a familiar esoteric signature was pulsing counteracting vibrations into his being. His anger gradually died down and his omnipresence slowly dwindled. The vibrational frequency of his being dropped ever so slowly, gently pulling him away from the states of Creation. Finally, Yeshua returned to a familiar etheric form in the Realm-Dimension of Akasha.

Priya's body pressed against his as the two of them locked lips in a deep, passionate kiss. Yeshua gently ended the kiss. Priya smiled and placed her right hand on his left cheek.

"I had to get you out of there before you destroyed too many lives," she explained with a kind smile.

"Thank you," Yeshua said. "I am sorry I let myself get carried away. I was not thinking."

"I know," she placed her right hand on his chest. "You are still a child. A multidimensional being, but a child, nonetheless. You have much to learn."

Yeshua summoned a chair and sank into it. A long white robe appeared and covered his body, but Priya dismissed his robe. She sat on his lap and nestled her naked body against his.

"But why?" Yeshua asked. "Why do they not care?"

Priya said nothing.

"They can easily end The Scribe and stop this madness," he raged and Priya kissed him again.

His features softened and the walls of Akasha ceased vibrating from the rage that bubbled and threatened to explode from his being. She gently pulled away and dished a stern gaze at Yeshua.

"You will never leave this place if you do not learn to control yourself," she said. "Do you understand?"

Yeshua nodded. Priya was his senior on the multidimensional scheme of things. Hence, he had to proceed with caution and wisdom.

"So you care," Yeshua said. "But you cannot help. Why?"

"I am not to interfere," she replied. "I must remain objective, as the transducer of consciousness to Creation. Only the senior multidimensional beings can help."

A moment of silence lingered between the two of them as Yeshua studied her.

"Also, there is more to The Scribe than you currently understand," she explained and straddled him.

She took his head and cradled it against her bosom. A sensation of warmth, calm, peace and... love, flooded his being. Yeshua completely relaxed in her arms.

I must trust her, he concluded. *This is not the Shadow of the Soul and I sense her good intentions to give me aide.*

"Besides," Priya gently stripped his head from her bosom and reached for his nether region. "Who says they don't care?"

She took him and guided him in. He did not resist, physically or mentally.

"What do you mean by-?"

He did not finish his question, not because of the tremendous feeling of ecstasy and exuberance that flooded his being, sensually, like nothing before. He did not finish his question because he found his answer.

"Kundalini," he said as Priya gyrated. "He turned me into a multidimensional being. He must have his reason, thus."

"For the record, I objected," Priya said and gyrated faster when Yeshua's body stiffened. "I did not think you were ready, but Kundalini thinks otherwise. I'm sure by now you have learned he's not to be trifled with."

"Ye-yes," Yeshua stammered from building pleasure. "I- I have had- my experience."

"You know what you must do," Priya slowed her gyrations. "Are you ready?"

But Yeshua never got the chance to say 'yes'. Priya did something with her hips that he never had the chance to process and a ripple of intense, ecstatic pleasure supercharged by Akashic energy washed over his body, cleansing him of his rage for the other multidimensional beings and propelling him to a certain level of maturity was replete with wisdom and caution, instead of blind emotion. He exploded in an orgasmic brilliance of light before he vanished from Akasha.

Yeshua awoke in his chamber in Egypt. Salemwalek and two other priests stared at him with stunned expressions on their faces. He propped himself on his elbows. He swept the chamber with his eyes before sitting upright on the bed.

"Master," Salemwalek exclaimed with joyous relief. "You have returned."

"Yes, Salem," Yeshua said with a smile. "I succeeded yet again."

"There was a bright flash of light right before you awoke, master," said a priest.

"The most amazing thing I have ever seen, master," another priest added.

Yeshua nodded. Then, he slid off the bed and slowly stood up.

"How long was I gone for?" Yeshua asked.

"Four years, master," Salem replied.

"I feel like I just took a nap," Yeshua said calmly. "I will walk around the city. It is a gorgeous day."

"Agreed, master," Salem said. "Returning from the Shadow of the Soul makes any day a gorgeous day."

Yeshua aimlessly walked the busy streets of Heliopolis. Later, a girl, no more than eight years old, ran up to him and offered him an apple. He smiled and crouched before he took the apple with his right hand. He ran the fingers of his left hand through the little girl's long, black hair.

"Thank you, my little friend," he said and bit into the apple. "For everything."

"You are welcome," the little girl replied. "Consider it a small gift for surviving the Shadow of the Soul... again."

Priya smiled, turned around and ran to play with some other children a few yards away. Yeshua smiled and chuckled as he shook his head.

"Now I know more about The Scribe, Priya," he said as he stood up.

He bit into the apple and resumed his stroll through the city.

"And I know how to deal with your rogue apprentice."

CHAPTER TWENTY-FIVE

DEATH BY GUILT

SHI'MON BLENDED WITH the crowd as they followed the criminal known as Yeshua. Some cheered while others jeered. After eating the Passover meal, Miryam went home while Yeshua and the rest of his apprentices went to the Garden of Gethsemane. There, Yehuda arrived with Roman soldiers and gave his master a kiss on the cheek, which identified Yeshua to the Roman soldiers and a few Pharisees who came with the soldiers. They hauled Yeshua away. Shi'mon's heart broke when they fastened his master's hands and feet in chains when they arrived at the Sanhedrin.

"Yeshua the Nazarene," High Priest Nefiki said. "Word is spreading that you call yourself the son of God. Is this true?"

"Your words, not mine," Yeshua replied calmly.

"We have our answer," High Priest Nefiki cheered, much to the delight of his colleagues and a few other among the crowd.

"Yeshua the Nazarene," Nefiki continued, "you have been found guilty of blasphemy against the Most High."

He gestured towards the Roman soldiers.

"Forty-nine lashes, please."

For putting Master through this, Shi'mon promised himself, *Yehuda must die.*

As strong as his resolution was, Shi'mon shunned his foolhardiness, despite his bold move to strike at one of the Roman soldiers who made to arrest the master, cutting off the soldier's ear. He had his reason for singling out this soldier.

"Stay your hand, Shi'mon," Yeshua had commanded. "This is not your fight."

Yeshua picked up the soldier's ear from the ground and reattached it, before willingly surrendering himself to the authorities.

Shi'mon winced and looked away when the first crack of the whip landed on Yeshua's exposed back. He squeezed his eyes shut.

Why did Master show kindness to that soldier?

A cauldron of emotions began to boil in Shi'mon's mind when he recalled something he witnessed a year prior. He glowered.

Was I wrong to follow him? he asked himself. *Is he a fraud? I need to know.*

"Why do I feel like I know you from somewhere?" asked a maiden.

Shi'mon jumped back a little, startled by the maiden's question.

"I do not think we have met, woman," Shi'mon replied harshly.

"I know you," she insisted and stepped closer to Shi'mon for a better look.

"I am sure I would remember if we ever met before," he replied dismissively and made to walk past her.

She stood in his way, blocking his path.

"Yes," she exclaimed. "I remember. You are one of his followers."

She jumped with excitement and turned around to share her discovery with some bystanders.

"You are mistaken," Shi'mon's eyes darted around in panic. "I do not know this man."

While the lady shared her discovery with some bystanders and pointed in his direction, Shi'mon dropped to a knee as if to tie his sandals and wormed his way through the crowd away from the maiden and those standing close to her. He emerged closer to the gate and for a moment, he locked eyes with his master, who screamed in pain as the whips tore the skin of his exposed back with every lash.

It is the least I can do to give him strength after I abandoned him in the garden, he said to himself. *But what could I do? The soldiers were ordered to arrest us as well.*

Shi'mon bit his lower lip as feelings of guilt riled in his psyche.

Master is trouble, he clenched his jaw to strengthen his resolve. *He brought this upon himself. Maybe he deserves this. Maybe this is Yahweh's way of punishing him.*

"Are you not one this blasphemer's apprentices?" a lad asked Shi'mon.

"I don't mingle with blasphemers, young man," Shi'mon replied and avoided the lad's gaze. "This is the closest I have ever come to this criminal."

"And you are a horrible liar, sir," the lad retorted and turned around. "Hey, everyone," the lad called out and gestured in Shi'mon's direction. "Behold, one of his followers."

But Shi'mon was gone before the lad finished his sentence.

I will not fall with this criminal, he told himself. *Yes, he is a criminal, a charlatan.*

Shi'mon teleported to the south wall of the Sanhedrin, away from the crowd gathered at the northern section.

Finally, some peace and quiet.

"So, is this where you hide like a coward while your master is tortured?" an elderly lady asked from the shadows.

Shi'mon staggered and almost fell to the ground. He thought he was alone.

"Look at you, acting like a caged rabbit," the lady stepped out of the shadows and approached Shi'mon. "Where is your loyalty, Shi'mon?"

"You mistake me for someone else, woman," he replied, ignoring the fact that this strange lady knew his name.

"Liar," she insisted. "Your name is Shi'mon and you are his apprentice."

"I do not know what you mean," he insisted. "I do not know this criminal."

As soon as he said those words, a rooster crowed, and Shi'mon recalled the master's words;

"Be aware that the time will come when you will betray me. On that day, you will deny me not once, not twice but three times and a rooster will crow to remind you of my words."

The shame, anger at himself, and the guilt became a combination of emotions too intense for his psyche to handle.

"I'm sorry Master," he cried with deep regret. "I'm so sorry. I never should have borne such thoughts against you. I had no reason to, despite what I thought I saw. I should have spoken to you about it. I should have trusted you. I never should have drawn those conclusions."

Shi'mon fell to his knees and tears rolled down his cheeks.

"You taught me about purpose," he sobbed. 'There's a reason for everything. And now, in your darkest hour, what did I do, as leader of your apprentices?"

Shi'mon beat his breast and tugged at his hairs on his temples. His heart came apart with regret and his soul shook violently with shame. Too late, no going back now. What was done was done. His act was final, etched indelibly on the walls of history and Akasha for all eternity, and he knew this. Pressured by his pride and need to salvage the situation, Shi'mon became his own judge, his own jury, and his own executioner. He tore his outer garments in twain, clawed the earth, and wept his heart out, punishing his psyche with thoughts and wishes of changing the past. Alas, despite all his training, he could not rewrite the past.

"My betrayal is unforgivable," Shi'mon, the fiery one, declared with passion most intense and supercharged this passion with all the etheric energy he could summon. "I deserve death and for my soul to suffer eternal damnation."

Shi'mon's psyche accepted this declaration as truth and final. However, neither was his body ready to be abandoned nor was it his time to die, creating a state of ethereal confusion within his etheric makeup. Thus, in this state of ethereal confusion, his soul, the barrier between his body and his spirit, was painlessly burned away into nothingness. In that moment, Shi'mon's eyes snapped open and they shone brighter than a thousand full moons. In that moment, Shi'mon became aware of his new status borne out of a transmutation of his physical form that came with the etheric consumption of his soul. He was now a soulless creature, and, in his soullessness, he found a new purpose.

"Yehuda, you are a dead man walking," he swore as he vanished from sight to find and facilitate the fatality of his archenemy, Yehuda.

A smile crept across the elderly lady's face who, a few moments ago, had also shape-shifted into the young lad and the maiden who questioned Shi'mon; three different forms from one person. Priya shape-shifted into a Roman soldier as she made her way through the crowd that cheered and jeered at Yeshua. She had a spiked whip in her right hand, the kind reserved for punishing the worst criminals. The ends of the whip left tiny trails in the earth behind her as she continued her walk towards the accused criminal that was Yeshua. Using clairsentience, she sensed the mixed emotions from the crowd; from those who were excited to witness the public thrashing of a criminal, to those who wished for a miraculous rescue of an innocent Jew from unjust punishment. When Priya was close to Yeshua, she leaned forward and brought her lips close to his ear.

"You are a big boy now," she whispered. "You can handle this. I am very angry with you, not just for surviving the Shadow of the Soul, again. I am furious because that sleuthing Kundalini turned you into a multidimensional being and I cannot read your script. I cannot see your purpose. You exist outside of Akasha and that drives me insane with rage. You are the first in all of Creation to receive such a special treatment. So, enjoy your blessing, and curse, while it lasts. But first…"

Priya stood up, lifted the whip high up in the air and crashed it on Yeshua's bare back, tearing skin and drawing blood; and, with every lash, the crowd went wild with ecstasy.

***

Crucifixions were not uncommon to Roman-occupied Israel. But that of Yeshua the Nazarene drew a record crowd of people. For three years, he walked among them, teaching them, healing their sick and even raising their dead. Yet, a day after the Passover, Yeshua was nailed to a cross like a common criminal and most of this record-setting crowd cheered on. However, when Yeshua spoke his last words right before his life expired, the earth shook in a violent earthquake and the veil in the temple that sealed off the Holy of Holies from the rest of the temple had ripped completely down the middle.

"The wrath of Yahweh is upon us," cried many as they fled for their lives.

Jeers turned to fear and fear turned to worship as many, including High

Priest Nefiki and those who conspired to have him executed declared, "He truly was the son of Yahweh."

No would touch his holy body on the cross. No one dared to; no one but Caleb, a goodly merchant from Arimathea.

"Sirs," he said to Nefiki and his cohorts. "Sabbath approaches and it is unwise to leave this man's body out in the open throughout the day of rest. With your permission, I would like to bury his body."

"You do whatever you want with that body," High Priest Nefiki had exclaimed. "We want no part of it. We now know that we have visited a curse upon ourselves and our children for this sin against the Most High."

Caleb hurried to Calvary. He had barely an hour and a half before the Sabbath. Yeshua's wife, mother, siblings and their children gathered in a mournful, grieving, wailing group at the foot of the cross unto which nails kept Yeshua's body fastened. He approached the family and addressed them all.

"I am truly sorry for this tragedy, fellow brothers and sisters," he bowed his head in respect. "The Sabbath approaches and I seek your blessing to bury your husband, brother and son. I have secured a piece of land not far from here. I have staff ready to prepare his body for burial before the Sabbath. Please, let me honor you and your son thus."

Miryam of Magdala, Yeshua's wife, turned a tearful eye towards her in-laws who all nodded their approval.

"What is your name, sir?" asked Miryam of Magdala.

"Caleb of Arimathea."

"Caleb, sir," Miryam broke down but gathered herself again. "On behalf of my family, thank you so much for doing this. We do not know how we can ever repay you. May Yahweh bless you and your family for many generations."

"No need to thank or repay me, madam," Caleb replied. "May Yahweh keep all of you strong during these dark times."

Caleb clapped twice and his team immediately went into action. Within an hour, his team took down Yeshua's body from the cross, prepared it for burial and placed it in a cave on the land he had procured. They sealed off the cave with a huge piece of rock and still had fifteen minutes left before the Sabbath.

Caleb returned to the inn where he was staying. He paid his team who helped him bury Yeshua a more-than-fair wage, much to everyone's delight and gratitude. The wooden piece on which the master's hands were nailed was still in his carriage. When he went to retrieve it and take it up to his room, one of the workers approached him.

"Let me help you with that, sir," offered the worker.

"That is kind of you, but I will take it myself," Caleb declined.

"Are you sure you do not want my help, sir?"

"You are a good man," Caleb replied paternally and heaved the wooden piece over his left shoulder with ease. "I may be more than half a century old, but I think I can handle a little bit of exercise," he added with a laugh.

"As you wish, sir," the young lad raised his eyebrows in surprise. "Be well and thank you once again for your generosity."

"You are welcome and thank you too," Caleb replied and went into the inn..

Caleb, who was The Scientist, who was also The Scribe, set the wooden piece by the door of his room and, at a time when glass had not yet been invented, he retrieved a test tube from his leather bag.

The Dimension of Time, he said to himself. *We, multidimensional beings, travel through time simply by accessing this dimension, and assume multiple roles at the same time in different timelines. 'Timeline', such a primitive word. Who was the fool who assumed time was linear in the first place?*

Of course I knew the blood sample Sasha brought in was not from Yehuda. I had to come back to this timeline, The Scribe wrinkled his nose in disgust, *and obtain this Yeshua's blood myself, especially now that he has survived the Shadow of the Soul TWICE. This means that his protoplasmic and etheric bodies have undergone a major upgrade, making his blood much more valuable than those of any of his soulless apprentices.*

The Scribe paused and idly tapped on his chin.

I still can't fathom why much of record in Akasha has been sealed off, he scowled in contemplation. *Even Akasha is unable to pull such a feat. I should know because, well, Akasha and I have a lot of history together.*

He held the test tube over the bloody portions of the wooden piece. Every molecule of Yeshua's still uncoagulated blood migrated from the wooden piece into the test tube under The Scribe's telekinetic pull. He corked the test tube and gave it an esoteric examination. He nodded with satisfaction.

"I'm not done with you, Yeshua," The Scribe spoke with an evil calm. "This state of not knowing bugs my essence and I don't like this strange feeling. Rest assured, I will find out why your purpose, your records, have been sealed off."

He stowed the test tube in the leather bag strapped to his hip.

"I shall pay you a visit shortly, Yeshua," The Scribe promised.

He walked away from the bloodless wooden piece.

"And when I'm done with you, I'll say hi to your wife and unborn child."

***

Yehuda half-walked and half-ran to the outer city. He was unsure why he chose not to teleport. The master had been right; nothing could have prepared him for this. His psyche quaked with unhindered guilt and his heart resonated with regret for not walking away while he had the chance to. The midday heat seemed to hammer extra hard on him, reminding him that something still existed called 'time', despite him losing track of it. He saw a sycamore tree in the distance and accelerated towards it, spurred by the sudden birth of an idea.

I may not know how to rewind time, he rationalized, *but I can walk away from it all.*

Yehuda made a rope manifest from the ethers. He could choose far more efficient ways to take his own life, but perhaps the dark poetry of a rope around his neck appealed to him the most.

Not that anything makes a difference, anyway, he thought.

He fashioned the end of the rope into a hangman's noose using telekinesis and placed it around his neck. He then climbed, instead of levitating, to a branch high enough to aid in his intent and tied the other end of the rope to the branch. Without the slightest hesitation, Yehuda closed his eyes and jumped.

His neck broke with a loud snap and his body dangled limply from the tree branch. But his neck healed as soon as it broke. Yehuda screamed in frustration and tried again. This time, the branch broke, and he landed on the ground, breaking his left ankle, which immediately healed itself. He looked at the broken branch on the ground and then looked at the branch stump on the tree. The stump looked perfectly and smoothly sliced, as if someone, or something, used an extremely sharp object to cut through the branch. He screamed in rage and punched the ground in desperation at the realization that Creation would not sign off on his suicide. A slight earth tremor radiated outward from the point of his punch. In his frustration, Yehuda had another idea. He reached into his pocket and retrieved the thirty silver pieces, his payment from the high priest for betraying Yeshua.

Maybe the object of my betrayal will be the object of my death, he said to himself.

Yehuda focused on the thirty pieces of silver in his right hand. He sparked the ethers into a ball of light, which engulfed the pieces of silver. When the light faded, a silver dagger with a six-inch blade rested in his right palm. He closed his right fist around the hilt of the dagger and cupped his left hand over his right hand. Yeshua closed his eyes and thrust the dagger, with both hands, into his heart. The pain was sharp and brief as the blade sliced through his flesh and dug into his heart. He felt his life slowly expire and a victory smile spread across his lips. He let go of the dagger, relaxed his body and surrendered to death's embrace. However, despite the claims of many, Yehuda's entire life did not flash before his eyes. Neither serenity nor peace flooded his soul. Instead, a bright flash raced across his vision accompanied by a feeling of burning which seared not his flesh but his soul. Pain…. Pain so intense, so indescribable, pulsated through every aspect of his being. Yehuda screamed so loudly that even the heavens heard. His heart spat out the dagger from his chest, casting it several feet away from him.

Even though Yehuda wanted out, his guilt would not let go. Even though Yehuda wanted to atone for the unatonable, his purpose would not let go. His master's death sealed his fate and there was no turning back now. Yehuda screamed again as the pain attained another crescendo. He crawled into a fetal position on the ground. His guilt glided across his psyche until it consumed his psyche to the point that only an alien, lifeless void tarried in its stead. He rose to his knees, turned his face towards the midday brightness of Solara and opened his eyes. Yet, as Solara burned deep into his retinas with a fury of the heavens, Yehuda was not blinded. He closed his eyes and bowed his head as the pain vanished as if it was never there before.

My wish to die has been granted.

Yes, he had died, but not in the flesh. The sensation of searing stemmed from the loss of his soul. Yet, in his death, in an irony that could only be borne of the esoteric, Yehuda's being pulsated with more aliveness than he had ever felt before. In that moment, in that instance of realization and total surrender, he opened his eyes, bright as they shone, to a new life of soullessness.

Yehuda stood up, walked towards the dagger and picked it up. The dagger glowed with a brightness that dwarfed even the brightness of Solara. He sighed and made the dagger disappear. Suddenly, something struck him in the solar plexus with enough force to slam him violently into the sycamore tree several feet away. If he was still human, he would have been dead on the spot.

"No one kills you but me, traitor," Shi'mon hissed through clenched teeth and zipped towards Yehuda, catching Yehuda in the face with his left foot. "Not even you."

Yehuda landed about twenty feet away as he absorbed the pain that shot through him.

"What an irony that you of all people should call me a traitor," Yehuda spat. "I saw you bury your tail in between your legs like the coward you are and abandon Master to save your sorry soul."

Shi'mon winced at the mention of 'soul' before he glared at Yehuda and charged towards him, fueled by unimaginable rage and fury. He flooded his body with supercharged chi. Yehuda saw Shi'mon was distracted by his words and seized the opportunity. He took a side step and caught Shi'mon by the neck. Using the momentum of Shi'mon zip, he spun around and threw Shi'mon's body into the sycamore tree. Bones snapped with several loud crackles, followed by a shriek of pain. But bones healed as soon as they broke, followed by a roar of rage. Shi'mon shook his head to catch his breath. Yehuda saw his opportunity.

Yehuda zipped towards Shi'mon, dropped low to the ground and propelled his body upwards, unleashing an uppercut into Shi'mon's gut. Shi'mon sailed about thirty feet in the air and on its way down, Yehuda zipped towards him and drove a knee into Shi'mon's ribs. But before Shi'mon's body flew away from the impact, Yehuda grabbed him by the right ankle and slammed his body into the ground like one would swing down an axe to chop some wood. Upon impact, the area around Shi'mon cracked in spider-web patterns around his body. Yehuda then jumped thirty feet into the air and whizzed downwards towards Shi'mon exposed spine.

Shi'mon, completely healed from splintered bones and internal organs turned to mush, rolled over as Yehuda's right foot sank six inches into the hard ground. Shi'mon spun around and drove his right heel on the outer part of Yehuda's left knee, shattering Yehuda's knee. Yehuda yelped in pain and collapsed to the ground. He flooded his body with supercharged chi and quickly healed his knee. Shi'mon used the moment of distraction and whooshed towards Yehuda, who was still on the ground. He seized Yehuda by the neck, lifted him in an arc above his head and slammed his body into the ground. The ground cracked around Yehuda's body. Yehuda caught Shi'mon with a brutal kick to the groin. Shi'mon's body sailed ten feet away due to the force of the impact. He regrew his crushed testicles before he landed on his feet.

Both men instinctively zipped away from each other and sparked the ethers. Light coalesced in the hands. The master had indeed taught them well. Double-edged swords with razor-sharp, four-feet-long blades formed in each archenemy's right hand. As they blazed towards each other for a deathly dance, something crashed between both men with enough explosive force to send them flying away from each other. Both men immediately resumed fighting stance and waited. When the dust settled, they saw Yochanan standing between them his arms folded and head shaking.

"If you two have not realized by now that you cannot kill each other like this," Yoch chuckled, "then you are even bigger fools than I imagined."

"Step aside, Yoch," Shi'mon hissed through clenched teeth. "I have a death to avenge."

"In time, brother," Yoch said, "you will learn more about Master's death than you are ready to know and accept in your current state of mind. But there will be no killing; not today at least and certainly not like this."

He smiled as his gaze darted between the newfound mortal enemies.

"Someone is smart enough to validate my opinion," Yehuda said.

Shi'mon was about to charge at Yehuda but Yoch raised a finger at him.

"Until the mission is complete," Yoch said, "there will be no killing OR any attempts at killing. At least, that was one of the things the master tasked me to do. So, I am supposed to be your babysitter until you two grow up."

"I do not need a babysitter," Yehuda scoffed and Yoch glared at him.

"For the sake of peace," Yoch walked towards Yehuda, "I suggest that you leave the group. In time, we will catch up. How does that sound?"

"I can do that," Yehuda agreed

Yehuda made his sword vanish.

"Thank you, brother," Yoch said.

Yochanan walked towards Yehuda and hugged him.

"I will see you around," Yehuda said, body trembling as he held back tears.

It dawned on him that Yochanan knew what he had done but did not judge him. Yoch, who was so young and yet so wise, still called him 'brother'.

"I will see you around," Yoch replied.

Yehuda nodded.

"See you around, brother," he replied.

"I will have your head, traitor," Shi'mon promised.

"And I would love to see you try, *your holiness*," Yehuda sneered, bowed at the hip before he vanished from their sight.

THE END OF PART TWO

PART THREE

GOOD MORNING SUNSHINE!

THE SCRIBE CROUCHED next to Yeshua's corpse.

"Here you are," he scoffed. "My alleged nemesis on Earth Realm."

He slowly unwrapped the bandages around Yeshua's head and pulled back the cloth that covered Yeshua's face. He pushed back a strand of hair from across Yeshua's left eye and ran a finger down his left cheek.

"So little accomplished," The Scribe smirked. "How do you plan on stopping me now, Yeshua?".

"With our help," said a voice that startled The Scribe.

He whipped around to find Salemwalek, Ramalesh and Grandmaster Chang standing in a triangular formation around him, each sage holding a staff in his right hand. A ball of light immediately coalesced in The Scribe's right hand, and black streaks of light flashed from it.

"You know what this is?" The Scribe asked, with a dose of condescension.

"Are we supposed to pee our garments because you wield the Light of True Death?" Salemwalek answered.

The three sages aimed their staffs towards The Scribe. Beams of energy exploded from each sage's staff and trapped The Scribe in a grey sphere of light.

"Did your masters not tell you never to play with esoteric fire?" The Scribe asked rhetorically as he raised his right hand above his head.

Instantly, the Light of True Death absorbed the surges of energy intended to hold him prisoner. Then, bright, orange flames beamed from The Scribe's sphere and consumed each of the sage's staff to ashes.

"I will deal with your insolence later," The Scribe smirked as he turned around to face Yeshua. "But first, I must ensure this imbecile dies a true death, and *STAYS* truly dead."

"And your pride has led to your demise," Yeshua said.

Yeshua no longer lay on the slab of rock. He stood at the right-hand corner of the tomb, glowing in a golden brilliance as he underwent a transmutation to a higher etheric constituency after resurrecting from his illusionary death on the cross of Calvary. He opened his right hand and the Light of True Death traveled from The Scribe's hand to his.

"I admit, I underestimated you, Yeshua," The Scribe conceded. "But, unique as you may be, my existence will not expire at your hands."

"Truer words have never been spoken, Chaos," Priya interjected as her form coalesced out of thin air. "This madness ends right now."

She closed her eyes, and two orbs of shiny black light coalesced in both of her hands as she spread out her arms on either side of her body. She aimed the orbs of black light at The Scribe. Yeshua raised his right hand above his head with the same intention. The ashes of the staffs of the three sages reconstituted themselves to form staffs, and the three sages aimed at The Scribe as well.

"It is good to see you too, Order," The Scribe said. "But you and I will dance later."

With those words, The Scribe clapped his hands once above his head, and a purple flame shot upwards from his feet to his fingertips. In an instant, The Scribe, also known as Chaos, The Anomaly, and The Scientist, was gone, leaving no trace behind and impossible to be tracked in all the dimensions of Creation. Priya let out a scream of rage so intense that it shook the earth like a rag doll.

"We will get him, Priya," Yeshua assured her.

"No. Chaos is mine and mine alone!" Order fumed and disappeared in beam of golden light.

CHAPTER TWENTY-SIX

UNLEASHED

AN AMBULANCE TORE through the streets of Bucharest like a predator fixated on a prey. Teeth clenched, eyes rolled into the back of her head, a patient, or more like a victim of a gruesome attack, convulsed so violently that three EMT's struggled to contain her naked, bloodied and badly mauled body. Her strength exceeded those of the gurney straps, which she had broken with relative ease the first time they tried to restrain her.

"What could have done this to her?" asked EMT #1.

"Maybe it was a bear," said EMT #2.

"Bears… don't… maul like… that," countered EMT #1 as he struggled with the victim's arm.

"Bear expert now?" asked EMT #2 rhetorically.

EMT #1 switched his position to sit on the bloodied female's left elbow. He used his hands to pin down her left shoulder and forearm.

His coworkers changed their strategy as well. EMT #2 sat on the victim's right elbow and pinned down her right shoulder and forearm with his free hands, while the strongest of them, EMT #3, sat on her knees with his back to her, and leaned forward to hold down her ankles with both his hands. The EMT's new positions seemed to work.

"Looks more like a dog bite," said EMT #2.

"If dogs have thumbs," EMT #3 said. "Look at her tummy."

The other EMT's noticed the patterns on the ripped chunks of flesh just above the victim's hips. The pattern indicated a huge hand print just above her hips; four fingers on her belly and a thumb on her lower back, as if she was grabbed from behind, just above the waist. The ambulance swerved to the right at the last busy intersection before the final two-mile stretch to the hospital.

EMT #3 resumed attempting to re-strap the victim's legs to the gurney.

Suddenly, the victim stopped struggling. In a final exhalation of air, she closed her eyes and her body relaxed to become perfectly still. The EMT's regarded one another and the victim, confusion written all over their faces. Slowly, they peeled themselves off her arms and legs and waited. Nothing happened.

"What's going on back there?" asked the driver.

No one replied.

EMT #1 pressed his left index and middle fingers on the victim's jugular. No pulse. He swallowed nervously and leaned until his cheek was close to the victim's nostrils. He held that position for a few seconds. No breath. He sighed and made to sit up. As he did, he never noticed the victim's lips peel into a grin. He never noticed her canines turn into long, sharp fangs. He never noticed how brightly her eyes shone as they snapped open. Most of all, he never got to fully appreciate his luck for his quick and painless death.

Patrick was in New Zealand investigating reports regarding multiple sightings of a nine-foot tall humanoid creature accused of abducting several children and women, when he received instructions from Shi'mon through telepathy.

'Bucharest: Locate and liquidate the Bright Eye.'

The suspect turned out to be a nine-foot humanoid creature, but she was not the abductor of the children and women. Instead, she was trying to help free them from the actual culprit; an interdimensional parasite that preyed on the human essence for survival.

Patrick neutralized the interdimensional parasite, returned eight out of the eleven children and women to their homes, and declared three missing, most likely dead. He also helped relocate the nine-foot creature to an unexplored area of the Amazon, where it found other creatures with similar features and traits, only these were about a foot shorter. Still, they welcomed her into their fold.

Patrick teleported to Bucharest. He followed the ambulance as it tore through the streets, whizzing through the crowd and traffic. He moved too quick for the normal human eye to consciously register his movements.

This will be an easy mission, Patrick shrugged *No need for UV bombs or decapitation. A little exposure to sunlight and Houston, we have a barbecue.*

The ambulance made a right turn. Patrick glanced at his watch.

Final stretch, he said to himself. *Save to assume the EMT's are already dead.*

A loud bang, the screeching of tires and the sudden stop of the ambulance froze Patrick and everyone in place.

Then, the rear tires of the ambulance suddenly left the ground for a second as if an insane amount of force yanked the ambulance off the ground. The roof of the ambulance caved outward at the same time. The rear doors of the ambulance flew open with a loud bang and the body of an EMT whooshed through the air like a baseball thrown by a pitcher. The body crashed through the windshield of a car that was slowing to a stop behind the ambulance, forcing the car to an abrupt stop. A six-car pile-up ensued. Gasps and screams erupted throughout the streets in the wake of the unbelievable.

Come on now, Bright Eye, Patrick remained calm. *Ashes to – what the -.*

The Bright Eye leaped out of the ambulance, dragging a terrified, bloodied, kicking, clawing and screaming EMT by the hair. The remains of two mauled, dismembered and disemboweled EMT's painted the interior of the ambulance in crimson and pink gore and guts. Another body, presumably the driver's, hung over the shattered glass partition that separated the front and the back of the ambulance. The brimming chaos on the streets hit a diminuendo as a cloud of confusion temporarily clawed its way through the collective conscious minds of everyone present.

Patrick wiggled his way through the gathering crowd, palm open, ready to spark the ethers into whatever was necessary. The Bright Eyes still maintained her human form, despite her body, face and hair being covered with blood and pieces of gore.

She's supposed to ash, Patrick snarled as he pushed his way through the crowd. *Wait, isn't that the chick from that show... Myths Hunters or something like that?*

Cell phones came out of pockets and purses and sheer stupidity and the search for social media likes and fame overrode the survival instincts of many. Patrick sighed pressed his earpiece.

"Track my location," he ordered. "Purge the internet."

"Affirmative."

He sparked the ethers into an EMP bomb and detonated. Every electronic device within a half-mile radius was instantly rendered useless.

Sorry, but not sorry, Patrick smirked.

Bright Eye Blades lifted the EMT over a foot above the ground by the EMT's hair with her left hand and drove her hand right through the EMT's gut. She retracted her hand from the EMT's gut and bloodied, internal organs hung loose from the dying EMT's eviscerated torso. She brought the EMT's face closer to hers, bared her fangs and sank them deep into the EMT's neck. She drank the EMT's blood in huge gulps to her satisfaction. She yanked her head backward, tearing off a huge chunk of flesh from the EMT's neck. Blood spurted from the EMT's jugular like a drinking fountain. Then, the pandemonium broke out.

Bright Eye Blades howled, filled with the feeling of untamed savagery, power and exhilarating aliveness. The overload in adrenaline dwarfed anything she had ever experienced, resulting in a rush that rocked her existential reality and thrust her into a realm of perception exponentially more heightened than that created by marijuana and cocaine, the only narcotics she had ever tempered with.

Blood and flesh; nothing ever tasted so good, she exulted in her mind. *Why did I have to wait all these years to discover such a delicacy? What is this feeling? Hallelujah.*

Every iota of her being resonated with the sensations of her current existence. Her taste, touch, smell and hearing went ablaze with fiery sensation. Even her vision was 200/200. And the best part of it all, she smelled the fear from every observer. She could taste the insane amounts of adrenaline they released, sending nuclear level reactions within her of hunger and thirst for their blood and flesh. This was ecstasy made manifest. This was perfection.

Bright Eye Blades dug her fangs again into the exsanguinating EMT's jugular.

Yes. Yes. Oh, freaking YES. This is the life.

Every cell in her body pulsed with a cataclysmic orgasm of its own. As she drank every last drop of blood with each pump from the EMT's dying heart, her body turned black, hairy and leathery, her knees broke backwards, her ears stretched and became larger and more pointy, and her mouth turned into a snout. She let the lifeless body of the EMT drop on the hot, blistering tarmac, lifted her eyes towards the sun and let out a skin-crawling, spine-chilling, soul-stealing howl of joy to signify the completion of her transformation into a daywalking luper. She turned her attention towards the crowd and zoomed in on a teenager, who was hitting his cell phone repeatedly in frustration. Her eyes met his. His fear fueled her lust like a catalyst to an explosive reaction. She bared her fangs in a grin of excitement and diabolical gusto before she zipped for the kill.

In a flash, the teenager realized just how foolish he had been to prioritize social media fame over survival. Death was a given. But even in the moment of realization, he still thought about the millions of likes, followers and subscribers his video would have earned him. He thought of the internet fame and all the chicks he would have scored. However, as the creature from Hell approached him for a kill, his dreams of a future that will never come to pass morphed into a nightmare of epic proportions. He squeezed his eyes shut and opened his mouth to scream. A second passed. Nothing happened. He opened his eyes.

"What just happened?" he asked himself.

He felt a sting in his throat and reached for it with his left hand. It felt warm to the touch. He retracted his hand and brought it to eye level. A thin layer of blood spread across the tips of his middle and ring fingers.

Patrick zipped, caught Blades' right wrist with his left hand, sank his weight and twisted his hips to the right. Maintaining pressure on Blades' wrist, he aligned his left forearm with Blades' right elbow. Blades veered to the left under Patrick's control of her arm. The claw of her left middle finger scraped the teenager's throat, leaving a paper cut on it. Patrick took a backward cross-step with his left leg in the same swift motion, twisting and turning Blades' right wrist violently. Her spine locked as her entire body helplessly turned about her right shoulder. Her right wrist snapped in several places, and her skull slammed on the scourging tarmac. Patrick raised his right foot to crush her skull against the tarmac.

Luper Blades parried his right ankle just enough to make Patrick miss his target and used the momentum of his descent to take him in an ankle lock as she rolled him over to her left. She now had the advantage, and Patrick's back was on the tarmac. She made to kick his groin to distract him before she shattered his ankle, but Patrick continued with the momentum of his fall, rolling over on his hands so that his back was towards Blades for a split second. Using brute force, he yanked his right leg forward as he rolled forward. Blades let go of his ankle and sailed through the air under the force of his forward roll. She rolled to cushion her fall and turned to face Patrick. The two opponents sized each other from a crouching position. Police sirens blared in the distance. Patrick sighed. Blades bared her fangs and growled. Then, they zipped towards each other.

To those who still dared to stay behind and watch, all they saw was a bloodied, feral, canine creature from Hell and a black, bald man disappear from a crouching position and, in a blink of an eye, a bloodied, feral, canine, headless creature's corpse roll on the tarmac till it came to a stop a short distance from its original position, while its head continued to roll until it came to a stop underneath a car. A second later, her headless body and head burst into flames, turned into piles of ash, a gust of wind blew the ashes away, and the black guy was nowhere in sight.

Patrick appeared in the restroom of a sushi restaurant in the heart of Tokyo. He walked out of the restroom in a freshly pressed dark-blue suit and matching shirt he sparked from the ethers. He retrieved a cell phone from his pocket, only as a distraction, and raised it to his ear. The phone was not even turned on.

"We have a serious situation, Father," Patrick said telepathically. *"The Bright Eyes are now daywalkers."*

"I know," Shi'mon replied.

***

Fr. Castro tried to hide his scowl as he blended with the many tourists at the Vatican.

'BLUE ALERT: RETURN TO BASE AT ONCE' the highly encrypted

text message had read.

My vacation cut short.

He thought about Rosanna; about how she cradled his head against her bosom to ease his anger. She understood he had to go. He loved her so much, and she reciprocated. His plan was to save enough money working for the O.R and then quit one day to start a family with Rossana. He could always stay employed after he quit. Someone with his skillset can never remain unemployed, unless they are handicapped or something.

Fr. Castro cursed under his breath again and reached into his khaki pants to retrieve a pack of cigarettes and a lighter.

No smoking on Vatican soil, he recalled.

He cursed again, a little louder this time, and returned the pack of cigarettes to his pocket. He lifted his face cap and dabbed at beads of sweat on his forehead with a red, cotton handkerchief. He stashed the handkerchief into his pocket and returned to taking photos, just like the thousands of tourists who flocked the capital city of the smallest sovereignty in the world.

"*Scuzi, Signore, parle l'inglesa?*" asked a tourist behind him in heavily accented Italian.

Fr. Castro turned around. A friendly, clean-shaven, mid-30's face greeted him with a smile. The tourist was about an inch taller than he was, with a strong build underneath his grey tee-shirt and white pair of shorts. His dazzling green eyes danced with politeness and the sun's rays seeped through a well-done crew cut.

Military, Fr. Castro thought.

"I'm sorry, sir," Fr. Castro lied in an Australian accent. "I don't speak Italian."

"Oh, you speak English," exclaimed the young man in a British accent.

His green eyes lit up even more.

"Wonderful. Perhaps you could be of help then?"

"Perhaps I could," Fr. Castro replied with a forced smile.

"Wonderful. How would you like to be a messenger to the rest of the world?" the young man asked with a fake grin.

Fr. Castro's narrowed his eyes, feigning confusion. He pressed a concealed button on his camera once to alert the order of possible, imminent trouble.

"I'm not sure I understand you, sir," Fr. Castro said. "Are you a reporter with a news channel?"

"No," the man replied. "But the world is about to know about us."

The stranger's eyes flashed brightly before returning to normal. Fr. Castro hit two buttons on his camera several times to confirm danger was present. The stranger closed his eyes and when he opened them, the brightness remained. He smiled again revealing elongated canines and pure evil radiated in his bright eyes.

Fr. Castro wasted no time. He hit a button on the camera, and UV light flashed from it straight into the stranger's eyes, temporarily blinding the Bright Eye. It screamed with maniacal rage and averted his face away from Castro.

Fr. Castro reached behind his oversized flannel shirt and retrieved his pistol. He fired two shots into the Bright Eyes' chin, and both bullets exited through the crown of its head. It hit the ground with a thud and mayhem broke out in the Vatican. Fr. Castro still had his weapon trained on the Bright Eye as he spoke rapidly into his radio.

"Bright Eye on the southeast corner," he said.

"Three more sightings reported," said a voice over the walkie-talkie.

"Holy crap," Fr. Castro cursed out loud.

"What is it?" asked the voice.

The Bright Eye started to convulse, and his back began to arch awkwardly. Its fingers elongated to claws, and its clothes ripped up and hung loose on its body as it morphed into a luper. It stood on its hind legs, towering over Fr. Castro by nearly a foot.

"It's not dead," Fr. Castro replied. "And it's not ashing."

The luper howled at him, yanking Fr. Castro from his state of paralyzing shock to full assault mode. He pulled out another pistol and turned the luper's body into a repository for silver-tipped bullets as he fired away. However, the luper barely slumped to a knee and nothing more. Fr. Castro cursed out loud and quickly reloaded his pistols.

"If I never see Rosanna again," he smirked, "I might as well go down with this abomination."

The luper swung its left paw at Fr. Castro's head. Fr. Castro ducked to his right and stepped closer to the beast. Using the luper's bent knee as a stepping stone, Fr. Castro lunged to the back of the beast, firing four rounds into the creature's head. Each bullet made a clean exit through the luper's face, but the luper only dropped to one knee. It turned around to face Fr. Castro and narrowed its glowing eyes. Fr. Castro gawked as the exit wounds slowly closed until the luper was completely healed. It grinned at him with defiance and mockery. Fr. Castro spat in its face and leveled his pistols at the luper.

"Go to hell," he screamed.

The luper prepared to zip and he prepared to fire. Suddenly, a black blur whizzed between Fr. Castro and the luper. The blur stopped, revealing a man completely covered from head to toe in a black combat outfit, wielding a sword with a four-foot long blade in his right hand. The luper fell in front of Fr. Castro, headless, and turned to ash.

"Scout the area," ordered his savior.

"Yes, sir," Fr. Castro replied and obliged.

So, the rumors were true. Fr. Castro thought. *The O.R. has a group of very 'special' agents led by a mysterious figure that only the big boss knew of. Cool. I should apply.*

Shi'mon and eight of his specially trained agents defused the attack at the Vatican as quickly as the attacks started. Shi'mon reached for his right ear and radioed an order.

"Release the EMP and bleach the internet," he said and left the chaos.

***

RBS News: *There have been multiple reports from London, Washington DC, Paris, Moscow, Jerusalem, Berlin, Bucharest and even the Vatican of strange creatures and psychotic people randomly killing and mutilating innocent civilians. Many sources describe their methods as horrific and gory…*

KPT Network: *What's most absurd is the fact that there are no video recordings of any of these sightings; like absolutely nothing on the internet. So much for living in the twenty-first century. But one common trend with all these reports is that all electronic devices within as much as a mile radius were fried. Some people are speculating that world governments know about this and are trying to keep it under wraps…*

TCB: *The President of the United States calls these 'vicious and senseless attacks' and accuses the UMAH and IMUS terrorist groups. But both terrorist groups, for the first time, issued a joint statement, saying, and I quote, "We bomb and behead infidels, not eat them,"*

Al Hassud News Network: *And who are these mystery people who suddenly show up and defuse these attacks? Reports talk of people moving too fast for the naked eye and these creatures turning to ash as soon as they are decapitated. You heard correctly; decapitated. Unfortunately, in the absence of concrete evidence, these claims remain speculations. Conspiracy theorists are having a buffet over these events. However, the similarity of the reports from different locations seems to suggest otherwise.*

CHAPTER TWENTY-SEVEN

FEELING THE REALM

"WHAT IS TAU'MA **thinking?" Yeshua asked.**

"Food, master," Mattityahu replied.

"What else?" Yeshua asked.

"And Hadar, master," Mattityahu replied using telepathy. *"She is my neighbor."*

Tau'ma sparked the ethers into a ball of hay and threw it at Mattityahu using telekinesis, but the ball of hay caught fire midflight and the ashes fell to the ground.

"Excellent work with the fire, Nathanael," Yeshua said.

"And good answer Mattityahu," he added using telepathy.

'Thank you, master," Nathanael and Mattityahu chorused.

'If you can spark the ethers into a ball of hay, why do you not spark the ethers into food?" Yeshua asked Tau'ma.

"I know not, master," Tau'ma shrugged and lowered his gaze. "Perhaps I may not be hungry after all."

"Or maybe you are just in love, brother?" Andrew offered.

"Not true," Tau'ma argued and bit his lower lip.

"We heard your thoughts," Andrew continued. "But even before clairaudience, you have always had an eye for Hadar."

Tau'ma glared at Andrew, who shrugged and smiled.

"You should tell her how you feel before Yehoyakim comes in and steals her from you," Andrew continued.

"Maybe Yoch, not me," Yehoyakim chimed in. "Marriage is not in my plan right now. I have things to take care of before I consider marriage."

"Pray tell, brother," Yehuda rolled his eyes. "What are these 'things' of which you speak."

"For your next test," Yeshua raised his voice, ending the conversation before it got out of hand. "I have a red cloak folded and placed on top of a rock. Let us see who gets it to me first. You all remember how I went up the hill to pray last night."

Yeshua did not even finish the statement and eleven of his twelve apprentices vanished from sight. Yochanan stayed behind.

"Well, everyone is off to the search already," Yeshua shrugged.

"Where is your cloak, master?" Yochanan asked.

"You are supposed to search for it," Yeshua said.

"You said you wanted to see who will get it to you first," Yoch stood up and straightened his garments. "You never said I had to search."

Yeshua regarded Yoch, nodded and snapped his fingers. Everything became still; from the fowls in the air, passersby, insects crawling on the ground, the dust, the wind… everything came to a perfect standstill, except for himself and his mentor. Yeshua beckoned at him.

"Walk with me," Yeshua said.

"Incredible," Yochanan exclaimed and glided towards Yeshua. "What did you do, master?"

"I encased us within a temporal bubble," Yeshua explained. "Linear time is moving at over 1,000 times less than its normal speed outside the bubble. No one outside our bubble will notice the difference."

"Amazing," Yochanan let his eyes feast on everything around him.

He glided towards a pedestrian, who was frozen in midstride. He waved his hand in front of the pedestrian's eyes.

"Nothing," he exclaimed. "Not even a blink."

He glided back towards Yeshua.

"How did you do that, master?" his eyes danced with excitement.

"By accessing the Dimension of Time, which is one of the states of Creation," Yeshua replied.

"Will you teach us?" he asked.

"No," Yeshua replied. "Accessing the Dimensions of Space, Time, Energy and Ether is reserved only for special beings in Creation. Unfortunately, you are not worthy and it is not a bad thing to not be worried. The level of responsibility and power that come with being able to access these states of Creation at will is far too grand for you all to handle without the blessing of one of these special beings."

"I understand, master."

Yochanan paused in thought for a moment.

"Master, you can see into the past and future, right?" he asked.

"Yes, I can."

"Can you travel into the past and future?"

"Yes, I can."

"Incredible," Yochanan beamed like an excited child. "This is the second year since your return to Israel and second year since our training started. So, are you saying you can go to the past, change some things, and everything we know now will change as well?"

"I can," Yeshua smiled at his cuteness. "I can even live in the past and future if I want to."

Yochanan's jaw fell and he stared unblinkingly at his mentor.

"And I can do all that because I can access all the states of Creation," Yeshua explained. "I can access the Dimensions of Space, Time, Energy and Ether at will."

Yochanan closed his mouth and swallowed. He opened his mouth to speak but Yeshua's words had rendered his speech useless. He staggered a little.

"The exercise I created about the cloak was merely a test," Yeshua continued. "Here, sit down."

He sparked the ethers into two, cushioned armchairs. They sat down and faced each other.

"Creation and the Creator are one and inseparable," Yeshua said. "Therefore, the Creator permeates all of Creation. Every realm has a representation of the Creator, of Consciousness. This representation is generally called Mother."

"Does that mean the Creator chooses to be a woman in the realm?" Yoch asked.

"No," Yeshua replied. "Mother is just a name. It has no bearing on any human attributes, be it physiological or psychological. Just like the Creator, it has no form. Yet, it can take any form it pleases."

Yochanan, the youngest of the apprentices, rubbed his chin as he furrowed his eyebrows in thought. His chin barely had any hair on it.

"Alright, master," he nodded. "I think I understand."

Yeshua flashed a kind smile, leaned back and crossed his legs.

"When a realm attains a certain level of spiritual evolution," Yeshua continued. "Mother chooses a creature on the realm who becomes a guardian to the realm. No one can vie for that title. Only Mother decides who her guardian is and that guardian holds that position, with Mother's blessing, for as long as Mother decides."

"What criteria does Mother use in selecting a guardian, master?" Yoch asked.

"That is a question for Mother," Yeshua replied.

"Can I ask her?"

"You can, but that does not mean she will respond," Yeshua replied. "I forgot to add; only the guardian can communicate with Mother, though sometimes, mother chooses to communicate with someone other than a guardian. But this is extremely rare. In fact, I have not seen any record of Mother communicating with creatures besides the guardians of the realm."

"Master," Yochanan moved to the edge of his seat. "Are you telling me this because you want to task me with finding the guardian?"

"Remember I told you that Mother chooses her guardian," Yeshua replied.

"Oh, correct," Yochanan squeezed his eyes shut and pursed his lips briefly. "My apologies. I forgot so quickly."

"No need for apologies," Yeshua said. "I do have a few tasks for you, though."

Yochanan straightened and scowled slightly to display his attention and focus.

"You will have to keep an eye out for Shi'mon and Yehuda," Yeshua explained. "You will know when that time comes. Can I count on you for that?"

"Of course, master," Yochanan replied with enthusiasm. "Anything."

"Good, now on to the next item."

Yeshua sat up and rested his elbows on his thighs.

"How good is your clairsentience?"

"About 100 cubits in range," Yoch replied.

"Good," Yeshua nodded. "I will increase the range of your clairsentience."

"To 200 cubits? 400?" Yochanan prompted.

"To the entire realm," Yeshua replied.

"By Yahweh," Yochanan exclaimed and sank into his chair. "How, master?"

"Psychic surgery," Yeshua replied.

"Psychic surgery," Yochanan spoke the words to himself as if he was in a trance.

"Do not burden yourself about that now, brother," Yeshua continued. "Another time and day."

"As you wish, master," Yochanan replied and sat up again.

"When the procedure is complete," Yeshua explained. 'You will be able to sense the realm's feelings because, as you know, the realm is very much alive. That means you will also be able to detect any changes in Earth Realm's esoteric signature as long as you are tuned in."

"Okay, master," Yochanan said. "Thank you for this honor."

Such faith, Yeshua's heart beamed with pride. *Such unwavering faith.*

"Well, I think the time has come for us to emerge from this temporal bubble," Yeshua stood up.

Yochanan stood up with him.

"The cloak is over there," Yeshua pointed at a boulder 27ft to their right.

"So close this whole time," Yochanan teleported to the boulder. "They are going to be so upset when they find out."

Yochanan lifted a flat rock on top of the boulder, revealing Yeshua's cloak.

"Ready?" Yeshua asked.

"Yes, master," Yochanan nodded and glided towards Yeshua.

Yeshua snapped his fingers. Linear time returned and everything moved as if nothing had happened. Yochanan's eyes wandered around in awe and fascination.

"Master, we cannot find your cloak here," Shi'mon said via telepathy.

"Okay," Yeshua replied.

A moment of silence lingered.

"Are you sure it is here, master?" Shi'mon asked.

"Did I ever say it was there in the first place?" Yeshua asked.

Many curses escaped the lips of two of the most foul-mouthed apprentices, Tau'ma and Mattityahu. One-by-one, the apprentices appeared in front of Yeshua. Their scowls of frustration vanished to looks of surprise when they saw Yochanan holding a cloak in both hands.

"Where did you find it?" Yaakov asked.

"Over there," Yochanan gestured towards a boulder.

"How?"

"It matters not, brothers," Yeshua interjected. "I gave a test, Yoch passed, the end. Lesson for today, learn to pay attention."

Yeshua smiled, much to the grumbling and rolling of eyes of the apprentices, except for Yochanan whose grin of victory remained chiseled on his face.

"Go home now," Yeshua bid them all. "We will resume training in two days."

One-by-one, the apprentices teleported away to their homes. Yochanan was the last to leave. He approached Yeshua and extended his arms.

"Your cloak, master."

"Thank you," Yeshua took his cloak. "Psychic surgery in six days."

'As you wish, master."

C. E. 2010

Yochanan sat in a Buddha pose on the black sand beach of Seme in the SW Province of Cameroon. The ~~riding~~rising tide slowly neared his legs as the yellow ball in the sky slowly turned orange and headed toward where the Atlantic

236

Ocean kissed the sky. He loved this beach, including the mountain to his back, which was the only active volcano in Central and West Africa. The locals loved him and always looked forward to his visits. They even gave him a name in their local dialect, which he still had to make the conscious effort to remember. An hour later, he stood up and headed for his hotel.

That night, he dreamed of… nothing, which usually happened whenever he kept his clairsentience constantly turned on. His body would rest, but his astral body scoured the realm, like a sentinel.

I'm no guardian, he told himself often. *But I will guard the realm regardless.*

The O.R. also did the same thing, protecting Earth Realm from all supernatural, extraterrestrial and paranormal attacks. He worked with the organization, only to Shi'mon's knowing.

An intense disturbance in Earth Realm's esoteric signature yanked his astral self back into his body. He bolted from the hotel bed and sat upright.

"Another portal," he hissed. "But this one is different."

Immediately, he teleported to the location where the portal was opened. He stood about 50 yards from the entrance to a cave on Mt. K2, wearing nothing but a pair of black, boxer briefs in the -20°F weather, but the winds blowing snow at 20mph created a windchill of over -40°F. Yochanan elevated his chi levels to render his body impervious to these deadly elements.

"Sinisters," he grinned and sparked the ethers into two daggers with footlong, razor-sharp blades. "Bring it on."

A faint chanting came from within the cave. He waited. Then, a five-foot-nine, slightly muscular, orange-skin humanoid creature with horns and a tail emerged from the cave, turned its back to him, knelt down and began incantations.

Why? Yochanan wondered. *Why did it not attack or flee? It acts as if I don't even matter, as if it has more important things to worry about.*

He read the kneeling Sinister's thoughts using clairaudience.

"Crap," Yochanan exclaimed and made to end the Sinister.

A portal appeared above the kneeling Sinister and a swarm of Sinisters emerged from that portal and immediately pounced on Yochanan.

202 and counting, he gritted as he swiftly beheaded four of them. *I must get to that Sinister before it completes its incantation.*

CHAPTER TWENTY-EIGHT

MARK OF A MOLE

"HOW DID THE Order know of our attacks?" Dreyko spoke with an icy calm that underscored the irony to his current sentiment.

"Guessing from their M.O.," Andrew replied swiftly. "At any given time, the order has agents in every major city in the world. Bucharest must have triggered and increased global presence."

"Logical," Danka's eyes narrowed to slits.

Andrew's expression and demeanor remained unchanged. Over the decades since his undercover mission within the Bright Eyes, Danka had gradually grown fonder of him. Providing The Twins with reliable, but selective, intelligence on the modus operandi of the O.R had helped to solidify his status among the Bright Eyes. Demonstrating unrivaled leadership, which came naturally to him being an apprentice of Yeshua's, quickly moved him up the ranks until he became Danka's confidant., a fancy title for 'most trusted Bright Eye and Danka's personal boy toy'. Andrew's duties included, among other things, providing Danka with adult entertainment, much to his displeasure.

"Thanks for taking one for the team," Shi'mon teased. *"We appreciate your sacrifice."*

However, his newfound status also invoked Dreyko's vengeful jealousy, but Danka's interest in him also meant he was under Danka's protection.

"Still, it does not explain how the order knew about Bucharest," Danka added.

Andrew clenched and relaxed his jaw.

"The Order keeps tabs on a lot," Andrew explained without skipping a beat.

He leaned forward and rested his elbows on the long table that sat eight of the top-ranked Bright Eyes in the Bright Eyes community; The Twins, himself, Sasha, Bischoff, Ernesto and two others. His gaze settled briefly on everyone present as he spoke, creating an air of confidence as he lied his way through his explanation, an act which came naturally from knowledge of the inner workings of the O.R.

"Remember, they deal in the paranormal, supernatural and extraterrestrial," Andrew continued. "They will respond to any claims of these genres. When the *Myth Huntsmen* received the video from him," he glared at The Scientist, "believe me when I say that the order increased its threat level alert given the nature of the video's content. You all know the rest."

"In hindsight," The Scientist said, "I admit I should have taken Andrew's counsel into serious consideration. Plus, I didn't think that the new breed would be taken out so quickly."

"I don't know of any creature that can survive a decapitation," Sasha spat with sweet sarcasm.

The Scientist blushed more from anger than anything else. After all he had done for these pathetic creatures over the past decades, the least they could do was show some respect. More than six decades after the destruction of the Berlin facility, he had finally been able to synthesize a serum that would turn these nocturnal, sewage-crawlers into daywalkers. The blood sample Sasha brought was useless but the sample he obtained from the wooden cross piece two millennia ago remained fresh and uncoagulated. He could not function in his full capacity as a multidimensional being while on Earth Realm. He could only function up to the current evolutionary potential of Earth Realm. As such, he had to wait for the next minor cosmic shift in the Dimension of Solaris, the dimension in which Earth Realm resides. This shift would usher the next minor phase of Earth Realm's evolutionary potential, which would in turn create the right atmosphere to synthesize the serum to turn the Bright Eyes into daywalkers.

This is 2010 and the Cosmic Clock is counting down, he seethed in frustration. *I hate Creation's rules. I could've easily accomplished this task of turning these Bright Eyes in to daywalkers as a multidimensional being. But no, I have to function using primitive constraints like linear time, which is not on my side right now. And why do I have to turn these creatures into daywalkers? Because as daywalkers, their etheric constitution will be different and ready to fully act as my catalysts when I unleashed the vibration of Chaos across Creation to undo it.*

***

Several attempts at synthesizing a serum resulted in failure.

What am I doing wrong? The Scientist wondered. *What is the common denominator between Shi'mon, Yehuda and The Twin's father, whatever his name is again? It has to be more than just soullessness.*

A few weeks later, he found the answer: emotion.

Yes. Somehow, these three had succeeded, albeit unconsciously, to isolate pure, untainted emotion. Shi'mon and Yehuda; consumed by guilt. The Twins' father (I still can't remember the man's name): overwhelmed by desperation. The Twins; an interplay between parental and animal DNA and an abominable lust for each other.

Danka's assumed biological father had 'died' presumably 'under normal circumstances', The Scientist suppressed a smile. *But one can never underestimate the power of artificial insemination under the guise of a spiritual visitation from an 'angel of the Lord'. And who was that angel of the Lord?*

This time, The Scientist managed a slight mischievous smile. He brought the test tube with Yeshua's blood into the palm of his hand using telekinesis.

So, how do I summon pure emotion? The Scientist sighed. *Emotions… such a primitive sentiment. But then again, Earth is a most primitive realm. I'm from Akasha and these human sentiments, or at least the way they function here, elude me. Despite functioning as The Scientist on this plane of existence, I don't even have a heart… literally.*

He cursed out loud.

To summon an emotion like these creatures do, I must relive an experience that was traumatizing to me, he concluded. *And I can think of only one; the moment I became Chaos.*

The Scientist relived the moment and experienced the full force of what he believed was the epitome of darkness and betrayal. That moment, despite its existence only in the past, became a seeming present reality. He visualized the feeling as a drop of water, which he dropped into the test tube. When he opened his eyes, the blood sample glowed with a pale, blue hue.

Finally, success.

The first tests on the Bright Eyes were a huge success. At first, they could not stay under Solara or UV light for more than twenty-four minutes. Their bodies adapted over the next few weeks and they could last for more than twelve hours under Solara or UV light. However, their inability to reproduce never changed.

Which I couldn't care less for, The Scientist told himself. *They can turn more humans into Bright Eyes if they feel the need to propagate their species. All I care about is their readiness at the etheric level to welcome the vibration of Chaos when I unleash it across Creation.*

The Scientist smiled with satisfaction.

I just created the first daywalkers on Earth Realm. My plan is on track so far. But did I ever doubt myself in the first place? I am Chaos. I am a purveyor of purpose. I am perfect and, therefore, my plan can only be perfect.

The Bright Eyes, just like the many unique creatures I have placed on strategic realms and dimensions across Creation, will serve as perfect conduits for the vibration of chaos I shall unleash. The chain reaction will be unstoppable. The outcome, the undoing of Creation, also known as pure perfection. Creation will be reduced to an unsullied singularity called Chaos, my own unsullied essence. This will happen when the Cosmic Clock completes its countdown to initiate the Great Reset. Before the last Great Reset, I did not exist and thus, Chaos did not exist. But with the last reset, I was spawned into existence and Chaos became a part of Creation. It is, therefore, inevitable that Creation must be undone to reflect my nature, Chaos.

***

"We should have heeded to your counsel, Andrew," Dreyko conceded and glared icicles at The Scientist. "However, I took the liberty of including one more location that was not a high priority target; Cameroon," Dreyko directed his spine-gripping stare towards Andrew. "Does the order, have any particular interest in Cameroon?"

"Not that I know of, your highness," Andrew faked confusion. "Unless that changed in the last sixty years."

"I do not think so," Dreyko continued. "And that is my point. Why would the order send an agent to a nation like Cameroon in the first place? Better yet, how did they even *know* of an impending attack in Cameroon? Unless one of you is their informant."

Dreyko's eyes narrowed as he glared at everyone around the table.

"I hate traitors" Danka hissed sadistically as she rose from her seat.

Andrew had never seen her so furious, so feral and… So fine.

Damnation, he cursed.

His cover was about to be blown, and all he could think of was how badly his testosterone drive was presently overriding his reason. An aura of fear and quiet panic smothered the room.

"Only six of us knew of this plan," Dreyko continued with his usual evil, calm demeanor, "my sister and I, Doctor, Andrew, Sasha, and Ernesto."

Dreyko leaned back in his chair.

"If you confess now, your death will be quick and painless.".

The tightening of his jaw, the narrowing of his eyes and the whitening of his knuckles as he gripped the armrests of his seat begged to differ, though. A deathly quiet filled the air of the room. No one even dared to blink, it seemed.

"So be it," Dreyko said.

Without warning, Dreyko zipped, grabbed Andrew by the throat and slammed his body against the wall.

Danka did the same to Sasha.

"You two are our prime suspects," Dreyko roared. "It seems as if your individual ties with Shi'mon and Yehuda have been rekindled."

"Now, which one of you will be the first to confess?" Danka roared as her face alone morphed into her beastly form.

Her glowing red eyes bored into Sasha's as Sasha struggled against Danka's death grip around her throat.

"I assure you, your highness," Andrew struggled to speak as Dreyko squeezed his throat, "I am not a traitor! I have been nothing but loyal to you two."

"Six seconds," Dreyko's baritone echoed across the room. "One, two, three."

"Your highness," Andrew said. "Please, don't do this."

"Four, five-"

"I'll see you two in hell," Sasha spat into Danka's face and teleported from the room, leaving Danka, snout agape with shock and grabbing at nothing.

"So, it was her," Danka growled as she regained her composure.

She delayed her transformation back to her human form to mask her relief that Andrew was not the mole.

A celebration is in order later, she promised herself.

"She even moves like Yehuda does," Dreyko agreed and let Andrew drop to the floor. "I want her captured, and brought back here, alive."

"Let me lead the search, your highness!" Andrew implored, picking himself from the floor. "I trained her in my combat skills, and I believe I am the best man for the job."

"And just how do you intend to do that?" Danka asked.

"I'll find a way," Andrew replied. "Let me find her, your highnesses. Please."

"Very well," Dreyko returned to his seat. "You bring her back, or I will have your head. Is that understood?"

"Yes, your highness," Andrew replied, knowing nothing would make Dreyko happier than to see him fail.

As Andrew turned to leave the room, a luper burst in with another luper in tow. She dropped to a knee.

"Kneel before our makers," she ordered the other luper, who quickly obliged.

"Forgive me, your highnesses," she said, initiating her transformation back to human form. "But I wouldn't come in like this if I didn't think it was important."

"Speak," Danka commanded.

"This is Cara from one of the villages nearby," she said. "I just turned her."

She turned her attention towards Cara.

"Return to human form," she commanded Cara.

Cara initiated her transformation back to human form.

"What do you mean you just turned her?" Danka walking slowly towards the two women.

The Scientist also walked towards the two lupers.

"Rise," Dreyko commanded before the luper could reply.

Both lupers stood up.

"Your highness," the lady swallowed nervously and cleared her throat. "I mean that she's now one of us and I'm still alive."

"And it keeps getting better," The Scientist exclaimed, grinning broadly while he gave both women a look over.

Dreyko approached the women, who trembled visibly with fear. He towered over them and regarded them as one would regard vermin for a few seconds before he did something no one had ever seen him do. He smiled and patted the bearer of the news on the shoulder.

"Your highness," Danka ordered.

The two ladies let out a heavy sigh of relief before quickly exiting the room.

"Are you getting this, brother?" Andrew asked telepathically.

"I am," Shi'mon replied telepathically. *"The Bright Eyes can now multiply their numbers indefinitely."*

CHAPTER TWENTY-NINE

COUNTDOWN

SASHA SAT CROSS-LEGGED at the entrance to a cave facing the ball of yellow in the sky as it gradually disappeared behind the horizon. Its glow felt warm on her skin, despite the snow that capped the peak of Mt. Kilimanjaro. The serenity of this mountain brought peace and tranquility to her troubled mind and aching heart, which yearned for the day she would become human again, free from the curse of being a Bright Eye. How this was going to come to pass eluded her. Yet, her faith remained as unshakeable as the mountain she sought solace from, a mountain she now visited more often ever since Andrew taught her how to teleport. At first, she would zip her way south, across two continents, a feasible but extremely exhausting feat, even for a Bright Eye.

This mountain testified to her most intimate and special days, as a human, with her one and only true love, Yehuda. The blessed hands of fate had brought them together. Sasha was picking mushrooms in the woods one day when some passersby attacked her. She fought, despite the dire look of the situation and the gods came to her aide in the form of a stranger, who seemed to appear from nowhere. He neutralized all eight of the assailants, leaving them with just enough strength and unbroken bones to carry their bodies to their horses. Patches of dried, black mud decorated his brown robe, unwashed face and unkempt hair and beard. She still sat on the ground, clothes ripped, arms and face bruised, when he walked up to her.

***

"Are you alright, milady?" he extended his hand towards her.

"Yes, sir, I am," she replied, taking his hand.

He helped her to her feet. She brushed the dirt off her hair and torn garments.

"A little bruised, but I am alright. Gratitude, sir. You saved me."

Sasha raised her eyes to meet his. She gasped, cupped her mouth with her hands and took an involuntary step back. In those eyes, a fire burned without heat. In those eyes, a cauldron of pain, loss, grief, anger, guilt, and shame bubbled with fiery intensity. She beheld a man who once had it all and lost it all. How could anyone blend total strength and utter powerlessness so perfectly? His eyes revealed a lifeless void that stretched into bottomlessness. A tear of sorrow ran down her right cheek, and the stranger had averted his eyes to the ground.

"You are welcome," he turned around and headed deeper into the forest.

Sasha just stood there, sobbing silently for a total stranger.

"You should head home now, milady," he added.

Sasha regained her composure and headed home. Her mother shrieked and ran towards her when she laid eyes of Sasha.

"What happened, my child?" her mother gave her a look over.

"I was attacked, mother," Sasha replied. "But I am fine, I assure you. A goodly stranger came to my rescue."

"By the gods, are you sure?" a panicked mother asked as the rest of her family emerged from the house, summoned by her mother's shriek.

"I am nineteen, mother," Sasha chuckled. "I believe I am old enough to know if I am not faring well?"

Her father came and gave her a look over before he gathered her in his loving, protective arms.

"You will tell us what happened once you get cleaned up," said her father.

Sasha's heart melted from the overflow of love from her family, a feeling she never grew tired of. As they headed home, her mind wondered to the days when she was homeless, wandering and foraging through the streets for survival, after escaping the orphanage with three of her friends.

The head nun at the orphanage was a vile creature of a human, who took pride in constantly reminding Sasha how worthless Sasha was, especially since Sasha's mother had dumped Sasha as a baby. Babies were bad for her flourishing career as a fancy lady and purveyor of erotic pleasures for men and women. The head nun's wickedness extended to every orphan in the orphanage. One day, Sasha made up her mind to leave the orphanage and live on the streets.

Maybe life will be better on the streets than in here, she thought.

And so, at age eight, she fled from the orphanage with two other girls and one boy. They lived on the streets, begging for food and coin. Many showed them kindness, others did not. Mr. Fowler, the baker, and his wife remained the kindest of them all. The couple fed them every day with three square meals for a whole year until a most unfortunate happenstance befell the goodly couple. A fire laid their entire business to waste, forcing the couple to leave the city and relocate to the village. Despite the couple's departure, Sasha and her friends survived the streets. Tragically, a few months later after the fire, one of her friends was abducted, and the other two died of a lung infection. Sasha had truly been alone for the first time in her life.

However, the hands of the gods were upon her. A goodly merchant saw Sasha begging for food one day and his soul ached with love for this child. He always provided her with food and clean clothes every time he came to the market.

"Tell me, child," he asked her one day. "Why are you on the streets."

Sasha told him her story. His heart ached and the tears flowed freely. He left that day and returned the very next day, three days earlier than normal. He found Sasha at her usual spot.

"I told my wife and children about you," he said. "And I asked them if they would not mind adding one more person to the family."

Sasha recoiled in shock and confusion.

The gods must be playing tricks on me, she thought.

"So, if it is alright with you," he had continued, "we would like you to become a part of our family."

The world went black as Sasha's mind could not handle the man's words and she passed out. She awoke later with the man's protective arms wrapped around her. She tried to say something but her words drowned in the tears of joy that flowed freely down her cheeks.

Sasha returned to the forest every single day in search of the stranger who saved her. Two months of searching proved unsuccessful. Still, Sasha did not give up and ventured further into the forest without consideration for her safety. Finally, she found him; more like he seemed to appear behind her, but she could have been wrong.

"Why do you seek me, milady?" he asked firmly but without intimidating her. "What is it you want?"

"I- I do not know, sir," she stuttered and averted her gaze. "I- I just wanted to say thank you…"

"You already did, milady," he spoke more softly.

"You are right, sir," she lowered her head to hide her blush. "I do not know why I seek you."

"What is your name?" he asked.

"Sasha."

"I am Yehuda."

"Pleased to meet you, Yehuda," she smiled and raised her head to meet his gaze. "You are not from here."

"Correct," he replied, turned around and started walking away. "And you should not be wandering in these woods like this. It could be very dangerous."

"But thank the gods you will watch over me, right?" she called after him.

Yehuda stopped and turned around slightly before resuming his walk. Sasha could have sworn she detected a faint smile beneath his thick, unshaved beard.

And so, it came to pass that over the next few months, Sasha and Yehuda forged a new friendship. The heatless fire in his eyes grew warmer, and a new form of life sprang forth within him. He trimmed his beard, combed his head, washed up and wore cleaner robes. Even before her attraction to his physique, Sasha had already fallen for the person behind the wall Yehuda had built around himself, a wall that was now full of many cracks and threatened to crumble to a pile of rubble. They kept the love relationship a secret for the moment. Despite the changes Yehuda exhibited, a feeling gnawed in the pit of Sasha's stomach that something seemed off-center about her lover; a feeling that usually vanished in the face of her feelings for him.

Alas, the gods dealt her a blow so low it changed her life forever. Her village came under attack one day just after sundown. She was returning home from her visit to Yehuda when she saw the orange glow in the night and the smoke rising in the air. The screams of fear and terror, as well as the crackling of burning, grew louder with each step she took as she ran towards the sight. The chaos was soul-snatching. The horror was spine-freezing. Sasha stood, rooted to the spot and unable even to scream. Her mother lay on the ground, blood gushing from areas where her left leg and right arm used to be. In the light of the flames, Sasha saw her mother's bloodied mouth move, as if she was trying to say something. Then, with as much strength as she could summon, her mother shooed with her right hand. Instead, Sasha took slow, dazed steps towards her.

A bestial sound from her left forced Sasha to look in that direction. Her knees buckled from soul-stealing fear and she fell to her knees. A creature that looked like the biggest dog she had ever seen, standing on its hind legs, held her sister's severed head in its right hand. It held her sister's headless body by the neck in its left hand. It lifted her sister's headless body and drank from the blood gushing out of the stump of her neck. It dropped her sister's body and head to the ground and darted towards her mother. It flipped its mother over using its left leg. Sasha averted her eyes and retched when the creature began to tear into her mother's gut with unholy savagery.

Out of the corner of her eye, she saw many villagers suffering fates similar to that which her family suffered: dismemberment and disembowelment from these creatures from hell. Some looked human, others looked like giant dogs. A man, stood unmoving in the center of the chaos, like a dispassionate observer of the mayhem and death that filled the air.

Maybe he is the devil himself, and these creatures are his soldiers, his demons, Sasha thought and wiped her mouth with the back of her hand.

The man she likened unto The Devil locked eyes with her. The Devil lifted his left hand and pointed in her direction. The creature that had taken her mother's life zoomed in on Sasha. It bared its fangs, growled and started walking towards her. Sasha stared into the glowing eyes of the beast, and suddenly, her features relaxed completely as a sweet calm seduced every cell in her body. Her body went limp, but her mind went into panic mode and her survival instincts kicked in. Yet, her body would not respond to her mind. In a final act of desperation and surrender, with the prospect of death by evisceration looming closer, Sasha unconsciously called out to her lover for help in her mind.

Yehuda teleported towards Sasha using her telepathic voice as a locator, half a micro second too late, unfortunately. He arrived just in time to witness a luper sink its fangs into Sasha's neck and zip away with her. Yehuda's world turned black with unimaginable fury. An evil darkness replaced the last ember of humanity the love of his life had fanned in him, and vengeance now resided where his heart used to be. He caught sight of a man looking at him. The man raised his hand and pointed in his direction. The remaining creatures with their bright, glowing eyes all turned their attention towards Yehuda and charged.

The man, who was The Scientist, noticed Yehuda's eyes turn bright as well. What followed would have been a blur to the average human eye, but to The Scientist, everything moved in slow motion.

"I didn't expect to meet you here, Yehuda," he muttered and smiled. "Let's see how you fare against my creatures."

In three heartbeats, Yehuda turned six lupers and seven chupers to ashes. He zipped towards The Scientist and slashed with the dagger he sparked from the ethers, but the blade slashed through nothing but air.

"I admire your skill, young man," The Scientist.

The Scientist turned around and headed for the forest, leaving Yehuda burning with white, hot rage.

"Don't worry," The Scientist added with a smug. "I'll take good care of her for you."

The Scientist vanished from sight before Yehuda could attack again. Yehuda let out a shriek of rage and frustration. He could neither track Sasha nor the man who just teleported away. Around him, flames crackled as properties and dead people burned in an unholy offering to the god of death and destruction.

A decade later, he found Sasha, who had been turned into a luper. Sasha blamed Yehuda for her family's unfortunate demise.

"Those creatures came to my village because of you," she screamed at him. "They came looking for one of theirs."

Yehuda sensed her pain using clairsentience and chose not to argue with her.

It took close to five years before her anger subsided, though the transferred aggression remained. She still did not know exactly which luper had killed her family and turned her because she never got the chance to witness the luper's transformation back to human form. She had simply awoken in a lair of Bright Eyes and realized that she was a part of them; a part of soulless creatures spawned from the Devil's loins. She hated them and herself with an unrivaled passion. Yet, she was wise enough to keep this hatred a secret.

One day, I shall have her vengeance, she promised herself. *My family's killer shall suffer a similar fate and I shall turn the rest of the Bright Eyes to ashes or die trying.*

Yehuda helped her redirect her cold fury for the Bright Eyes into a source of motivation. Sasha moved from lover to apprentice. One day, Yehuda finally told her his story, and her heart shrank with pity for him.

"I still cannot believe that you are the one they called Judas Iscariot."

The world and his brothers vilified him, the Bright Eyes wanted him, or his blood, and Shi'mon, his archenemy, and The Order wanted him dead. Yehuda certainly was the most wanted man in the underworld, and she was probably the only person who truly loved him. From then on, she swore to work with him and take out the Bright Eyes.

***

Sasha snuggled into a comfortable position as Yehuda's body materialized behind her. Her heart ached with longing and the need to be held and comforted. She closed her eyes and enjoyed the peace of being held in his strong, protective arms. She gently held his left cheek in her right hand as their lips and tongues met. The most wanted man in the underworld caressed and kissed the crown of the head of the most wanted woman in the underworld.

"So, what's the plan?" she asked with her eyes closed.

"We're working on it.," he caressed her long black hair. "We have a bigger problem, though. They can now multiply their numbers beyond the threshold."

Sasha bolted upright and stared at Yehuda in the eyes.

"That's not good," she exclaimed.

"Understatement," he confirmed. "Andrew just told us. As soon as you left, a Bright Eye brought in a new convert. Said she had just turned the other, but she was still alive."

"There are seven-plus billion humans in the realm, Yehuda," Sasha exclaimed. "Seven-plus billion people who could be turned into day-walking Bright Eyes. This could be-"

"The end of humanity," he completed her sentence for her. "Not unless we do something to stop it."

"Oh my God, Yehuda," Sasha cupped her mouth as fear for an unwanted future furrowed down her spine. "We must act now."

"You think we don't know that?" he exploded.

He took a deep breath.

"I'm sorry, my love." he apologized.

"Yehuda, are you there?" Shi'mon asked telepathically.

"Yes, brother. I'm here."

"We have a new development. Gethsemane. Midnight local time."

"Alright, what is it?"

"The Twins just made contact. They have a proposition for us."

CHAPTER THIRTY

AFFIRMATIVE ACTION

"SO, HOW DO you want us to proceed, your highnesses?" Andrew asked.

"Capture and convert," Danka replied.

"As you wish, your highness," Andrew agreed. "Are we to be covert about it? When do we start? I apologize for the questions, but the more information we have, the better we can carry out your orders"

"No need for apologies, Andrew," Dreyko replied. "You have proven yourself trustworthy, yet again."

Andrew bowed slightly to conceal his surprise at Dreyko's compliment.

"And no, we will not be covert about this," Dreyko added. "Start now."

"Thank you, your highness," Andrew said. "But I fear we may be overlooking something."

"Speak," Danka commanded.

Keep up the show, you… Andrew stayed his thoughts.

"I believe The Scientist will agree with me on this," Andrew gestured towards The Scientist. "Despite the evidence we have, I recommend we observe the new convert for a few days. If nothing unwanted happens to her, then we can initiate conversion."

The Scientist narrowed his eyes while The Twins slowly nodded.

"Keep talking," Shi'mon said telepathically.

"Will you just shut up," Andrew yelled telepathically. *"I need to concentrate."*

"Okay, okay," Shi'mon replied. *"I'll let you work your charms."*

"No time for jokes, brother," Andrew scolded.

"Fetch the new convert," he ordered a guard by the door.

"Yes, sir," the guard clapped his heels once and dashed away.

He returned a minute later with the new convert. She bowed her head when she stood in front of Andrew.

"How long ago was the conversion?" he asked the lady.

"Less than an hour, sir," her body trembled visibly.

"Doctor?" Andrew asked in a friendly manner.

"I agree with Andrew, your highnesses," The Scientist said, shifting his gaze between Dreyko and Danka. "Let us observe her for a few more days."

"I agree with them, brother," Danka met her brother's gaze. "Just a few days."

Dreyko remained silent. Andrew used clairaudience to listen to his thoughts.

I would rather begin the conversion at once, Dreyko thought. *But it appears these fools are right. Plus, I must support my sister, especially in public, in spite of her bedding that fool. Anyway, I will deal with him later, permanently.*

"Perhaps we can proceed with the 'capture' phase for now and hold off on the 'conversion' until after the observation period, your highnesses?" Andrew offered. "If nothing happens to the new convert within that time, then we can turn the captives."

"What in Yahweh's name are you doing, brother?" Shi'mon screamed telepathically.

"Buying us time without giving up my position," Andrew replied calmly. *"I can't attack The Twins by myself right now, and The Anomaly is here."*

"Good idea" Dreyko finally agreed. "Commence with the capture at once. No babies or children, at least for now."

"I'll lead the mission myself," Andrew offered. "If it pleases your highnesses."

"You are a true soldier, Andrew," Danka said with a smile. "But Bischoff can handle the mission just fine. Besides, you also have Sasha to hunt, do you not?"

She turned her attention towards Bischoff and nodded,

"Your highnesses," Bischoff half-jumped, half-stood up from his seat as he affirmed his orders.

He rallied the rest of the members at the meeting. They zipped out of the room, leaving Andrew with The Twins and The Scientist. An awkward moment of silence lingered in the air.

"I must admit, that was wise of you, Andrew," Dreyko said.

"You give me too much honor, your highness," Andrew bowed his head.

"Very well deserved," Dreyko continued. "My sister was right about you."

Andrew registered Dreyko's subtle warning.

"See. I told you not to sleep with the bitch," Shi'mon scolded him telepathically but Andrew ignored him.

"Your highnesses, there is another small matter I believe we ought to address," Andrew raised his head.

"The Order," Danka said and Andrew nodded.

She knows him that well, Andrew heard Dreyko's thought and clairsentience revealed Dreyko's jealousy.

"What about the Order?" Dreyko clenched his jaw.

"Your highnesses, they have been our nemesis for the longest time," Andrew said. "I propose we lure them into a trap and get rid of them once and for all."

"That would require an irresistible bait," The Scientist interjected.

"What if we told them about our recent turn of events?" Andrew proposed.

Confusion caressed the faces of The Twins and The Scientist.

"Think about it," Andrew explained. "What better way to create a sense of urgency than to let them know that the one leverage they had over us was gone? The pressure will fall on their shoulders to act swiftly to prevent the eradication of the humans."

"I am going to choke you," Shi'mon could not believe his telepathic ears.

"Shut up," Andrew wished he could punch his brother in the nose.

"Besides, from what I hear," Andrew continued, "their present leader is an egomaniac. I say we feed that ego till it leads to his demise."

"Really? Is that what people say about me now?" Shi'mon asked rhetorically.

"Your words, not mine," Andrew replied. *"You've given sermons about yourself before, haven't you?"*

"So, you're saying we just inform them about our plan to initiate a worldwide conversion of humans to Bright Eyes," The Scientist said rhetorically, leaning forward and clasping his hands in front of him.

"Worldwide conversion," an evil grin spread across Danka's face. "I like the sound of that."

"Convert or die," Dreyko mused with the words.

"The end of humanity," The Scientist concurred. "And the rise of a new, dominant species."

"A new world with your highnesses as their leaders," Andrew added.

"Their gods," The Twins chorused together and looked at each other.

"Still want to choke me, brother?" Andrew's sarcasm was sharp even via telepathy.

Shi'mon was silent.

"You're welcome," Andrew added.

"Call the Order," Dreyko ordered, and Andrew obliged.

"You better not be speechless when you pick up the phone," Andrew warned Shi'mon.

The phone rang twice, and someone picked it up.

"Museo delle Maschere di Milano, come posso auitarla?" a charming male voice said in Italian.

"Your highness," Andrew put the phone on speaker.

"I want to speak with your boss," Dreyko spoke calmly.

"Of course, sir," said the male in English "With whom am I speaking, please?"

"Dreyko Pakola."

They heard the receptionist swallow nervously.

"One- one moment, please" he stammered.

"Hello?" Andrew recognized Shi'mon's voice.

"Is this the boss of the order?" Dreyko's rudeness was not unusual.

"I am," Shi'mon replied flatly.

"Hello to you as well,' Dreyko attempted to put some humor in his voice but fared poorly. "I wanted to inform you about something."

Fourteen seconds later, Shi'mon summoned Yehuda using telepathy.

***

"It's time then," Yehuda said, as he appeared behind Shi'mon.

"Master said we would know when the time was right," Shi'mon approached a rock that held so many memories for them and the rest of the apprentices.

Shi'mon and Yehuda seemed to be just two out of the many pilgrims who visited this holy site called the Garden of Gethsemane. This was the garden their master visited after his last supper with them before his arrest and subsequent crucifixion. They stared at the rock in reverence; the rock where their master knelt by and prayed for strength, the rock on which beads of sweat trickled down his temples as droplets of blood. While their master prayed, Shi'mon and ten of the apprentices had fallen asleep, and Yehuda was on his way with Roman soldiers to finalize his betrayal of their master.

"The last meal we had with Master," Shi'mon started saying but his words died in his throat.

Yehuda stood in reverent silence. He remembered his two-thousand-year enmity with Shi'mon. Master was dead, betrayed by him, and denied many times by Shi'mon.

Purpose or not, Shi'mon's hatred for me was justified, Yehuda sighed as his thoughts churned in his mind. *Even before I betrayed Master, Shi'mon was furious at me for my atrocious indiscretions. I was wrong on every account and to this day, my regret is still as intense as it was 2,000 years ago.*

Two thousand years later, Yehuda still knew no peace. Two thousand years later, he still did not have the courage to face Miryam, talk less of her daughter; Master's daughter. Yehuda spared a glance in Shi'mon's direction. He rejected his instinct to listen in on Shi'mon's thought.

The man is far cry from perfection, Yehuda squared his shoulders and stared blankly ahead. *Still, his hatred for me is justified. Before Master's death, he was just angry at me; really angry. But after Master's death, that anger had morphed into hatred, which I reciprocated, more out of a mix of self-preservation and transferred aggression than anything else. I mean, who was he to judge me? Being our leader didn't give him the right to be my judge and executioner.*

Yehuda swallowed, took a deep breath and let it out.

Well, we both share one thing in common now, he shrugged slightly. *Our guilt for our individual roles in Master's death made us soulless. Regardless of the past, we have a problem much bigger than our soullessness et al. Humanity is facing the threat of extinction and we must find a way to cast aside our hatred for each other and work together to stop this. The Bright Eyes cannot win. Their victory will spell the extinction of humanity.*

Before they moved to stop the Bright Eyes, they needed an esoteric upgrade and to have this upgrade, they would have to individually face an even greater enemy on fair, unsullied terrain in no other location than the Shadow of the Soul.

"We must waste no time," Yehuda said suddenly.

Shi'mon did not move. Yehuda understood why. He too was reliving his moments of guilt. Neither of them had visited this location for nearly 2,000 years.

"We must go," Shi'mon said a minute later and Yehuda nodded.

They joined a tour and walked with the tour until they came near a sycamore tree at the northern part of the garden. They then stepped behind the tree and summoned a barrier of invisibility on the other side of the tree so that no one saw them teleport. Even if anyone did, no one would remember seeing them in the first place. They appeared in a vast desert of snow and temperatures that would cause a normal, unprotected human to freeze to death almost instantly. However, these former apprentices of Yeshua elevated their chi to counteract the inhumane elements of this place.

"I remember the first time Master brought me here," Yehuda spoke with fondness and smiled for the first time that day. "First time I ever saw snow."

"I know," Shi'mon replied, also smiling at Yehuda for the first time in over two millennia. "Antarctica is most amazing and intriguing."

"There it is," Yehuda said, pointing to his left.

They teleported to the flat top of the structure Yehuda had pointed at. It stuck out at about a hundred and fifty feet above the snow. To the untrained eye, this tip of the eight-hundred-foot pyramid, completely covered in the purest of white marble, would have been invisible in the harsh blizzard.

"Would you mind doing the honors?" Shi'mon gestured downward.

"The honor is for the leader," Yehuda replied.

"And I defer that honor to you," Shi'mon countered and stepped back.

Yehuda nodded.

Maybe there is hope for us after all, he thought.

He dropped to a knee, evaporating the snow around him with his chi in the process. He traced two symbols with his right index finger on the marble, which appeared as golden glyphs. He stood up, and Shi'mon stepped close to him. A beam of white light beamed upwards from the pyramid's top and engulfed them, teleporting them to a pitch-black chamber in the pyramid.

"Let there be light," Shi'mon commanded.

The chamber registered and accepted his level of awakening. It resonated with his esoteric frequency and lit up, but not from any light source in particular. The illumination manifested from the sparking of the ethers.

"Behold. The Hall of Death," Yehuda's eyes wandered around the chamber.

The walls, ceiling, and floor stretched to nothingness, to oblivion, though they constituted part of the pyramid. The pyramid served as a portal between Earth Realm and another level of existence that the apprentices were about to visit for the first time. Four greyish gold sarcophagi hovered in the center of the hall, each facing a different and opposite direction from the other. Each sarcophagus appeared to be fashioned from a single chunk of crystal vibrating with a frequency that clairsentience revealed was otherworldly to Shi'mon and Yehuda.

"Master never told us what we would find in here," Yehuda said.

"True," Shi'mon agreed. "But he also said to trust ourselves and be patient. We chose this path for a reason, and Creation will see us through."

"Even when we are facing true death?" Yehuda asked rhetorically.

"We must first choose the right sarcophagi," Shi'mon reminded him.

"Or let them choose us?" Yehuda offered.

Both men glided towards the sarcophagi and waited. They emptied their minds of all thought and emotion and became still by their own nature. After what felt like an eternity, two sarcophagi opposite from each other glowed and hummed with the sound of *OM*. The two men met each other's gaze, nodded, and each man walked towards a humming sarcophagus. A handprint slowly manifested at the crown of each sarcophagus. Both men reached out with their right hands towards the handprints. Sparks of energy danced between their palms and the handprints until their hands settled into the handprints. The handprint felt warm and tingly to the touch.

A click punctuated the resonating *OM* sound. The lid of each sarcophagus levitated weightlessly in the air, though each lid looked like it weighed over a ton. Each apprentice floated into their respective sarcophagus, which appeared to be bottomless on the inside. They hovered within the bottomless void of their respective sarcophagus as the lids slowly descended to close them in.

"Good luck, brother," Yehuda called out.

"See you soon, brother," Shi'mon called back, and the lids sealed shut.

The two men were instantly plunged in pitch blackness. They lay in there, waiting to see what would happen next. They lost all sense of time and space as they waited. Nothing.

Then, Shi'mon blinked and found himself on a beach with sparkling gray sands. He wore a pair of green shorts and a flowery shirt and a fishing rod rested in his hand. He cast the fishing line into the sea.

"Did you catch anything yet?" a voice asked from behind him.

Startled, he whipped his head around. His eyes fell upon the most beautiful, flawless and perfect sight he had ever seen, wearing nothing, except for a bikini that barely covered her ample bosom and nether region.

"Who are you?" Shi'mon asked.

Shi'mon's fishing line disappeared, the beach and sea vanished, and he found himself in a chamber with white marble, seamless walls, and floor, wearing a white robe and sitting on a bed that was seamless with the floor.

"Hello Shi'mon," a voice greeted him warmly. "You can call me Priya. Welcome to the Realm-Dimension of Akasha. Welcome to the Shadow of the Soul."

CHAPTER THIRTY-ONE

PRELUDE TO DENIAL

SHI'MON WAS ON his way to visit Yeshua one evening to seek his counsel on something. He thought it best to visit after dinner hours. The evening breeze felt cool on his face. When he was close to Yeshua's house, he heard some faint moaning coming from the house.,

"It appears I picked a bad time to visit Master," Shi'mon smiled. "I shall see him later. This can wait."

He turned around to leave but a movement a few hundred yards up the hill caught his attention. He made to ignore it, but a second glance revealed Yeshua heading down the hill.

"Who, then, is in Master's house," Shi'mon's eyes popped in shock. "I must make certain for myself."

So, instead of returning home, he hid in the bushes and waited. His shoulders slumped with disappointment at Miryam.

"Of all the people," Shi'mon shook his head. "Why, Myriam. Why?"

And who are you committing adultery with, Myriam, Shi'mon's mind raced. *I wonder how Master is going to handle this.*

Excitement brewed in his gut. Then, when Yeshua stopped a stone's throw away from his house, Shi'mon's excitement turned to confusion.

What is Master doing?

Yeshua waited for over five minutes, which felt like an eternity to Shi'mon, before he called out.

"My love, are you home?"

Within seconds, the naked figure of a man quickly crawled out the back window, clutching his garments in his hands.

"Yes, my love," Myriam replied. "I am home."

Shi'mon scowled and burned with fury when he recognized Miryam's partner-in-sin. Worse, a harsher reality dawned on him. Yeshua was aware of the affair.

"And if Master is aware that his wife is committing adultery with Yehuda, why is he not doing anything about it?" he wondered. "Unless-"

Filled with so much disgust at the situation, Shi'mon could not finish his sentence as Myriam opened the door and kissed Yeshua in the mouth. He turned around and retched violently.

***

"I do find it interesting that your master did nothing about the affair," Priya said calmly.

Priya hovered close to Shi'mon, who sat on the bed, teeming with fury and disgust.

"Maybe he was in denial," Shi'mon offered.

"Oh no, no, no, no, NO, Shi'mon," Priya countered. "He definitely was aware of the affair. But he must have had his reasons for not doing anything about it, don't you think?"

Priya inched closer towards Shi'mon.

"Or maybe it was just a sick fantasy of his. Besides, this is not the only time you saw something that made you, um, 'question' your master, is it?"

"There is a reason for everything," Shi'mon said the words like a mantra. "If he knew about the affair, and tolerated it, it must have been for a reason. I trust my master."

"What about now?" Priya waved her hand in the air and the scene changed.

***

Shi'mon crouched behind a tree in a small garden on the outskirts of Jerusalem. The moonless night offered extra cover of darkness. Yochanan, the master, and another young man, a Roman soldier sat around a small fire. They seemed to be having a regular conversation.

Nothing wrong with Master comingling with the Gentiles, he rationalized. *We met him once with a Samaritan woman and he taught us not to judge others. Still, I dislike the Romans.*

Shi'mon strained to eavesdrop on the conversation. He could not hear a thing.

Too bad Master has not yet taught me clairaudience. And why am I even following Master?

Shi'mon tried to shrug off his own question but failed woefully.

Ever since I realized Yehuda and Myriam were living and sin and that Master condoned it, I could not help but question Master's integrity, he thought. *First, it was the Samaritan woman, then the adultery, and now, Roman soldier is involved.*

Shi'mon leaned against the try, gazed into the starless sky and shook his head.

Is Master really the Messiah? Is he really the Son of Yahweh?

He returned his focus on Yeshua and the group in time to see Yochanan and Yeshua standing up together. Shi'mon narrowed his eyes. Then, Yeshua took Yochanan's face in his hands and brought his face closer to Yochanan's. Shi'mon exploded in a conundrum of anger and disgust. Extreme disappointment welled up in his chest as he squeezed his eyes shut and bit his lips to stifle a scream.

***

"Do you remember that night, Shi'mon," Priya asked telepathically, with a note of victory in her voice. *"Do you remember what your master did with those two men?"*

"I remember," Shi'mon replied telepathically.

His eyes welled up with tears of disgust for his master.

"Why do I have to relive this? This is not fair," Shi'mon cried out telepathically.

He swallowed, steeled his resolve and returned his focus on the screen. The images appeared to have been paused. Priya waved her hand and the images resumed playing.

***

When Yeshua pulled his face away from Yochanan's, Marcus stood up. Only then did Shi'mon realize that nothing but a thin cloth covered the Roman soldier's body. The three men then disappeared into a cave nearby and did not emerge until first light.

***

"I told you," Priya took a huge bite of an apple. "Sick fantasies."

"This cannot be," Shi'mon forced himself to say.

"Believe me, my dear," Priya rebutted. "Your eyes do not deceive you."

Shi'mon recoiled slightly at Priya's words. Something about the way she said it clawed at his psyche.

"Your eyes do not deceive you."

Why did she say it like that? He wondered.

Suddenly, his moment of clarity hit him.

"What I saw that night was from my vantage point," he exclaimed. "But I am in the Shadow of the Soul and I can watch everything from a different vantage point now."

His eyes beamed with excitement as he rewound the images using the power of will. This time, he changed his line of sight to align perpendicularly to Yeshua and Yochanan. He let out a huge sigh of relief when he saw everything that actually transpired that night.

"Master never kissed Yoch," he chuckled. "He was training Yoch on the

Breath of Life."

He turned a gaze of gloat towards Priya.

"You know," he spoke with vindication in his voice. "Transferring, through breath, chi infused with etheric energy supercharged in a specific way. It can be used to reanimate, de-aminate or even give someone an esoteric upgrade."

"I know what the Breath of Life is," Priya rolled her eyes and tossed her half-eaten apple to the side.

The apple disappeared before it hit the floor.

"And look," Shi'mon pointed at the screen. "Master is performing an esoteric surgery on the soldier. These usually take hours and this one in particular lasted all night. I later learned that his name was Marcus. Master must have special purposes for these two. I mean, Yoch got training on the Breath of Life before everyone else, including me, and this Marcus… Well, I guess we will know soon."

Priya yawned and rolled her eyes again.

"No sick fantasies," Shi'mon exclaimed with relief, finally feeling the weight of a two-thousand-year old burden coming off his psyche. "There is a reason for everything."

"Touché," Priya admitted. "But what about this?"

"You should have been there, my love."

Shi'mon could identify that voice in his sleep. His gaze fell to the floor, his shoulders drooped, and his heart sank like a ship's anvil to the bottom of the sea of his stomach. He could not turn to face her. He dared not face her. Two millennia of guilt and pain, multiplied a thousand-fold in the Shadow of the Soul, would not allow him to turn around and face the bearer of the voice. Yet, a pair of gentle hands took him by the shoulders. Shi'mon could not resist the loving touch of his one, and only, true love as he let Rania turn him around and lift his chin up until their eyes locked into each other's.

"You should have been there, my love," she said again.

"I am so sorry, my love," he replied as tears ran down the corners of his eyes.

Priya glided over twenty feet away and summoned a chair. A grin of mischief spread across her face.

"There was nothing I could do," he added weakly.

"How about we find out?" Rania said sternly.

Forced by something seemingly beyond his control to use clairsentience, Shi'mon felt a side of Rania he had never felt before; her rage. He cowered and a cold chill crawled all over his body like a constrictor about to swallow its prey. Rania waved a hand in the air and summoned a scene.

***

The fourth day of the month of Adar. Rania, her two daughters, and four grandchildren were getting ready to go to the market together. Shi'mon was supposed to meet with them later at the butcher's shop. He was friends with the butcher, and they wanted a good discount on some veal.

"I have a quick errand to run and I will meet you all there," he promised them.

For thirty-six years, he hunted Yehuda, the traitor, to no avail. Then, he heard rumors of a stranger in a remote land in the Far East, who had 'miraculous powers and had never aged a day' since he arrived in those lands more than a quarter of a century ago. Shi'mon himself never aged and he had explained to Rania why he never aged.

"I love you and that is all I care about," Rania had replied and sealed her words with a deep, passionate kiss.

That kiss helped him maintain his sanity. That kiss kept him going. Still, he had unfinished business with Yehuda.

Shi'mon teleported to the village and found Yehuda in the marketplace.

"Meet me by the hillside now or these people will find out what you can do," he spoke via telepathy.

"Fine," Yehuda agreed.

After creating mini craters, leveling a few hills, uprooting a few trees, breaking and healing bones, crushing and healing internal organs, their hatred for each other eroded their sense of reason to realize the futility of their fight.

"My love, help."

Shi'mon thought he heard Rania call out to him via telepathy.

But how can this be? he wondered and continued fighting.

"My love, ahh."

Shi'mon no longer felt his connection to his wife. He immediately teleported to the butcher's shop but he was a few seconds too late.

***

The scene then rewound itself to a few seconds prior to his arrival. This was the first time Shi'mon witnessed the horrors of the day his family was taken away from him.

***

The earth shook with the most violent earthquake Jerusalem had ever experienced. Almost every building stood as a pile of rubble and dust. He saw panic and fear seize come alive in his family's eyes as Rania gathered everyone close to her. His heart shattered into too many pieces to count when Rania raised her hands, in a final act of desperation, courage and unconditional love, to shield her family, his family, from the crumbling walls of the butcher's shop. Two seconds times infinity later, he saw himself appear near the rubble.

Shi'mon turned his face away from the screen and wept bitterly.

***

"So, tell me, my love," Rania's fury pulsed with such intensity that it could choke the life out of a raging bull. "Where were you?"

She grabbed him by the throat with one hand and slammed him on the floor. His guilt, regret, pain and self-loathe took away every ounce of resistance in him.

"I should just die," he said.

"No, no, no, my love," Rania shook her head at him and picked him up to his feet. "You will answer me before you die."

Rania kicked him in the groin with so much force that Shi'mon sailed four feet in the air before he crashed into the ground. Excruciating pain seared from his groin to the rest of his body.

"You put your foolish pride before you own family," she towered over him.

"I am sorry," Shi'mon spoke barely above a whisper.

"Sorry?" she snarled. "SORRY? Is that all you can say, Mr. Leader? Are you just going to sit there and feel sorry or are you going to be a man, a leader, and do something about it?"

"What is it you wish for me to do, my love?" Shi'mon asked weakly, still laying on the floor. "I cannot bring you all back to life."

"Did you hear me ask for that?" Rania snorted before she straddled him and grabbed a fistful of his gown. "I want retribution. I want payback."

"Anything, my love," Shi'mon pleaded. "I will trade my life for yours, our children's and grandchildren's. I will give up eternity, everything I have and everything I am, to be with you all again."

"That's very good to know," she said, her lips peeling into an evil smile. "Because, here's your opportunity. I'll ask you again; why were you not there to save us?"

"Because I was...," he started saying and then stopped.

He breathed in deeply and then continued.

"Because I was out there trying to kill Yehuda."

"Are you saying Yehuda is to blame for you not being there to save us that day?" Rania cocked an eyebrow.

Actually, Yehuda is to blame for my family's death, he thought. *If he had not had the affair, if he had not betrayed Master, I never would have hated him like this and I never would have been out there trying to kill him....*

He sat up and Rania slid off his body.

My family would still be alive if it was not for him.

The chains of guilt broke and smelted into a red, hot fury; fury at the reason behind his family's death. As such, all prospects of forgiveness burned away from the touch of his fury and a renewed hatred and decree of death emerged in its stead. Rania crouched next to him and brought her lips to his ear.

"Yehuda is responsible for our deaths, is he not?" she insisted.

"Yes, he is," Shi'mon agreed.

"So, what are you going to do about it?" Rania asked.

"Yehuda must die a true death," Shi'mon replied.

"Say it again."

"Yehuda must die a true death," Shi'mon spoke more firmly.

"Again."

"Yehuda must die a true death," Shi'mon screamed.

"Then, my love, you should rejoice because you are in the right place," she turned her head to stare straight ahead before adding, "and time."

Shi'mon followed her gaze. When he saw what she meant, a dark presence possessed his psyche and erased everything he considered to be himself. Yehuda smiled at him at first, but something happened and the smile disappeared from Yehuda's face. Rania inched closer until her lips just brushed Shi'mon's earlobe.

"Go get him, my love," she whispered.

"With pleasure," Shi'mon replied.

Using clairvoyance, Yehuda saw Shi'mon undergo a transformation from soulless to something beyond soulless, right before Shi'mon zipped towards him for the kill.

He has failed already, but I shall try to save him, Yehuda sighed. *And herein lies my final and hardest test in the Shadow of the Soul.*

"One down, one to go," a grin of victory graced Rania's face as she shape-shifted in to Priya.

This Priya, formerly Rania, turned towards the other Priya, who had just finished eating her apple. Both Priyas dissipated into gray mists, slithered through the air and merged into a single form.

"Indeed," Priya agreed and took a bite of an apple she had just made manifest.

CHAPTER THIRTY-TWO

SEDUCING A SCORPION

"HUSH, MY LOVE. Just relax," she cradled his head on her bosom.

Her heart beat against his temple and her left breast blocked his vision; a feeling Yehuda never grew tired of, even after 2,000 years. He closed his eyes as Miryam worked her magic on him.

"I've missed you so much, Miri," he said softly.

He nestled against her bosom some more and he ran the fingers of his free hand between her lower lips. Miryam parted her legs some more to grant him full access. Here, in the Shadow of the Soul, every feeling, including their lust, adult passion, and culmination, was multiplied a thousand-fold.

"2,000 years," she replied. "But you're here now, and that's all I care about."

"I know this is not real," Yehuda slowly peeled himself away from her body, stood up and stretched. "But I might as well enjoy myself while it lasts."

"Oh, my love," Miryam cooed over Yehuda's chiseled body.

Miryam slid off the bed, hugged Yehuda from behind and ran the fingers of her left hand over his chiseled chest and abs. Her firm breasts pressed against his back, invoking near-insurmountable feelings of desire in his loins. His chest heaved heavily while be became hardened and extended.

"Is this what two thousand years of working out does to the human body," she giggled like an excited school girl.

Yehuda spun around, picked her up and threw her on the bed. Another round of erotic frenzy followed. With each pulse of pleasure, Yehuda's psyche slowly sank deeper into a bottomless sea of non-remembrance.

Remember why you are here, his subconscious called out to him.

He ignored the voice as Miryam straddled and gyrated him in ways she had never done before. His eyes rolled to the back of his head as he sank deeper into that bottomless sea.

This is not real, his fading subconscious said.

Yehuda jolted slightly and blinked several times. Miryam's body stiffened as she gyrated faster in an all-too-familiar prelude to an explosion.

Wake up.

Yehuda catapulted out of the bottomless sea as Miryam screamed with sheer, savage ecstasy and collapsed on top of him under the weight of sweet satisfaction.

"This is not real," Yehuda said.

"Remember when we first met?" Miryam asked.

She keeps ignoring me every time I say this is not real.

He gently pushed her off his body and summoned a sheet over his body.

"I do," Yehuda replied.

***

"Excuse me, sir," Yehuda said. "I am Yehuda from the village of Kerriyoth."

"Hello, young man," said the merchant. "How may I help you?"

"I am looking for Sheikh Abdul's shed," Yehuda replied. "I must meet with his emissaries and I hear they are in town today."

A young lady of exquisite beauty emerged from the back of the store.

"Daughter, come here," said the merchant. "Do you know where-"

Yehuda heard nothing after that. He stared at the young maiden as if he was in a trance. Her lips moved. The merchant's lips moved. They gestured and even pointed in one direction. Yet, Yehuda just stood there, mouth open, focus 100% trained on the most beautiful woman he had ever laid eyes on.

"Young man?"

Yehuda jerked back to reality.

"A thousand pardons, sir," Yehuda bowed his head and kept his eyes averted to the ground. "I meant no disrespect. Your daughter..."

He could barely finish his sentence. He heard a chuckle.

He is going to kill me now, Yehuda thought.

"It is quite alright, young man," the merchant said. "You may gaze upon me."

Yehuda lifted his gaze, nervously, and tried to focus on the merchant, but his eyes kept drifting towards the merchant's daughter.

Miryam, Yehuda reminded himself. *He called her Miryam.*

"The Sheikh's shed is two streets down, third shed to the left," the merchant shook his head in amusement. "You will not miss it."

"Thank you, sir," Yehuda bowed his head. "I bid you good day, then."

He turned around and left the merchant's store. Five paces later, he hurried back to the merchant's store.

"Sir, forgive my boldness," he swallowed nervously. "But I would like to speak with your daughter."

Over the next five months, Yehuda and Miryam's love grew stronger still and Yehuda paid her regular visits at her father's store. He learned that her father was training her to be an heiress to his business, especially since she was an only child. One day, Yehuda had some news for Miryam.

"I have built some good amount of trust with the Sheikh's emissaries and they have agreed to take me with them on their business journeys," he announced with much excitement. "I shall learn the ways of merchants, amass some wealth and return here in no more than two years to ask for your hand in marriage, if you will wait for me, my love."

"Why, my love?" Miryam sobbed. "Why do you have to leave? My father can instruct you in the ways of the merchant."

"I must find my own way, my love," Yehuda explained. "Please, I need your support. Knowing that you will wait for my return is all I need to keep me going."

After much talk and deliberation, Miryam agreed to wait for him.

Eight months, an Arabian emissary came to Miryam's father's store.

"Greetings, sir," he said. "Are you Benyamin, father of Miryam?"

"I am," Benyamin replied. "How may I help you?"

Miryam sat on a stool next to her father. She was on her feet at the mention of her name and a strong sense of foreboding gripped her stomach.

"I bring word about Yehuda, the one whose heart beats for your daughter," he replied. "I am afraid it is word of unwelcome tidings. The caravan with which Yehuda traveled was attacked three moons ago. No survivors were found."

Miryam lost consciousness. She awoke a few minutes later to a world wrought with pain, grief and a deeps sense of loss. For many moons, she sealed her heart from the world and lived in a dark place of loneliness and sorrow, until a goodly man came to their store one day. He reeked of wisdom and virtue and her world went ablaze with the fire of aliveness and hope. It was love at first sight.

"I must say, sir," Miryam boldly stepped up to this stranger. "You must be a sorcerer of sorts to invoke my curiosity, thus. What is your name, sir?"

"Yeshua, miss," was the reply. "I am a Nazarene from Galilee and I came here looking for the most valuable item here."

Benyamin watched with joy in his heart to see his daughter come alive as if by magic. He dared not interfere in the chemistry that flared between these two.

"Forgive my rudeness, Yeshua Sir," Miryam stepped closer. "But you do not seem to be the rich type. So, speak your heart's intent. You never know, you may see it fulfilled."

Yeshua smiled and stepped closer. He was barely a foot away from her now.

"I speak my heart's intent, miss?"

"Miryam."

"Miss Miryam, I speak my heart's intent," Yeshua continued. "I seek the most valuable item here... and I am looking at her right now."

Six months later, Miryam was wed to Yeshua and six months later, Yehuda returned. After several attempts, he finally had some private time with Miryam.

"You promised to wait for me," he raged.

"I was told you died when your caravan was attacked," Miryam sobbed. "I mourned for you, you know."

"We were attacked, yes, but I survived," he gritted his teeth in frustration.

"And how was I to know, Yeh?" she asked.

Yehuda kicked the wall in anger, hurting his foot in the process.

"I tried to send word to you," he explained. "Without success apparently."

"I am sorry, Yeh," Miryam sniveled.

"You can leave him," Yehuda proposed.

"You have lost your mind," Miryam spat. "I cannot leave him and not because I fear being stoned to death."

She put a hand on his shoulder.

"I still have feelings for you," she explained. "But I love my husband. He's a wonderful man in so many ways and I cannot leave him for any reason, not even for you. I am sorry."

She turned around to leave.

"And I think it is best for us not to meet like this anymore," she added and ran away into the night, ignoring Yehuda calling after her.

Yehuda was fully aware that this man, Yeshua, was not at fault in anyway for Miryam not waiting for him. Yet, he needed to channel his anger and frustration and assign blame on something. He could not hate Miryam even if he tried. As such, Yeshua became the psychological embodiment of his anger and jealousy. To make everything worse, this Yeshua was starting to become a local sensation; teacher, healer, miracle worker, you name it. One day, Yeshua approached him out of the blue.

"I want you to become an apprentice of mine," Yeshua had said to him.

Something beyond this Yeshua's charisma warranted that he accept Yeshua's proposal. Besides, it represented a great opportunity to meet Miryam sometimes. His relationship with Miryam remained platonic until it progressed to adultery. Even then, Miryam still refused to leave her husband. From then, he swore to take matters into his own hands. From then, he started devising ways to get rid of Yeshua permanently. Meeting with the Hight Priest presented the perfect opportunity to see his dream come to pass. Finally, Miryam would be his.

***

"But your plan failed," Miryam said.

Yehuda buried his face in his hands and wept.

"I was naïve and stupid, and I paid a high price," he spoke between heavy sobs. "All I wanted was to be with the one I loved. Now, I can only hope for Master's forgiveness."

"But I am here, my love," Miryam cooed. "We can be together."

"Perhaps," Yehuda steeled his resolve and stood up.

The sheets fell off, revealing his naked body. He turned around to face Miryam.

"But I know you are not my Miryam," Yehuda added. "Besides, I let her go a long time ago. Whatever you are, the sex was great and all, but I am on a mission and time is of the essence."

"Well then," Miryam shapeshifted into Priya. "The timing could not be better."

Priya changed the scene with a wave of her hand. Yehuda saw Shi'mon with someone who looked like Rania. Using clairsentience, he sensed all of Shi'mon's pain, guilt, shame, anger, and fury. Using clairvoyance, he saw everything that constituted Shi'mon disappear, signifying Shi'mon's failure in the Shadow of the Soul. He panicked for a moment.

"I can still save him," Yehuda said the words more to himself than to Priya.

"He's gone already, Judas," Priya's voice had a malicious hiss in it. "You know why he's angry, don't you?"

"I can still save him," Yehuda rebutted.

"He's coming for you, Judas," Priya insisted. "Just like your name indicates, you betrayed him."

"You wish," Yehuda fought off Priya's insidious propaganda with powerful declarations and conviction.

"If he kills you here, you die," Priya whispered in his ear. "You said it yourself. You have a mission."

Priya inched towards him, the sheets falling from her body. She pressed her skin against his skin, but he summoned clothes over his body. She smiled and stood next to him, her body now covered in a perfectly fitting white, sleeveless, ankle-length, silk dress. Yehuda turned and glared at her.

"The question now is," she smiled. "How far are you willing to go to protect the mission, Judas?"

Yehuda knew what he may have to do in the end.

One life to save billions more, he said to himself. *Brother has failed and therefore, brother has already died a true death.*

He sighed and readied himself.

I am sorry, brother.

Shi'mon whizzed towards him and he whizzed towards Shi'mon as well.

The two Priyas from either camp looked at each other and smiled. The two Priyas dissipated into the air in gray mists and coalesced into one. A chair came out of the floor as she eased herself into it.

"Beautiful," she grinned and took a bite of an apple she just summoned. "So beautiful."

The two apprentices had danced this dance a countless number of times before. Each man could predict the other's move before it happened, like a deadly game of chess. However, Yehuda changed the rhythm. Instead of fighting back, he started neutralizing Shi'mon's attacks, invoking deeper feelings of anger and frustration from Shi'mon.

"We must stop fighting, brother," Yehuda tried to reason with Shi'mon as he took a right sidestep when Shi'mon swung a left uppercut at him.

He turned his hips to the left and, using Shi'mon's momentum, placed his right knee as leverage on the back of Shi'mon's left knee, and caught Shi'mon's left forearm with his left hand. Then, applying pressure on Shi'mon's left scapula with his right hand, Yehuda spun Shi'mon in a semi-circle until Shi'mon lay face down on the marble-like floor, unable to move.

"Master is dead because of you," Shi'mon snarled and glared at the floor. "My wife, my children and grandchildren died because of you."

He struggled to break free, but Yehuda held him fast.

"No, brother," Yehuda spoke calmly. "I did not kill Master, and I certainly did not kill your family."

"You're a dead man, you traitor," Shi'mon hissed.

Yehuda's body came off the floor when Shi'mon used brute force to push himself from the floor. Shi'mon turned his right shoulder inwards, creating leverage to partially free his left arm. Yehuda felt fingers reaching for his inner thigh before sharp pain exploded from where his skin got pinched. Yehuda let out a scream and let go of Shi'mon, who quickly seized the opportunity to deliver a series of bone-crushing punches and kicks until Yehuda found some space to zip away from the onslaught.

"Don't you get it, brother?" Yehuda pleaded. "This is the Shadow of the Soul. Here you face YOUR darkness, not anybody else's."

Shi'mon zipped towards him but Yehuda zipped away.

"And the only darkness I have is YOU," Shi'mon spat and zipped again towards Yehuda, but Yehuda zipped away.

"The only darkness one has is that which resides in oneself," Yehuda argued using telepathy. *"Think about it, brother. Master knew of his death before it happened; he accepted his path. We all accepted our paths."*

His words seemed to catch Shi'mon in his track for a second and Shi'mon did stop attacking.

"Besides," Yehuda added telepathically, *"Master is still alive, isn't he?"*

"But my family is not," Shi'mon yelled and attacked.

Shi'mon attacked with maniacal and psychotic rage. Yehuda landed a combination of punches and kicks, which temporarily numbed Shi'mon's limbs.

"But I did not cause the earthquake that killed them, brother," Yehuda continued calmly and telepathically. *"If you can just be honest with yourself for a moment, then you will see why you're so bent on my demise. You blame me for Master's death, whereas you did not hesitate to deny him three times that night."*

"I was justified," Shi'mon tone of voice was heavy with emotional exhaustion. "I thought Master was having sexual relations with other men. I thought he condoned his wife's adultery with you. I thought Master betrayed us all; betrayed ME. My denial of him was justified!" he yelled and zipped.

He whooshed towards Yehuda, but Yehuda evaded his attack.

"But you were wrong, and now you know it," Yehuda rebutted via telepathy. *"And about your family, it was their time to leave the realm. There was nothing you or anyone could do to change that."*

Shi'mon took a knee. His shoulders drooped as the shell that he had become gradually began to fade away. Yehuda took a step towards him.

"They had served their purpose, brother," Yehuda added. *"You must see and accept that."*

Shi'mon shook his head in rejection of Yehuda's true statements.

"No," Shi'mon spat and stood up. "You betrayed Master and distracted me from my family at the time of their death. Their blood is on your hands. Blood for blood, you must pay with yours."

Yehuda heaved a heavy sigh of resignation.

There's only one thing left to do now.

He took another step towards Shi'mon and met Shi'mon's glare.

"Master told us to be our brother's keeper," Yehuda said via telepathy. *"He also told us there is no greater love than he who is ready to lay down his life for another."*

Yehuda opened his arms.

"If my death brings you peace and freedom, then please get on with it," he continued calmly. *"I forgive you and bear you no ill-will. The mission comes first and you must see to it that the mission is successful. The fate of our species now rests in your hands, brother."*

He closed his eyes and opened his arms wider, inviting Shi'mon to fulfill his life-long wish.

An evil grin of victory graced Shi'mon's face.

"Finally, after 2,000 years, I shall have my wish," he rejoiced. "The bane of my existence shall die and die a true death."

Shi'mon sparked the ethers into a dagger. The dagger appeared in his right hand. He closed his fist around the hilt of the dagger, blazed towards Yehuda and struck him in the heart.

"Yes," he cried with victorious relief. "Finally, I am-"

His grin vanished and confusion creased his face as a moment of realization struck him like a bolt of lightning. Shi'mon met Yehuda's eyes, which reflected his peace and surrender. Yehuda's legs gave and he collapsed towards the floor, but not before Shi'mon caught him in his arms. Yehuda managed a weak smile. His right hand went up and took Shi'mon by the shoulders.

"It's alright, brother," Yehuda said via telepathy. *"I bear you no resentment or ill-will. I hope you finally find peace and, much more, I hope you succeed with the mission."*

Everything that constituted his esoteric makeup slowly began to dissipate, while Shi'mon's esoteric makeup slowly returned to normal, prior to his failure.

"Say hello to the team for me, please," Yehuda added. "And tell Sasha I'm sorry I had to do this."

Yehuda's hand fell from Shi'mon's shoulder and his body completely relaxed as he died the true death in the Shadow of the Soul. Shi'mon quaked with sorrow and sadness at the realization of what just transpired. Yehuda, his former mortal enemy, had sacrificed himself and taken his place in true death.

"You had to choose between killing me and saving me by dying the true death in my stead," Shi'mon shook his head in awe and profound appreciation. "This is a test that I don't think I would have passed. But you did, brother. You did."

And then, his heart broke and he wailed like a child.

"You must go now," Priya said. "You can mourn him later."

"What about his body?" Shi'mon asked.

"Don't worry about that," Priya replied. "He will be erased from Creation, and that includes your memory too."

"Oh," Shi'mon did not understand Priya's words.

He returned his attention towards Yehuda's dead body in his arms.

"I owe you my life, brother," Shi'mon let Yehuda's body slide to the floor. "Thank you, and I will see you later."

As he stood up, a pair of huge, crystalline, green eyes manifested about 24ft from him. The fanned-out head of a cobra complimented those eyes, followed by the entire body of the creature. Kundalini, the Serpent of Consciousness started sliding its way towards him.

Shi'mon waited in perfect stillness of body and mind, transfixed by the sheer power and energy pulsating from this esoteric creature. The Serpent raised and spread its head, bringing it barely inches away from Shi'mon's face. It stared into Shi'mon's eyes; its crystalline eyes changing colors as its stare dug deep into the nothingness within Shi'mon. Then, it lowered its head to Shi'mon's feet. Kundalini wrapped itself three-and-a-half times around Shi'mon's body, with its head extending two feet above the back of Shi'mon's head. It opened its mouth, bore its long, golden fangs and plunged them into the crown of Shi'mon's head. Shi'mon screamed as a surge of energy that felt like chi multiplied a million-fold rippled across his body, infusing every fiber of his physical and etheric anatomy with power, energy and aliveness he had never experienced or conceived of before. Blinding, white light beamed from his mouth, nose, ears and eyes.

Shi'mon jerked awake in a sarcophagus in the pyramid in Antarctica. The lid of the sarcophagus lifted in the air by an unseen force. Shi'mon stepped out of his sarcophagus and glided towards the other sarcophagus that housed his brother's mortal remains, supposedly. He placed a hand on it. Deep sadness smothered his soul. He closed his eyes and smiled.

"My soul is back, brother," a tear rolled down each eye. "And I am upgraded, all thanks to you and your sacrifice. I shall not fail, brother. This, I promise you."

He stepped away from the sarcophagus, closed his eyes and turned his face upwards. His being pulsed with a new kind of energy and power that came with his upgraded essence. A beam of bright, white light engulfed him in the Hall of Death and brought him back to the top of the pyramid. He teleported back to their rendezvous point. Sasha hugged him.

"Something is different about you," she remarked.

She gave him a look over and grinned.

"A lot is different about you," she added.

"Thank you for noticing, Sasha," he smiled.

"Wow, you even smiled," she added and play-punched him in the triceps. "Where's Yehuda?" she asked, looking past Shi'mon.

Shi'mon's smile vanished and he did not reply. Sasha managed a slight nod and clenched her jaws to stifle the welling of emotions within her. She failed. Her knees buckled and she sank to the floor. Shi'mon caught her. She spasmed and sobbed against his body. He held her in his arms for a few minutes while she cried her heart out. Then, he knelt beside her and took her by the shoulders.

"I will explain everything to you later," he said with firm resolve. "Time is off the essence and we have the Bright Eyes to defeat. I need you to be strong for now. Can you do that for me, please?"

Sasha sniveled and nodded.

"Good," Shi'mon gave her a smile of encouragement. "I have a gift for you."

"What is it?" Sasha dried her eyes.

"Hold still," Shi'mon said and took her face in his hands.

He opened his mouth slightly and inched closer as he gently pulled down her chin to open hers. Sasha recoiled with horror at what she thought was about to happen. But when the energy hit her, her body relaxed in total non-resistance. She grabbed Shi'mon by the back of his neck and locked lips with him, as if Shi'mon was a long, lost lover. She pressed her lips against his. She sucked and imbibed this invigorating and intoxicating flow of energy that flowed from him as if her life depended on it. Her gesture was nothing akin to passion or lust. Her gesture resulted solely from the feeling generated by receiving the Breath of Life.

Every iota of her being rippled with life and energy like she had never felt before. She throbbed with power so intense it threatened to tear her apart ether by ether. She stripped herself away from Shi'mon, inclined her head towards the ceiling and screamed as beams of brilliant, white light exploded from her eyes, ears, mouth and nostrils. She closed her eyes and brought her gaze forward.

Shi'mon used clairvoyance to admire the beauty of her newly-given soul, even before she opened her eyes, which flashed with a new kind of brilliance. He smiled. So many centuries of living a life full of guilt and lust for vengeance had made him forget much of his training. However, after surviving the Shadow of the Soul and recovering his soul, the memories returned, including that on giving the Breath of Life. Watching Sasha's esoteric rebirth brought him joy, peace and a new sense of purpose.

"So," Shi'mon said. "How does it feel having a soul again?"

Sasha was speechless. More tears streamed down her cheeks, but this time, they were tears of joy.

"You've said enough already," he smiled at her. "And you're very welcome. Now, are you ready to take on some Bright Eyes?"

Sasha's expression turned stern and serious.

"You bet I am," she replied with unwavering confidence.

Sasha stood up and dried her eyes.

"For humanity and Yehuda," Sasha exclaimed.

"For humanity and Yehuda," Shi'mon affirmed and stood up.

Their eyes flashed in unison, and they both teleported to the lair of the Bright Eyes. They had less than forty-two minutes before the slaughter was scheduled to begin.

CHAPTER THIRTY-THREE

RULES OF ENGAGEMENT

WELCOME TO MY abode", Dreyko's voice boomed across the empty ballroom of the medieval castle when Sasha and Shi'mon emerged out of teleportation. "I almost lost hope about you making your appointment."

"Good to see you too, Dreyko," Shi'mon replied flatly.

Dreyko looked down at Shi'mon and Sasha from the twenty-feet high balcony like an eagle looking down at its prey. The ballroom was large enough to host two hundred guests. Danka stood to his left, Andrew stood to Danka's left, and The Scientist stood to Dreyko's right.

"I would say it is good to see you, Sasha," Danka's coldness caressed every syllable of her words. "But I do not believe in telling lies."

"Still spreading those hind legs for Andrew and Dreyko?" Sasha spat.

Andrew placed his right hand on Danka's shoulder as she made to leap over the balcony.

"Your highness, she's mine, remember?" Andrew said. "She's not worthy of your time and effort. I give you my word that I will make her wish she was never born. I will do this in your honor and glory."

Danka's features softened but her scowl and glare lingered.

"I want to watch you keep your word," Danka commanded.

"As you wish, your highness," Andrew bowed in her direction.

"That's right, Andrew," Sasha said. "You tame that bitch. After all, that's all she is; a stinking, sex-crazed, psychotic, bitch of a mistake of Mother Nature's."

Danka regarded Sasha for a second before she erupted in knee-slapping laughter, which invoked looks of surprise on everyone's face, including Dreyko.

"Look who is talking," she said, wiping fake tears from her eyes. "Have you looked at yourself in the mirror lately?"

"Actually, she has, Danka," Shi'mon stepped forward. "And that is part of the reason why we are here."

Shi'mon increased the size of his voice box by manipulating his anatomy using the power of will. In doing this, he amplified and tripled the range and amplitude of his voice.

"I know you all can hear me," his voice echoed across the ballroom. "I know what you all dream of. I know what you all long for."

He spun around slowly as he spoke, taking his time to let his words worm their way into the minds of the Bright Eyes hiding in the shadows.

"You want to live again, to feel human again. You want your souls back. You want a cure."

He continued to pace the ballroom.

"I have good news for you all. Sasha has looked at herself in the mirror lately and do you know what she saw? She saw a new person, a new being because she has her soul back."

Shi'mon let the many gasps of awe and shock ripple across the ballroom.

"There is a cure for soullessness," Shi'mon add. "And I have that cure."

More gasps and murmurs seeped into the ballroom. Dreyko raised his hand and silence immediate smothered the ballroom.

"You speak of a cure as if we are diseased," he scoffed.

"Soullessness is an esoteric disease, Dreyko," Shi'mon replied.

"Be that as it may, what makes you think we want to be cured of this 'esoteric disease'?" Dreyko asked, sneering at 'esoteric disease.'

"Do you speak for yourself or everyone else?" Shi'mon asked.

"Where I go, they go," Dreyko snarled.

"Then choose wisely, I beg of you," Shi'mon pleaded.

My oh my, Master would be most pleased to see brother trying to talk some sense into his enemies' heads, Andrew remarked. *Whatever happened to him in the Shadow of the Soul. He's much different now.*

Dreyko glowered and banged a fist on the stony balcony, causing cracks to spread around the point of impact.

"*WE* are the new creation," he bellowed. "*WE* are on top of the food chain and we will eradicate humanity."

"This *IS* remarkable," The Scientist nodded.

His sudden and unexpected remark drew everyone's attention towards him.

"I thought I created the perfect creatures for my purpose, only to realize that there just may be a better creation standing right in front of me."

"What are you talking about?" The Twins asked at once.

The Scientist leaned over the balcony.

"Tell me, Peter," The Scribe asked Shi'mon, ignoring The Twins. "How's

Akasha doing these days?"

"She sends her regards," Shi'mon replied dryly.

"I'm sure she does," The Scientist replied smugly.

"Peter? What is going on, Doctor?" Dreyko demanded.

"You don't even know who you're dealing with, Dreyko," Shi'mon said calmly. "We don't either, but our master calls him The Anomaly, Akasha calls him Chaos and he-" Shi'mon pointed at The Scientist, "- is NOT your friend."

"Touché," The Scribe, or The Scientist as the Bright Eyes called him, replied and turned to face Dreyko. "And if you had attended Sunday school, the name 'Peter' should've struck a chord with you. But you were too blinded by your need for world domination that you could not even see half-a-step in front of you."

He gestured towards Shi'mon.

"That man right there, *your highness*," The Scribe sneered at 'your highness', "is one of the Twelve Apostles of Jesus in the bible. Did you know that he also has a brother named Andrew?"

Andrew teleported away from Danka's side and stood alongside Sasha and Shi'mon. The color drained from the faces of The Twins as reality finally hit them in the solar plexus. Then, Danka's expression changed from shock, to blinding fury and finally, an evil half smile appeared on her face.

"Now you know how the order has always been ahead of you every step of the way."

"You knew all along," Danka glared at The Scribe. "And you never cared to say a thing?"

"Do not waste your energy, Danka," Shi'mon advised. "There is really nothing you can do to him. He only let you feel like you were in control."

"But why?" Danka asked. "Why go through all that trouble?"

"I am a purveyor of purpose," The Scribe replied. "And purpose is something that eludes your puny intelligence."

He turned his attention towards the open ballroom and spoke out loud for all to hear.

"Right here, right now, the fate of humanity is at a fork. To my left," he motioned towards The Twins, "the mutated spawns of soulless creatures and to my right," he motioned towards Shi'mon and his group, "creatures who were once soulless but are not anymore. May the better species win and decide the fate of humankind."

With those words, The Scribe gradually faded into thin air.

"What's the plan, brother?" Andrew asked.

"Sasha will relocate the prisoners to safety and return to help in the fight," he replied. "And after the fight, we will return the prisoners to their respective homes. But first, you need a soul."

Shi'mon bid Andrew come closer. He took Andrew's face in his hands and parted his lips. Andrew parted his and the Breath of Life flowed from Shi'mon's mouth to Andrew's. When he finished administering the Breath, Shi'mon let go of Andrew, whose eyes glowed brighter than those of a Bright Eye. His body also glowed for a few seconds before the glow disappeared. Many gasps and murmurs erupted from every corner of the ballroom.

"Thanks, brother," Andrew searched around. "Where's Yehuda?"

Shi'mon shook his head slightly and Sasha clenched her jaws.

"We will mourn him later," Andrew steeled his resolve and turned to face The Twins at the balcony.

Suddenly, the murmurs died as Dreyko's voice rang across the ballroom.

"These abominations are what stand between us and world domination," Dreyko thrust a finger in Shi'mon and his team's direction. "So, tell me, my loyal subjects, what do you choose: a life of hiding in the dark, lurking in the shadows like creatures ashamed of their identity, or an eternity as day-walking rulers of Earth Realm?"

Howls and chattering of teeth emanated from everywhere as Bright Eye nation chorused its choice. Shi'mon, Andrew and Sasha stood in a triangular formation and readied for an attack.

"This is it, people," Andrew said.

"For humanity. For Yehuda," Sasha clenched her fists.

Andrew and Shi'mon nodded.

"Comrades," Dreyko's voice bellowed again.

A deathly silence swept across the ballroom.

"Attack," Dreyko ordered.

A swarm of hundreds of Bright Eyes zipped towards Shi'mon, Andrew and Sasha from every hidden corner of the ballroom.

Sasha teleported to the prisoners. Shi'mon and Andrew whizzed among the Bright Eyes. Heads rolled and headless bodies turned to ash.

"Need a hand here," Sasha called telepathically. *"There are over a thousand of them."*

"Dreyko must have done some more abductions of his own," Andrew said telepathically and cursed. *"And conversions, as well, from the looks of it."*

"Go help Sasha," Shi'mon ordered Andrew. *"I'll take care of the Bright Eyes here."*

Andrew teleported to her location.

The Twins watched intensely from their vantage point on the balcony. The Scribe had made them look like fools in the presence of their subjects and they could do nothing about it.

I will deal with him later, Dreyko promised himself.

He traced a circle in the air.

The random attack from the Bright Eyes suddenly became more organized. Some arranged themselves into three concentric rings around Shi'mon.

One millisecond:

Five Bright Eyes, consisting of three chupers and two lupers formed the first barrier. They had no weapons.

Easy kills, Shi'mon noted.

Two milliseconds:

A second group, five lupers and six chupers, arranged themselves behind the first barrier. Each Bright Eye had either a sword or a machete in hand.

I can take out about three of four of them, but not without them doing me some major damage, Shi'mon assessed. *Might even lose a limb, or worse case, my head.*

He could regrow body tissue, but there was no way around decapitation. Still, the worst lay ahead.

Three and four milliseconds:

Eight chupers and eight lupers formed a third barrier behind the second one and each Bright Eye had a sword or a machete.

Now I am doomed, he surmised. *I can teleport away, but the Bright Eyes must be taken out today. The mission comes first, always. They cannot be allowed to infect the realm with their cancer. Andrew and Sasha will just have to finish the job.*

He drew a quick breath, sparked the ethers into another sword and charged.

Five milliseconds and real time:

Shi'mon turned the first barrier of Bright Eyes into ash in a flash. When he zipped for the second barrier, however, the unexpected happened. A loud explosion, followed by blinding light, boomed across the ballroom, stunning everyone especially the Bright Eyes. A brilliant object blazed along the third barrier. Dispossessed weapons clanged on the stony floor of the ballroom as piles of ash gathered in the stead of many a Bright Eye. The brilliant object then blazed to a stop next to Shi'mon.

"You know how to make an entrance, don't you?" Shi'mon guffawed.

"Good to see you too, brother," Yehuda smiled.

Yehuda's eyes dazzled with intense radiance and many sparks of energy and power danced between them like electricity. The Bright Eyes trembled visibly and slowly retreated at the sight. Sasha and Andrew rejoined the group.

"Brother," Andrew cried for joy and slapped Yehuda on the back before Sasha yanked him towards her and planted a deep, passionate kiss on his lips as tears of joy ran down her cheeks.

"Noooo," Dreyko raged.

"I have neither seen nor heard of any creature resurrected from true death," The Scribe interjected, as he appeared next to The Twins, who did not seem to care about his sudden reappearance.

"This keeps getting better," The Scribe smiled with fascination.

Then, his expression creased with deep concern.

"Someone, or something, is changing my script and it is not Akasha," he said. "She wouldn't dare."

He heaved his shoulders as he began to dematerialize.

"And I do NOT like not knowing," he vanished completely.

"But how come, brother?" Shi'mon asked.

"It is best if I show you," Yehuda replied.

Yehuda summoned an enormous amount of energy and tapped into the Dimension of Time. He encapsulated the four of them in a temporal bubble in which linear time slowed down by over a thousand times. Everything outside the temporal barrier moved so slow they appeared to have frozen in place: from the Bright Eyes retreating, the particles of dust in the air, even the waves of sound as they traveled.

"I don't know how I'm able to do this," Yehuda said via telepathy. *"But I am certain that this is neither Master's doing, nor was it part of my training."*

Then, Yehuda tapped into the Dimension of Time once again and the four of them experienced a suction force that pulled them into a void. Yehuda accessed the Dimension of Space and the four of them relived his final moments in the Shadow of the Soul as if they were in a super-high-definition, five-dimensional, virtual reality.

***

Shi'mon had just been engulfed in a ball of light and Yehuda's dead body lay on the ground. Priya shook her head as she glided towards his lifeless body.

"What a waste," she said telepathically.

"Says who?" Kundalini hissed soundlessly and slithered towards Yehuda.

Priya whipped her head towards Kundalini, incredulous of Kundalini's words.

"No," she glared at the creature using telepathy. *"He is not worthy."*

"Know your place, creature," the serpent whipped its fanned head towards her.

Its crystalline eyes burned cold, green flames at her. Priya cowered.

"Who are you to tell me if he's worthy or not?" Kundalini hissed its fury at Priya.

"I am Akasha," she yelled out loud.

"And I am Kundalini," it towered over Priya. *"I existed long before you were created, even before The Logos was created. I do not interfere with your work. I even speak with you only as a courtesy. But you will no longer interfere with my work or question my judgment. Unless you need a reminder that not all multidimensional beings are equal. Are we clear?"*

Priya cowered and averted her eyes. She did not reply. Kundalini lowered its head until its crystalline, cold, green, flaming, eyes hovered mere inches from hers.

"ARE – WE – CLEAR?" it enunciated every word of the question.

"Yes," Priya replied.

She knew better than to let her ego get in the way. When last that happened, Chaos had been born and nearly a perfect cycle later, she was still trying to set things right.

Kundalini turned away from her and slithered its way towards Yehuda's lifeless form.

"I am Kundalini, The Serpent of Consciousness. I am a bringer of death, and a giver of life," it hissed and coiled once around Yehuda's lifeless body.

"This is a great moment for all of Creation," it coiled the second time around Yehuda's lifeless body.

"Behold, the first of its kind to be reborn from true death," it coiled the third time around Yehuda's lifeless body.

"Welcome, to a new being, to a new kind of life," it completed half a revolution around Yehuda and spread its head over Yehuda's head so that it faced the same direction as Yehuda faced.

Kundalini then propped Yehuda's lifeless body upright.

"See what I see. Feel what I feel," it bared its long, golden fangs.

"Rise, Yehuda of Keriyyoth," declared Kundalini, The Serpent of Consciousness, and buried its fangs into the crown of Yehuda's head.

The brightness was so intense that Yehuda's body became the brightness itself as Kundalini injected the venom of a new kind of consciousness into Yehuda. Priya, despite her opposition to Kundalini's decision, had to admit that the event was the most glorious she had ever beheld in her entire existence. Yehuda became the human embodiment of some energy, or life force, that was impossible to describe, and that energy, that life force, that consciousness was Kundalini itself.

Hence, the grand entrance in the ballroom.

***

Yehuda emerged from the Dimension of Space, returning the four of them to the plane of existence in which Earth Realm, and the ballroom, tarried.

"Wow," Shi'mon exclaimed, feeling at a loss for words.

Sasha and Andrew agreed.

Yehuda emerged from the Dimension of Time, causing the temporal bubble to dissipate. Linear time continued its regular flow. Less than a millionth of a microsecond had elapsed during the entire process. As such, only Shi'mon and his team were aware of what had just happened. None of the Bright Eyes could consciously process such an infinitesimal loss of time.

Anna march in with a group of ten other Bright Eyes.

"What are you imbeciles waiting for?" she barked. "End them lest I lay all of thee to ash with mine own hands!"

"Didn't anyone ever tell you this is the 21st century, and no one talks like that anymore?" Sasha taunted.

"And did you ever wonder by whose hands your family fell?" Anna asked and a wicked smiled appeared on her face as she transformed into a luper.

A dark fury possessed Sasha's psyche as the memory of the night her family fell returned in a flash.

"Go get her, Sash," Yehuda said.

Anna howled at her in defiance and bared her fangs.

"With pleasure," Sasha hissed and blazed towards Anna.

CHAPTER THIRTY-FOUR

NATURAL SELECTION

ANDREW BLURRED AND zigzagged among the Bright Eyes wielding a sword with a five-foot, double-edged, razor-sharp silver blade he had sparked from the ethers. Many of the Bright Eyes he turned to ash were his students. The others were strangers, recent converts. Still, heads rolled and piles of ash gathered in the wake of decapitated Bright Eyes. Eight Bright Eyes with swords, machetes and scimitars surrounded him, forcing him to cease blurring through them. A luper charged from the front and another from his left. The tip of a four-foot long medieval sword pointed to his back, ready to sever his spine if he stepped back. He had only one option. He whizzed forty-five-degrees to his right, cutting through the liver of the luper who attacked him from the front and driving the heel of his right foot into the solar plexus of a chuper in front of him. She rolled backward to cushion her fall, settled on her toes, bent her knees and leaped forward, fangs bared and scimitar cocked.

Just like I taught you, Andrew smiled.

Andrew pivoted on his left heel. Using the momentum of his spin, he brought his sword down on her neck. At the same time, he swung his right hand in an upward arc and his blade cut off the head of the luper with the sliced liver. Two heads rolled, two bodies turned to ash. The remaining six Bright Eyes attacked in a chaotic formation. Andrew smiled. The first Bright Eye, a chuper, swung at his neck, right-to-left, with his axe. At the same time, another chuper traced a downward arc with its scimitar from left-to-right, aiming to slice him across the torso. Andrew dropped his body towards the floor and rolled forward. The axe and scimitar sliced through air as Andrew sparked a second sword from the ethers. Using the momentum of the roll, he leaped upwards, cutting through the torsos of the chupers, halving both of them.

Six seconds until they reattach themselves, Andrew thought.

Andrew landed among the last four of the Bright Eyes. He stomped the outer knee of a luper. The luper's patella shattered in a loud snap and soft tissue came apart from bone. The luper howled in pain and its weapon clanged on the floor as it fell to the floor and clung to its useless knee. In the same move, Andrew turned his body to the right and thrust his sword into the side of a chuper's abdomen. The sword made a gory exit on the other side. In a show of sadistic savagery, Andrew used his body weight and pulled the sword outward, causing the chuper's tummy to look like a repulsive smile of a clown filled with blood and severed guts. The chuper collapsed to the ground with a bestial shriek of pain.

Six seconds to heal.

Invigorated and empowered with a new surge of energy and power from the Breath of Life, Andrew moved too fast for the last two of the Bright Eyes to track. Two piles of ash collected where they stood after he blazed past them. Andrew took one final zip past the two healing Bright Eyes on the ground and turned them to ash. The entire assault and counter-assault on the eight Bright Eyes that attacked him lasted exactly 4.8 seconds.

Shi'mon flowed through his attackers like an all-consuming lava, burning the Bright Eyes to ash. Forty-eight hours ago, their howls and shrieks of pain would have been music to his ego. He would have relished the feeling of ripping their heads off or crushing the beating hearts in his bare hands. He would have savored in the sheer savagery of the slaughter, and sadistically too. But not this time. Instead, His heart sank with each Bright Eye that turned to ash.

Using clairsentience, he felt the last trace of their humanity evaporate from their soulless bodies right before they turned to ash. Clairaudience captured their thoughts. He felt their unbridled gratitude, happiness and peace that came with the freedom death offered.

I would save them all and make them human again if they let me.

But they did not. They had chosen otherwise out of fear, ignorance or both. They feared what they believed The Twins would do to them if they chose to become human again. They feared the unknown that lay beyond returning to their humanity. They feared facing their guilt for all the atrocities they committed as Bright Eyes. Shi'mon shook from the overload of the overwhelming emotions and the many thoughts thrust upon his clairsentience and clairaudience from the dying Bright Eyes. They welcomed death as opposed to the hell that awaited them as humans.

Sasha slammed her right shoulder into Anna's chest, sending Anna crashing into the stone wall. As Anna shook her head to clear her vision, Sasha grabbed her by the throat, lifted her in the air and slammed her body into the stone floor. Many cracks radiated away from the point of impact of Anna's body. Sasha snarled, balled her right hand into a fist and brought it down on Anna's face. However, Anna rolled on her right shoulder, away from Sasha's fist of fury. Sasha punched a six-inch deep hole into the stone floor. Anna rolled back towards her left, driving her left shoulder into the back of Sasha's elbow. Sasha's scream of excruciating pain came a millisecond after the rapid snaps of her elbow that broke in several places.

Anna continued her roll over Sasha's body until she faced Sasha. She used the momentum of her roll to land a left uppercut into Sasha's chin. Sasha's body sailed ten feet across the room. Something whizzed past her left ear before she heard a loud crack as something blunt slammed into her spine, stopping the trajectory of her body. The pain rendered her voice box useless. A set of claws dug into her shoulders before she reached the floor, hurled her in the air and bashed her body six times into the stony floor before a wall of the ballroom accelerated towards her. White, hot pain flashed before her eyes before everything went black for a split second. She fell to the floor in a helpless heap and faced the ceiling. Sasha supercharged her chi to initiate the healing of her shattered bones and internal organs turned to mush as Anna face turned human.

"To think you could ever best me in combat," Anna loomed over her.

Anna wrapped the claws of her left hand around Sasha's neck.

"I have given some thought as to which of thine family tasted best," she dug a claw of her free right hand into Sasha's open, bleeding chest.

Sasha grunted and groaned as Anna twisted her claw. A few ribs sticking out started slowly retreating into place as Sasha healed her body. Anna removed her claw from Sasha's chest and sucked it dry of the blood. She shuddered and her eyes rolled to the back of her head.

"Thine mother was the best, but thou. Oh my."

Anna panted from the surge of energy that coursed through her being unlike anything she had felt before.

"Such intensity," Anna exclaimed. "Such power. What *ART* thou?"

Anna's face transformed back to chuper form and she bared her fangs in a prelude to drain Sasha dry.

"Your nemesis," Sasha hissed.

Sasha finished healing her body while Anna raved about her blood and its invigorating power. She drove a right uppercut into the back of Anna's elbow, almost tearing the elbow apart completely. Anna howled in excruciating pain and let go of Sasha's throat. Sasha landed on her feet and immediately side-stepped to Anna's right. She slid her right forearm underneath Anna's right triceps and slipped her left forearm over Anna's right forearm, sinking her weight at the same time. She then clasped her hands as she clamped Anna's right elbow to her chest, just below her neck.

Then, Sasha quickly rotated her body in a semicircle, bringing her left and right arm down, her chest upwards and crashing her left foot into Anna's right calf, pinning Anna to the ground as she straightened her posture, all in a single motion. Anna's body remained in place but her right elbow and shoulder violently twisted in unnatural angles. Anna's scream barely drowned the crackling of her right elbow and shoulder as they broke in several places. For good measure, Sasha zipped so quickly away from Anna that she ripped off Anna's entire right arm from her body. She cast the severed arm aside.

Anna howled and collapsed to the floor as she reached for the stump that used to be her right arm with her left hand. She writhed and wailed in the pool of blood that gathered from the bleeding stump in her shoulder. Sasha walked towards Anna and grabbed her by the throat.

"I want you to look into my eyes as I end your pathetic existence," Sasha said lifting Anna's face to her eye level.

Anna's eyes rolled to back of her head as the bleeding stopped. However, she could not regrow a new arm and desperately needed her severed arm.

"Look at me," Sasha commanded.

Anna weakly trained her gaze towards Sasha.

"I want this to be the last thing you see before I make you suffer something far worse than what you did to my family."

She applied pressure just below Anna's jaw, forcing her mouth open.

"This is for my family," Sasha said between clenched teeth and opened her mouth.

A blue flame shot out from Sasha's mouth into Anna's. Sasha looked like a human dragon breathing blue fire out of her mouth. The flame burned with heat, sparked from the ethers and, forged with a powerful will. Only a will of similar strength and above could extinguish it. It consumed Anna from the subcellular level. It burned her at the etheric level, causing Anna pain and agony that words could not formulate.

Unlike the other Bright Eyes before they died, Anna's eyes did not even flash for one last time. Her final moments were devoid of gratitude, happiness and peace. She went into nothingness, sadness, confusion, and oblivion. She turned to ash not even knowing what had just happened to her; only that her existence had come to a most unexpected end.

Sasha lowered her hand covered with Anna's ash. Five centuries of pain, grief and lust for justice suddenly crashed on her like an avalanche as closure set in. Her body spasmed uncontrollably, she sank to her knees from the weight of emotional exhaustion and wept her heart out, uncaring of the fight that still raged around her.

The power surged through every fiber of Yehuda's protoplasmic and etheric constituency, taking over everything he believed was himself. He pulsed so much with this newfound power that he did not need to decapitate the Bright Eyes. A simple laying of hands and the Bright Eyes puffed to ash. As he glided through the Bright Eyes and gave them the touch of death, the words of Kundalini, right before his resurrection, came to mind. How he remembered, he was unsure.

Perhaps, I was not fully dead? he wondered. *Maybe during my resurrection, a temporary fusion of essences occurred between mine and Kundalini's.*

As if possessed by another entity, Yehuda suddenly stopped his attack on the Bright Eyes. They attacked him, they hit nothing but air.

"I am Kundalini, the Serpent of Consciousness."

He levitated about twenty-feet off the floor, opened his arms wide and closed his eyes. Every Bright Eye, including The Twins, stared at him in confusion and awe as fear slowly took hold of their hearts.

"See what I see! Feel what I feel."

Specks of light coalesced into a transparent serpent of light and curled three-and-half times around his body. The serpent fanned its head above his head. Yehuda and the light image of Kundalini opened their eyes at the same time. Two pairs of flaming orbs burned with a dazzling brightness where their eyes used to be, and sparks of energy danced around their eyes in jagged patterns. Without warning, beams of bright, white light shot out from the two pairs of eyes, merged into a single beam and washed over the Bright Eyes on the floor. Every Bright Eye, about sixty of them remaining, turned into ash. Then, Yehuda slowly descended to the floor as the luminous manifestation of Kundalini slowly vanished. Yehuda collapsed to the floor in a helpless heap and returned to his normal self as Kundalini's essence became dormant.

"What just happened?" Andrew asked, still incredulous.

"Kundalini," Shi'mon replied.

He sat on the floor and cradled Yehuda by the back of his neck.

"For a moment, Yehuda was its vessel."

"Too bad my form can only handle a tiny fraction of its power," Yehuda chimed in weakly.

His head spun and his vision was hazy. He activated his chi to heal himself from whatever damage Kundalini's manifestation had done to him.

"Too bad we didn't use it on them," Andrew said, gesturing towards The Twins on the balcony.

The Twins overhead them and relaxed the tension in their bodies. They met each other's eyes and nodded before turning to face Shi'mon and his group.

"Andrew and I will take the bat," Shi'mon said loud enough for Dreyko to hear. "I am sure he wants to do many things to Andrew."

"Sasha and I will take the bitch," Yehuda said out loud to Danka's hearing.

He stood up and stretched his muscles as he completed his healing

"We all have unfinished business," Dreyko said.

Danka kissed Dreyko deeply and passionately for a few seconds. She stared into his eyes after their lips parted.

"Let's finish this, brother."

Dreyko smiled and nodded.

The Twins leaped over the balcony in human form. Danka landed on the ground on four limbs but slowly stood on her hind legs, towering into an eight-foot tall, incredibly beautiful luper with thick, pristine white fur. Dreyko had transformed into an eight-foot tall, hideous-looking, cross between a human and a bat, with a six-foot long pair of wings. He flapped his wings steadily, with each flap sounding like a massive gust of wind, until his feet gently touched the floor. An eight-foot tall, hideous-looking, cross between a human and a bat flexed his shoulders and folded his wings. The Twins flashed and maintained a red glow as they assumed attack positions.

"That was a remarkably quicker transformation than last time," Yehuda said.

"Indeed," Shi'mon concurred.

"If you weren't such a mean bitch," Yehuda taunted Danka, "you would have made an excellent pet."

Danka roared, not howled but Dreyko remained silent.

Danka whooshed towards Yehuda and Sasha, but they zipped in opposite directions. However, in classic chess mindset, Danka had read their move and veered to her left instead. Her left paw caught Yehuda's gut, ripping most of it out. He yelped in pain as bloodied flesh and guts hung out of his torn abdomen. Danka spun on her left heel and sank her right claws into Yehuda's left shoulder, digging as deep as possible into flesh, muscle, and tendon. Yehuda professed his pain with an eardrum-ripping scream.

Sasha made to blaze to Yehuda's rescue, only to be stopped by Yehuda's body hurtling towards her at the speed of zip. His body slammed into hers with so much force that the impact sent both of them flying across the ballroom towards a wall. Danka bounded faster than their bodies sailed through the air and drove her right shoulder into their entangled bodies with the force of a minivan doing 80mph. The extra force from Danka's charge accelerated Yehuda and Sasha into the wall, causing them to crash into the wall with greater force. Many cracks appeared in the wall from the point of impact of their bodies. They landed on the floor, sprawling in a pile of broken bones and battered bodies, until they stopped in front of Danka's hind paws.

Danka scooped Yehuda and Sasha off the floor as if these two were pillows; Yehuda with her left paw and Sasha with her paw. She hurled Yehuda over her head and slammed his body into the floor to her right and did the same to Sasha, slamming Sasha's body to her left. She picked them up once again, leaped thirty feet into the air and crashed their bodies into the floor with an acceleration of 5g's. Yehuda and Sasha coughed out blood as ribs shattered into many pieces and dug into their lungs and healing internal organs. Danka leaned forward, burying her claws deep into their chests and licked some of the blood flowing from the corner of Yehuda's mouth. Her red orbs turned bright white, her chest puffed out, her neck arched and she inclined her head towards the ceiling as her body went rigid from the immense surge of energy and power unknown to her that pulsed through her body. A howl of excitement escaped her snout. She lowered her head and inched closer towards Yehuda's left ear.

Was that her soul returning? she wondered. *Is this why The Scientist wanted their blood?*

Danka howled again.

No, this is just a taste of something much, much bigger than getting my soul back.

"I do not know what you have become. But, I must admit, I absolutely love it,' she growled. "Now you will know just how much of a bitch I am when I drain you of every drop of your blood."

Danka raised her head, roared and bared her long, sharp fangs before she went for Yehuda's jugular.

Shi'mon streaked towards Dreyko from the front while Andrew came in from Dreyko's left. What looked like a half-smile stretched across Dreyko's face. He shifted slightly to his right, just out of Shi'mon's path, and extended his left leg, tripping Shi'mon who stumbled wildly from the momentum of his acceleration. Andrew, unable to change his course quickly enough, crashed into Shi'mon. The siblings tumbled in a chaotic heap about eight feet to the right. Dreyko zipped towards them, grabbed each man by the ankle and banged their bodies together as one would clap a pair of slippers together.

Shi'mon and Andrew hands coming up to shield their faces did not offer enough protection for the bones snapping, flesh tearing and internal organs getting squished. Dreyko flung them into the wall for good measure. He savored the way the two men collided with the wall. Dreyko then whooshed towards them and plunged his fists into both men's guts, pinning them to the wall. Warm blood and ground guts flowed over his hands. He retracted his fists and both men collapsed to the floor.

"Pathetic," Dreyko sneered.

He turned to see how his sister fared. Satisfied, he returned his attention towards Shi'mon and Andrew.

"I was looking forward to something close to a challenge," he lifted Andrew off his feet by the throat as Andrew's open abdomen gradually closed up and jagged, protruding bone pieces retracted into his body. "Despite your complete waste of my time as opponents, you brought me a gift."

Dreyko bared his fangs and plunged them into Andrew's jugular. His glowing, red orbs changed to a white brilliance and his body stiffened as energy and power surged through his body. He retracted his fangs, arched his neck, inclined his head towards the ceiling and clattered his teeth to produce glass-shattering soundwaves before he plunged his fangs again into Andrew's jugular.

Yes, yes, YES, Dreyko beamed as an intoxicating and invigorating aliveness infused his being like he had never, ever felt before. *I can feel it. The return of my soul and much, much more.*

The rush reached a crescendo, his eyes attained a maximum level of brilliance and the surge became steady. Still, Dreyko drank from Andrew.

I want every... last... drop... of... it.

Sasha used the last bit of strength she had regained during her brief moment of healing and threw her body against Danka's, knocking Danka off Yehuda and preventing her from biting Yehuda. As both women rolled away from Yehuda, Danka ended up on top of Sasha. She pinned Sasha to the floor and sank her fangs into Sasha's jugular. Sasha screamed.

"Noooo, not again," she raged from anger, desperation and fear before Danka slipped a claw over her throat and tore her throat out.

Sasha tried to speak, to scream, to make a sound. Nothing, except for the gurgling in her throat as she gradually choked on her own blood. However, she realized something much worse. Her vision grew dimmer and the blood oozing from her throat had almost stopped flowing. Her body grew weaker by the second as Danka sucked the blood out of her with three times the force of that of a house vacuum cleaner.

She's not turning me, Sasha thought. *She's killing me.*

Sasha used the last of her might to reach for Yehuda, who lay sprawled on the floor, weak, semi-conscious and still healing. A feeble gesture; yet, she had to feel him one last time before she died. Yehuda's left hand was mere inches from hers, inches that felt like a million miles. Finally, she touched his fingers and a smile blessed her face when he weakly turn his head and meet her eyes.

At least, I found closure for my family's death, she thought. *And now I die, happy to know that I am saving the love of my life.*

She took his hand, used the last of her strength to give it a squeeze before the cold hands of death gently took her away.

Yehuda saw Sasha's eyes growing dimmer by the second. He felt her squeeze his hand once before her hand fell limply to the floor.

Why does she look like a dried out, Egyptian mummy? he wondered.

He narrowed his eyes and shifted his attention in time to see Danka retract her head from Sasha's neck and roared. Déjà-vu. Twice, he found her, twice she saved him and twice he lost. Rage fueled his being like he had never felt before and an incredible amount of adrenaline flooded his body. He did not know how, and neither did he care, but he healed instantly and completely.

Blinding, white-hot, pain erupted from the left side of Danka's ribcage. She howled and sailed ten feet in the air before she landed on the ground. She took a fighting stance and waited for her next attack. A streak accelerated towards her. Yehuda telegraphed a downward, right punch and Danka raised her left paw to parry, leaving her chin exposed. She fell for Yehuda's trap. He rammed his left knee upwards into her chin with the force of a wrecking ball, shattering her jaw and breaking off many fangs.

Danka rolled backwards from the impact but immediately assumed fighting stance. Her only defense was an offense. As such, she leaped, paws extended and a toothless snarl graced her snout. Yehuda sidestepped to his right and drove a right uppercut to her partially healed ribs, shattering them to splinters. Danka howled in pain and collapsed to a knee, cradling her shattered ribs with her right hand. Yehuda slipped in front of her, cupped her occiput with his right hand to hold her head in place as he drove his left knee towards her chin. Danka used her left hand to block the attack and bounded to her hind legs.

In one fluid and graceful motion, Yehuda shifted his weight to his right as he slipped his right hand under Danka's left arm. Cradling her left forearm on the back of his neck, and resting his right hand underneath her elbow, he straightened his posture, aligned his body with hers and held her left arm in an elbow and shoulder lock. Then, he zipped in a complete circle. Danka's left elbow and shoulder crepitated with the breaking of several bones into splinters. She let out a heart-rending roar, borne out of paralyzing pain, and collapsed on the floor.

Yehuda let go of Danka's useless left arm and leaped in the air. He accelerated at 6g's and crashed his knee into Danka's spine, shattering several vertebrae. Danka's body went limp from loss of motor functions due to the attack on her spine. Yehuda then cupped her forehead to hold her head in place. Focusing every etheric iota of strength, anger, fury, rage and vengeance boiling within him to the tip of his middle, intermediate phalange, he cocked his right hand. The tip of the intermediate phalange of his right middle finger traced a bright arc in the air as he brought it down on Danka's second cervical vertebra, the axis, with enough force to turn sixty bricks to dust.

The impact resulted in an explosive brightness of light and energy. Soulless or not, the spine and the brain control the functions of the body and Yehuda's punch severed Danka's spine. The only reason Danka did not die instantly was because of the esoteric upgrade she obtained from drinking Sasha's blood. Yehuda let her forehead hit the floor before he stood up and flipped her over with his foot. He took her by the neck, squeezed and lifted her off her feet.

Shi'mon saw his brother's eyes grow dimmer. He switched to clairvoyance and saw his brother's aura fade away until it was gone. He switched back to regular vision and met Dreyko's eyes, holding an unrecognizable, desiccated body of what used to be his brother. An emptiness flared within him and a singularity was birth in its stead: the death of Dreyko. In an instant, his recovery was complete, and he charged. He drove his shoulder into Dreyko's sternum, sending Dreyko flying towards the wall at over 60mph. Andrew's dead and desiccated form hit the floor with a thud. Instinctively, Dreyko spread his wings and held them open like an aerial brake, causing him to come to an almost complete halt.

Shi'mon snarled and blazed towards Dreyko and rammed into him at the hip. However, Dreyko folded his left wing, inclined his body to the left and tossed Shi'mon into the wall with Shi'mon's acceleration. He crashed into the stone structure, but the singularity within the void in him numbed him to the pain. He rolled forward from the impact with the wall and streaked towards Dreyko. Dreyko took a step to the left and brought the full force of his knee upwards towards Shi'mon's solar plexus.

He stopped 4ft in front of Dreyko and stomped at the knee Dreyko aimed at his solar plexus. The sudden impact caused Dreyko to trip forward and Shi'mon unleashed a fiery, left uppercut that connected with Dreyko's chin with the force of a sedan moving at 50mph. Dreyko's mandibles came apart in many broken pieces and his fangs flew from his mouth in every direction. As Dreyko's head lurched backward and his body sailed in the air, Shi'mon zipped in the air to maximum height. Then accelerated downwards at 6g's and rammed Dreyko in the sternum. The crash on the floor left many jagged cracks spreading across the floor around Dreyko's body like an extraterrestrial spider web.

Shi'mon loomed over Dreyko, who needed over eleven seconds to heal his body completely. Whatever last trace of peace and serenity he had acquired from his visit to the Shadow of the Soul had disappeared, leaving room for the singularity that beckoned him like a choir of sirens. He flipped Dreyko over on his belly with his right foot. Then, he grabbed the base of Dreyko's right wing with his right hand and ripped it off Dreyko's scapula. Dreyko unleashed the most horrific and monstrous scream Shi'mon had ever heard. He reached for Dreyko's left wing and tore it off as well. Another monstrous scream escaped Dreyko's throat; screams which, to Shi'mon, sounded like a sanctifying symphony from a soprano. He glanced at Yehuda in time to see Yehuda deliver the spine-severing strike on the back of Danka's neck.

Shi'mon then drove a downward punch on Dreyko's thoracic vertebrae for good measure, severing Dreyko's spine and resetting his healing time. Dreyko's body went limp from loss of motor functions. Shi'mon grabbed Dreyko by the back of the neck, leaped with Dreyko in the air and smashed Dreyko's face into the stone floor. Pieces of flesh and bone splattered around Dreyko's head. Dreyko groaned as Shi'mon flipped him over on his back and lifted him off the floor by the neck. His face was gone, pieces of his skull stuck out from his brain and a bloody hole remained where his mouth used to be. Shi'mon brought Dreyko's face close to his.

"I offered you a simpler solution, and you refused," he hissed. "Now, you will wish you had chosen more wisely."

Simultaneously, Shi'mon and Yehuda opened their mouths and breathed the Breath of Life into Dreyko and Danka respectively; only this time around, the breath was not a giver of life. They infused the Breath of Life with every bit of negative energy and emotion they could muster; from the guilt, anger, fury, hatred, and everything else they had let go of after their return from the Shadow of the Soul, to their current states of mind forged from the loss of those most dear to them. It flowed from their mouths and into The Twins', burning them with a fire that was both real and unreal; burning them with a fire that was both hot and cold. It flowed from their mouths, not as bright, blue flames, but as bright red-indigo flames.

And the flames burned. They burned The Twins at a subcellular level. They burned at the etheric level. They burned at their very essences. They burned and consumed all that they ever were and all that they had ever conceived themselves of becoming. They burned their illusions and reality. The Twins groaned from pain beyond bearing and description. The suffering was succinct at a surreal level.

They burned. Oh yes, they burned. From inside-out, they burned. By Creation itself, they burned. By the curse of their choices, they burned. And by the cries of countless creatures whose lives they had cut short, they burned.

And so, The Twins died, with no knowledge of what happened to them. No surrender, no hope, no joy, no happiness and no peace in their death; only oblivion, and an emptiness that could not be explained. They burned straight to nothingness, without even turning into ash, as if Creation itself shunned the very thought of ever having them as a part of its history.

CHAPTER THIRTY-FIVE

REDEMPTION

FINALLY, IT WAS over. The Twins and the Bright Eyes were gone. Shi'mon turned to face Yehuda. The victory over the Bright Eyes had come at a very high price. Shi'mon knelt beside his brother's desiccated, mortal remains. Yehuda sat on the floor and cradled Sasha in his arms. Silent tears traced Yehuda's cheeks, and Shi'mon brushed a hair from his brother's face. His heart ached with so much pain he could not even shed a tear. Yehuda leaned forward, closed his eyes and kissed Sasha softly on the thin, dry line that was her lips, hoping against hope, that she could return his kiss.

"I wish with all my heart that you could come back to me," he spoke via telepathy, as if Sasha could hear him. *"I'd gladly take your place if I could."*

Suddenly, Sasha's chest heaved upwards as she sucked in a huge lungful of air. Yehuda's eyes snapped open. A pale, blue mist oozed from his mouth into hers. Sasha, eyes closed, sucked in the mist. It took him a second to understand what was happening. He screamed for joy and kissed Sasha with so much passion that he feared he might be suffocating her.

Sasha grabbed the back of Yehuda's neck and held him fast as if letting go would spell her death. Her clairsentience kicked in. She felt life-giving energy course through her body, sparking every cell of her body to life and supercharging her chi. Strength and vitality returned to her body. Her clairaudience and clairvoyance came alive. She heard her heart pumping, the blood flowing through her blood vessels, the air whizzing in and out of her lungs, neurons firing impulses throughout her body, the ignition of the energies of her physiological processes and everything in between. Her aura and eyes glowed brighter by the second as she imbibed more of the mist from Yehuda. Then, her clear sentience merged with Yehuda's and tears of joy streaked down her cheeks. She gently broke the kiss and met his loving gaze.

"I felt you; all of you," she said softly and placed a hand on Yehuda's chest. "Your thoughts, your emotions, your everything."

"You look so beautiful, my love," Yehuda smiled and sniveled.

They both laughed softly. Sasha sat upright and nestled against his chest.

"Would you really have given your life for me?" she asked.

"Anytime, any day," Yehuda replied.

They smiled at each other and kissed each other again before Yehuda turned towards Shi'mon.

"He's your brother," he said to Shi'mon. "You kiss him."

The three of them broke into laughter. Shi'mon turned his attention towards his dead brother lying in his arms.

"I am certainly not going to kiss you," he said softly and laughed a little.

Shi'mon laughed because he knew how to bring his brother, the last of his family by blood, back to life.

"What Yehuda did not explain when he showed us what happened to him in the Shadow of the Soul," he adjusted Andrew in his arms. "Was that he gave his life for me. He took my place because I failed."

Shi'mon glanced in Yehuda's direction. Yehuda nodded and gave him a smile of encouragement.

"I may never get the chance to pay him back," Shi'mon continued. "But I will pay it forward. The same unconditional love he showed me… I will extend it to you, brother. As Master said, 'No greater love exists than one who is ready to lay down his life for a friend.' And you and I are more than friends."

He turned his attention once again towards Yehuda and Sasha.

"We are family," he said.

"He's so sweet," Sasha leaned towards Yehuda and whispered loud enough for Shi'mon to hear.

Shi'mon sparked the ethers into a tennis ball and tossed it in her direction using telekinesis. She deflected the ball using telekinesis and stuck out her tongue at him.

Shi'mon smiled, closed his eyes and visualized unconditional love as life-giving energy flowing from his heart to his brother's. He turned on his clairvoyance. A golden aura formed around Andrew's body as the life-giving energy flowed into him. The aura shone brighter with every passing second. Andrew's chest heaved outwards as he took in a huge lungful of air. When Andrew opened his eyes, they shone with a white brilliance and pulsed with life. His body rejuvenated from ancient-Egyptian mummy to its original form. Shi'mon let Andrew fall to the floor as he stood up.

"Very funny, brother," Andrew rolled his eyes.

Shi'mon extended a hand and Andrew took it. He helped Andrew to his feet. Yehuda and Sasha joined them, and the four hugged in one embrace for over a minute. No words were said, audibly or telepathically. Yet, in that silence, everything was said from the very core of their hearts. Then, they teleported to Shi'mon's safe house in Rome.

"I believe I noticed a chuper getting away," Yehuda said.

"Saw him too," Shi'mon affirmed.

"Agent Patrick," Shi'mon called telepathically.

"Yes, your supremacy," Patrick replied telepathically.

"Chuper on the loose," Shi'mon said.

"On it, boss," Patrick replied.

"And one more thing," Shi'mon.

A few seconds later, Patrick affirmed Shi'mon's orders and terminated the telepathic link.

This should be easy, Patrick said to himself.

***

Paris by night. A young lady walked in steady steps down a dark street on her way home.

9 pm, why take a taxi when the night is still so young? she thought. *Besides, I enjoy the feel of the breeze on my face, better than my date tonight. So much for online dating. Men. Great sales pitches, pathetic deliveries.*

She was five-foot-eight inches of stunning beauty. A short, dark, green dress covered her body, a body which professed many religious trips to the gym. But she had never been to the gym; not even for a second. Despite her exquisite physique, her personality remained her biggest head-turner. She rocked her six-inch, high-heeled shoes as if they were sneakers.

"Care for some company, my fair lady?" a voice called out in broken French from a dark alley she walked by.

She ignored the stranger and continued walking without breaking her pace.

Who the hell still referred to any woman as 'fair lady' these days? She thought. *Fine. Let's end this quickly.*

The stranger zipped and snatched her into a darker alley a block away. The stranger, the last chuper, bared his fangs to feed and forge a companion for himself. To his surprise, the lady's arm shot up and held his throat in a death grip. His eyes bulged in shock at the immensity of her strength. He tried to break free, despite his realization that he was no match for this... whatever this lady way.

"You had seven-plus billion people to feed from," she smirked. "Yet, you chose me. You really deserve to die."

In the darkness of the alley, her eyes flashed green. The chuper trembled with morbid dread..

"What… are… you?" he asked between chokes.

"You'd never understand," she replied and ripped the chuper's head off with her bare hand.

The chuper turned to ash. The lady blew the ash off her hand.

"Thanks for taking care of my assignment," a man said to her.

Who was this man who did not even flinch at her decapitating this creature with her bare hand? she asked herself. *Maybe he was in shock?*

She straightened her dress and gazed at the silhouette of the tall figure against the streetlights.

His aura indicates he's not evil, she thought. *And he must be accustomed to creatures like this one. He even called it 'his assignment'. Regardless, he's still a stranger.*

She made to walk past the man.

"I know who you are, Marissa," Patrick said telepathically.

She froze and turned to face him.

Only family calls me by that name, she thought. *And I don't think I've met him.*

"I'm Patrick and my mentor was your father's apprentice," he added telepathically.

Patrick extended a hand. Marissa nodded, took it and gave it a firm shake.

"It is time, isn't it?" she asked telepathically.

"Yes, it is," Patrick replied. *"And my mentor summons you."*

***

Yochanan slashed away. Bodies dropped and disappeared. More than 200 Sinisters rushed towards him on the north face of Mt. K2, in the Himalayas. Somehow, the Sinisters had found a way to create a portal between their realm, Nimbu, and Earth Realm. Yochanan had to stop them at all cost. However, he gravely underestimated their numbers. He could easily handle up to sixty of these creatures by himself. But killing 200 of them before the incantations stopped seemed an impossible feat to achieve and he had no time to call for backup.

If I can just get to the Sinister chanting the incantations.

Suddenly, the mountain began to tremble, a phenomenon which created a hum.

It's now or never.

He leaped over the swarm of Sinisters, heading towards the Sinister doing the incantations. Seven Sinisters threw themselves at him in mid-flight to derail him. He took out four of them before he hit the ground and decapitated three more before leaping again. The incantations stopped, and the Sinisters all stood still. Yoch slashed at the chanting Sinister, but he was a slash too late. An invisible force slammed into his body and threw him away from the mouth of the cave. Yoch landed in a crouching pose and readied for another attack. None came. He looked around. The Sinisters were not attacking. They were all prostrated on the ground and facing the cave.

A seven-foot, naked, humanoid male with an orange skin tone stepped out into the open, unfazed by the elements at more than twenty-five thousand feet above sea level.

"It's him," Yoch frowned. "He's out."

A Sinister approached this giant, dropped to both knees, lowered his head to the ground and offered his leader a fur coat that was fashioned specifically for his leader. The leader nodded his acceptance of the offering. Two female Sinisters hurriedly took the coat from their comrade's hands. They placed it over their leader's shoulders, and he shrugged on the coat for proper fitting. The two females and the male retreated, heads bowed to the ground and without turning their backs to their leader. Yoch turned on his clairsentience. Fear and awe filled the air with a much deeper ferocity than the elements on the world's second highest point above sea level. He dismissed his dagger and straightened, his presence inviting a cold look of condescension and disdain from the giant.

"You must be one of those I have heard so much about," said the giant via telepathy.

"Rest assured, creature," Yochanan replied in kind. *"We will crush you."*

The creature scoffed.

"You are aware that you are heavily disadvantaged, right?" the leader said. *"And I am not speaking of numbers."*

As much as Yoch hated to admit it, he knew this creature was right. His ego was badly bruised, but his wisdom got the better of him.

"We will meet again, creature," Yochanan promised and teleported away.

The creature stared blankly ahead for a few seconds as if lost in thought. Then, he returned his attention to his subjects.

"The hour has finally come, my people," Maduk spoke aloud. "It is time to take back our inheritance. It is time to take back Earth Realm."

And the Sinisters chanted their agreement.

***

"You're a hard man to find," The Scribe said.

He slid on an empty stool next to the man.

"You could have picked a better bar, you know that?" he added.

The man took a sip from his mojito and kept staring blankly ahead. The Scribe signaled to the bartender, a young lady barely in her twenties.

"A double, please" he asked in Portuguese.

She flashed a radiant smile and obliged.

"A toast," The Scribe offered, but the man continued to ignore him.

"What do you want?" the man finally asked in a cold monotone.

"Let me show," The Scribe placed his left index finger on the man's forehead.

In a flash, the man witnessed the obliteration of the Bright Eyes in all its gory detail. When The Scribe retrieved his finger, he grinned with pleasure at what he saw. The snarl on the man's face was almost poetic. The glass of mojito in the man's hand shattered into tiny pieces, startling waiters, waitresses and a few customers.

"No need to worry," The Scribe tried to calm everyone down as the man slid off his chair and headed for the door. "Just an accident."

He slid his hand in his pocket, sparked the ethers into a $50 note and slid it towards the bartender.

"For everything," he said and dashed after the man.

"Would you like to meet the man who stole your soul and slaughtered your children?" The Scribe asked when he caught up with the man.

"He's a dead man walking," Marlo spat.

His eyes flashed from pale blue, to bright red and then back to pale blue as he marched angrily into the night in search of Yehuda.

***

"Maduk is here," Yoch slammed his palm on the table, frustration and shame welling in his stomach. "Damn my pride. I didn't expect 200 of them."

"You did well, brother," Shi'mon tried to reassure Yoch.

"You were smart enough to leave the area, though," Yehuda added. "This is Maduk we are talking about, you know."

"We'll get him next time, brother," Andrew interjected, tapping Yoch on the shoulder. "Together. As a team."

"Family," Sasha interjected.

"Yes, I forgot," Andrew chuckled. "Family."

Shi'mon rolled his eyes. Yoch nodded his gratitude for their support. Suddenly, a grin appeared on Yoch's face.

"I take it I don't have to babysit you two anymore?" his gaze darted between Shi'mon and Yehuda.

The two men looked at each other and nodded slightly.

"We're good," Shi'mon replied and Yehuda nodded.

"We're family," Sasha whispered and giggled.

"Keep this up and I just may change my mind," Shi'mon teased.

"Too late," Sasha shrugged. "We have witnesses."

"Did I miss something?" Yoch asked with a look of confusion on his face.

"Don't mind her, brother," Yehuda replied with a smile. "Short story."

"If you say so," Yochanan shrugged. "And what am I supposed to do with these diapers? It's been two thousand years, you know."

Andrew rolled his eyes, Yehuda shook his head and Shi'mon glared at Sasha. Sasha, though, erupted in laughter, invoking looks of confusion on everyone's face, including Yoch.

"So," Shi'mon sighed. "We eradicate the Bright Eyes, and Maduk shows up."

"No rest for us," Yehuda yawned and stretched. "Speaking of rest, you need an upgrade, Yoch."

"And how are 'rest' and 'upgrade' even related?" Sasha asked.

"I wonder myself," Yoch agreed.

"But seriously," Shi'mon said. "You do need an-"

He stopped in the middle of his sentence. He raised his left hand to his face. The green crystal on his ring pulsated with green light. He looked at his brothers, and they all had the same look of shock and most of all… fear… on their faces.

"Wh-what's going on?" Sasha stammered.

They had faced dangers a-plenty before, including The Twins; twice. Never had they ever been afraid of anything or anything. This was the first time she saw them show fear in their demeanor. The men regarded one another, as if lost for words. Finally, Shi'mon spoke up.

"He has been set free," Shi'mon replied and swallowed. "Someone or something has let him out."

"Who?" Sasha asked as she herself was infected by the fear that radiated from these three apprentices of Yeshua.

***

The chopper flew at a low altitude over a part of the Grand Canyon that remained inaccessible to tourists, hikers and even Native Americans. The crew consisted of eight men: two pilots, a protective detail of three former marines, now-soldiers-for-hire donning full commando gear, two priests, each with a tattoo of a six-pointed star on the back of their right hands, the emblem of the Cult of The Morning Star, and self-made billionaire Ethan Pitts, owner and president of Pitts Solar Company. Ethan held a flat, circular, grey piece of marble, about six inches in diameter, and half an inch thick. A needle spun lazily on the grey surface.

"What's that, boss?" asked Mercenary #1.

"A compass," Ethan replied.

"Looks like nothing I've ever seen," said the soldier. "It ain't pointing north."

"'Cause it ain't that kinda compass," Ethan replied dismissively.

Mercenary #2 elbowed Mercenary #1 in the lower ribs. #1 got the message. *Best I keep my mouth shut,* he concluded.

Suddenly, the needle tilted slightly to the left and stopped spinning.

"Veer left," Ethan ordered the pilot.

"ROGER that," affirmed the pilot.

The chopper veered left and flew for about a minute before the needle on the compass began to spin wildly.

"We land here," Ethan said.

"ROGER."

Four minutes later, everyone but the pilots left the chopper.

"You," Ethan pointed at Mercenary #3. "Stay with the chopper. You two," he gestured at #1 and #2, "follow us."

Ethan held the compass in front of him as he slowly spun around, waiting for a sign. Suddenly, the compass yanked his hand forward with so much force that he almost tripped and lost his balance.

"This way," he grinned.

After about a hundred yards of walking in the sunny, clear-sky, 97°F of dry heat, the compass would not allow him to take another step.

"It must be over there," he pointed straight ahead.

"Crazy fools," Mercenary #1 whispered to his comrade.

"Crazy rich fools," Mercenary #2 rebutted. "And we're getting paid to babysit. So, just shut up and stay focused."

"You need to get laid, bro," Mercenary #1 teased. "You're so- holy-"

The mercenaries immediately trained their weapons and aimed as an invisible veil seemed to peel away about 50 yards from them to reveal a Native American sitting stone stiff on a stool, except for his blinking eyes. The Native American had white markings on his face and wore a Native American tribal outfit including headwear.

"Hear that, man?" asked Mercenary #1.

"The hummin'?" replied Mercenary #2. "Damn right, I do."

"Think it's coming from there?" Mercenary #1 gestured towards the Native American.

"Yeah," replied Mercenary #2. "Some weird stuff is goin' on here."

Many expletives escaped the lips of Mercenary #1.

"The Guardian," the billionaire exclaimed. "He who neither eats nor sleeps. He whose sole purpose is to guard Earth Realm's most notorious prisoner and herald to our lord and master."

Ethan Pitts danced with excitement and glee.

"I've waited for this moment my whole life," he rubbed his hands together.

"Come no further," commanded the guardian via telepathy.

"I done spent too much time and money to get here and you expect me to just turn around and walk away?" Ethan scoffed. "Do you know what I had to do to get this compass? The sacrifices I made?"

He held out the compass towards the guardian.

"You wife and baby girl's deaths will be avenged," the guardian replied via telepathy.

"Not if my lord and master has got something to say to that," Ethan replied.

He held out the compass to his right. A priest took it from his hand.

"I will get what I came for, guardian," Ethan snarled. "One way or another.".

"Then may the curse of the condemned remain upon you here and in the afterlife," the proclaimed using telepathy.

Suddenly, Mercenaries #1 and #2 screamed, dropped their guns, fell to the ground and writhed in the dust and rocks. Mercenary #3 saw their faces and arms break into sores and rot away until nothing was left of them but their clothes and boots; not even their skeleton. It all happened in less than seven seconds, seven seconds of heart-rending, spine-chilling, soul-snatching screams to underscore the pain and suffering that befell those two before they perished. However, his boss and the two priests remained unaffected. Ethan pulled a revolver from his belt and leveled it at the guardian's head.

"Your petty sorcery has no effect on me," Ethan sneered.

"Your fate is already sealed," the guardian said via telepathy.

Ethan fired a single shot. A trickle of blood rolled out of the bullet hole in between the guardian's eyes before he slumped to the side.

"Screw this," Mercenary #3 exclaimed. "I didn't sign up for this crap."

He made to flee to the chopper. However, a priest raised his right hand and pointed a finger towards him. Instantly, Mercenary #3 levitated into the air and let out a gut-wrenching scream right before he imploded, scattering flesh, blood and guts all over the ground and on the chopper. The pilots raised shaking hands in the air in surrender. Ethan stashed his gun away and headed for the boulder. The priests followed closely behind him. Ethan stopped and the priests walked past him until they were about 20ft away from the dead guardian. One of the priests reverently placed a manuscript on the ground. A six-pointed star drawn in crimson ink graced its thick, black front cover. The priest flipped through the pages of the manuscript, made of human flesh and written with blood until he came to a page that contained the drawing of a winged humanoid creature with fangs, two horns and a tail. Then, both priests bowed their heads twice and began their incantations in an alien, unholy-sounding language.

Thick, dark clouds gathered, snuffing out the sun, and the winds blew with the intensity of a Category 1 hurricane. Lightning illuminated the skies and thunder boomed across this part of the Grand Canyon. The priests continued with their incantations. Suddenly, the part of the Grand Canyon directly in front of their vision phased in and out until it disappeared entirely like a virtual reality of the esoteric kind. A perfectly spherical boulder, 13ft in diameter, appeared with the phasing out of the esoteric virtual reality. A constant hum reverberated from this boulder that was clearly extraterrestrial and even extradimensional in every regard. The priests continued to chant until the slab in front of the boulder rolled away to reveal an opening in the boulder.

"Behold the prison," Ethan said the words with reverence and awe.

One of the priests ceased incanting while the other continued. He stood up and removed his black, hooded robe. Thick, black and yellow smoke billowed from inside the prison. More streaks of lightning filled the skies, claps of thunder boomed and the winds picked up speed. The storm increased to a Category 3 hurricane. The smoke converged into a human form, and golden light carved out a human silhouette with wings that spread out from its scapulae. The figure approached the naked priest. The naked priest closed his eyes and opened his arms.

"I offer myself to you, wholly and unreservedly," the priest cried out into the storm. "Take me as thine vessel and use me as thou will."

"As if you ever had a choice," the winged figure of smoke and golden light replied in an eerie, cold, emotionless tone of voice.

It glided and disappeared into the naked priest.

"Behold, Lucifer's General," Ethan cried for joy and fell on his knees. "Behold, the King of Demons."

More flashes of lightning and roars of thunder filled the atmosphere in this part of the Grand Canyon, churning the storm to a contained Category 5. The possessed priest, who was now the vessel of the most powerful demon in Creation, turned around to face the other priest and Ethan. It opened its eyes, a pair of fiery yellowish, red orbs, with energy and power flying from them like sparks of electricity. Suddenly, golden flames burst outwards from his eyes, ears and mouth as the demon let out a scream that was a blend of so many cycles of pent-up rage and a joyous cry of liberation.

"Finally, I am free," it cried. "After all these cycles, I am free. The moment has come. I will destroy Earth Realm and everyone and everything in it."

The priest and Ethan prostrated themselves in front of their master, and chanted, repeatedly.

"ALL HAIL BEELZEBUB! ALL HAIL BEELZEBUB! ALL HAIL BEELZEBUB! ALL HAIL BEELZEBUB!"

THE END OF PART THREE

AUTHOR NOTES AND CONTACT INFORMATION

Thank you very much for reading *The Bright Eyes*, Book One of *The Soulless Ones*. I hope you enjoyed reading it.

Follow me on social media: ***@elonendelle***

Facebook Page: ***Leo E. Ndelle***

YouTube Channel: ***Eloverse***

Visit my website for more information about me and the series:

www.eloverse.com

Email me: ***email.elone@gmail.com***

Leave a rating and review.

Please take a moment to read a sample of Book Two of the series titled ***An Archangel's Ache.*** Enjoy!

BOOK TWO

AN ARCHANGEL'S ACHE

KAZUK SAT ON his throne. Yes, it was *HIS* throne. It had been a few cycles since he had assumed the role as the King of the Realm of Hell, and The Scribe better not keep the King of Hell waiting. Kazuk was growing more and more impatient with every passing moment. But his impatience was a mere substitute for his feeling of inadequacy vis-à-vis The Scribe. Yes, there was absolutely nothing he could do to this being. Kazuk clenched his jaws in frustration. He decided to focus more on the things he could control, like his realm. Yes! Hell was his realm and under the mantle of his leadership, there had been many changes.

Kazuk was not the original leader of this cesspool of a realm. The Realm of Hell was an uninhabited realm in Celestia's vicinity. But after the Great Rebellion in Celestia, those who had risen against Michael and his host had been defeated, and the defeated had been banished to Hell. But their banishment had left them without their leader and her next-in-command, Zukael, who now went by Beelzebub, as these two were imprisoned in other dimensions that were known to Michael alone. As such, the leadership role for the fallen was vacant. But even Malichiel, now Metatron, the master strategist of the rebellion, did not care to assume that role. Kazuk had decided to seize the opportunity, and he was not the only one who coveted the role.

And so, the battle had raged on. Being an underdog and master strategist, Kazuk had blended sharp wit and supreme skills with the sword in a game of smarts and brute strength. Twenty sought the throne and thirteen fell within a snap of the finger. It was down to seven, and while Kazuk had entertained his six opponents in a dance of more death and damnation, he chose to exhibit a public display of his strength and skill for all in Hell Realm to see. When he was tired of toying with his prey, the predator that was Kazuk beheaded each of his opponents with swiftness and savvy.

He let the angel light streaming from the severed heads of his adversaries bathe his feet as he picked up the heads one-by-one. Hell Realm watched in fear as he walked in slow, calculated steps towards the empty throne, with three severed heads in each hand. The unspoken message was loud and clear. It was one of total dominion and zero tolerance for any form of opposition. It was a promise of strength and leadership like Hell Realm had never seen before. It was an affirmation of the hope of returning to Celestia, with or without their former leader, Luceefa. It was a wordless speech heralding the dawn of a new cycle for Hell Realm and its inhabitants.

Kazuk turned around and faced his new kingdom. His eyes slowly swept across the realm as a deathly silence washed over Hell Realm. Seemingly satisfied, he raised the heads of his slain victims in the air and let them fall on the stairs. The heads rolled down the stairs and ended at the feet of some terrified creatures. Kazuk then rested both hands on the smooth, marble-like armrests of the throne and lowered his body, mired in the angel light of his slain opponents, into the throne. His bride manifested from thin air by his side, descended a few steps in front of him and faced the Realm of Hell.

"Creatures of Hell Realm!" she spoke out loud in the sonic frequency of Hell Realm so that every creature from every corner of the realm could hear her. "Behold Kazuk, your new leader! Your new King!"

Fire and heat blazed. Ice and cold froze. Hounds of Hell howled, dropped on all fours and buried their snouts in their paws. Pain, suffering, pestilence, and all things evil echoed. Lost and fallen creatures cowered and shivered. Demons dropped on their knees and lowered their heads. Trumpets sounded and Hell itself was rocked as if in a hell-quake. And all of Hell chanted:

"ALL HAIL, KAZUK! ALL HAIL THE KING!"

Kazuk then reached for his wife. She accepted his hand and sat across his lap. Lithilia kissed the King of Hell passionately on the lips and Hell Realm erupted in praise.

Made in the USA
Monee, IL
06 April 2020